CW00340747

TIME WILL TELL

172/500

TIME WILL TELL

The Chronicles of the Sight
from
The Golden Tome

N. A. Preece

Book Guild Publishing
Sussex, England

First published in Great Britain in 2009 by
The Book Guild Ltd
Pavilion View
19 New Road
Brighton, BN1 1UF

Typesetting in Meridien by
SetSystems Ltd, Saffron Walden, Essex

Printed in Great Britain by
Athenaeum Press Ltd, Gateshead

A catalogue record for this book is
available from the British Library

ISBN 978 1 84624 368 4

Contents

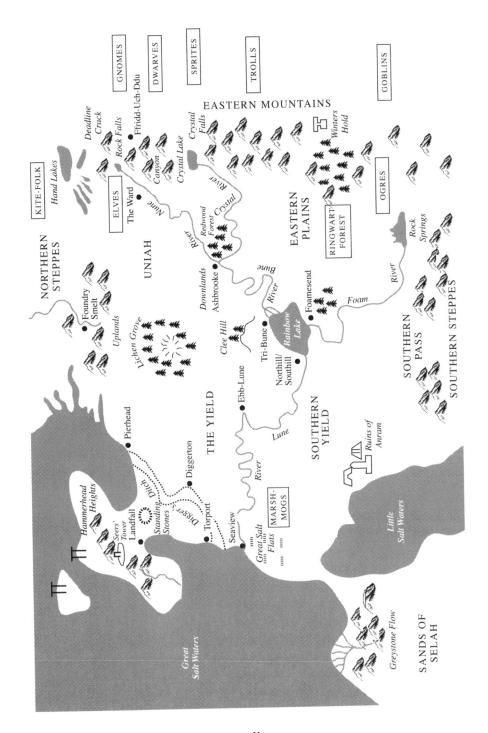

Introduction

Where does one begin? Usually at the beginning, but this must start at a different place and time.

It is much like the creating of a new cut diamond by a master artisan; he studies it. Then when he is ready and he has chosen his plan the artisan lovingly and carefully shapes the diamond into a priceless gem. Much, it is true, is due to the rare and precious material formed under immense pressure but it takes the touch of a master's hand to create the jewel. Thus, something that before was sought after is now priceless.

Someone owning the jewel would think no deeper than the lustre it has now and would tell its story from the time of its purchase.

A diamond has many sides and angles and can be appreciated from all aspects but it must be remembered that although it is multi-faceted, it is still the same stone. This story is about such a jewel. A diamond in the making, but one of flesh and bone and you shall see what becomes of him.

Let me start; here . . .

Prologue

Seers' Tower is a proud and defiant, almost timeless, edifice. It is home to the Council of the Sight. It is an ancient body of seers, eight in number, who watch over the affairs of all who live in this land. The Tower is eight-sided with eight towers that soar eight storeys high and is sheltered by the shadows of the Hammerhead Heights; it is protected by the deep still waters that surround the rock on which the Tower stands. Bright and clear like a beacon in the glorious light of day, yet dark and mysterious as it melts into the night at the setting of the sun. It can be enticing yet foreboding. It really depends on the individual who approaches as to how it appears from the outside; all who do so with good in their heart have no need to fear; although you probably would feel some trepidation upon seeing it for the first time. Do so with evil in your heart and no amount of subterfuge will hide it from the Sight for long. They have a way of knowing who is friend and who is foe. They thought they were safe in their own company, but events have taken a surprising turn and there has been intrigue and suspicion where once there was mutual respect and trust. A seer has rebelled against the age-old order; setting himself as master of the land, imprisoning the others behind an energy barrier set between them and the outside world. Things will never be the same again, now that some of the old laws have been rent out of time. Unless the banishment is undone and the seers freed from the Tower, untold suffering will settle upon the folk of this land; some have already felt its cold touch and perished.

How long has the Tower stood? No one can remember. Its walls were and are as silent to that question as the waters that surround it; however, let me tell you of that which is inside the walls of the Tower. As I have said, it has eight sides and eight towers, each one the home of a seer. They are led by the dwarf, Terra Standfast. He adopted this name when he became a seer, inheriting the right to lead by virtue of his appointee, also a dwarf who was in his turn the leading seer and also known by that name. (Each adopts the name of their predecessor when they are

1

inaugurated into the Sight.) Terra has overall responsibility for the other seers and for the land, and more particularly, over the power within the Tower itself; his is a heavy responsibility indeed.

Others of the Sight are Liam Card-reader, an elf; Emerald Star, a water sprite; Auger Wind-rider, a Dwarf; Eden Yield-keeper, a female elf from the Eastern Lowlands; Elise Saranya, a woodland sprite; Urim, the keeper of the Tome, a human being (of whom you will hear a great deal more); and Ebon Lodestone, also a human being and newest of the seers. These are the eight who currently wear the mantles of their individual responsibilities and presently form the body of the Council of the Sight.

They are the only residents able to withstand the demands of life in the Tower; true there are others who serve, but in a different way. They too are protected under the care of the seers, enabling the day-to-day affairs of the running of the Tower. However, they can only serve for a limited time before the influence of the Tower inevitably requires them to return to their homes in the villages nearby for a season. Those who serve in the Tower are eighty – I was about to say people but that would be misleading – they comprise, from time to time, men and women, elves and sprites, dwarves, the occasional gnome (though they are not usually willing participants) and others.

The Tower is approached by one means only known to you mortals, by way of the ferry, a rough hewn timber platform that clanks its way across the silent waters. Echoes resound along the ravines of the nearby Heights as the chain, slick from timeless usage, rides roughly over the cogs and pulleys. Drops of water splash without sound back into the lake as if reticent to leave their mother for long. The chain links the bank of the lake to the stub of volcanic rock that thrusts itself out of the cold stillness like an angry fist, clenching the base of the Tower in a vice-like grip. The dark waters are silent and cold; so cold it can be felt even at the height of summer. However, within the Tower it is a different story altogether.

One enters through the only gateway that links it with the outside world, at the south of the Tower, between the imposing buttresses and chiselled archways interspersed with places of concealment for defence. Under the oppressive weight of the gates and portcullises and then across the double drawbridge that connects the outer bailey with the main body of the rock, one enters a surprisingly warm, bright flagstone courtyard. Although the sun can only bathe the whole of the courtyard with its rays at the summer solstice, due to the height of the towering walls, there is no darkness cast from them. There is shadow where the rays of the sun cannot reach but there is an unusual brightness about the place.

At the centre of the courtyard, a shaft the size of a cartwheel plunges into the depths of the rock. Out of it there emanates a soft pulsating glow that gives a warm and pleasant ambience in contrast to the leaching cold of the granite walls, dispelling the chill of the waters outside. One feels immediately cheered and less oppressed upon entering.

Lines of luminescence flow from the shaft to each of the eight towers; travelling along conduits in the flagstones, disappearing under the walls of the inner building through arched inlets set into the base of each tower. There is a gentle, almost inaudible, hum from far below the courtyard that is carried up the shaft and is unnoticeable upon entering the courtyard, but it soon impinges itself upon your consciousness. It is said that too long an exposure to it will cause unpleasant results to the unwelcome visitor, which is why there is a constant coming and going of the folk who serve the Sight. Only the seers are immune to its influence and can stay within the confines of the Tower indefinitely. Without the protective care of the seers, it would drive you out of your mind with its intensity. According to popular folklore, it has done so on a number of occasions in the past when the seers and the Tower have been besieged. Man has not always understood the mystery of the Sight and the seers have been looked upon with caution and mistrust from time to time. The seers, however, are not always present at the Tower themselves; they travel throughout the land observing life and applying a gentle touch here and there to keep things on the correct course. There are always at least two who remain behind, tending their duties to the Tower; not many people know this about them. There are stories, it is true, of contact between the inhabitants of the lands and one or more of the seers but evidence of this is hard to find, for they leave as unobtrusively as they come; like a shadow that catches the corner of your eye, then they are gone.

At least, that's the way it used to be – times have changed; the way the Sight views things has had to change. They would not be

3

called the Sight for long if they did not. No, things have changed quite dramatically. It is rumoured abroad that there has been a split from within and that one of the seers has risen up in rebellion against the old ways. As you have been informed, this is no false rumour; it is true and is a most startling and unnerving turn of events. Each of the seers was chosen, hand-picked by the voice of the Sight, nominated by the outgoing member before their time was finished. They can and do die, but their lives are not numbered in years as you would measure yours. Rather they are measured by the times and the events of the land, one episode after another; they have seen the coming and going of the great and ignoble alike.

These are no ordinary beings, not any more that is. For once the eight mingled with mortals, until, called upon by fate, shall we say, to take upon themselves, as protectors, the mantle of the Sight. Each of them in their place; eight mantles with eight rods of power and eight seats in eight towers; together in perfect symmetry holding the rods of power; a lock on the gateway between this land and another. Now, cross your fingers; for it is customary to do so if you are superstitious. Even if you are not you would do well to do it at the mention of anything other-worldly, or just at any time one believes that one should, to ward off ill-fortune.

So this is where the story starts: to recount to you the events that ensued following the rift within the Council of the Sight, and in particular the record of one of their number – Urim Tome-keeper; all of which is recorded in the Golden Tome. You shall be told of these things as they happen and as long as there is the Sight to do so the affairs of this land will be recorded for all time. To give a faithful rendition of the events that brought an ordinary boy to the attention of one Ebon Lodestone, formerly of the Sight.

Chapter I

Jon's Challenge

In the darkness something stirred. It made Jon jump and brought him from out of his half sleep into a state of near panic but all he could hear now was the thumping of his heart as it pounded in his chest. He lay there, wrapped in the warmth of his blanket and heavy travel cloak, at the centre of his favourite clearing in the Redwood Forest not too far from his home. The skin of his cheek itched, as if a tiny insect were crawling over it, and he felt the hairs on the back of his neck stand on end.

He had been uncomfortable, ill at ease with the woods when he settled down for the night. All during that day he had had an uneasy feeling; as if someone had been watching or following him. He had lost count of the times he had stopped to look over his shoulder, to listen for any strange sounds. He had even hidden for a while beneath a fallen tree, concealing himself under its tangled foliage, listening. He had given up hiding eventually, telling himself that he was being stupid; yet the nagging uncertainty of being followed or watched continued, so much so that the spot between his shoulder-blades felt as if a knife were penetrating his flesh.

He could not get rid of the feeling and several times had almost abandoned his design to sleep in the woods for the night. He had tried to convince himself that he was being foolish and that he was imagining things; he had not entirely succeeded. As evening had drawn in, Jon had made camp in the small clearing he knew so well; he had lit a cheering fire in the usual spot, to dispel his fears as much as the cold night air that was settling upon the ground.

He had visited here so many times in the past, but this was his first visit since his mother had taken ill earlier in the year and died; he had not taken it particularly well. She had been his rock.

He had not known his father (he had disappeared before Jon was born) and knew very little about him. His father and mother had been together for only a short time when he had disappeared. Some said that robbers had killed him; others that he had just abandoned her. Jon did not pay much heed to them. He only knew that his mother had loved his father and had never lost faith in him. She used to tell him that, no matter what people said, she felt that he would never have deserted them. That he must have met with an accident that had prevented him from coming home. She and Jon had sat in the fields nearby for so many balmy summer nights, his head in her lap. As she stroked his hair lovingly she would tell him of the times she and his father had had together and of their dreams for the future, which were never realized. She had loved him until the day she died, calling his name – David – softly as she drifted into the next life, leaving Jon broken-hearted and alone. He had buried her in the churchyard, at the foot of the old yew tree, which he could see from the cottage window. He had grown up in Ashbrooke, a market town on the borders between the northern Yield and the Plains of Uniah. He had become reclusive since her death and had shunned the company of others, venturing out infrequently; only Anna had understood, encouraging him in her own silent way; she had been his only friend.

She had been mute since birth but was full of life. He could never stay sad for long when she was around; the room would light up when she walked in to it. It was she who had persuaded him to take some time out in the forest to escape his self-imposed prison; he just needed to be away from the memories that the cottage held and find peace in the woods.

Now the chill of the evening had turned downright cold; at least he felt it had. He felt robbed of the warmth he had had snuggled into his blanket, more by a sense of trepidation than of fear. Something most definitely was not right. He was wide awake now; the exertions of his day's journey forgotten in a flash the moment he was roused by that sound, whatever it was. He was as familiar with these woods as he was with his own backyard and knew there was little to cause him concern or harm; but he was concerned now.

What was it he had heard? He was not quite sure; he just knew it was not right; he felt it was not right. He hardly dared to breathe, though he could feel his heart thumping in his chest and the blood rushing through his ears so loudly it seemed that he could discern little else. Jon loved the forest because of the freedom he felt there and the solitude; there was no one to disturb his musings; he could be one with the trees and at peace with the land. He was not a great one for socialising with the townsfolk of his home, in Ashbrooke. He did not think he was antisocial, just reserved, private; he preferred to be alone (though he would have been grateful for some company right now). He was tense, he could feel his body cramping, he was aware of the discomfort of a cold sweat under his armpits that made him squirm involuntarily. Lying there on his side facing the glowing embers of the fire, he knew that his earlier misgivings had not been wrong. Was it in his imagination or had he really heard a noise? No, he was certain it had been real and not imagined. He felt sure that whoever or whatever it was that had been following him was nearby. The shadows seemed to gather around him and to intensify whilst the night sounds quieted and stilled. A ruddy glow illuminated up to the edge of the clearing but darkness lay beyond like a thick velvet curtain. The dying light of the fire picked out the underbrush and turned the fronds of the plants into strange shapes. Jon felt the pulse in his neck jump as his heartbeat quickened; the sound of leaves rustling nearby sent it into convulsions; his scalp seemed to shrivel on his head, tightened by the deepening furrows on his brow.

He had never been as anxious as he was now. Indecision crippled him; should he wait for something to happen? Should he jump up in an effort to catch whatever it was off guard and somehow seize an advantage? What should he do? The indecision was as debilitating as his fear.

He could not have called for help even if there were anyone to hear his cry; his mouth felt as if it were made of wool. He tried to swallow but there was no spit.

Slowly, hardly daring to move, he unclenched his grip on the cover that he had drawn up around him. Feeling towards the only comfort he had, a large hunting knife secreted under the knapsack he was using for a pillow, he closed his hand around its hilt.

Jon tried to summon up all of his courage, he was not of great stature, and just five foot nine, but felt he could handle himself

7

in a fight if needed. That time might be now; he had to do something.

He froze mid thought. Standing at the edge of the clearing, gazing right at him, was a hooded figure. Jon could see him quite clearly, despite the dying light of the fire. The figure was wearing a long black robe, much like those worn by the friars at the abbey (Jon thought that's who it was at first). The robe appeared worn with age and had obviously seen better days.

He could see the man's features under the hood as he was wearing it high on his head. Greying dark hair, the pinched rugged face of a man in his mid to late forties, chiselled unshaven jaw and soft eyes.

He held within a tanned hand a stout staff, as black as his robe. He did not appear to be threatening, but there was something about his face that caught his attention; there was something familiar about him. Was this the cause of his stupor? How long had he been standing there? Jon had not seen him emerge from the forest shadows. Several moments passed and neither of them moved or said a word. Jon realised that he needed to breathe and let out his pent up breath and then gasped for air. His heart rate steadied a little and he was about to ask who he was when the man spoke.

'Hello, Jon, I'm sorry to have made you jump like that, mind if I join you?'

After a little while that seemed an age, Jon stuttered nervously.

'No . . . Not at all . . . I mean . . . yes . . . well . . . Who are you?'

His anxiety had turned to astonishment and bewilderment. This man whom he could not recall ever having seen or met before in his life, yet looked familiar to him, had him at a disadvantage.

The man stepped closer in a fluid, easy manner and sat on one of the logs placed around the fire for that purpose. He raised the cowl from off his head and by doing so immediately seemed less threatening. Jon definitely felt he should know him and asked tentatively. 'Do I know you from somewhere?'

His eyes, sparkling and alive, seemed to dance in the waning light of the fire, warm, soft and kind.

'No, Jon. We have not met before this night, though we are

kin to one another you and I. I am your uncle. I am called Urim; your father was my brother.'

Jon felt stunned at the declaration. He had never heard his mother talk of him having an uncle, but it would explain the feeling he had that he knew the man.

'I know you must find this all very confusing and I don't blame you. You probably were unaware of my existence.'

Urim bit nervously at his bottom lip, something Jon knew that *he* did on occasion.

'I have been engaged elsewhere. I came when I was able to; unfortunately news travels rather slowly where I come from. I am sorry for your loss, Jon, she was a wonderful woman.'

He looked at his feet and let out a time-weary sigh.

'Sorry I didn't get to see her this time, before she died that is.'

Jon found himself slowly relaxing in his presence; he could sense a great sorrow upon his uncle as he spoke to him about his mother. That sounded so strange, his uncle, it would take a while for that to sink in and for him to feel comfortable with the idea.

He could not help but feel at ease with him; there definitely was something about the stranger that struck a chord with him. There was a resemblance, something about his features and his voice that persuaded him to believe that this was indeed his uncle. He could hardly believe that this was happening. His discomfort and unease with these events were melting away, as the early spring frost melts at the rising of the sun.

He could not explain why he felt like this, he just could not help himself. Something about the man, something in his eyes that communicated to him that he was telling the truth; that they were kin.

Urim looked up and smiled a toothy smile, his tanned face creasing around the eyes. 'Your fire could do with a bit of life in it.'

He stabbed at the dying embers of the fire with his staff, a blue spark jumped out of the ashes and flames grew steadily until the clearing became brightly illuminated. The warmth dispelled the night chills and chased Jon's own chills away; his jaw dropped in amazement.

'I believe we may talk a little easier over a bite to eat and a hot drink to keep out the cold.'

He placed two coins on the makeshift table by the log on which he sat, draped the folds of his sleeve over them and tapped his staff against the base of the makeshift table. There was a brief flash of blue light and when he pulled back the sleeve of his cloak, Jon's jaw dropped. There on the table were two plates of stew and two mugs of chicory, steaming and welcoming. An enticing aroma filled Jon's nostrils and he realized he was hungry; his mouth watered and his stomach rumbled but he eyed the offerings with suspicion.

'Well, perhaps you will forgive the theatrics; I do love to show off occasionally. Come, eat, then we shall talk and I will explain all I can. Time enough for that I believe.'

He cast a look around them, out into the darkness beyond the light of the fire, then turned his attention to the food and commenced to eat. Jon could not resist; he really was hungry. From out of his covers he pulled himself up into a sitting position and sat opposite Urim on the log he had been resting against. He put his cloak about his shoulders to protect himself from the chill. Hesitantly at first, then more eagerly as the juices titillated his taste buds, he tucked into the most delicious coney stew he had ever tasted. He had not tasted anything so good for a long time; he had eaten earlier but cheese and fruit, nice as they were, did not compare to this.

Jon eyed his uncle warily as he ate. He was not yet fully convinced by what he had heard, but did not feel unduly threatened by his behaviour. If he had meant him any harm he could have done so before now. He began to settle, to relax his guard, and asked, 'How did you conjure up this food? That was some trick.'

Urim's gaze shifted towards him and he momentarily stopped chewing to give Jon a wearisome look before a broad smile stretched across his face followed by a soft chuckle. He finished chewing his last mouthful, put down his plate, took up his mug of hot chicory and cradled it in his hands to better warm them.

'Understand, Jon, the food and drink were not conjured up from thin air, I am unable to do that. They were . . . "borrowed" from another place, or rather purchased. I expect that at this very moment there is a bemused innkeeper scratching his head in confusion. He is probably wondering where on earth his two bowls of stew and two cups of chicory have gone and why there are two coins where he thought he had left the food and drink. I never take without giving, that is the law by which I stand. I live and honour it as best I can.'

He paused for a moment, as if considering what next to say or how it should be said; again he chewed nervously at his bottom lip.

Jon sensed that there was much more to know than what Urim was telling him and his suspicions were aroused again, what was he hiding? Jon was curious and needed to hear more if he was to believe anything Urim told him. He encouraged him to say more. 'Humph.'

Urim shook his head as if he could hardly believe what he was saying himself.

'The tale is long in the telling, Jon, too long for now but you shall know, that I promise you.' He looked off into the distance of an inward stare.

'Yes that I promise you. Now, let me apologise for causing you concern, I realise that this is all quite a shock for you. Had there been a better way I would have chosen it but I am bound by certain factors that I cannot explain to you now. It's all to do with the timing of events. I'm afraid I couldn't have made myself known to you before now because . . .'

He paused and lent his ear to the night air. His eyes searched inwardly before settling on Jon. 'You were being hunted.'

The words stunned Jon to the core.

'Hunted?' he exclaimed loudly, almost upsetting the remnants of his meal from off his lap and choking on the mouthful of chicory he had just begun to swallow, then in a more subdued voice, 'Hunted? By what?'

Jon's tone was filled with incredulity and fear. He had been right! Something *had* been following him but he had not thought himself to be hunted. The hairs on the back of his neck bristled again and he gave an involuntary shudder as a cold chill swept through him. Urim held up his hand and quieted him.

'I'm afraid so, Jon.' He spoke quietly and softly. 'You are unfortunately in not a little danger, which I am afraid is partly my doing. That is why I have travelled from Seers' Tower to help you. Permit me to fully introduce myself: I am Urim, keeper of the Golden Tome and of the Council of Seers, you might have heard of us as the Sight.'

Jon had indeed heard of the Sight; there were many stories and legends of the seers circulating in the towns and villages. Was this person Urim indeed one of the seers of whom he had heard so much? Was he indeed his uncle? Fantastic! He was astounded and awed if it were true.

'Yes it's true,' Urim said as if he knew his thoughts. Well, they would not be too hard for him to read as they were written all over his face. 'I also have need of your assistance.'

Urim looked at Jon earnestly as if trying to gauge his reaction.

'This is incredible.' Jon finally blurted. 'You're a seer. Well I've heard of a seer called Urim of course, there are lots of tales about him, but they go back for hundreds of years and you're not that old, are you! Are you?'

'No, I'm not that old.' He chuckled and lowered his head in amusement. 'I am from a long line of seers named Urim; you see it is more a title than a name. I currently hold that title and have done so for a relatively short time in comparison to others.'

Jon was speechless and did not know what to say; he struggled to fully comprehend what Urim had just told him. He felt he would wake up any minute now to find himself safely tucked up in his cot at home. He squeezed his eyes tight shut and half opened one to test his reasoning. He was really sitting in the clearing he had visited so many times before. There, sitting across the fire from him, was not only a long lost uncle, but also a seer: Urim, the one they called Tome-keeper, sitting here in front of him as large as life.

Excitement, incredulity and fear all intermingled in his mind from what Urim had just told him.

'Hunted? And you need my help?' Jon quizzed, looking at him through his half open eye, squinting. 'Hunted?'

Urim confirmed with a slight nod of his head.

'And yes, I do need your help.'

'Hunted by what, or shouldn't I ask? And you're sure it's me you need, not someone else?'

'Yes I am sure it is you who can help me. And it is not what hunts you, it is who hunts you. It is another seer, Ebon Lodestone, who seeks you. Fortunately his vision is not as clear as mine and he lacks a certain privileged knowledge that I have. Jon, believe me when I tell you that if I could have avoided this dilemma I would have done so. It is just far too complex to explain now, though you will ask it of me. When the time is right I will tell you all there is to know, but it is too dangerous for you to know too much at this present time.'

Urim paused in his explanation, or lack of one. He reached across and gently placed a reassuring hand on his shoulder. Looking him squarely in the eye he said, 'I am come to help you achieve what you must achieve. I believe you to be ready, Jon, you have to be, but time will tell. That is all I will say on the matter for now, other than to promise you that as I have said one day you shall know all that you need to know.'

Urim's eyes seemed to penetrate deep into Jon's seeking perhaps to know the thoughts that lay beyond. Jon shifted uncomfortably, avoiding the searching gaze of the seer, feeling his face flush and wondering whether, as a seer Urim really could see and know his thoughts.

'It is no surprise to me that you find this all too much to take in.' Urim grimaced, chewing his bottom lip nervously. Jon looked into the fire that still burned brightly without any apparent fuel. 'Had there been a better way or a different time I would have chosen it, but I am bound.'

It sounded almost like an apology but there was sadness and regret in his tone. 'What we do with our time is so important, we shouldn't waste it. It is something that rules our lives, today's mistakes are tomorrow's regrets.' There was a distinct edge of melancholy and a slight tremor in his voice. 'Well, Jon, we must do the best we can with . . .'

He stopped mid sentence, jumping to his feet, and in one fluid movement waved his staff over the fire, returning it to its previous state, that of a dull glow; the clearing was plunged into darkness, which gradually lifted as his eyes adjusted to the gloom once more. Gesturing Jon to be still and silent, his eyes closed, Urim cocked his head the better to hear for any tell-tale whisper that would carry in the cold night air.

'We must go from here.'

Leaning toward Jon he whispered, 'They are coming. They have discovered us and sense a kill; gather your things into a bundle, make them think you are lying by the fire asleep, take only that which you must; make haste, lad, and quietly, or we may not last the night.'

That last statement probably did not need to be said but it gave

13

Jon an increased desire to do exactly what had been asked of him; he was ready in a moment.

Jon nodded once to Urim and followed him silently out of the clearing, into the dark towards the north, in the direction of the Uplands.

Jon had spent a lot of time in the woods on his own and prided himself on knowing his way around them and being able to recognize the tracks made by the woodland wildlife. Looking back swiftly over his shoulder he could see the dull glow of the camp fire; it emitted just enough light to make out a shape that looked for the entire world as if he were still lying there. His attention reverted to the present task, that of following Urim into the woods. The darkness seemed deeper, but he knew that it was just the effect on his eyes after leaving the firelight behind. There was a good moon tonight and his eyes adjusted quickly; just as well for he had to weave between the saplings and bushes that thickened around them. They moved like ghosts, avoiding making any sound that might betray them.

Jon had no idea of what time it was. He guessed it must be after midnight from the position of the moon, which he glimpsed above the lofty canopy of the giant redwoods. He was still adjusting to the relative gloom of the forest after leaving the glade and the light of the fire. His mind questioned what he was doing skulking around the forest in the dark following someone he had met only minutes ago. He did not really know if what he'd been told were true; he could not help believe the things he had heard, yet he questioned what he was doing. Here he was following a stranger, who professed to be his uncle, whom he had never heard of before. Here he was being led away into the cold and dark, away from the warmth of his camp fire on the pretext that he was being hunted. How did he know it was not Urim, if that was his real name, who had been following him all this time? That Urim was the one of whom he had to be afraid. All these arguments made sense to him as the voice within him argued against trusting what the seer had told him, yet he *did* trust him. He was certain that they were related to each other because there was such a strong resemblance between them: the same height, the same colour eyes, the nervous gnawing of the lower lip. These were obvious signs to Jon that Urim was who he said he was, that he could and should trust him. A shriek from a startled forest creature that ended abruptly from somewhere behind him made him glance over his shoulder nervously.

Somewhere off to his right he heard something shuffle through the underbrush, a small mammal skittered across his foot making him jump; he wondered who was the more scared, him or the creature. The cold air away from the fire made his lungs hurt and his breathing quickened in response to the exertions of hurrying and the fear that was building inside him. He was just about to ask Urim why he had not approached him earlier in the day, when a great howling wail went up into the air from behind them. He almost jumped out of his skin and it chilled him to the bone.

He instinctively spun around towards the mêlée that had erupted. It came from the direction of the clearing, from where they had been but a minute ago.

'If you value your life, follow me and do exactly as I say.' Urim hissed the words between his teeth adding urgency to his words.

Jon was almost swept from his feet as Urim grabbed him, whispering hoarsely, 'Follow me or you're as good as dead, pay no heed to whatever is happening back there, keep close to me.'

Another chilling shriek pierced through the cacophony of sound that only hinted at what might be occurring back at Jon's camp. So Urim was right: he had been hunted. They had obviously discovered that their intended victims had escaped them and were venting their displeasure and frustration in some way amongst themselves. He imagined the campsite was being turned upside down and his belongings scattered all over the place in their fury at his escape.

He struggled to keep up with the seer as they dodged their way through the trees and underbrush; they tried not to make too much noise though it could not be helped. Sap-filled branches would swish back into place having been brushed aside as they ran; one thing was for certain, he had to trust Urim now.

The seer seemed to know his way around these woods as he continued unerringly to beat a path away from the baying and howling of their pursuers. Doubtless they *were* being pursued by them and, if they were found, well he dared not think about it. Jon did not question that Urim was right in saying that this night would be his last if he did not keep up; he stuck to him like glue.

Urim did not seem to worry much now about the noise that

they were making as they fled through the forest. He just seemed intent on getting as much distance between them and whoever it was who was after them. Who did Urim say it was: another seer? Why would another seer want to kill him? He had always believed that they were kindly disposed towards the inhabitants of the land and helped care and nurture it. Jon was a little confused to say the least.

He almost ran into Urim as he stopped dead in his tracks. He dropped his knapsack that he had been reluctant to leave behind and fumbled to retrieve it.

'Try not to be so clumsy!' Urim sounded off to Jon in a loud whisper of annoyance, then more kindly as he placed a reassuring hand on his shoulder and smiled. 'We need to be careful.'

Jon just nodded embarrassed by his clumsiness. He always had been a bit accident prone, and hefted his pack over his shoulder determined not to be a nuisance to the seer. He had always felt that he was a burden to have around when he was with his friends in his younger days. He had not been particularly good at the things that the others did and they had been cruel in their teasing; as youngsters are. It had left him with a lot of insecurities. He crossed his fingers in superstition to ward off bad luck when thinking of anything negative.

He came out of his reverie; distracted by a sudden movement to their right, Urim grabbed his arm and half dragged him for the first few steps until Jon could regain his footing. They made no attempt to conceal their movement; Jon guessed that the time for stealth was past.

Whatever Jon had seen moving was close enough to be aware of them so there was no point in trying to hide now. He could sense that they were being pursued at a pace and heard what sounded like a frantic attempt to catch up to them.

Tiny branches were slapping into his face and body now, stinging as they hit, and no doubt leaving red welts on his arms and legs. No time to worry about that now, he just wanted to get away. Urim forged the way ahead with Jon close behind, clutching on to his backpack as best he could. Urim suddenly veered to the left pulling Jon off balance. An arrow whizzed past his ear with a swish of air and imbedded itself with a dull thud in the tree just to his right. Urim slewed off the track they had been on and Jon realized that if they had not changed direction at that

16

precise moment in time the arrow would have found its intended victim. He gulped and swallowed hard when he realized that Urim had been right and meant what he had said about being careful. They really did intend to kill him. He believed now, without any shadow of doubt, that Urim had been telling him the truth.

Urim again stopped, suddenly gesturing him to be quiet and still.

'Whatever happens, do not move or say a word, I need to concentrate and must not be distracted.'

For what seemed to be an age they stood in silence against a large tree, cloaked in its shadow.

All around them there was the thrashing of bushes and whoops and shrieks, rough, coughing snarls and barks. Somewhere close by he heard a long, subdued, throaty rattle of a growl. If he had had any warm blood in his veins before, it had now turned to ice. Shivers went up and down his spine. He knew the voices of the forest but this was something else, something so foreign to this place that it was terrifying. His heart thudded in his chest and felt it would give out at any moment. His chest heaved from the exertion of running and stumbling from their pursuers.

He tried to keep his breathing low but still his heart pounded and his lungs burned for want of sufficient oxygen. He kept as still and as quiet as he could, fearful of betraying them both to the stalking creatures that were so close at hand.

Jon felt a buzz in the air as if there were a swarm of bees around him and his ears began to ache a little. He tried to equalize the pressure by holding his nose and blowing; that helped but he could still feel rather than hear the buzzing around him.

'What *is* going on?' he questioned silently, not daring to utter the words. He stole a glance at Urim who seemed to be in a deep trance; he was looking fixedly straight ahead, his left hand grasped his staff so tightly that his knuckles whitened, his right hand held out ahead of him. In his palm was what looked like a miniature golden book that was pulsating with a blue light.

He did not seem any the worse for having fled through the forest and certainly did not look perturbed by the unusual buzzing noise. Then he realized that it was Urim that was causing it, but how? Why?

Jon looked around, he recognized where they were, they stood just short of the edge of another clearing in the forest. They had kept shy of the open and hugged the shadow of the tree, keeping them hidden from the view of any would-be assailant.

The ground dipped slightly towards the middle of the clearing where, in its centre, there was a pool of clear water; the light of the moon sparkled in its dark mirror-like surface. There was only one tree in the clearing, on the opposite side of the pool, a weeping willow, long tendril-like branches tickling the ground, its leaves softly rustling in the gentle night breeze. He heard the approach of the creature before he saw it and prepared for the worst. Surely Urim could hear it too; why didn't they run? Why had they stopped here? Question after question flashed through his mind. He felt anxious, alarmed at the approach of who-knows-what? He flinched at the sudden appearance of the creature as it crashed through the nearby undergrowth. He had never seen its like in the forest or anywhere else around here. He doubted he would ever come into these woods alone again if such creatures as these were abroad. It stood hunched on squat, sturdy hind legs, covered with black matted hair; it reeked of decay. He guessed that it was about seven feet tall; he could hear its laboured breathing, which fouled the air as it snorted from the exertion of trying to catch them. The stench was almost unbearable; the pungent odour wafted on the air, filling his nostrils. It almost made him retch; he could feel himself gagging and struggled not to do so and give them away.

He could see the thing quite clearly as it surveyed the clearing from eyes that were high up on its head. Its snout was long above rows of razor sharp teeth, protruding from its jaws. This thing resembled a bear but its head was more like a reptile. It was testing the air, seeking for any tell-tale smell of them that lingered. Why had it not seen them or caught their scent? It was so close to them that he dared not move or say a word. Urim was most emphatic about that and he believed in him now. Jon observed the creature with dread and fascination; its eyelids fluttered like a butterfly over emerald green eyes. They had slit pupils with a transparent membrane protecting them. It had coarse, rank hair, matted with grime covering its body. He wondered where such a creature could live. It did not look too comfortable in its stance but its muscular forearms were far too short for walking on all fours. Its back legs were stocky and twice the girth of Jon's legs. He began to recollect a description of a creature that had been captured some years ago in the marshland on the southern borders of the Yield. It had escaped soon after, killing three of its captors and leaving the other one for dead. A marsh-mog they had called it. Yes, he was convinced this was indeed a marsh-mog.

What was it doing here? Why had it not seen them? He could not understand; was it blind? It did not seem to be, because it was searching the clearing intently. The creature shifted from one great leg to the other as if excited by something, anticipating, awaiting the command to pounce. As Jon was studying it, a movement caught his eye just beyond where it was standing; another one. 'How many more were there?' he asked himself. His reverie was cut short by a movement in the clearing. Trying to keep sight of the marsh-mogs out of the corner of his eye, and see what had attracted his attention, Jon saw a figure by the willow tree leaning nonchalantly upon his longbow. There was a second figure, squatting by the brook, filling a drinking flask with clean water.

They had his full attention now; he recognised them from descriptions he had heard given by travellers from the east: gnomes, the antithesis of a dwarf. Everything good there was about a dwarf was counterbalanced by the bad in a gnome. To look at them, dwarves and gnomes did not appear to differ greatly. The only real way you could tell a dwarf from a gnome was by the beard. A dwarf would never be seen without his beard whereas a gnome could not grow one and would rather be boiled in oil than have one.

They were dressed in hunting greens, the customary dress for gnomes. They were seasoned hunters and had assisted trappers from time to time but could not be trusted as far as you could throw them. They could turn on you as quick as a flash betraying you to whoever gave them a good deal. The bile rose in his throat when recalling the tales he heard of their treachery. What he would not give to be able to get one of them in his hands. He had wondered sometimes what he would do but had never been able to satisfactorily come to any conclusion. He might never find out and that would be fine by him; but there, just a little way off, tantalisingly close and unsuspecting, were two gnomes. They were probably the ones who had been tracking them earlier and had narrowly missed skewering Jon with that arrow. Had it not been for Urim grabbing his arm and the sudden change in direction, he would no doubt be dead or injured and in their hands at this very moment. Jon felt it strange that the gnomes seemed so relaxed and confident about being out in the open clearing, taking no thought for cover or concealment. They were as comfortable as if in their own backyard, not a care in the world. Had they given up trying to catch him? Were they playing some sort of game with them?

The faint yet audible sound of decaying leaf mulch shuffling underfoot just off to his left caused him to stiffen. He had almost forgotten the marsh-mogs. As he looked in the direction the noise had come from he was shocked to see three of them standing about twenty feet away in a group.

Further on from them were two more and as he scanned the shadows at the edges of the clearing he could see movements between the trees, more were gathering. He felt absolutely petrified, yet Urim seemed completely unaffected by the whole situation, standing there as before, only now he was frowning, deep in concentration. He was aware of the buzzing noise still and noticed that Urim's staff was glowing with a pale blue luminescence.

A sharp, barking yelp from off to his left made him jump. From all around the clearing a great howling and clamouring arose, making his blood curdle. The gnomes, who had been so apparently at ease before now, were looking very alarmed and turned frantically one way then another in confusion and bewilderment.

They tried shouting out to the baying creatures but whatever it was that they were trying to say became drowned out by the tumult from the company of creatures filled with a blood-lust. Other sounds mixed with those of the marsh-mogs; Jon guessed that there were other creatures than they in their company.

A long, low, growling snarl intensified to become a screaming howl, like a wolf that had been on the prowl and was now calling the pack to order. Jon could scarcely hear himself think. The din from the pack was so loud he could feel his insides reverberate. Then all at once, as if set off by some signal, the creatures rushed the gnomes, eager to get at their quarry. Still Jon could not understand what was happening. Why were they attacking the gnomes? Surely it was he that they wanted.

CRACK!!!

The air shook with a roll of thunder, and green lightning crackled out of the darkness of the forest, dissipating into the night. The noise reverberated around the whole area, hurting Jon's ears, deafening him momentarily. He instinctively covered his ears with his hands and closed his eyes. Too late of course, the ghost of it echoed through his skull and the memory of the lightning flash was imprinted into his eyelids. Even Urim flinched and grimaced as if in pain yet he maintained his stance and concentration determinedly.

When he looked up he could see no sign of the gnomes, just a mass of black hairy bodies quivering in fright, yelping like so many whipped dogs.

Out of the forest shadows opposite where they stood strode a shrouded figure, much like Urim in appearance. Jon was bemused, shocked and frightened; he had not expected this. He remembered what Urim had said, that he was being hunted by another seer. 'What was his name?' he asked himself, trying to remember. 'Ebon, that was it, Ebon Lodestone.'

Like Urim, he wore a black cloak over a black robe that reached to his ankles; it was secured at the waist by a large, black leather belt. He wore the hood of his cloak well down over his head so that Jon could not discern his features; it was almost as if he had no face, making him look even more menacing and mysterious.

He strode purposefully up to the centre of the clearing amidst the cowering marsh-mogs and other wolf-like creatures, gesturing them to move away. A large, grey wolf-hound loped along beside him, coming to heel when Ebon stopped; another hooded figure followed him a little way behind but he could not make him out amongst the marsh-mogs.

'So my fine friends, we have brought you to task at last.'

He rolled his head back and laughed briefly.

Jon saw that one of the gnomes raised an arm towards Ebon; the tunic was tattered and torn, bloodied from what must have been a frenzied attack upon him.

'Well I must say that I hadn't expected this; two for the price of one? You managed to evade my net before, but now I have

21

you and I shall not be so remiss as to lose you again. Bring them; carefully. I wish to question them, if they die, you die, painfully.'

He strode back into the forest following a rough track north, towards the Uplands. The gnomes were treated with much more respect by the creatures now that *their* lives were accountable.

Jon watched silently, transfixed by what was unfolding before him, not daring to move. The creatures carried the gnomes out of the clearing in Ebon's wake along the track, subdued by Ebon and in fear for their lives. It was reminiscent of a wake; hardly a whisper was heard, just the trudge of many feet on the dusty animal track.

Jon looked at Urim. He was perspiring and seemed to be weakened by his efforts; the small book he held was no longer glowing and he was clinging to his staff to steady himself. Jon offered assistance but Urim shook his head, managing a weak smile and a nod of his head to indicate that he was OK. Urim squared his shoulders and took in a couple of deep breaths, placed the miniature book back into the pouch at his side then said, 'Well, Jon, there's no going back now. From here on in it's a difficult road, one that I can only help you with a little, though it's a journey that you must take if all is to be put right. Let's go to your home, Jon, we will be safe there for the moment but we can stay only a short while.'

Looking down the track that Ebon and his troop had taken he said, 'We must travel a different course than Ebon's this night. I need to rest and you no doubt have many unanswered questions. I need a good strong mug of chicory and I hear tell that you make a good brew?'

He smiled engagingly at Jon and gave him a friendly slap on the back. He spun around and walked briskly in the opposite direction to which Ebon had gone, saying over his shoulder, 'If we make good time we could be there for breakfast.'

Jon was caught off guard by Urim's comments and manner but quickly determined not to be surprised by anything the seer did or said again, not after what he had just witnessed. One thing Urim was dead right about though, Jon did have some questions that he wanted to ask; and they needed answering!

Chapter II

Urim's Tale

They walked side by side along the dusty, rutted road. The night receded as dawn approached and the golden rays of the sun broke through the clouds as it rose higher into the sky, dispelling the dark terrors of the night; the light cast their shadows along the road in front of them. It was not much of a road, just a cart track really, but it carried a lot of traffic at times, particularly when the trappers came to the village after the summer season. The day was breaking the cold grip of night as they made steady progress, heading back to Jon's home, a small cottage near the chapel in the centre of Ashbrooke. A cock crowed somewhere off to the left from one of the outlying farmsteads and they heard cattle lowing, eager for the morning milking to begin. They had not said a word to each other since leaving the forest. Jon was still a little suspicious of Urim; there was something not quite right about all this. For instance, how did he know which direction to go to where he lived, how much more did he know about his life? There may be many more things about Urim that would surprise and concern him. The more he thought on him, the more bemused he became and the more questions he needed answering. However, this was not the right place; Urim had promised him answers when they got to his home, and he would have to wait until then. The one thing that could not wait was how they had managed to escape when a marsh-mog had stood just lengths from them? So he asked.

'Oh, I simply exchanged the outlines of the gnomes for ours; the creatures thought that the gnomes were us, whilst we merged into the shadows, seemingly becoming part of the tree, making us invisible to them. Quite simple really but it took a lot of concentration to effect the required transformation.'

Urim responded as if it were an everyday occurrence and did not offer any more explanation than that.

23

Jon glanced towards him, keen to know more but Urim stared fixedly at a spot about ten steps ahead of him as they walked; he obviously had no intention of engaging in any further conversation for the moment.

Jon could feel the warmth of the sun on his back as it gathered strength. He usually enjoyed this time of the morning and relished the crispness of a new day. He could breathe in the fresh, clean air, washed by the early morning dew and marvel as the mist gathered in the hollows as if veiling the earth as it slumbered. Today though, his thoughts were far from the beauty of the morning; darker images still played across his mind; he shuddered involuntarily. The forest was several leagues behind them now, he was eager to be home, usually it was the other way around and he would be wishing to be in amongst the trees. He looked back towards the forest, silhouetted against the rising sun, dark, as it had never appeared before. He wondered whether they were safe from Ebon and the marsh-mogs. He guessed they were otherwise he felt sure that Urim would not appear so relaxed about them travelling along the track through open country.

Despite his fatigue, the seer was setting quite a pace and Jon had to walk briskly in order to keep up with him. Still he said nothing and Jon thought it best to honour his silence for the while. He cheered up when they crested a rise. He had not paid too much attention to where he was in relation to the road they were on until then; he had been too intent on his thoughts. There, below them, nestling between the Crystal River and the River Nune, was his home town of Ashbrooke. It lay sheltered from the north winds in winter because of the surrounding Downs and its being in a depression at the confluence of the two rivers. The rolling Downs were lush and verdant with crisp green grass, ideal for the farming of sheep and cattle where they could graze contentedly; all was right with the world, he mused, whilst there were sheep in the fields. He grinned in relief at the familiarity and normality of the place. His mood brightened at the thought that he would soon be tucking into a hot mug of chicory and possibly a few eggs as well. Amazing how cheering the thought of hot food and drink could be to the soul, he thought.

Jon could see the chapel tower near his home; it was the first building in the town to catch the rays of the sun each day. Soon the whole town would awake from its slumber and bask in the welcoming blush of the morning sunshine. The town was still and quiet; only the sound of the rivers flowing gracefully through the centre disturbed the silence. Occasionally there came a bleat from a lamb on the hills or the chirp of the birds as they flew from branch to branch. He wanted to run down the track all the way home, then remembered Urim and decided to repress the urge and guide the seer to his home. He wondered if perhaps Urim may already know where he lived; he seemed to know everything else about him.

Jon noticed Urim falter in his step as they topped the rise and wondered whether he was ailing from fatigue. He caught a glisten in his eye and then he sneezed, again and again. Urim begged his pardon to which Jon gave the traditional response, then without another word between them they walked on and into the town centre.

Urim *did* seem to know the way. Jon let him take the lead a little at each crossroads and junction; he never faltered from taking the right one. All the way up to the back entrance of the cottage; Jon hardly ever used the front door. Urim reached out for the latch, only then did the seer come out of his daydream and remember that Jon was with him.

'Your pardon, Jon, I was forgetting myself, this is your home.'

He was very different from the Urim of last night and Jon began to feel concerned.

'Is anything the matter, Urim? You seem a little distracted.'

Urim cast an eye down the alleyway alongside the cottage towards the chapel.

'I'll be fine once I have rested.'

He spoke with a small falter in his voice.

Jon gave him a look that belied belief in what he had heard, lifted the latch and stepped inside the back garden; it wasn't much but it had kept him busy with tending to the vegetables following his mother's death. Life was different for Jon here; he felt safe, secure from the ways of the world. This cottage was where he had grown up, where his mother had taught him, where she had died; it had been his refuge and, eventually, his prison. Were it not for Anna, the only person who really knew him, he would have stayed here, cocooned in its security. She had not given up on him throughout his struggle to come to terms with the loss of his mother. She understood how he felt; she had lost both of her parents when she was just nine years old. Although she was dumb, she could communicate to him in a way that transcended words. A soft, gentle touch on his arm, a look from her dark eyes, made all the darker by her porcelain skin, clear and fine. She had been the one that had encouraged him to go to the forest yesterday and get away from the village for a while. She would be amazed at what had happened; *he* was amazed!

They entered a small room at the back of the cottage; it smelt musty but not unpleasant, so he opened a window to let in the fresh air. Moving through to the parlour, he opened that window too. He noticed that there was still no sign of life from the town and began to feel concerned. Was everything as it should be? Where was everyone? A thought caused him to stop midway through opening the window. What if Ebon had come here first! What if he had killed all the townsfolk!

'Mornin', Jim.'

'Mornin', Frank; luverly day ain't it.'

The two men continued their conversation as they passed by the window. Jon started, held his hand to his chest to steady the beating and laughed to himself. Stupid fool, he thought. As if! He reprimanded himself for being so fanciful and dramatic; always thinking the worst. 'I'll boil some water and fix us some chicory. I think there's some ham and eggs in the larder. Maybe the bread could be freshened in the oven, or perhaps you could whiz up something from somewhere?'

He half expected Urim to use his staff again, to light the fire and produce steaming drinks just as he had last night. Apparently not; he just stood there at the window, looking out at the chapel. He made no move to respond; they had spoken only briefly the whole way home as Urim had explained the manner of their escape.

Jon shrugged his shoulders dismissively and busied himself getting a fire started. They had soon sated their hunger on the delicious ham and eggs along with a large wedge of granary bread; all washed down with a warming mug of hot chicory.

The meal finished, they both sat in silence. Jon leaned back in his chair, rubbing his tummy with a contented smile on his face. Urim cradled his mug of chicory in his hands and stared into it, much as the travellers do when they tell your fortune from the patterns left in the dregs.

Jon studied him. He was a mystery; a fascinating and bewildering enigma. There were so many questions he wanted to ask but he did not know where to start.

Urim leaned back in his chair, resting his head on the wall behind him, eyes closed. After a while he opened his eyes and fixed Jon with his gaze.

It unnerved him because it was plain to see the family resemblance now; it both unsettled and reassured him all at the same time.

'You have a lot of questions to ask of me, Jon. In time you will have all of them answered; for now I will tell you what I can.' He spoke as if reading his thoughts.

Jon was particularly interested in hearing what the seer had to say. Urim had been unwilling to talk earlier so he was not going to stop him now. He encouraged him, eager for an explanation of why he was here and what was going on.

Urim closed his eyes as if piecing together the threads of what he was going to say. After a moment or two he leaned forward and looked Jon in the eye.

'You must understand that what I have to tell you may only raise further questions. More importantly, it would be disadvantageous to know too much at this moment in time. I have to ask for your forbearance.'

He leaned forward as he spoke, as if he were pleading for his understanding.

Jon could clearly see that Urim was deeply earnest; he knew somehow, beyond a shadow of doubt, that he was a friend. The conviction he felt was so strong that he did not doubt it for a minute. He looked back at him squarely and nodded.

'It would probably be better if I just told you all I can, I'm sure that along the way, many of your questions will be answered.'

He went on to tell of treachery in the Sight, of duplicity, jealousy, pride, arrogance and of ambitions of power. Urim and Ebon were seers in the Council of the Sight, the only men amongst the eight who held title. The leader of the Sight was a dwarf named Terra Standfast, that being his title. For many hundreds of years all had been in harmony, each seer serving in their place and taking the title of their predecessor on their passing. Always the same types of individual for the required role, whether it be man, dwarf, elf or sprite. Each had accountability

27

to the Council as a whole, no one being greater than the other. Each knew their place in the order of things.

Only Terra Standfast and his predecessors held the 'chair of final verdict' and he was held to be the leader of the Council of the Sight. This had been sustained and unquestioned for centuries, from the founding of the Sight. That is until a certain man took the title of Ebon Lodestone. He was young, as was common, and had been selected and groomed for the succession on the passing of the then incumbent Ebon.

Once inaugurated at the passing of the old Ebon, a kindly man who had done much good throughout the land in his time, he had wanted to change things so that everyone got a chance, as he called it, to be the leader of the Council. Of course he would be the first to have this privilege because it was his idea and it was only just that he should be the first. They overruled him of course and he outwardly appeared to accept the decision, but inwardly he plotted and schemed to take control. Urim had befriended him and treated him like a younger brother, encouraging him to learn his duties well and to perform them as befitted a seer. Ebon did so at first but soon tired of it and wanted more. He had sounded Urim out on supporting him. Being cautious, Urim agreed with him in order to discover his true intent but kept Terra Standfast informed of developments.

Months went by and Ebon feigned loyalty to the Council, all the while making alliances with those who thought as he did. Over a period of time he gathered knowledge from ancient books he found deep in the library of the Tower. One night he told Urim that he was ready to make his move, he knew now how to take control and wanted Urim to support him in the forthcoming meeting.

He had agreed in order to allay any concerns Ebon may have had, and then sought out Terra Standfast so that he would be forewarned of Ebon's plans. The stability of the Council must be maintained.

They convened in the central chamber beneath Terra's dormitory as usual; each seer sat at their appointed place. Ebon was accused and evidence submitted, he was asked if he had anything to say. They expected that he would deny all the allegations; but he surprised them all by denying nothing. Quite the contrary, he boasted of his ambition and turned on Urim accusing him of duplicity, of treachery and denounced their friendship. As far as Ebon was concerned Urim was no better than the rest of them and could join them in their fate. He snatched his staff from the table before him (all seers placed their staffs on the table in front of them when convened for a council) and slammed its head onto the table. Green light exploded from it and the other seers' staffs melted into the surface, becoming one with the wood, before they could lay hands on them. Without them, their powers were limited at best. Ebon's fury was plain for all to see; cursing the Sight and promising revenge for imagined slights against him. He sprang for the door before anyone could stop him and sealed the others in the chamber. He had gone throughout the Tower taking things from each of the seers' dormitories, the servants and domestics never guessing that anything was amiss, only thinking that he was fulfilling a charge to do so by the Council. No one knew of any problem because the chamber was soundproof from within and the other seers could not raise the alarm; they could do nothing to stop him.

As he left the Tower he somehow engaged its powerful defences against an imaginary assault. He put up an impenetrable shield that shimmered like a veil of rising heat; it obtained its power from the central shaft in the courtyard: power pulsed along the conduits in the flagstones up through the eight towers, then rising above Seers' Tower like a great upturned bowl that completely covered the area surrounding the Tower. Somehow he had created an illusion within that the edifice was under attack by another force. The power came from within the Tower itself. Thereby, it was both attacking and defending itself in a continuous cycle that would not be broken. Nothing could get in or out of the Tower. Ebon had the whole land at his mercy and he wanted to be the ruler of it all, no matter what the cost. To help him achieve his ambition he surrounded himself with others who sought power and influence. Amongst them, gnomes, trolls and weak-minded men who sensed a chance of glory.

Urim continued.

'Fortunately, after several attempts, one of the seers managed to get out, however the Tower and the other seers are still in the grip of Ebon's charm.'

'It was you? You were the one to get out. How did you do it?'

Urim paused for a moment. Jon guessed he was reliving the events of his escape.

'I told you that my tale would engender more questions; the answer to that is not important at the present. What is important is that we stop Ebon from wreaking havoc in the land and find a way to end the cycle of power that holds the seers captive in the Tower. I have already tried and failed in the attempt. All I succeeded in doing was to alert Ebon to my being there. Somehow by using the talismans he had stolen, he gained knowledge about you, that we are related as it were; he hopes to get to me through you. Jon, I know where Ebon can be found and what his purpose is but we must leave here by tomorrow at the latest, though I would prefer now, if we can.'

Jon nodded and hurried his preparations for the journey. Fired up by Urim's words he wanted to help him free the seers and to assist in whatever way he could.

Urim wandered over to the window that overlooked the church. Looking out of the window he said softly, 'She is buried over there, your mother, in the graveyard by the tree?'

'Yes. It was the spot she had always wanted. She bought the plot not long after my father disappeared; she always used to say that it's best to be prepared, you never know what might happen.'

'She was a very wise lady; you must miss her.'

Urim clutched the curtain that hung at the window, not looking at Jon as he spoke.

Jon went quiet for a moment and lowered his head; he chewed nervously on his lower lip. 'She was everything to me.'

'I am sorry that I wasn't here to see her. It wasn't possible. You see, there were certain conditions incumbent upon me when I was sent here.'

He moved wearily away from the window and sat at the table clasping his hands. Jon looked to see if anything further would be added to that statement, but there was nothing forthcoming. He took the plates into the kitchen, shouting over his shoulder, 'Where are we going, and how long do I need to pack for? You'll need something too, there's a spare satchel in the cupboard under the stairs.'

Jon returned to let Urim know how to open the door; it was a little tricky and you had to have the knack. He was surprised to see that Urim had already opened it and was pulling the satchel from its hanger.

'Oh, I see you've already done it; that was lucky.'

Urim stuttered a little as if he had been caught with a stolen apple in his hand.

'Oh yes. It wasn't difficult. Not for a seer I mean. We'll be away for some time, probably a couple of weeks, no more. Take what you can easily carry; we don't want to be weighed down by too much. We'll purchase food along the way and hire lodgings, although we will need to be discreet, we don't want to draw attention to ourselves.'

Jon looked at the seer dressed in his worn, black robe and said, 'I think we might do so anyway. You don't often come across a seer in these parts!'

'Hum, no, but then you do see the friars as they commune from town to town. We will have to avoid taking the coach and walk just as they do. That way I will pass as one of them.'

Jon shrugged and accepted that Urim was probably right; after all that's who he had thought Urim was when he first saw him.

There was a knock on the kitchen door that startled Jon; Urim sighed and sat at the table resignedly.

'I'd hoped to forego this moment. Come on in, Anna.'

Urim looked very uncomfortable and clasped his hands tightly; his face paled a little. Turning to Jon he said, 'Tell her nothing. It is vital that we keep as much to ourselves as possible.'

Jon cocked his head to one side but nodded his agreement. There must be a good reason not to say anything but he did not understand why he could not say anything to Anna; anyway it might not be her knocking on the door.

Sure enough, it was Anna. She poked her head around the door, frowning quizzically. A broad grin spread across her face when she saw Jon and she flushed slightly. The grin vanished though when she saw Urim and the quizzical look returned.

Jon beamed, delighted to see her. 'Hello, Anna, come on in. Have you had breakfast?'

Anna closed the door behind her. She was a mute so communicated with Jon by means of sign language.

I saw you were back. Is everything OK? What's happened? Who's the stranger?

31

'Yes, I'm fine; he's my uncle, we met in the forest last night; he saved my life.'

He glanced at Urim and stopped short of any further explanation.

Anna noticed that they were making preparations for a journey.

Are you leaving again so soon? Where are you going? What's happened?

'I'm not sure where we're going. My uncle has asked me to go with him because he needs my help.'

Anna was not keen on this news; glaring at Urim suspiciously, she signed to Jon.

You're going with him? You don't know anything about him? I didn't think you had an uncle?

Jon spoke quietly and turned so that Urim couldn't hear.

'No, I know. Quite a surprise isn't it. I'm pretty certain I can trust him though, I believe him to be genuine, you only need to look at him to see the family resemblance.'

Anna did look closer and softened a little; she could see a resemblance. She was still concerned and upset that he would be leaving. Being quite feisty in nature, she was not going to let this go; she was a tenacious person and strong willed.

Then I think I'll come with you, she signed back resolutely.

Jon shot a glance at Urim, wondering what his reaction would be to Anna accompanying them. Urim sat at the table and stroked his forehead as if trying to iron out its creases.

'Unfortunately, dear Anna, it is not a journey that concerns you and you would do well to stay here.'

Jon and Anna were both shocked: Urim could read her signing. What other surprises did he have in store for them, Jon wondered.

Urim's voice was tinged with emotion as he continued.

'You see, it is a matter of fate that dictates what we do and what becomes of us. In this case I foresee that only ill would come of your journeying with us. So I must insist that you do not come.'

Well, talk about a red rag to a bull. Jon had never seen her so incensed. He decided to duck out of this fight, because that is what it was going to be, albeit a battle of wills. He did not want to lay odds on who would win. He knew that Anna was nothing if not determined, he did not know about the seer.

She went into fast mode with her signing and stood her ground, ending in a defiant stance with hands on hips. Thrusting her jaw forward, daring Urim to deny her the right to do what she wanted and to go where she wanted, when she wanted.

Jon tried to keep up with her signing and to translate but Urim gently waved a dismissive hand in his direction. Then, when she had finished, he faultlessly signed back. *My goodness, Anna, how I love your passion. It is so refreshing.* He carried on by speaking. 'But as I have said, this journey is not for you to undertake. Please do not mistake my statement as a denial of your ability. It is simply a statement of fact. You would be ill-advised to come with us. Let me explain.'

He went on, a soft smile upon his lips and a gentle light in his eye.

'It does you credit to show such passion and concern for Jon. I can assure you that his safety is paramount to my being here. He is kinsman to me, in fact my nearest kin and I would never ask him to do anything that would damage his welfare. There is something that I must do and can only succeed if Jon comes with me. His contribution to this venture is vital to its success.'

'Excuse me, Urim. Why am I a vital part to this? I'm no one of any consequence. Why is it so vital that I go with you?'

Jon was confused. He had agreed to go with Urim, indeed he felt an inner compulsion to do so, but he had not been told that it was vital for him to go.

Urim looked at Jon as if reluctant to say any more but knew he had said too much to go back now.

'That is something that you will discover for yourself when the time is right. Remember that too much information can be destructive as well as informative. Once again I have to ask for your trust and patience, I ask a lot I know, but it is necessary.'

He bit nervously at his lip.

Jon did the same.

All three of them were silent for what seemed an age. Gradually Anna's stance wavered and she relaxed, resigned it seems by the strength of Urim's tone and his demeanour; signing back to them she declared, *Then I must go with you, what you are saying only convinces me more that I need to go; someone has to look after you. Besides, there is nothing to keep me here.*

She glanced quickly at Jon for a second and continued.

The Hooper family can easily get another housemaid; I know several who would jump at the chance. I'd be doing them a favour.

Jon was a little stunned by all this but was quite happy for Anna to be with them, he knew she could take care of herself; she was no shy domestic that's for sure. He was glad she wanted to go, on reflection, it was exactly the sort of thing that he would expect her to do.

Urim hung his head and clasped his hands more tightly as if trying to wring a more solid argument from them. It was apparent that he was not happy with this. Lifting his head and levelling his gaze at Anna, he said, with great conviction and determination, 'That is the worst thing that you could do. As I have said, this journey is not one to be undertaken lightly and certainly there can be no place in it for you. You cannot come.'

He was resolute and it was plain that no amount of arguing would dissuade him from it. Anna stood there, hands on hips and red faced; she was furious with Urim for the stance he was taking and could see no way around it. She stamped her foot petulantly and stormed out of the cottage, slamming the door shut so that it juddered on its hinges.

'Well that went well.'

Jon reprimanded Urim and rushed out after her. He caught up with her at the end of the alleyway leading into the street.

'Urim's right, Anna, we don't know what lies ahead and goodness knows how long we shall be gone.'

He tried to calm her down but he only succeeded in making her more agitated but he spoke more kindly and shyly as he added, 'I wouldn't want anything to happen to you. I want you to come with me, *us*, but I can understand Urim's point. You're much better off staying here. If only to please me; I don't want to see you hurt.'

She calmed visibly and blushed disarmingly. This was the first time Jon had ever hinted at anything other than a casual concern for her. She had loved him for many years, hoping that someday he might love her in return, hardly daring to think that he might. Here he was though, showing that there was hope. They had been like brother and sister and she appreciated his brotherly concern.

She stilled and settled her deep brown eyes on his. She drew into him, wrapping her arms tightly around him. Resting her head on his chest, she could hear the thudding of his heart. With tears in her eyes she drew back from him and kissed his cheek.

She clasped his hands in hers and nodded submission to his request. She wiped her tears away with the back of her hand then signed, *If you think it best, Jon, I will stay.*

'I do.'

Then be careful. I don't trust him and I don't like him. Are you sure about this?

'Well, as sure as I can be, but I will be careful.'

She reached up and kissed him again, giving him the tightest hug, almost crushing him in the process, then she turned and walked briskly away, wiping at her face as she went. Jon stood for a while looking after her. He wished he had had the courage to tell her how he felt, but they had been as brother and sister for so long. He did not know whether she would feel the same for him. He chewed on his lower lip nervously and returned indoors.

Urim was still sitting at the table, hands clasped. He seemed troubled. He covered his eyes and cleared his throat then pushed himself up from the chair.

'Come then, Jon, we have no time to lose, we must away. The longer we stay here, the more danger there is for the townsfolk. Are you ready?'

'Yes, I think so.'

He gathered his belongings together. He looked around the room as if it would be the last time he would see it, ingraining it into his memory. He packed the last of the food from the pantry into his backpack.

'Right, I'm ready, let's go.'

They walked out into the sunlight of a glorious autumn morning. Under any other conditions Jon would have been in high spirits. Today, though, he felt both subdued because of last night's experience and at the same time a little excited at the prospect of an adventure. With one of the seers as a companion, this was likely to be a significant one.

They turned north, out of Ashbrooke, away from the security of his home and the past, into the uncertainty and insecurity of the future. He had nothing more than the trust he had in the man who had revealed himself to be his uncle, but more amazingly, a seer of the Council of the Sight.

*

They stopped for a brief rest at midday on a grassy slope by the roadside, sheltering in the shade of a small copse of birch trees, to rejuvenate themselves with a spot of lunch. The waning summer sun still had sufficient strength in it to warm the air around them pleasantly, creating a sense of contentment within them.

'Why did we come this way, Urim?'

'Because this is the way we need to go to where we shall meet with Ebon again.'

Jon stopped mid bite of his biscuit.

'Ebon? I didn't think we wanted to go anywhere near him.'

'If it could be avoided, we wouldn't but we must retrieve something from him before he has the opportunity to use it.'

'Oh! What's that?'

'It is something that will increase his knowledge and power, giving him the advantage over us if we do not first obtain it.'

Urim fell silent but Jon was bursting to know more.

'So this thing that Ebon has, I take it that he doesn't know how to use it then.'

'Correct.'

He was getting nowhere fast.

'So where are we headed?' Jon asked, hoping for a better answer than he had received so far.

'We are heading for Foundry Smelt.'

Jon choked on his last mouthful of biscuit.

'Did you say Foundry Smelt? But that's a good four days or more from here.'

'It is indeed,' Urim confirmed as he sat and relaxed against a fallen branch.

'So shouldn't we get going?'

'There is time yet.'

Something about Urim was really irritating Jon; he was far too relaxed about starting again and he was being deliberately uncommunicative. He decided not to press the matter but to leave things to Urim; after all, *he* was the seer.

They sat and watched the trickle of movement along the road as every now and again the occasional hay wagon would trundle past. A goose herder encouraged his flock along the road to the forthcoming poultry market at Ashbrooke.

A lone traveller coming from Ashbrooke caught his attention. He watched the traveller's progress towards the crossroads near where they sat as there was nothing better to do while Urim was being so unresponsive. He was carrying a backpack much like his own and was kitted out for a hike.

Jon noticed that there was something odd about this person and then he realized that it was not a man, it was a girl. Not just any girl though, it was Anna.

He shot a quick glance at Urim. He was impassive, as if he had expected her to follow them; it was almost as if it were planned.

She approached briskly and in good humour, waving toward them as she climbed the gentle rise to where they were. A broad smile on her face as if to say, 'You can't stop me from going where I want to go.'

Urim was not amused; he took her by the arm and gently but firmly steered her away from Jon so as to be out of earshot. Not that it mattered because Jon would be able to read her responses anyway. He decided to stay well out of this. Anna could handle herself and he did not want to argue against her not coming because deep inside he wanted Anna to come along. She would be a hard nut to crack if Urim was to get her to go back, which was clearly his aim. This should prove interesting, he thought to himself.

Urim was not happy; he went through many emotions from appealing to common sense, through pleading and frustration to exasperation. She would not be moved from her resolve to accompany them.

Jon gave a slight chuckle of delight when he saw Urim hold up his hands in surrender and back away from her. It was clear that he was used to getting his way in any discussion; Anna had squared up to him at every point; Urim had met his match.

He stalked off in a huff ahead of them on the track. He snatched his pack from off the ground and slung it across his shoulders. Jon thought that the food that was in it would probably not be worth eating after such treatment, but that was up to him.

Jon caught up with Anna and said, 'You really shouldn't have come . . . but I'm glad you did.'

She beamed at him to hear him say that. She giggled in her own silent way and linked arms with him as they hurried to catch up with Urim.

Their journey continued but this time with one extra traveller.

Chapter III

The Journey Begins

There was a noticeable change to the air this morning; the wind had shifted overnight and blew from the south, bringing with it warmer weather. It was a welcome relief from the light frosts of these past few mornings of their journey. They had managed to secure accommodation each night, until yesterday, when a sudden storm had held up their progress. They had sought shelter in a cave that they had discovered when the storm struck. They had been soaked by the sudden downpour and had had to dry their clothes around an open fire; they were, as luck would have it, able to cook a hot stew from the scant provisions that they were carrying in their backpacks, otherwise they would have had to have eaten cold fruit and biscuits. It was fortunate that they had anything at all; their objective was to have spent the night at the Spotted Cow tavern that Urim had told them of, just a few more leagues up the trail.

There they would have enjoyed a warm cot for the night, having dined heartily on a meal of beef and mushroom pie, washed down with a steaming mug of chicory. Ah, the thought of it had made Jon's mouth water; instead they had had bean stew. Welcome as it was on occasion when you are expecting it, but when you have beef and mushroom pie on your mind; well, it comes in a poor second. He had hoped that Urim might produce something for them to eat, just as he had done when they first met, but Urim had said that there was food available, and that there was no need for him to 'use magic' when they could provide for themselves. Jon had not been very happy, but had had to concede his point.

The air was thicker today and it tickled his nose making him feel as if a sneeze was imminent; no matter how he twitched his nose, it still tickled. One look at Anna told him that she too was feeling the effects of the change in the air. Her eyes were red, as if from lack of sleep and she was rubbing at her nose. Something in the air was clearly causing an irritation to their senses. Urim did not appear irritated by it though, other than the occasional sniff.

'Not far now,' Urim said encouragingly, as he prepared to continue the journey.

Jon felt relieved to hear it but if it was not that far why hadn't they continued on in the rain and benefited from the comforts of the tavern? He had spent a restless night tossing and turning in an effort to get comfortable so was looking forward to a good lunch when they reached the tavern. Maybe they would have some pie left over from last night's supper; that would be nice.

'If we get started now we could have a late breakfast at the tavern instead of biscuits and water. What do you say to that?'

Jon did not need telling twice; the thought of dry biscuits was not as appetising as ham and eggs with buttered toast and a cup of chicory, seated beside a nice warm fire.

He looked across at Anna who nodded vigorously to indicate her own desire for a cooked breakfast rather than the one they were to have had.

He could almost smell the bacon and his stomach growled in anticipation at the prospect of the food; his mouth watered. Suddenly the day had a whole new appeal to it and his attitude changed from being grey and downcast, much as the weather had been yesterday, to keen and alert. A new energy filled him and he smiled for the first time since being drenched in the rain yesterday afternoon.

He really had been a misery; normally he did not mind a little rain but at home he was usually able to dry himself quickly and get into crisp clean clothes. All he had was the spare set he carried in his pack but he had worn them already and they were in need of washing. The good thing about it was that they did not smell, at least he did not think they did but he had pressed his nose into them just to make sure. Urim and Anna were in the same situation as he; so what if they did smell, he thought, he would not be alone in that; besides, they could have them cleaned at the tavern later today.

'How long before we reach the tavern, Urim?'

'Not long.'

That was all he said, offering no further insight or attempt at conversing with them on the matter.

'Are you ready, Anna?'

She nodded and shouldered her pack.

Urim stood waiting for them and was ready to go; so off they set, down the leafy slope to the track that led to Foundry Smelt. They would make for the tavern first for a bite to eat for breakfast and clean clothes of course.

'We should be there in just over an hour, maybe two,' Urim said over his shoulder to them as they followed a few steps behind him.

Although it meant that breakfast was not too far away, it made Jon annoyed at Urim, now he knew how close they had been to the tavern, but he did not say anything out loud. He just mumbled under his breath about how he and Anna had had to sleep on the hard ground through a cold night in a cave instead of in a warm, comfortable tavern. Then he considered how he might have felt if they were to have trudged through the mud and rain for a couple of hours longer yesterday. He admitted to himself that either way he would have been annoyed with Urim. 'Oh well,' he thought, 'at least the worst is over and we can have that hot meal.'

'We must enter the tavern in daylight. Strangers are looked upon with mistrust in these parts, especially if they arrive after the sun has set. It tends to get dark early down in the valley because of the foundry, and the smoke lies heavy in the air at this time of year; you can probably feel it.'

'That's why they had not carried on yesterday,' Jon thought to himself, 'because they would not have got there in time.' So it was the foundry that was upsetting their eyes and noses. If only Urim had said; he wouldn't have been half so annoyed.

Anna was looking the worse for wear from the polluted air; her eyes were bloodshot and appeared as if she had a streaming cold; she was not in a good state at all and was glad to hear that the tavern was nearby.

'I've heard tell that the air is better in Foundry Smelt than in the area around it. Is that true, Urim?' Jon asked, hoping that it would be.

'So I have heard. We would do well to obtain the shelter of the tavern where you can refresh yourselves before continuing on. Salve can be purchased to block out the emissions and so protect your nose and your eyes.'

Urim said no more and urged them onward.

The day should have brightened as the morning lengthened and the sun rose higher, but there was a gloom in the sky before them, a thick black cloud that defied the sun's rays to penetrate it. Underneath that cloud was Foundry Smelt; they could not see it yet but there was no mistaking where it was.

The trees thinned and gave way to pleasant farmland as they passed through the countryside; they saw fenced-off fields and scattered settlements, homesteads and barns. People were busy tending to the affairs of the day, whether for themselves or an employer; all worked hard at their tasks. Domesticated animals were being tended to and the sounds of cattle and sheep drifted in from the open fields reminding Jon of home. As they continued on, the fields and crofters' cottages gave way to clusters of houses. The tickle in his nose was becoming almost unbearable and Anna was fading fast, her energy being sapped by the pollution. How could people tolerate such a thing? How could they breathe? Yet they seemed not to suffer any ill effects and carried on as if the air was as pure as in the mountains.

They topped a rise in the road and saw the land stretch out before them in a broad valley. Jon stopped dead in his tracks. He had heard tell of the smelt from travellers but could not have imagined anything like that which was before him now. At the centre of a large valley lay Foundry Smelt. It was huge. Black with the grime from the forges; one could almost feel the heat from here.

It sat like a spider in the midst of its web, strands of habitation stretching outwards like the spokes of a wheel. The buildings followed the courses of the three roads he could see and the numerous streams that seemed to flow into the centre with no apparent outlet; his gaze was drawn to the thick black cloud that hung above it.

Columns of smoke climbed into the air, countless numbers of them rising from the chimneys of the forges. It looked as if the cloud was a giant creature straddling the smelt on hundreds of spindly legs. He had never seen anything like it and felt as dumb as Anna; lost for words. The sun was climbing towards mid-morning but there was a gloom hanging over the whole valley as the strength of the sun was unable to penetrate the soot-laden cloud.

The countryside changed dramatically from that which they had been passing through earlier. Ahead of them was a landscape devoid of colour; everything was a dull grey. No grass grew; there were no farms or any sign of animal life. All that lay before them was the smelt, dominating the valley. Encircling it, just a few leagues down the road, he saw buildings, houses and shops that formed a ring of habitation around the smelt. These were obviously the homes of the people who worked at the forges and supporting industries. They appeared to have built them so as to be out from under the cloud; so that they were able to gain some benefit from the sunlight at some point in the day. There were more buildings that followed the roads in, two or three deep on either side, connecting the whole together. Jon could see the one they were following passing through the houses ahead of them going north on into the smelt and two others, one from the east and one from the west. They were both likewise lined with a jumble of buildings fighting for their own space. He assumed that there was another one just like these on the opposite side, coming in from the north.

The buildings ahead of them caught his attention; several of them were larger than the others and signs hung above their doors. From his position at the top of the rise he could see that they fronted onto a small square but were too far away to distinguish what the buildings were. He assumed that they were taverns and that one of them was the Spotted Cow that they were to have lodged in last night. He was awe struck by the sheer immensity and dreariness of the scene before him; the enthusiasm he had felt beforehand for visiting the place waned considerably. He no longer relished the prospect of entering this polluted valley, amidst the grime and dirt, having been used to the clean freshness of the countryside. Urim seemed set to do so of course and it was too late to turn back now; besides, he needed something to eat and the tavern ahead promised to deliver that at least. Jon wondered whether anyone else seeing Foundry Smelt for the first time felt the same way he did or was he just being 'a country boy'? He caught Urim looking at him and Anna with a wry smile on his lips and a twinkle in his eye as if something amused him.

'Don't be too disappointed, my friends. Many people feel the same way you do about this place. In fact the only ones I've heard speak fondly of it are the metal masters themselves. They take great pride in their skills and are fiercely protective about it. So don't go upsetting any of them with anything you might say. Now, let's see about something to eat shall we?' He started off down the road; Jon and Anna just looked at each other, shrugged their shoulders resignedly and followed him.

Jon's mind filled with questions; at each turn of events more questions arose that he wanted answers to than he received. For instance: the metal masters to whom Urim referred; he had heard tales about them, how you never saw one far from his beloved forge and that if you did, you should treat them with respect; unless of course you wanted to end up needing medical care. As they tended to be very large and muscular individuals, no one had ever had the courage to ask whether this was the case.

He had no recollection of having met one of them himself; he felt sure that he would have remembered if he had, but he had heard stories of incidents in the taverns where someone, rather the worse for drink after an evening of revelling, had said something amiss. He had never seen anything himself but he had seen the results of one such incident. One of the local farm labourers who worked near Ashbrooke, Martin Groombridge, spoke with a whistle now after he had lost a tooth during an encounter with one of them some years back. Martin did not like talking about it so rumour and speculation abounded as to what really happened; no doubt the story had received embellishment over time.

A loud sneeze from Anna brought him out of his reverie; she was not bearing up well with this change in the air and was clearly in some distress. Her eyes were red and tears were running freely down her cheeks; Anna did her best to wipe them away but that only seemed to make it worse.

Urim signalled for them to make haste. Jon felt concerned for Anna's condition and wanted her to receive respite from this awful pollution so helped her on her way. His stomach was beginning to growl angrily at the thought of food nearby so did not need any further persuasion to follow.

He was feeling a little apprehensive and uncomfortable; he put it down to his disappointment in his impressions over Foundry Smelt but was unconvinced that that was the cause. As they descended towards the group of buildings ahead and the long awaited hot meal, he could not help looking back over his shoulder with an uneasy feeling. He was sure that there was something back there that was not quite right.

What it could be, he had no idea, but he was seldom wrong about his sense of awareness. He tried to brush his concerns aside, to talk himself around to being sensible and not to be so imaginative. It worked for about five seconds then he found himself looking over his shoulder again.

'Stop being stupid, Jon.' He scolded himself as he helped Anna along the road.

Urim was a little way ahead of them and had been eager to get to the tavern; Jon supposed that he too was hungry. Then he noticed the seer falter in his step and stop, he cocked his head to one side as if listening for something and as they drew abreast of him they heard it too. A rumble and a thudding vibration through the ground, he could feel it through the soles of his shoes. Whirling around and catching them both off guard, Urim unceremoniously grabbed hold of them and threw them into the ditch at the side of the road. There were sparse hedgerows growing there and they went sprawling in a tangle of twigs and dried leaves at the bottom of the ditch. Jon landed heavily but Anna had a softer landing; on top of him, which made him wince as her elbow caught him in the side, knocking the wind out of him. At least she fared a little better than he did on landing in the bottom of the ditch; but they were both left tangled amongst the body of the bushes and his side hurt him.

He had not seen where Urim had gone. He had supposed that he too had jumped into the ditch after them but was nowhere in sight.

'Blast it, uncle, what do you think you're doing?' Jon fumed from the bottom of the ditch, nursing the pain in his side.

Then the sound of a coach and horses being driven at speed brought him to awareness of more than his immediate predicament. He stopped struggling and listened to the sound as it closed upon them. The horses thundered by, as if running for their very lives, pulling a coach that swayed as it careered along the dusty roadway. Jon caught sight of the driver but could only see his cape, flapping in the wind the carriage created, as it flashed by, causing a choking cloud of dust to rise from the road.

This did not help their sufferings at all. As if the pollution from the forges of the smelt was not bad enough; they were left coughing and spluttering on the dust of the roadway.

Eventually they dragged themselves out of the ditch, untangling themselves from the branches of the bushes that clung to them as if reluctant to let them go. Dusting himself down carefully, due to the discomfort in his side, he saw that across the road there was no hedge or ditch. 'If only Urim had pulled us to that side of the road,' he thought to himself, 'rather than pushed us into the ditch.' There would have been plenty of room for the coach to have gone by and they would not have had to suffer the indignity of the ditch. Where was Urim anyway? He was nowhere in sight.

'Great. What are we supposed to do now?'

Anna sneezed loudly.

'Bless you,' he said, and then noticed that she was holding her arm and a look of pain was on her face.

'What's the matter, Anna? Have you hurt your arm? Let me see.'

Well, it had not broken thank goodness but she needed some attention. Maybe it was a sprain or even a dislocation. Jon was not very good at medical aid and decided that with or without Urim he had to get her arm seen to and that's what he was going to do. He held her gently and helped her along the road towards the tavern as she cradled her injured arm in the other. He tried to help as much as he could but he was also aware of his own discomfort and could probably do with being looked at himself. He did not think that he had broken a rib; it was not too painful, probably just bruised.

The dust from the road that had stirred up with the passing of the carriage was settling back down and made breathing a lot better. Nevertheless he would be glad to get indoors, away from this bad air. He suddenly saw the funny side of their situation and could not help laughing at their predicament. All that came out was another wince as he felt the pain in his side and tried not to laugh. Anna, with tear-streaked cheeks that were all the more visible due to the grime and dust that caked her face, tried to join in the laughter until she too remembered *her* injury.

They were a sorry sight to behold. They stumbled along trying not to laugh at themselves and each other, for each tickle of humour brought a reminder of the pain that they each had.

45

'Where is Urim?'

Anna just looked at him with an 'I told you so' expression on her face before reverting back to one of pain.

'Come on; let's get you to the tavern where we can ask for assistance. Urim can look after himself. He's obviously not bothered about us.'

Anna nodded in agreement.

They met no other travellers on the way as they stumbled along the road, like a pair of wounded birds, towards the tavern. He was right: it was the Spotted Cow; this is where they were to have lodged. Turning to Anna, he caught her attention and suggested that they say that they were brother and sister, so as to avoid any problems or questions. He knocked on the door. The inn had closed now as the breakfast rush had been and gone. He knocked again.

'We're closed,' a person replied from inside the tavern with a broad accent. Jon knocked again.

''Enry, go and see who that is making all this fuss and tell 'em we're closed.'

The door opened just wide enough for whoever was inside to push his head through to deliver the message but when he saw them he opened it wider. Before them stood a rather rotund, middle-aged man dressed in red cotton breeches and a blue shirt, unbuttoned at the collar. Over them he wore a stained, white apron and on top of his balding head was a lopsided chef's hat. He held a large serving spoon in his hand that dripped some sort of gravy on to the floor.

'Now then whoever you are what's all this commotion about; didn't you 'ear my sister say . . . that . . . we're . . . closed,' he blustered in the same broad accent, but his voice trailed away as he took in the sight before him. 'Well bless my soul. Martha, sister dear, come and look at what we 'ave 'ere. Two sorry looking packers if ever I did see,' he bellowed over his shoulder towards the kitchen.

They heard the woman approaching, mumbling under her breath about getting the food ready in time for lunch. She was equally rotund. She had rosy cheeks and was puffing for breath as she walked. She wore a blue, long-sleeved dress, gathered at the waist and covered by a full length apron, much like her brother's. She had dark, wiry hair gathered up under her white

46

linen bonnet, which she was pushing back into place with the back of her flour-covered hand.

'Oh, brother dear, must I do everythin' myself,' she scolded her brother teasingly; she took one look at them and raised her hands in surprised alarm, exclaiming, 'Oh you poor dears; don't just keep 'em standing at the door like that, 'enry, let 'em in. Come and sit down you poor things. Why you look half done to death you do. Come and sit down by the fire.'

She continued to fuss over them, hardly stopping to draw breath and guided Anna gently to a seat by the fire; clearing tables and chairs aside and making room for them to pass.

'Well come on, 'enry, stoke up the fire and get some o' that heat into 'em and fetch me two bowls of stew from off of the stove.'

Henry obediently did as instructed, giving Jon a wink and a smile as he did so. He gathered from that that he had become accustomed to the way she spoke to him and did not seem to mind; he appeared to be a very amiable chap.

'Now then, you just come and settle yourself down next to your young friend 'ere and tell me all about it. What's 'appened to you two?'

She looked at Anna expectantly and dabbed at her face with her apron to wipe away some of the dust from the road.

Anna gestured to the woman that she was unable to speak and glanced at Jon to explain for her and that she had hurt her arm. Just as he was about to do so, the woman grabbed her and pulled her to her ample bosom exclaiming, 'Oh you poor dear; can't you speak? Oh you poor thing; whatever are we going to do?' She held her at arm's length, took another look at her and pulled her to her bosom. Rocking her to and fro she exclaimed all the while, 'Oh you poor, poor dear, you poor child, what a shame it is.'

Finally Anna was able to release herself from the woman's embrace whereupon she gave a mighty sneeze and nearly toppled off the chair with the effort of it. Anna was taken aback by all this and was trying to point out that she had hurt her arm.

The woman noticed she was cradling her arm and exclaimed in a high squeal of alarm, 'Oh you poor thing; let me look at that, you poor dear child; and not a voice to tell Martha about it neither.'

She busied herself in applying a serving towel as a sling to help support Anna's arm. Jon was almost in tears with the whole thing; with the extraordinary behaviour of their benefactor and from the pain he felt in his side each time he made to laugh; he did not know whether to laugh or cry.

Martha reached down and picked up a bowl of warm water from the fireplace and gently washed Anna's face. All the time fussing over her and chattering away about what terrible times there were, what with strange folk coming and going. Not that they were unaccustomed to strangers here but things certainly were more strange than usual.

Henry returned with the food and Jon offered him two florins for the stew but he waved it away. 'Not at all, young sir, we've no mind for payment when a good deed is required. Isn't that right, sister? We wouldn't 'ear of it. You just sit there and gather your strength. I'll get you a mug of chicory each to wash it down with.'

Off he went again to get the promised drinks.

Jon thanked him for the stew and ate it with relish; not quite the beef and mushroom pie he had been hankering after, but tasty all the same.

'You just tuck in to that stew, young 'uns, before it gets cold. We'll leave you two alone for a while 'cos we've got to get the lunch ready for our customers when they arrive.'

Martha was in her element and was fairly clucking like a mother hen with a brood of chicks. They sat quietly, eating the stew, as their hosts bustled around getting things ready.

Jon could not remember eating a better bowl of stew for a long time; it was as good as the one Urim had provided that night in the forest; he wondered whether it came from here. How did he do that sort of thing? he mused, fascinated by his abilities. Maybe one day he would find out how he did it.

For now he was just content to rest by the fire and to enjoy the mouth-wateringly tasty stew. It was certainly better than the food they had been eating these past few days. He looked around him and took in the place now that he had a chance to do so. He had been in the inn at Ashbrooke a few times and the other taverns on the way here, so was not unaccustomed to their appearance. This one though was the oddest he had ever seen.

48

The chairs and tables were of different sizes, probably so as to accommodate all sizes of customer who might call; they were packed tightly in to seat as many as possible. The place was clean and free from dirt; it looked as if the floors were scrubbed regularly anyway. It was a large room, about twice his height, adorned with all manner of bric-à-brac. Some he recognised whilst some he most certainly did not, and he did not have a clue as to what their purposes might be.

The strange thing about the place was the different sized furniture. A group of tables and chairs on one side of the fireplace were small, as if for children, whilst on the other side they were of normal height and proportion. Then on the other side of the room near a second, larger fireplace, were massive refectory style tables and benches.

He was bemused at the serving area along one side of the room. It had been built in three different stages. At the point closest to them the counter would reach his midriff; he could have almost used it to sit upon.

The next stage was of a more familiar height where he could stand more comfortably and lean upon it without difficulty. The third stage was around chest height and it would have been difficult for him to receive any service from there. Curious, he thought. Then it occurred to him, it would be a place that many different types of individuals would frequent as they came to do business with the metal masters, as Urim called them. Foundry Smelt was a crossroads between three different types of people. The metal masters, who were of large stature, and hence the larger tables and service counter. Individuals from Jon's own land traded and conducted business of whatever nature, and then dwarves. They would come here, to the Northern Uplands from their native homeland in the Eastern Mountains, for the superior crafted metal tools and weapons.

Jon wondered just what they ought to do for the best and decided that they should wait here at the tavern for a while. Firstly because they needed to rest and enjoy some good food and secondly they both needed to have a bath; and third, they might have the opportunity to put on some clean clothes. He did not have a clue as to what Urim was intending they do here at the smelt. Better that they sit and wait for Urim to turn up, as he believed he would. Urim would know that this was the place they would head for after they had become separated. At least he hoped he would; where else was there for them to go?

The rest of the morning passed by and lunch came and went; along with the various locals who used the tavern for their midday meals as well as a place to meet. They appeared eager for some juicy piece of gossip or the opportunity to brag of their business prowess. There was a real hustle and bustle about the inn; both Martha and Henry were busy seeing to the needs of their customers. It was obviously a good place to frequent; the food was good and the ale strong. They must be busy all the time as they employed a man who tended the bar and two girls who served the hungry crowd.

After the lunch time rush had subsided, Martha came across to them and said that she had sent for a young man who would tend to them. She did not have much of an idea about medicine but had heard that a physician from the Ward was visiting someone nearby. The Ward was a place of healing run by elves some days travel from here. He would be here soon to check on them. Jon had thanked her and again offered to pay for their hospitality.

'Lord, taint nothin' to me, my lad. Only too pleased to 'elp. Now if you're lookin' for somewhere to stay, I can offer a room for the night at a reasonable rate.'

'Thank you, you're very kind, ma'am; we'll let you know about the room. You see we're waiting for a friend. He's a . . . friar from . . . from our area and we were separated when we . . . when we had our accident.'

'Oh, I see; well, we'll keep a lookout for 'im and send 'im in your direction, so to speak,' Martha said, but it was clear that she did not really understand. Anna's arm was quite painful and her elbow had swollen slightly so that it was awkward for her to move it. Jon's side was also quite sore. He noticed one of the girls, who had been clearing things away, stop and nod in their direction to a young pleasant looking chap who had elfin features. This was obviously the physician that they had sent for and would tend to their ailments.

He drew near and smiled a welcome.

'Hello, my name's Hamill. I was asked to come and see two travellers who were in need of some medical attention. I can tell

50

without looking any further that you are both in need of my services.'

Jon warmed to him instantly. He had never met an elf that he did not like; true he had not met many of them, but the stories he had heard were all favourable. They mostly kept themselves in the east country, where the Ward, their medical centre was located. Anyone in need of help was welcome there but not everyone could get there; so they travelled, as part of their student years, learning and practising their healer's art around the country. It was an instinct behaviour and indicative of their nature to heal the sick and afflicted.

'Have you travelled far?' he asked. He seemed genuinely interested.

'Yes, we've come from Ashbrooke, to the south; do you know it?'

'Why yes I do. I came through there just the other day. What a commotion there was on market day. Were you there then?' Hamill asked as he tended to them, providing a salve for the irritation caused by the polluted air, then putting Anna's arm in a proper dressing and sling.

'No. We left the day before. Why? What happened?' Jon asked, knowing that Anna would be as curious as he.

'There has been all sorts of talk going on of strange creatures in the forest. Some of the farmers have said that livestock had gone missing overnight and they'd heard strange noises. Someone even said he'd seen a big black creature like a bear but with a long reptilian head; speculation has been rife about what's going on. They even said they were going to organize a search party for one of the farmers who had gone missing.'

Jon and Anna exchanged horrified looks; they knew what it all meant. It was Ebon and his gnomes trying to get hold of Jon; he had obviously grown bold; either that or he was desperate.

Why was it that he was after him? he asked himself. What had he done? Why was he so important to the seer? Where was his involvement in all of this and where was Urim? He simply had to know the answers or burst. He determined that the very next time he saw Urim he would demand the truth.

Jon asked Hamill what had happened on market day at Ashbrooke on behalf of them both, leaning forward in his eagerness to know what had occurred.

Hamill replied with infuriating indifference. 'Don't know, I left on the coach the next day and headed for this place as I heard that one of the metal masters was in need of medical treatment. I've not long finished with him; lucky for you that I was not far away.'

Hamill was very talkative and went on to explain what he did.

'I am required to obtain as much experience as possible, from whatever source I can, before I qualify to serve in the Ward as a senior physician. I got here to attend to the metal master as quickly as I could, arriving yesterday on the mail coach; I find that the best way to travel, don't you?'

Hamill finished his work, fastened his pack and asked, 'So, what are you going to do now?'

Jon looked at Anna. She shook her head slightly and signed, with difficulty, that she thought they should take Martha up on her offer and book a couple of rooms for the night. He nodded and said to Hamill, 'We're waiting for a friend so will probably stay for the night to rest up.'

'Good idea. It would be wise to rest that arm of yours for a week if you can, you've badly twisted the ligaments and you need to rest them.' Turning to Jon, he said, 'You need to avoid any strenuous movements too. The tissue between your ribs is inflamed and could cause much more pain if it isn't treated properly. I'm staying at the Packers Lodge across the way so if you need me, just send for me. I'll be there until tomorrow when I head back to the Ward. Nice talking to you. Sorry I've got to go. There's someone else who's in need of my services. Remember now, rest, that's the best medicine anyone can have.'

Jon thanked him for his help and offered payment.

'Thanks but that's not required; when we take up the oath, our services are to be offered free of charge; I am happy to have helped. Have a good night.'

'Thank you for your kindness, Hamill; hopefully we won't have to call on your services again but thanks for the offer. I also hope that we can meet again in better circumstances.'

They were a little sad to see him go; they had been grateful for his company.

The evening was drawing on and the place was starting to fill up again. Jon asked Martha if they could have a couple of rooms for the night and a hot bath would not go amiss.

'A hot bath it is, no worries, but I've only got the one room left now, it's got two cots in it though; would that be agreeable for you and your sister?'

Anna blushed slightly but nodded her consent so Jon paid over the two florins, with another for a meal of beef and mushroom pie each before they retired for the night.

They sat at the same table, after having taken their baths and put on some clean clothing. They had also arranged for the laundering of their other clothes to be ready for tomorrow morning. The salve that Hamill had given them had worked a treat and Anna was feeling much better, her eyes had lost their redness and she had stopped sneezing; he felt much relieved too.

The tavern was fairly busy with various folk coming and going and they had seen a number of the local people, in appearance much like themselves, but they had not seen any dwarves. What Jon most wanted to see was a metal master and he was not disappointed when some of them came into the tavern.

It was no wonder that people generally left them alone as they were tall and heavily built. Being in close proximity to them was quite a daunting experience; they were amiable enough, casting only the briefest of glances their way upon entering the inn. They sat at the larger tables on the other side of the room and took no further interest in the two of them. They were all fairly similar in build with thick, bushy hair and beards; some were dark, some blond; but red hair seemed to predominate.

Jon and Anna enjoyed their meal by the fire and finished it off with a cup of fruit wine, relaxing in the warmth and security of the ambiance within the inn. No one took much notice of them and they fairly forgot the rigours of the past few days as the local people sang to the tune of a pipe and drum.

A group of dwarves came and sat nearby but they kept themselves to themselves and nobody paid much attention to them; dwarves were frequent visitors to this part of the land. One dwarf did sit apart from the others, in the darkness of an alcove where he kept his hood over his head concealing himself within its shadows. He got up and left soon afterwards, although they did not see his departing; one minute he was there sitting alone, then he had gone. Jon did not pay him much heed and soon forgot him as raised voices and a scuffle between two of the locals who had had some sort of disagreement caught his attention.

53

Whatever it was, it could not have been much of an argument because they resolved it amicably enough and the two of them were soon laughing and drinking together again.

As the evening wore on, Jon started to become a bit concerned about Urim. He felt sure that he would have found them by now. Wherever he had disappeared to, whatever it was that he was doing, it should not have kept him away from them for this long. He determined not to fret about it; it would not change anything. Maybe he would turn up in the morning. 'It's more likely to be the middle of the night,' he added as an afterthought to himself. Jon's musings were interrupted by the gentle touch of Anna's hand on his arm. He had not meant to shut her out; it was just that he was concerned and did not want her to worry. He stared at her across the table; a sweet smile played upon her lips, her dark eyes sparkling in the firelight. He found himself drawn into their depths and realized that he had been staring at her open mouthed, entranced by what he beheld. He had never been in love with anyone but guessed that he was now; if what he was feeling was anything to go by. He thought how pretty she looked and held her hand at one point. Reassuring her more than anything; though he did feel his stomach knot up when she smiled at him and gently squeezed his hand.

He had always been kindly disposed towards her because of her being a mute and had made the effort to learn sign language to make it easier for them to communicate. She had appreciated this and they had become good friends, more like brother and sister really. He now knew, as they sat there looking at each other, that he loved her; he probably had done so for some time; he just hadn't been aware of it. Strange that it had taken this journey together for him to become aware of it. Still, he could not be certain of her feelings towards him and was painfully shy about the whole thing. What if he was just imagining it, he would feel a right fool and would probably ruin their friendship. No, better to say nothing until he was certain of how she felt towards him.

They had not communicated much to each other during the course of the evening; they were both very tired and he asked her, 'Are you ready for sleep?'

Yes. I am tired. What about you?

'I can't keep my eyes open any longer.'

Chapter IV

Follow my Leader

They rose from the table and made their way through the crowd to the rear of the inn. The bartender escorted them up two flights of wooden stairs to their room at the top. Jon and Anna had used the room earlier and had put up a dividing curtain between the cots; Jon had hung a blanket over a line that he had fastened from one side of the small room to the other; it did not give Anna total privacy but it was better than none. The bartender was a strong, swarthy person with broad shoulders and a barrel for a chest; he was also short of a few teeth and his nose had been broken at some point in time; possibly from his boxing days. Jon had noticed some paintings of a bare-knuckle fighter hanging on the wall behind the bar and realized that they were of the bartender when he was younger. He had obviously been success-ful as there were many trophies in a line on a shelf above the bar that he kept. Jon thought that he probably had to enforce the 'rules of the house' from time to time and needed to be able to demand respect from the patrons. Despite his appearance, he was courteous towards them and lighted their way to the room.

The light from the small candle lanterns that they carried cast eerie shadows against the walls as they ascended the wooden stairway; night lights had been placed on the landings but they provided insufficient light for them to see where they were going.

The room was fairly basic and utilitarian but comfortable; at least it would mean that they had the chance of a good night's sleep. A fire crackled in the stove that stood at the side of the dormer window, helping to keep the room warm and free from any cold draughts. Turning to the bartender, Jon said, 'We were expecting our uncle to meet us here today. If he should turn up, would you let him know where we are?'

He pressed a token into the palm of the man's hand and thanked him. The bartender touched his forehead in acknowledgment and backed out of the door promising to do so if he should see him. Jon heard him move along the landing, floorboards creaking as he went, and down the stairs, closing the door behind him that led into the bar and shut out the sounds from the tavern. Turning to Anna, Jon asked, 'Do you want to use the washroom first?'

Anna nodded, gathered up her nightshirt and wash bag then took the lantern Jon proffered her after he had lit a candle that was on a shelf by his cot.

He looked out of the window, down at the square below. There was no moonlight; the cloud of pollution that hung heavy over this part of the valley prevented any direct illumination. Only lanterns placed on the sides of the houses lit the way for those who returned home after a night of merriment.

Light spilled out onto the square from the open doorway of a neighbouring tavern. Two men emerged from across the square; arms around their shoulders like long lost friends now reunited. The sound of music and laughter from others still enjoying the revelry carried in the night air. They made promises to each other to meet again the following night 'for another little drink', as one of them put it, before going their separate, though noisy, ways.

The sound of their boots on the cobbled courtyard resounded through the night and echoed down the alleyways as they made their way home. A dog barked nearby then yelped as one of the men swore and landed a well aimed kick in its direction; having no doubt trodden in something rather unpleasant.

'Bloomin' animal, look what you've done. Perishing nuisance; aww, what a mess! The missus'll kill me.'

Jon smiled at the welcome the man was likely to receive from his wife upon his return home; he wondered whether she would have given him an earful for being drunk anyway, let alone bringing in the dog's mess.

Anna returned and smiled self-consciously as she scurried to her cot. Jumping in, she pulled the covers about her shoulders. Jon closed the window in order to keep as much pollution out as possible; he went to clean his teeth and get ready for what he hoped would be a good night's sleep. On the way back along the landing he stopped to peer out of a side window that afforded a panoramic view over the rooftops of the surrounding buildings. It was dark so he could not see very much; the staircase was gloomy; a night light burned in a niche just above the first landing, casting flickering shadows against the rough plastered walls. From the floor below he could hear another occupant snoring gently, his repose possibly aided by an evening's socialising earlier in the tavern.

As he turned to knock on the door to let Anna know he was coming back in, he heard a creak of dry wood on the staircase. It was as if someone had trodden on a loose stair tread and stopped, not wanting anyone to know that they were there. Jon froze in mid motion; standing still as a statue, he felt his ears twitching involuntarily, just as a cat's would do when hunting. He waited for what seemed an age, listening, waiting for another sound; none came, other than the snores from the first floor.

Everything was eerily still; he let out a sigh, realizing he had stopped breathing, and castigated himself for being so jumpy. He peered over the balustrade but could see no one; the stairwell was empty; another creak of dry wood, giving under pressure made him start.

He held tightly onto the banister rail and looked down at his feet; he rocked to and fro on the ball of his foot. Creak, creak. He laughed nervously with relief as he realized that it was he who had caused the creaking on the floor.

He crumpled inwardly, relaxing his tensed up nerves. 'Stupid fool,' Jon breathed out to himself. 'You're getting as nervous as a kitten, pull yourself together.'

He took a couple of uneasy breaths and tried to calm himself down; Jon shook his head in disbelief at his being so stupid. He knocked on the door before entering their bedroom and went to his side of the room where he busied himself getting ready; he had been looking forward to a good night's rest. His side still felt very sore and he was grateful for the prospect of a comfortable mattress to sleep on. He settled down into his covers, blew out the light and whispered, 'Good-night, Anna.'

He tried to sleep, but despite his fatigue, he could not. He worried about what they were going to do. Urim had disappeared, leaving them to fend for themselves and Jon had no idea what to do next.

He had pretty much decided to wait for another day to see if he could discover what had become of the seer. After that, well, they would just have to return to Ashbrooke. 'What else could he do?' he asked himself. He had hoped that Urim would have found them by now; surely he knew that this is where they would be!

It all seemed like such a waste of effort on their part to just give up after having travelled all this way; and for what? He certainly did not want to have to turn tail at the first little problem that they encountered and go home without accomplishing their goal.

He recalled how Anna had withstood Urim, insisting on coming along on their search to find a way to release the seers. Urim had been dumbstruck and mumbled under his breath, obviously not happy with things and frustrated by her determination. Jon had simply been a bystander but had observed their exchanges with more than a little amusement. He knew Anna was quite a formidable force to deal with, she would not give way; once she had made up her mind to do something, she did it.

He was roused from a deep sleep by Anna shaking him back to semi-consciousness.

'Humph . . . what . . .'

She placed a hand over his mouth so that he would not make any more sounds. He raised himself up onto one elbow trying to drive the cobwebs from his mind. It was still dark outside and there was only a little bit of light coming under the door from the night light in the hall. Anna was obviously concerned about something; he could just make out her worried expression in the gloom. She gestured towards the door, indicating for him to listen. After a moment they heard the noise of a creaking floor-board or stair-tread. Jon listened for a moment then placed his hand on hers and said reassuringly, 'Don't worry, Anna, it's just the movement of the wood responding to the changing temperature.'

He could feel that it was cold and his breath condensed as he exhaled; the fire in the little stove had gone out. He could see that she was unconvinced. She shook her head and pointed to the door again, only this time with some urgency and determination.

He cocked his head to listen some more without hearing anything else but pulled back the covers and fumbled around for the lamp on the table nearby. The light hurt his eyes, even though it was a small lamp that gave off only a subdued light. He put his breeches on and stood by his cot.

Anna stood close by in her nightdress, hugging herself in the chill air. Ordinarily Jon would have been embarrassed but all he could think was how beautiful she looked; softened by the low light she was a delight to behold.

'Put on your cloak and I'll show you there's nothing to be afraid of.'

She looked down at herself, realizing that she could not very well stand there in her nightdress. She had not given it a thought before but blushed now and hurriedly pulled on her gown. Jon turned away, despite not wanting to and thought, as he smiled to himself, that it was a bit late now to turn his head, but he did so anyway. He was looking towards the door but all he saw in his mind's eye was Anna.

He was distracted from his reverie by a movement under the door; he saw a shadow, cast by the light in the hall, moving out on the landing and he froze; he heard a floorboard creak and the shadow stilled.

Time stood still. He stood rooted to the spot, petrified, unable to move; his eyes widened and his jaw dropped. A sinking feeling made his stomach churn; he could not believe what he was seeing.

The door handle was slowly turning. Someone out there was coming into their room. He watched and as if in slow motion the door swung open . . .

He gasped in surprise and relief.

'Urim, you gave me a start. Where have you been? What's been going on? Have you found out what we need to know?'

The questions just came out in a rush. Urim stood still, framed in the doorway and silhouetted against the light from the hallway, his hood covering his head. He gestured to them in the dim light of the lamp that Jon was holding in front of him to be quiet and to follow him. Jon wanted to protest, to demand Urim answer his questions before they went anywhere. He knew, however, that if Urim wanted them to be quiet and go with him, then there was a good reason for it.

Holding the lamp in front of him in one hand and holding Anna's hand with the other, he followed the seer out of the room, along the landing and down the stairs. Several times he side-stepped a floorboard and indicated for them to do the same so that they were able to navigate them without making any noise. They made their way along a narrow corridor at the foot of the stairs and out a door at the rear of the tavern into an alleyway.

Urim did not seem to need a light to guide him, moving unerringly through the gloom; they needed the light of the lamp, however, as it was difficult to follow the seer due to his melting into the night, concealed by his long black cloak. They zigzagged their way along the narrow alleyways; creatures of the night skittered out of their way as they splashed through the puddles. They avoided, as best they could, the detritus left by uncaring occupants and pedestrians.

Jon followed closely in Urim's quiet footsteps, keeping a tight hold on Anna's hand as they slipped through the darkness. They dodged from one alleyway to another, pausing only momentarily, so as to remain unnoticed, as an occasional inhabitant passed by.

The air was heavy with oxides and soot. Even at this early hour of the morning the forges were hot and the atmosphere acrid from their discharges. They heard the sounds of bellows and hammering from time to time as they passed the shadows between the smithies. Anna was nursing her arm that was still hurting from their fall into the ditch yesterday. It was obviously still sore and she winced occasionally but gave him a reassuring smile and nod of her head when he looked inquiringly at her.

Together they followed Urim, wondering where he was taking them at this time of the night and why. Jon could not help being suspicious of everything that Urim did but put his concerns to the back of his mind, berating himself for being such a doubter. A couple of times he thought he had heard someone behind them but could not discover anything when he turned round to see who it might be.

He recalled his feelings that day in the forest when he had been certain that someone had been following him, before Urim had 'introduced' himself. He had the same feelings now and had tried to convey them to the seer but he had simply signalled for him to be quiet and continued onwards. Jon guessed that if they really were being followed then if anyone would know it, Urim would. They stuck to the shadows, quiet as mice.

Urim was as silent as the grave, moving with agility and haste but not too fast that they could not keep up with him. Anna held firmly on to Jon's hand; he could sense the tension in her body. He wanted to comfort and reassure her but could only squeeze her hand every now and then and give her encouraging looks. He dared not look away from Urim for too long for fear of losing him as they dodged from one place to another.

Their footsteps echoed along the maze of narrow walkways as they went along routes that were dryer and free from rubbish. Jon had no idea where they were or where they were going but trusted in the seer. Despite his curiosity and frustration of not knowing where Urim had been or where he was taking them, he thought he knew him well enough to trust him. He felt confident of him and was, now that he thought of it, amazed that he had ever doubted him. He felt a strange kind of warmth within him towards the seer, a loyalty that he had not felt before. The more he thought on it, the more sure he became of him. He felt as if nothing could harm them and that as long as he kept following the seer, all would be well. He relaxed so that he began not to care where they were going, just so long as he followed Urim. It was almost a compulsion: to keep following the seer.

In stark contrast, however, Anna was becoming more and more concerned and tugged at Jon's sleeve several times, trying to communicate her anxiety to him at their situation.

They stopped as they reached the end of a series of short turns; ahead of them lay an open square lined with buildings, much like the one outside the Spotted Cow tavern where they had been lodging.

Staying concealed by the shadows, Urim pointed to an inn opposite them. A large gateway to the side led into a courtyard and stables; as he looked into the courtyard Jon caught sight of a movement by one of the doorways. A small figure moved in the dark and there were three short blinks of a light. The seer signalled for them to follow him; skirting the square and still keeping to the shadows as much as possible they made their way to the stables and entered a coach house. Inside was the coach that had almost run them down the other day; Jon recognised it as there were few coaches on the roads. It was covered in dust and just off to the side the horses were feeding from a rack.

When they were inside, the door shut quietly behind them; the warm feeling that Jon had felt wrapped around him fell from his shoulders like a stone. He had a bad feeling about this now; the hair on the back of his head stood on end and he breathed in sharply.

There was a scratching at the door; he heard a low woof from a large dog outside. Turning to look towards the door he saw the small cloaked figure they had seen earlier open the door; in trotted a large grey wolfhound; he gave a cursory sniff in their direction then went to heel by the side of the seer and licked the proffered hand.

Jon's mind was in a whirl; he recognised the animal immediately: it was the same dog that he had seen in the forest that night when the marsh-mogs had attacked the gnomes in the clearing. Still holding Anna's hand, he drew her closer to him, placing himself in front of her protectively. Jon bit nervously at his bottom lip; he held his lamp, now burning low on oil, towards the figure who had led them here. He stood facing them in the darkness, still with his head covered by the hood of his cloak, but there was no disguising him now. As the seer lifted the hood from off his head instead of revealing the dark hair and gaunt features of Urim he exposed the blond curls and sneering lip that belonged unmistakably to Ebon. Anna had not seen the dog before so it held no significance to her and she had only heard of Ebon, not seen him. When he lifted the cowl from off his head she gasped involuntarily. She had had her misgivings about following the seer from their room earlier and had tried to convey her concerns to Jon, but he had been so sure. He was so confident that they were doing the right thing that she had held her reservations and trusted in his judgment.

She had felt reassured as time went on and had begun to feel placated; she had even felt warm and trusting towards Urim. Not any more; like Jon, that feeling had vanished when they entered the coach house.

'Thought I was him, didn't you? Well, as you can see, I'm not.'
Ebon's tone was menacing and gloating.
'He's not the only one who can play games.'
'No, you're not him; not even close.' Jon's barbed response did not go unnoticed.
Ebon's smile faded slowly; darkness clouded his eyes as he took in Jon's remark then snarled back, 'Don't mess with me, boy; you may find your little girlfriend wouldn't like it.'

Jon got the point and said no more. He was scared, furious and desperate to get both Anna and himself away from here and out of Ebon's grasp.

Ebon bristled with contempt.

'You think him so good, well let me tell you; he's not so good. He's a deceiver, a fraud. I know you think he's your uncle; he told you that he was didn't he, boy? You see I know who he really is, and he's not your uncle. He doesn't give a fig about anyone else; all he's concerned with is his precious duty to the Sight.'

Ebon watched Jon closely and relished the effect his remarks were having on him.

Jon did not know what to say. He was stunned by what he'd heard but wasn't sure whether to believe him or not; he knew Ebon to be a liar but then he only had Urim's word for that. Jon had had his doubts about Urim; but everything he said made so much sense; it all felt true and there was the resemblance between them. Jon checked himself in his thought process. He was not sure he wanted to reach the conclusion where his thoughts were taking him. Could it be that Urim had misled him? Could it be that he was not his uncle? He did not know what to think or who to trust any more. He just wanted for this to be over, to be safe, back home again in his cottage in Ashbrooke.

He found himself wanting to believe what Ebon was saying but dared not hope. His emotions were in turmoil. He stood there in the gloom, shocked and vulnerable, feeling isolated and alone. His dilemma was should he keep faith with Urim, or believe what Ebon was telling him?

He suddenly knew what to do. After his experience with them both in the forest, he knew where his allegiance lay. Whatever his doubts he must place his trust in Urim – whoever he was.

He squared his shoulders and faced Ebon defiantly but held his tongue. Holding tightly to Anna's hand he eyed the door judging whether they could make a dash for it and escape. He guessed not.

As if discerning his thoughts the dog sauntered over to the door and sat on its haunches, making it impossible for any attempt to flee that way. He looked for any other way out of there; there was only the door with a barred window above it.

'So, not willing to believe me then? No matter; just thought you ought to know. I'll save what I know for a better time.'

Ebon smiled a crooked smile. Though his face would have been considered a handsome one in any other circumstances, his evil intent shone through, marring his good looks. He was enjoying his position of being the holder of knowledge that would be of interest to Jon; he teased Jon with the promise of knowledge but was unwilling to give it; for when he did, Ebon would lose his position of power. A look of sheer glee lit Ebon's face; he was relishing the whole experience.

'I had intended killing you out of hand and be done with it but I am intrigued with what would happen if I were to let you live a little longer. Besides, I don't believe you would want any harm to come to the little lady now, would you?'

Ebon spoke softly but there was no doubt about his intent. He nodded to his accomplice who stood by the door holding the latch as if preparing to leave.

'I have a task to fulfil. As much as I am enjoying our little conversation, I'm afraid we must depart.'

He turned to leave then stopped just as he was going out of the door to add, 'Oh, by the way, I shouldn't think about trying to escape. The only way in or out is through this door and my dog Khan will be staying right here; so I'd advise you not to attempt getting past him. Not that I mind you understand; do as you please. I'm only telling you to avoid anything happening to your pretty friend. There is some food in a basket in the coach with a bottle of mulled wine should you so desire; it's not poisoned, I don't do things that way; it's so distasteful. We may be gone for some time so would you mind seeing that Khan gets his bone? It's in a package with the basket. Try not to miss me.'

With a mock bow towards them he stepped through the door and locked it shut.

'Well what now?' Jon asked himself out loud. He looked dejectedly at Anna. She was nursing her arm. Without the support of the sling Hamill had given her it must be giving her some discomfort; he rubbed his side unconsciously.

I take it that was Ebon? she signed to Jon and had a worried look on her face.

Jon nodded and sighed.

'I'm sorry, Anna. I should have questioned what was happening; I just felt so sure it was Urim. He must have used a sort of mind spell on us to make us think it was him, heck, it was him, I could have sworn it was Urim.'

He looked around them and admitted to himself that there was no other way out, just as Ebon had said.

What do you suppose will happen now?

'I don't know.' He lied. He knew only too well that Ebon planned to kill them both. Why they were still alive he had no idea; but he was glad they were. Ebon had some use for them yet otherwise they probably would be in the next life already. He crossed his fingers superstitiously to ward off ill fortune. His stomach rumbled.

'Fancy something to eat?'

He rummaged through the basket in the coach and found the food and bottle; then noticed the greased paper package containing the bone. He removed the wrapping and an idea came to him. Maybe the bone would be his means of getting the dog away from the door so that they could make their escape.

He jumped down from the coach and winked at Anna, showing her the bone and nodding in the direction of the hound.

'Maybe we can distract the dog away from the door by enticing him with the bone and get the door open.'

She nodded eagerly in agreement.

Jon started towards the dog, bone out in front of him, waving it in the air enticingly so that he would catch the scent better.

Khan stood up and sniffed the air, licking his lips and wagging his tail, but as Jon drew closer he began to snarl and curl his lips back over his teeth. They were intimidating to say the least and he thought better of getting any closer. He backed off a little and tossed the bone into a corner onto some straw. It was a big bone, rich with marrow, and it landed with a thump. 'Go on boy; go on Khan. Get the nice bone.'

The big dog looked at it hungrily and made a step towards it, licking his lips in anticipation but he did not move any further. Instead he issued out a very low growl towards Jon and sat down. He continued to glare at Jon and growl for some time. When Jon made a move towards the bone to try again he raised his hackles and made a half lunge towards him. He certainly made it known that they had better not try anything with the bone again. The animal was unhappy with not being able to have it; but nothing, it seemed, would make him move away from the door.

It seemed that his fear of his master and the repercussions if he was to fail in his duties overrode his basic instinct and desire for food. He simply would not be moved and Jon had made an enemy of him.

In any other circumstances Jon would have had pity on the poor animal, lying there with doleful eyes, resting his head on his paws. Whenever Jon made a move towards the bone, he would jerk his head up and growl; so it stayed where it was.

Jon and Anna sat in the coach and ate the food that Ebon had left for them without another word passing between them – Anna because she could not and Jon because he did not know what to say. He sat brooding on their situation, trying to think of some way out of this.

John opened his eyes with a start and realized that he had been asleep. Anna too had dozed off and was just waking. Had Ebon put something in the drink to make them sleep? He thought it unlikely because they would probably still be asleep. No, they were simply very tired. He looked out of the coach window and saw that they had been awakened by the noise of Ebon returning. He was alone. Khan immediately pounced upon the bone that had been tantalizing him for all this time, though Jon had no idea as to what time it was. Khan licked the bone once slowly as he held it between his paws, eyes closed as his taste buds exploded along his tongue. He opened his eyes, looked straight at Jon and emitted the meanest growl he could before turning his full attention to his meal. He obviously had not appreciated having been made to wait to devour this delight.

Ebon was pacing the room.

Evidently things had not gone as he had expected them to because he was in a bad mood, muttering and cussing under his breath. He stopped once or twice to study Jon and Anna, scowling at them as if they were the cause of his annoyance. They probably did play a part in it but clearly things were not going to plan for Ebon.

Jon opened his mouth to throw a jibe at Ebon about things not going well; turning to look at Anna he decided that it would be better for them both if he just kept his mouth shut. He did not want to make their situation any worse than it was.

Anna touched his arm to indicate that she wanted to sign to him.

What do you think we ought to do?

Jon signed back to her so that he did not disturb Ebon or let him know what it was they were discussing. He turned his back so that the seer could not see what he was doing.

I don't know what to do for the moment. I think we just need to be patient and hope we get an opportunity to escape. Maybe Urim will find us.

Jon did not hold out much hope but he did not want to frighten Anna with any thoughts of not being able to get away.

'What are you two up to? Don't think I don't know you're up to something,' Ebon said petulantly.

'Well there's no getting away from here. Pretty soon now I'll have what I want; then you will have no further need for concern about anything.'

That sounded ominously more like a promise than a threat and it worried Jon that they might not be able to get out of this fix. Where are you, Urim? He almost wished for him to appear like some redeeming angel.

Chapter V

The Forge

A staccato rap on the door made Khan bark; Ebon sprang towards it and spoke softly through a gap in the wood. A few words passed between them, and then he opened the door and admitted the small cloaked figure who had accompanied Ebon when they left earlier. Jon realised now that the figure was not a lad at all, but was a gnome. They spoke in low tones so Jon could only catch the occasional word, something about forge, time and chest. Anna could not help by her lip reading as the gnome kept the lower part of his face covered and Ebon had his back to them.

Ebon nodded and turned to look at them with a smug expression on his face; he fixed Jon with a cold look in his eye.

'You will both come with me; don't try any tricks or my friend here will be only too pleased to kill your little girlfriend without a moment's hesitation. We wouldn't want that now would we?'

Ebon jerked his head in the direction of the gnome.

So that was why he had them both, to act as hostage, one for the other. She was to be the means to ensure Jon's compliance; behave or she pays the penalty. Jon bridled his anger, but clenched his fists in rage and frustration at being 'held to ransom' in this way; there was nothing he could do about it. His dislike for Ebon was growing by the minute.

'I'll find a way, Ebon; so help me I will,' Jon hissed through clenched teeth. Were it not for Anna he would have gladly flattened him at the risk of injury or death to himself, just for the satisfaction it would bring.

'Thanks for the warning. I'll be careful.'

Ebon dismissed Jon's comments as if they were mere empty threats, as indeed they were all the time Ebon held the upper hand.

Ebon pulled his cape around him and started towards the door.

'Follow me; come Khan.'

The big dog was reluctant to leave his bone but came to heel, tail between his legs. He gave another low growl towards Jon; clearly he was not going to forget what Jon had done. The gnome opened the door and signalled for them to go. He held the door while they exited: Ebon and Khan, followed by Jon and Anna. The gnome, unpleasant creature that he most obviously was, took up position just behind Anna.

Jon noticed that he kept his hand within the folds of his cloak, presumably on the hilt of his gnomish blade. There was no chance of a break away from them like this; the gnomes were renowned for their skills as assassins and their efficiency with a knife. Their preferred method of dispatch was a slit throat. Apparently they enjoyed feeling the life drain away from their victims as they administered death at close quarters. Gnomes considered it of great importance to be able to do this skilfully and silently; Jon had the feeling that this gnome knew how to do just that.

Jon followed Ebon without fault. He would not give any cause for the gnome to do what he no doubt wanted to do anyway; all that was stopping him was Ebon's command.

He wished now that he had listened to Urim and sided with him in making Anna stay in Ashbrooke. If she had, she would not be in this danger now. Then he remembered that she had followed them and insisted on coming; if Urim was unable to dissuade her, he supposed that no one could have.

They moved swiftly through the dark streets, taking less caution over being observed than before, though they met no one. Not that it would matter because as a seer he could cause them to blend into the night. Then a thought struck him. Why had they had to be so cautious before? Could it be that Ebon was not so adept as Urim!

After they had traversed only a few streets and alleyways Ebon stopped outside one of the many smithies in the area. He signalled for the gnome to go first then turned to them and said in a whisper, 'One sound or move from either of you will be your last.'

Jon knew that he meant it.

The door creaked open and the gnome signalled for them to enter. The forge was unattended it seemed. Anna pulled on his coat sleeve and nodded across to one of the bays; sticking out from there were a pair of large booted feet. The gnome had obviously dispatched the occupier so that they could use it; but for what purpose?

Ebon strode over to where the person lay and nodded in satisfaction.

'You didn't kill him did you? I can't afford any problems here; not yet anyway.'

The gnome shook his head and backed away, hands held out, palms up, in denial of killing him.

Ebon motioned towards Jon and said, 'Good. Now then, set the traps and get that manacle on him, I don't want him escaping this time. There's no Urim to help you with any more tricks here, boy.'

He used the name Urim almost as a curse, emphasising his displeasure at the sound of it. The gnome secured a chain to a post nearby and with the manacles at the other end placed them on Jon's wrists with little concern for his skin or feelings and laughed in his face. His breath stank of garlic; Jon could smell it even through the covering over the gnome's face. Anna sat next to Jon on a bale of straw and inspected his wrists; she applied a little of the balm that Hamill had given them for their eyes in the hope that it would give some relief. It had worked on their eyes; maybe it would help Jon's wrists from becoming sore from chafing.

Ebon brandished his staff and stamped it to the ground with a resounding thump. Jon wondered whether anything should have happened as a result of that action but nothing did. 'I should have made an end of it in the forest had it not been for the interference of that meddling . . .' His voice trailed off into a hoarse cursing under his breath. He seemed to be trying to control himself, as if there were some force that was driving him in his anger. 'He did a good job, I'll give him that,' Ebon continued, distracted and rambling over his thoughts. 'I hadn't planned for that. It wasn't until we got to the edge of the forest that I realised what had happened. Too late. One of my gnome guards almost dead and the other badly injured and YOU . . .' He raised his voice and spun on Jon with a venomous tone. 'You gone; well, he won't fool me again, that I promise you. What I can't understand is how he got here in the first place; but I mean to find out and you my boy will be the means of me doing just that.'

'How do you propose to do that? I'll not help you,' Jon said, trying to sound more convincing than he felt.

Ebon laughed and spread his arms in mock surprise.

'But you already are; you can't help it. All the time I have you I have the means to spring my trap to foil Urim and to kill him. I could kill you now and have done with it but I am uncertain as to what might happen with you out of the way. So for the moment, you stay alive. Not that I would be concerned if I had to kill you, so don't go thinking that you're safe.'

'Urim told me all about you. How you tricked the other seers and locked them in the Tower; well if Urim got out, so can the others.'

'Oh have no concerns about that, dear boy; there is no question as to them being able to escape. They can't and won't. I've seen to that. They can't interfere with my plans and by the time they figure it out it'll be too late. I shall be in control.'

'Urim won't let you,' Jon blurted.

Ebon feigned surprise. 'Oh! You think so do you? He won't do a thing whilst I have you and you won't do anything all the time I have her.'

He chuckled with glee. 'So you see things have turned out quite nicely for me after all, despite your meddling, Jon.'

He said his name deliberately, coldly, and then added mockingly, 'Promised to tell you things, has he? Promised to explain everything to you has he? Tell me, *Jon*, Why hasn't he done so already?'

He stood hand on hip with a raised, questioning eyebrow. 'I'll tell you why he hasn't; because he can't. He dare not; but I can; I know all about him and you . . . you insignificant pup. Maybe I *will* tell you!'

Ebon saw Jon's reaction; though he tried hard not to betray his need to know, he could not help it.

'Yes, I thought you'd be interested. Hmm! Now here's a dilemma.' Ebon feigned questioning himself by stroking his chin in contemplation. 'Should I let the cat out of the bag so to speak? Should I open a can of worms?'

His countenance darkened as if he was full of rage and spat the words at Jon. 'Not until I want to.'

Ebon span on his heels and walked over to the forge where the gnome was endeavouring to get the temperature up by using the large bellows that he operated by a foot pedal. Ebon began pacing again, urging the gnome to work faster.

Jon wondered whether to believe him or not; he seemed genuinely to know more about Urim and himself than he had thought. He knew Urim was keeping something from him; was it true what Ebon had said about Urim not being his uncle? If so, then who was he and why claim kinship? Could it be that Urim was his father?

Jon had latched on to that idea not long after Urim had appeared because of the likeness between them and the fact that Urim knew so much about him, his mother and the cottage. It was too much for him to consider right now and he put it to the back of his mind. Although he had had initial misgivings about Urim, he had proved to be fair and honest. He had told Jon that there was more to know; that he would tell him when the time was right to do so. He had not deceived him in that. Whereas Ebon had been anything but fair and honest. His very actions cried out to Jon that he could not be trusted. Urim, on the other hand, showed that he could be counted upon; hadn't he saved his life that first night back in the forest?

Being his uncle could account for that; but if what Ebon had said were true – about him not being his uncle – the question remained: Who was he?

So the circle of uncertainty and doubt went around and around in his head. He finally decided that he should follow his instincts and trust Urim; but where was he? Why did he leave them at the roadside, injured? Why had he not returned? More importantly, would he find them in time and free them from Ebon's grasp? The next time he saw Urim, if he ever did, he would demand he answer these questions. What he *did* believe was that Ebon was a liar and untrustworthy. Only in as far as his threats of violence could Jon believe that Ebon was telling the truth. He certainly intended doing them harm at some point, as and when it pleased him. When, Jon asked himself, would they cease to be useful to him? He had no idea.

The gnome dragged a small chest out from under a canvas in one of the stalls. It was almost as big as him and was obviously heavy because he had to drag it across the floor leaving deep marks in the earthen surface.

'At long last I will be able to have what I need. Get it open, now.'

The gnome grabbed a hammer and cold chisel and commenced work on the hasp securing the lid of the chest. Jon could see markings and scratches on it; as if earlier efforts had been made to get it open. Sparks flew off with each strike of the hammer, but to no avail. He next tried using a long lever; he made no impression on it; the hasp and padlock remained defiant. Ebon scolded the gnome for his efforts.

'I told you that wouldn't work. Get the forge as hot as you can, we'll melt it off.'

'Lost your key?' Jon could not help from commenting and smirked at their apparently futile efforts.

Ebon spun angrily around, clenching a fist at Jon and seethed. 'Don't push your luck, boy.'

Jon got the point and decided for the safety of them both, particularly for Anna, he would refrain from any further confrontations with Ebon; at least for now.

They sat in the shadow of the loft where Jon was secured and watched as they tried to get the chest open. Filled with exasperation, Ebon turned on the gnome and gave him an earful of abuse. They could feel the heat in his words as the gnome submitted to the torrent of abuse that was being piled upon him.

Not many gnomes would tolerate such treatment from a man; but Ebon, being who he was, it made all the difference.

Quite unexpectedly the door to the forge opened and in stepped one of the largest men he had ever seen. He was even taller than the metal masters he had seen at the Spotted Cow. Despite the door being large he had to duck his head to avoid striking it against the wooden lintel. He had a mass of red hair with a thick red beard to match and was wearing the traditional thick leather apron that the metal masters wore. He was clad in long, heavy breeches and a long-sleeved top with sleeves rolled halfway up his arms. He had muscular arms covered in thick red hair and numerous areas of scar tissue, presumably from working at the forge.

'Brutus I need to borrow . . .'

His words trailed off into silence as he took in the sight of the rogue seer and gnome working at the chest by the forge, with

Jon and Anna huddled together under the loft, Jon chained to the post as if he were a mule.

'What's going on 'ere then? Where's Brutus?' he demanded in a voice thick and low that boomed out across the room.

Before anyone could move or say a word, Khan had launched himself at the throat of the big man, with a blood-curdling snarl. Quick as a flash and belying his size, the smith stepped aside, ducking slightly and twisting so that the dog missed him. As the hound passed, he caught it with the back of a massive hand, slapping the brute away so that he landed in a crumpled heap. He yelped and lay still.

He was not dead; Jon could see him breathing but he was unconscious.

The gnome whipped out his knife and came at the smith in a flurry of movement. He moved so fast he seemed like a blur, parrying with one arm and lunging then slashing with the other. He changed his knife from one hand to the other in a blink so that you could not tell which hand held the knife. The big man stood firm awaiting the one move that would be the decisive one.

Out of the corner of his eye he saw Ebon move forward also and raise his staff. He searched around frantically for a weapon of some sort, anything that would prevent Ebon from harming the smith.

Before he could act, Anna grabbed a coal rake, propped against the wall nearby and ran at Ebon.

Distracted by her charge he levelled his staff at her.

'No,' Jon yelled and stumbled forward hampered by the chain, grabbed her around the legs and brought her down on to the straw, just as a flash of green power sizzled over their heads. It erupted amongst the stack of coal sending chunks of it every-where with a blast that hurt his ears.

Anna winced as she landed, hurting her arm again but at least she was still alive and had not ended up being roasted by the fire from Ebon's staff. Jon had not seen the effect that the power unleashed by a staff could have on anyone but guessed he was not too far off the mark.

The scuffle and noise of the affray had aroused attention from the street; Jon could hear others approaching. Ebon was scarlet with fury and would have turned on them were it not for the smith catching hold of the gnome as he made his move. Disarming him, he threw him at the seer so that they landed in a heap by the forge.

There was quite a commotion going on outside as people endeavoured to gain entry to see what was going on inside.

Ebon searched frantically for a way out and yelled in frustration like a madman. Standing over the gnome, who lay unconscious at his feet, Ebon clasped something that was secured around his neck on a long chain; putting it to his lips it emitted a shrill sound whereupon he and the gnome became engulfed in a swirling wind and vanished from sight. A mini whirlwind rose up in the smithy shop. It spun round and round, howling in anger, gathering strength as it did so. Several individuals, almost as big as the smith, finally gained access to the smithy just as the small whirlwind burst through the door. The men saw it as it blasted past them, scattering them across the forge shop. They rose to their feet and crossed their fingers to ward off bad luck as it rushed past them howling with fury, scattering everyone aside who stood in the way, out into the street and disappeared into the dark.

'What was that?'

'I guess that was Ebon making good his escape,' Jon said in response, noticing that Khan had also vanished along with Ebon and the gnome.

They had been trying to gain entry into the smithy for a minute or two but it was as if something had been barring their way until now. They looked around warily, not knowing what to expect next. What greeted them was the sight of two Southlanders, one of whom was manacled to a post, and the big smith standing in the centre of the shop.

Jon aided Anna gently to her feet and made sure she was unhurt, setting her down on the straw bale. He asked tenderly, concerned for her condition, 'Are you hurt?'

She smiled back at him weakly and nodded that she was fine but held her arm protectively.

'Who are you, and where's Brutus?' The big man demanded.

Jon nodded over in the direction of the booted feet, saying, 'I guess that's him there; I don't think he's dead, just unconscious.'

'He better not be dead, for your sake,' the smith said as he firmly but gently pushed Jon aside in order to see if his friend needed help.

The men hurried over to see if their friend was in need of any medical assistance; he was still out cold and had received a nasty clout to the head. Blood was congealing around a wound at the base of his skull. He would have an almighty big headache when he came around and it would be a while before he could lift a hammer again. Other than that, he appeared to be in good shape, groggy but stable.

They helped carry him out on a makeshift stretcher to receive the attention he needed whilst someone went ahead to alert a medical attendant that they were coming.

Just as they got to the door a heavily cloaked man walked in carrying a staff.

'Wasn't that the bloke who was here just now? Grab him someone,' one of the men shouted but no one moved; they were all a little spooked by what had happened and were reluctant to end up like Brutus.

The cloaked figure stopped and threw his hood back from off his head.

'Urim,' Jon exclaimed in his joy and relief at seeing him again. 'It's all right, he's with us, and he's not the same one who was here just now. This is our friend . . . he's my uncle,' Jon added with conviction as he looked at him squarely.

Urim looked him in the eye and smiled. 'Thank you, Jon.'

'Where the heck have you been these past few days?' Then more angrily: 'We could have been killed. Why didn't you come for us?'

'I am afraid I was . . . detained. How are you both? I see that Ebon has been busy. Ah! I see that we have secured the chest; excellent. Our first objective has been achieved.'

'What?' Jon was completely bemused.

'I am sorry not to have been with you. I am afraid that my absence was necessary in order to have obtained the chest, or at least what's in it.'

Jon stood open-mouthed in disbelief at what he was hearing; he found it difficult to take in that Urim had deliberately left them to the mercies of a lunatic seer and a murderous gnome in order to obtain this chest.

'You knew about all this?'

Urim replied without flinching. 'Yes. I knew that Ebon would come to Foundry Smelt to try and open the chest, for this is where the metal binding's hasp and lock were made. He thought, wrongly, that the tools that made them would also unmake them. I could not interfere until the chest was discovered. It was but moments ago that I knew the exact location of where it would be and sent help; just in time too by the sound of things. I *am* sorry, Jon, Anna, to have had you go through all this but as I have said it was necessary. I know how you must be feeling.'

'How can you?' Jon said accusingly. 'How can you possibly know how we feel? You leave us alone on the road without a word, injured and lost, not knowing what to do or where to go. You disappear goodness knows where. We're abducted at midnight by Ebon, thinking it was you. Held hostage and almost had our throats slit by that murderous gnome, then almost fried by Ebon's staff. How could you possibly stand there and say that you know how we feel?'

Urim stared at the floor and kicked the dust with his foot, looking awkward and abashed.

'You are right and justified in what you say; and in feeling the way that you do. It pained me to have left you but it was necessary at the time for me to make myself scarce. I also needed to discover where Ebon was headed. He was in the coach that passed us on the road.'

Urim was clearly feeling very awkward in what he was saying. Jon could not help softening his stance and hear what the seer had to say.

'Believe me, both of you, when I say that if I thought for one minute that you would have come to harm . . .'

He did not need to finish the statement; everyone present felt the passion of his conviction and concern towards them both.

There was an awkward silence for a moment dispelled by a dry cough from the smith who was standing by the forge; an intrigued spectator.

'Would anyone care to let me know what's going on?' he asked, looking at first one, then the other.

'Your pardon, smith . . .'

The big man interrupted Urim in his apology.

'My name, Southlanders, is Braun and I am metal master 'ere, not smith. Brutus is a smith, one of my apprentices and I'd like to know just what is going on 'ere and who it was that floored 'im!'

'Again I ask for your pardon, metal master.'

Urim bowed his head to Braun in recognition of his status and continued. 'I am Urim of the Council of Seers; this is my nephew Jon and his friend Anna from Ashbrooke. We have come to claim the contents of that chest that was of such curiosity to the others you saw. Ebon, an acquaintance of mine, has stolen various items from Seers' Tower; I believe you may be familiar with the place?'

Braun nodded and gave Urim a look that meant many things, like 'Am I supposed to be impressed' and 'You haven't told me what I need to know yet'. He stood arms folded, waiting for more information.

Urim stumbled on. 'Yes, well, it would appear that Ebon's accomplice, a gnome named Carver I believe, "floored" your Brutus in order for them to use the tools and forge here. They were endeavouring to force the chest open to take that which it contains when they were interrupted by you.'

'Tell me then, seer, how it was that a gnome, no bigger than my leg, could possibly have been able to inflict said blow to the back of the 'ead of my friend, who was twice his height?' Braun made a good point it seemed.

They all three, Jon, Anna and Braun, looked at Urim to see what he would say to that.

'Huh! You make a good point, sir; may I suggest that he was tricked into bending down to inspect the chest, where the gnome would then be able to deliver the blow thus.' He demonstrated how he thought the gnome had overcome the smith.

'You make a good point too, seer. I accept that it could have been as you have said. They were a suspicious pair; and they did have this lad secured to the post, so I think I am inclined to believe you. Come, lad, let me loose you from your bonds.'

Braun picked up a large set of cutters and snapped the manacles off Jon's wrists. They had not been on very long but they had already made his wrists sore, despite Anna's ointment. 'So they were after what's in this chest were they? Well, let's see what's inside that's of so much interest to them.'

Braun made to force the lock on the chest but Urim stopped him.

'No, wait; you will have no more success than they had like that. It was made here many centuries ago, protected by the ancient skills of your forebears, with a little embellishment of our own. You will need a key.'

'And I suppose you have it do you?' The metal master enquired.

Urim slipped his hand into a pouch that hung at his waist and drew out a thin gold chain; attached to it was a tiny key.

Urim knelt in front of the chest and inserted the key into the lock; it started to glow. He turned the key and mumbled something in a strange language under his breath. The lock fell off the clasp and into his hands and stopped glowing.

They all stood, mouths open in awe.

'My goodness; I've never seen anything like it; that were never made 'ere. I'm sure o' that,' Braun gasped in wonder.

'Ah but it was. It's just had a little embellishing with white magic,' Urim countered.

'Wow, that was neat,' Jon whispered in amazement.

'*Yes. Neat*,' Urim repeated. He smiled and looked for the entire world as if he were a little boy with a new toy. His excitement showed for just a second or two then he was the familiar serious Urim again. He lifted the lid carefully between gentle fingers as if frightened it would shatter if handled roughly. He reached inside and lifted out, just as carefully, a small roll of parchment secured in an emerald green ribbon. Strange markings were visible on the outside; words possibly, but not in any language that they knew or recognised. Except Urim.

'Dwarfish,' he muttered almost reverently. The scroll sparkled in the reflected light from the lanterns. He tried to undo the ribbon but it only clung tighter the more he tried to undo it. He muttered the same words he had done before but still with no effect.

'Hmm! We will have to find someone who can help us solve this conundrum. For now I think we could all do with a bit of sleep. This has been a long night and it's not finished yet.'

He placed the parchment into a pocket within his cloak and closed the lid of the chest; it shut as if there were a vacuum inside. Urim clicked the lock back into place; it shone briefly, just for a moment, from within its workings, then faded into cold grey steel.

Turning to the metal master, Urim asked as politely as he could, 'Master Braun, might we ask a favour of you? We are in need of somewhere to stay for the remainder of the night and as the hostelries will all, no doubt, have secured their doors hours ago, I wondered whether you could suggest a place for my companions and me to rest. As you can see, the girl is hurt and in need of recuperation.'

Braun straightened himself and responded, as was customary in these parts when anyone requested aid, 'I would consider it an honour, sirs and young lady, if you would accept the humble lodgings of my own home not many streets from 'ere.'

'Thank you, Master Braun. We gratefully accept your noble offer.'

The formalities said, they bowed heads towards one another.

'Allow me a few moments to secure the forges, here and in my own shop next door, and I will escort you there.'

Braun doused the forge here quickly then left, presumably to do the same to *his* forge.

Urim asked Anna, 'Are you OK? How are you feeling? Is your arm too painful?' His concern was genuine and sincere.

I'm fine, Urim. Thanks for asking.

'I'm fine too, Urim; thanks for your concern,' Jon said with an indignant look on his face.

'Oh, I can see you're OK; I knew you would be. He dared not hurt you, at least not yet; you are too valuable to him for you to come to any harm, but he is rather unpredictable, so I kept a close eye on things.'

Jon was taken aback, not just with what Urim had said, but also with the implications of what he had said.

'What do you mean, "you kept a close eye on things"? You were nowhere to be seen.'

Urim drew them both closer. 'Exactly; it was as I said: necessary, to all intents and purposes, for me to be absent. That way Ebon would show his hand and I could be free to observe and act when and if necessary. Did you not feel, Jon, that you were being followed when Ebon led you from the tavern?'

Jon recalled now that he had felt as if someone had been following them.

'That was me, but I kept myself hidden from Ebon. It wasn't by accident that Braun and the others arrived when they did. They weren't aware of it, but I placed an impression in their minds to come here. I truly am sorry to have kept you in the dark about this. It was the only way to succeed; and you have succeeded. Well done both of you.'

Urim smiled encouragingly.

Jon would have quite happily thumped him there and then and Anna looked as though she could have spat acid at him. He had used them; and neither of them was happy about it at all. Jon began to wonder at what Ebon had said about Urim being a fraud. He saw now his duplicity; serving only his own ends. He chewed nervously at his lower lip. Maybe there was more to what Ebon had said about Urim than he had given credence, he thought to himself; one thing was for certain, he would not trust Urim so readily again.

Braun returned to the forge shop.

'I have decided to believe that you are friends and can be trusted; at least, let us say that we fight the same foe. It was quite apparent that you were being held against your will by those people. Brutus regained consciousness and confirmed that it was indeed just as the seer 'ad said. If you would follow me I'll lead you to my home where you can rest until morning. It's not far, just a few streets away.'

Jon had no idea what time it was, so he asked Braun. 'What time is it, Master Braun?'

'It is still quite early, not yet four of the clock, young sir. My apprentice, Brutus, was stoking the fires of the forges ready for some work that needed completing rather urgently for some customers. Darned impatient these dwarves; said they wanted to be away by morning. Well, this 'as put me back a bit now. I shall have to find someone else to help me once I get you settled.'

They had gone but a few lengths from the forge shop. Jon turned to speak to Urim but he was nowhere in sight. He could have sworn that they had stepped over the threshold one after the other, yet Jon was alone. Anna and Braun were just ahead of them. Braun had turned to look to ensure that they pulled the door shut. He was just about to come back to investigate why Urim had not come out when Urim emerged and pulled the latch, securing the door.

Nobody locked anything here. Strange for a place that specialised in making locks amongst other things but apparently no one would think of stealing from anyone else; besides, the penalty for any crimes committed here were quite draconian.

They continued on their way and reached Braun's home within a couple of minutes. It was a large place; everything was much larger than that to which they were accustomed in order to accommodate the larger framed northerners of Foundry Smelt.

'Excuse the state o' the place – I weren't expecting visitors. I'm afraid it's a bit small, but I think it will serve your purposes.'

'What? A bit small! Master Braun, it's huge.'

Braun looked at them in bewilderment then laughed.

'I reckon it is by your standards, young sir. Aye, I reckon it is.'

Turning to Urim, he said, 'You'll excuse me from staying to settle you in. I have to get back and sort out what to do about that work I promised.'

'Of course; thank you for your kindness. We'll be fine.'

Urim bowed slightly to the metal master, who returned the courtesy then departed, leaving them to fend for themselves.

Jon settled Anna into a large chair near the fire. It was still warm and the embers were still glowing slightly. After a little coaxing it burst into flame, warming the room. Anna had soon settled into a light slumber.

'I'm shattered,' Jon said under his breath. Urim made no effort to respond; he was lost in the flames of the fire, caught in an inward stare.

'We should rest while we can; there will be precious little rest for us in the days to come.'

The seer was a constant amazement to him. Unfathomable. He determined more than ever to solve the mystery of who Urim really was. He had some thoughts, but they were not developed enough for him to lay any credence to them; yet.

Braun reflected on the strange goings on of this night as he walked back to his shop more by instinct than with any conscious thought. He was brought back to the present by a commotion ahead of him: folk were dashing around and he became aware of them shouting, '*Fire! Fire!*'

He looked up for the first time since leaving his home in the street behind him. He saw the unmistakable glow in the sky that signified a fire had taken hold of one of the buildings ahead.

It was a constant hazard in the smelt; forges were kept burning around the clock; otherwise they cracked and needed replacing. Somewhere in the foundry, a smith or a metal master would be working at his forge and fires often broke out.

An icy hand gripped his heart; fearing the worst, he ran as fast as he could and came upon the scene he had dreaded. His shop and that of his apprentice were ablaze. A number of volunteers formed a chain of hands passing buckets of water from an underground tank, designed just for this purpose. There were many of them at strategic points around the smelt. It would be a matter of damage limitation now as the fire had taken hold. The workshops were beyond saving; it was the adjoining buildings that they were trying to save now.

He rushed forward in an effort to try to save something of use but realised it was too late. The heat from the flames was too much for even one like him who was used to the heat of the forges. All he could do was to help save the other buildings and watch as his business turned to ashes right before his eyes.

Two hours later it was all over. Along with those whose job it was to fight fire wherever it occurred, helpers were damping down the charred ruins of his once busy and prosperous forge. As the blackened timbers cooled Braun sifted through the debris for anything that was salvageable but found little of any worth. He guessed what had happened; he had secured the forges, they were safe when he left them. In all his born years he had never left a forge unless he knew it to be safe. No. This was no accident. Someone had deliberately set fire to the buildings and he had a good idea who.

'Blast that gnome,' he whispered threateningly under his breath. 'When I catch up with you, it will be a bad day for you and that seer of yours.' He promised himself that, no matter what, he would see this through to the end. For Brutus's sake as well as for his, for he was out of work too unless he could attach himself to another master. The forges were not much; but they were his, free and clear. Now there was nothing but a pile of ashes and some broken dreams. He thought then to check for any sign of the chest that had caused so much of a problem but could find no trace of it; more than likely it had been incinerated in the intensity of the flames.

It was mid morning by the time Braun walked dejectedly into his home. Urim was washing at the bowl, having slept soundly for the last few hours and was feeling refreshed. Jon and Anna were still sleeping, one on each of the huge cushioned chairs by the fireplace.

'Good morning, Master Braun,' Urim started to say but did not finish his sentence as he noticed the look of him as he entered with smudges of soot on his face and clothing, with a whiff of charred wood he carried around him.

'What's the matter? What has happened?'

Then Urim stuttered as he said, 'Oh my; it's the forge. It's burned down hasn't it? I feared as much when we left.'

Jon and Anna were awake by now and caught the end of what Urim had said.

'What's that? What's burned down?' Jon asked, bleary eyed but gaining awareness rapidly.

The big man sat down wearily on a chair at the table, exhausted by his experience and bitterly disappointed at the loss of his forge shop.

'He burned my forge,' he said finally through gritted teeth and banged his fist on the table making Anna and Jon jump. He fixed Urim with a determined stare.

'That there gnome, o' that friend o' yours, seer, has burned my forge down and with it the chest or at least I couldn't find any sign of it.'

They were all silent for a while, taking in the meaning of what had happened, no one caring to break the uneasy silence.

The big man straightened with resolve and stated, 'Wherever you go from now on, I'll be with you. I need to see the end of this. No use trying to stop me.'

He held up the palm of a big hand towards them.

'I have nothing here now; besides, I've a feeling that that gnome will be crossing your path again and when he does . . .'

Braun clenched his fist out in front of him as if he were already wringing his neck.

'There may be more than you bargain for on this journey,' Urim cautioned.

'Well that may be; but I am coming with you.'

It was clear that he had made up his mind on this.

Jon and Anna both looked at each other in amazement and then at Urim.

Urim nodded thoughtfully. 'We leave as soon as everyone is ready.'

As Urim turned away, Jon thought he caught a slight smile on the face of the seer and a glint in his eye.

84

Chapter VI

Alliance

They went with Braun to take a look at the burned-out shell of what used to be a profitable forge shop. The smell of charred wood was strong in the air and grew stronger as they drew nearer to where his smithy had, until yesterday, stood. As they approached, Jon noticed a small group of what he at first thought were children, then realized that children do not have beards or carry swords and axes; they were dwarves.

There were ten of them standing beside a small cart, drawn by a piebald pony, and were looking quite bemused at the sight of the charred remains. They were dressed in the standard clothing of short tunics and hose with stout boots.

One of the dwarves who carried a polished staff saw them approaching and, recognizing the metal master, hailed them.

'Master Braun. What has occurred here?'

Braun said to Urim as an aside, 'These are the dwarves I told you about. I'll have to tell them that I am no longer able to fulfil their order, though I suspect that they already know that by now.'

Then turning to the dwarves he said, 'Good day to you, sir. I am afraid that I am unable to deliver your order; as you see I have no forge to work from and what I had completed has been lost to the fire.'

Jon noticed that each of the dwarves' tunics had a logo or badge on it, which Jon took to determine which house or family they belonged to. One of the dwarves carried a bow slung across his shoulders with a full quiver of arrows. His badge depicted a bow and arrow, so possibly, Jon thought, it could be an emblem of their particular skill.

Urim had stayed with Jon and Anna but was listening intently to what Braun and the dwarf were saying. He tried to catch the

85

attention of the metal master so that he could be invited into the conversation. As if on cue, Braun indicated the seer, nodding in their direction; he did not wait for a second opportunity. He walked quickly over to them and, after being introduced with the customary bowing and shaking of hands, engaged the dwarf in hushed tones. Jon wished he knew what all the talking was about but did not want to appear rude by going over and butting in. He guessed that he and Anna were mentioned as they all turned to look at them at one point. He had hoped that he would be invited into the conversation too, but he was not, which annoyed him somewhat. Then he had an idea and turning to Anna asked her, 'Can you lip read what they are saying, Anna?'

She nodded and while reading what was being said, began to recount it to him by signing as best she could with her injured arm.

Apparently Braun had told the dwarf about the cause of the fire and that Urim had discovered the scroll with dwarfish writing on it. Urim was asking if they would be able to translate it for them.

The dwarf had responded by saying that if he could see it then he might be able to.

Urim had agreed and they were all going to go back to Braun's house where they could see the scroll and examine it under more suitable conditions.

Urim came over to them while Braun invited the dwarves to his house for some refreshment.

'We're going back to Braun's house with the dwarves so that they can have a look at the scroll and hopefully translate it for us. We can't exactly show it to them here in the middle of the street so Braun has offered his house to afford us some privacy.'

Back at Braun's house Urim and the leader of the dwarves, whose name was Javelin, examined the scroll while the others waited patiently and exchanged polite conversation. Jon discovered that the badges on the dwarves' coats were indeed an insignia of their family and trade or skill; also that each dwarf would take the name of their acquired skill. Javelin, the leader, took his name from his skill with the spear while Archer's was because of his ability with the longbow. Tracker and Trapper, two brothers, had similar motifs as they were from the same family but they differed slightly due to their various skills. Carter carried the symbol of a wheel in his badge because he had duties regarding the transportation of their goods. Roper, who had a talent for knots, sported the symbol of a coiled rope with an intricate knotted end. Blade was a renowned swordsman amongst the dwarves whilst Bowman was adept with a crossbow.

Runner and Seeker also served after the manner of their names as a messenger and as an intelligence gatherer, or in other words, Jon supposed, a spy. All of these skills passed from father to son down through the generations. Jon envied them the time that they had had with their fathers and wished that he had had that same opportunity. All of his knowledge was self taught and compared to Tracker he was a mere novice. Yet he felt proud of his achievement in the art of tracking and had won several competitions back home. He wished that he could have time to learn a little from Tracker about his skills.

Their assignment from the dwarf army was to obtain new weapons from the metal masters. They were preparing for an anticipated battle with the gnomes of the upper Eastern Mountains. There had been a lot of activity lately and forays into their land by the gnomes that had resulted in some losses both of dwarves and their property. Things were becoming very unstable between the two races, as Archer had put it with a glint in his eye as if eager for a fight.

The group of dwarves were part of a larger contingent based on the borders between the gnomes and themselves. They had already encountered trolls and goblins from the south that had been stirred up against the dwarves by the gnomes. Unfortunately with Braun's forge destroyed and their order of weapons with it, they had to obtain a new supplier.

Urim showed the scroll to the dwarves and hoped that they would be able to reveal what was written on it.

'Well, what do you make of it, Javelin? Can you translate what is written on it and can it be opened?'

He studied it for a few moments then called Seeker to look at it.

'What do you say, Seeker? Do you recognize anything here?'

He studied it carefully and replied after a while, 'No, I cannot make out what it says. It is a very old form of dwarfish; you will need an expert to decipher this. Sorry I can't help.'

He shook his head as he moved away from the table.

'Ordinarily I would recommend that you ask the Council of the Sight at Seers' Tower but we have heard that the Tower is inaccessible due to some field of energy that surrounds it; is that so?'

'You are correct, Seeker. I am at the moment unable to enter the Tower. It is for this purpose that I need to find answers as to how I can remove that barrier.' Urim stated the fact with a hint of frustration in his voice.

Javelin called the dwarves together and conferred with them in their native tongue; there was much nodding of heads and stroking of beards as they talked together. Eventually Javelin turned and addressed Urim, saying, 'It has been decided that four of us will accompany you to the dwarfish capital of Ffridd-Uch-Ddu in the Eastern Mountains. There we believe that certain of our scholars will be able to assist you in determining the writing on the scroll. Archer, Trapper, Tracker and I will act as your guides whilst the others will stay to locate a new supplier and await completion of our weapons order.'

Braun looked at Urim quickly then offered a suggestion.

'I will gladly help them do so if you will grant me a few minutes; I will introduce one of you to my friend Malachi. He has a forge not far from here and is a good master smith; I am certain he will supply all that you need. Who will come with me?'

'Seeker is my secondary and will take command of the others. He will go with you.'

Seeker nodded in acceptance of the order from Javelin and went with Braun to meet with Malachi.

Urim beamed with delight at the decision of the dwarves to accompany them.

'We are grateful for your help and to have your company. When would you be ready to leave?'

'We have but to await the return of Master Braun and to collect some belongings from the tavern we are lodging in. Otherwise we are ready to go,' Javelin declared.

Jon tugged at Urim's sleeve. 'We need to return to the tavern *we* stayed in to collect our belongings and clean clothes.'

'Very well then; at which tavern are you lodged?' Urim asked the dwarf.

'We are at the Spotted Cow; the best tavern this side of the Crystal River.'

'But that's where we were staying!' Jon exclaimed in surprise.

'Yes. I thought I recognized you and the girl. You were rather conspicuous, the pair of you. Stood out like a sore thumb you did; but then we are used to being observant at all times.' He winked at Anna and grinned playfully.

It was getting on towards lunch time when Jon knocked on the door to the tavern; they had not opened the tavern yet after the breakfast session had closed and were probably still preparing for the lunch time rush.

'We're closed.' The response came from somewhere within.

'I think we've done this before,' Jon said as an aside to Anna with a wink; she smiled back and giggled silently.

'It's Jon and Anna; we stayed here last night. Don't you remember? Anna and I had some treatment from Hamill the physician.'

There was a brief silence then the sound of footsteps approached. The door opened and Henry popped his head around the side of the door.

'Well, bless me if it ain't. Come on in, young 'uns. We wondered what had happened to you both. Is this your uncle?'

Then noticing the dwarves, he asked, 'Are you all together?'

'Yes. Yes we are. May we get our things? We shall be leaving and wondered whether our laundry was ready.'

'Yes indeed, come on in all of you. We were about to open up for lunch anyway. No doubt you will want something to eat afore you go.'

Henry invited them all in, delighted at the prospect of a large group wanting lunch.

'That's an excellent idea,' Javelin said before anyone else could speak.

Anna nodded, eyes wide with the prospect of a good meal; Jon too was feeling rather hungry. They all looked at Urim pleadingly; he smiled playfully after a while and nodded in agreement.

'Very well; it does make sense for us to eat before we go, but we must be away afterwards, no dilly-dallying.'

'Then it is settled. Sit yourselves down.'

Henry guided them to a couple of tables, one for the dwarves and one for Jon, Anna and Urim, suited for their sizes. Braun sat on the other side of the room at a more suitable range of furniture.

Martha emerged from the kitchen with rosy cheeks from the heat. Wiping her hands on her apron she made a beeline for Anna.

'We were that worried about you we were. Isn't that right, brother?'

Henry made to answer but Martha just carried right on.

'No one saw the going of you and we didn't see you for breakfast. We wondered what had happened to you. Still 'ere you are safe and sound; you found your uncle I see.'

She turned to Urim, placing her hands on her broad hips, scolding him.

'You ought to be ashamed of yourself leaving these two poor young 'uns wandering about by themselves. In such a state they were, brother, weren't they?'

Again Henry made to answer but Martha did not give him a chance to speak. Instead he lifted his hands in submission, smiling broadly to himself, and went off to get them some drinks.

'Fair gave us a turn you did. We didn't know what to think. Cots all a mess and bags left on the side. Looked for the entire world as if you 'ad vanished into thin air.'

Looking at them carefully and making sure that Anna was OK, she relaxed and stopped fussing.

'Oh well, can't stop 'ere talking all day. I've got things to do. Now be sure to say goodbye when you leave. I don't want any more worry on your account you 'ear me now,' She scolded playfully and scurried off back to the kitchen.

Henry returned with drinks and told Jon and Anna that their belongings and clean clothes were in a side room ready for them to collect when ready. Henry told them what was on the menu for today; they ordered their meals and relaxed while they waited for the food. Urim provided payment on behalf of them all and requested some fresh supplies to take with them.

'We thank you for your service, sir. You have some fine food here. We particularly like your stew. Isn't that right, Jon?' Urim winked at Jon as he said it.

Jon smiled broadly in response. 'Yes indeed. We particularly enjoy your stew.'

He stifled a giggle. So Jon had guessed right. This was the place where Urim had 'conjured up' the stew they ate that night in the forest; it still remained a mystery though as to how he had done it.

The tavern started to fill with local workers, some of whom Jon recognized from yesterday and the staff busied themselves taking orders then delivering platters of steaming hot food. A buzz of conversation filled the tavern along with the clatter of cutlery and crockery; it was obviously a busy and popular place.

Archer leaned across and said to Jon, 'Just as Javelin said: this is the best tavern this side of the Crystal River.'

He nodded and returned his attention to his meal.

They made a strange sight; not so much the dwarves, for they were common visitors to these parts. Urim and the two Southlanders attracted a little interest from folk as they entered; other than that, they were left to themselves to enjoy their meal.

Just then, who should come in but Hamill. He saw them at the table, smiled and crossed the floor towards them. Jon was just about to introduce Hamill and Urim, when Urim stood, extended his hand and greeted him warmly.

'You must be Hamill; I am very pleased to meet you. Forgive me, we have not met before today, my name is Urim. I wish to thank you for taking such good care of my nephew and my niece yesterday.'

'You are entirely welcome I'm sure, but I did no more than my duty,' Hamill said, taken aback a little with the exuberance of the greeting.

'Nevertheless, I am grateful to you. Jon told me of your attentiveness towards them both. Will you join us?'

He looked at Anna who smiled disarmingly and signed *Hello* to him.

'I don't mind if I do. Thank you. How are you, Anna? Does your arm feel any better? I trust you have been resting it?'

Anna indicated that it was still sore but thanked him for asking and smiled the kind of smile that would melt even the hardest of hearts. Hamill did not have a hard heart; he dissolved into the empty chair opposite her with a stupid grin on his face.

'I'm fine, Hamill, thank you for asking,' Jon stated sarcastically. He did not like the way Hamill was looking at Anna. He was more than a little disturbed by Hamill's attention to her; he did not realise it but he was displaying clear signs of jealousy.

'Oh I'm sorry, Jon. Of course I am concerned for you too. How are you feeling? Let me look at your side.'

He lifted Jon's shirt and felt along his bruised ribs. Jon flinched and grimaced.

'That's fine, just a bruise. It will be right as rain before you know it. Just don't go overdoing things,' Hamill reassured him.

'I had hoped to find you both here; I wanted to check you over before I returned to the Ward.'

'You're going back to the Ward?' Urim asked with interest.

'Yes. I'm going to catch the mail coach this afternoon; if they have any space.'

'We're travelling that way ourselves. Why not come with us?'

Jon gave Urim a withering look and shook his head slightly, not wanting Hamill to travel with them.

'Thank you. That would be fine; would there be room in your carriage for me?'

'I'm afraid we don't have a carriage, Hamill,' Jon interjected. He was hoping to dissuade him from joining them. 'We intend to walk.'

That did the trick it seemed. Hamill showed disappointment and alarm. He did not like walking too far.

'Ah well, in that case I'll try my luck with the mail coach if it's all the same with you. Thank you for your offer though. Well, I must be going if I'm to make it in time. Look after yourselves; look me up when you get to the Ward. Goodbye.'

They said their farewells and Hamill left to catch his coach, much to Jon's satisfaction. Not that he disliked him; in fact he had taken a liking to him when they first met. He just did not want him around Anna. He fooled himself with thinking that he was simply being protective of her but deep inside he knew it was more than that.

'Why did you invite him to join us, Urim?' Jon asked, trying to conceal his emotions.

'I thought he would be of assistance to yourself and Anna along the way. Did you not want him to come with us?'

Jon could not find a suitable response so turned his attention back to eating in an effort to avoid any further discussion.

When they had finished lunch, they collected their belongings, along with their fresh supplies, and started off.

Henry and Martha waved them goodbye with an invitation to return again soon. 'Mind you look after that girl, young man.'

The dwarves took the lead followed by Urim, then Jon and Anna, then Braun at the back. They had not gone far when they heard a cry from behind them. Turning, they saw Hamill running to catch them up.

'I'm glad I caught you; I'm afraid there was no space on the coach so I returned to the tavern and they said you had just left.' He gulped for breath. 'Would you mind if I join you? I'm not one for walking really but the next coach isn't for two days.'

'Of course, that's no problem at all, Hamill; you are most welcome.'

Urim turned and winked at Jon, placing a reassuring hand on his shoulder.

Hamill attached himself to Anna and Jon. It was clear he intended to stay with them for the duration of the walk.

'At least it will only be for a couple of days,' Jon thought to himself. When they got to the Ward they would part company.

Jon had mixed feelings about it; he was grateful to Hamill and could not help liking him; it was just that he felt uncomfortable with his obvious attraction towards Anna. He was looking forward to seeing the Ward. He had heard so much about it and had always wanted to visit, but usually the reason anyone would go to the Ward was if they needed medical treatment of some kind.

What really excited him was going to Ffridd-Uch-Ddu, the dwarves' capital; not many Southlanders got to see it. Here he was going to see both the elves and the dwarves in their own environment. He would be the stranger, not them; now that was something to remember. He would have some fine tales to tell his grandchildren, if he ever had any that is. He had no plans as yet on settling down with anyone and felt awkward about the idea; besides, he needed to find someone who would have him. He found himself looking at Anna and a strange warmth flooded over him; he could feel his cheeks reddening.

He looked at Hamill and he cooled. He was not sure how he felt about him but it was clear that Hamill liked them, particularly Anna.

They had applied the salve to their eyes before leaving the tavern and it certainly helped to diminish the effects of the pollution. They all, apart from Braun, were glad to be leaving Foundry Smelt and its oppressive black cloud.

He had lost everything with the fire, only his house remained and he had arranged with a friend for it to be rented out until his return. So there was nothing to tie him to the place, which enabled him to leave without too many reservations, and he seemed cheerful enough. Besides, he would be back someday; he just did not know when. His resolve to catch up with Ebon and the gnome was clear. What he would do when that time came was not so clear. Time would tell.

Due to their late start from Foundry Smelt, they did not reach the main coach house at Hoarley Vale as they would have liked so they settled for a small guest house by the name of Green Lodge in one of the villages along the way. The weather was fine and had improved the further they travelled away from the black cloud that was ever present above the smelt. They had travelled well and Urim was pleased with the progress they had made.

Braun had been somewhat disgruntled, which Urim had expected, and had walked some of the way engaging him in conversation in soft tones. Jon guessed that he was employing some sort of relaxation inducement on him because he had calmed considerably after a while. The dwarves had marched uncomplaining, as expected; they were in good spirits as they were on their way home and were in buoyant mood. Tracker and Trapper talked almost non-stop and were obviously good friends as well as being brothers.

Archer had walked some of the way with Jon and explained that dwarves lived for around two hundred years. Trapper and Tracker were youngsters at only sixty years old, which is why they were so loud. 'Teenagers', Archer had called them with a smile. Dwarves took things very seriously; after all, life was a serious matter and was too short to be frittered away. He did confess though that there were times when a good song would rouse their spirits.

Anna and Jon had borne the journey well and were accomplished backpackers. Hamill, however, had not done so well. Being unaccustomed to hiking for any great distance, he was more than glad to stop for the night and rest his sore feet.

Following a more than fair dinner, though not of the standard of the Spotted Cow, Urim took Javelin aside and had a short conversation with him out of earshot. Javelin nodded a few times and tugged at his beard before they returned to the others, addressing Jon and Anna. 'We shall set up a watch throughout the night. Urim has told me what happened to you last night so we will take turns at the watch. I will stand guard first for two hours followed by Archer, then Trapper and then Tracker. The rest of you can enjoy a good night's sleep. From what I have heard, you could do with it.'

Jon and Hamill were to share a small room at the top of the house with a connecting door to Anna's room. Urim and Braun would share a room next to the dwarves on the first floor. Javelin settled himself at a table with a flask of the dwarves' favourite brew, relk – strong enough to bring tears to the eyes of the most hardened of drinkers – and a long clay pipe. 'I'll be fine here. Don't you worry; you can sleep safely tonight,' he reassured them as they climbed the stairs to their various rooms.

Jon awoke to a gentle shaking. He opened his eyes and saw Anna smiling down at him. *Come on, sleepy head, or you'll miss breakfast,* she signed with difficulty because of her bad arm. He stretched and groaned, reluctant to leave the warmth and comfort of his covers. He would have been quite happy to have stayed where he was but realised that was an idle wish and tossed back the covers once Anna had gone. It was the thought of a good breakfast that had levered him out of his cot; the enticing smell of bacon had wafted through the door as Anna closed it. He was hungry.

'Come on, Hamill. Time to get up; we've a long way to go today.' He dressed after a quick wash using the bowl on a table by the window. Hamill groaned and turned over, pulling the covers tighter. 'Please yourself,' Jon thought and went to join the others. They ate a hearty breakfast, having been much refreshed from their night's rest and were just getting ready to leave when Braun noticed Hamill was missing. 'Where's Hamill?'

They all turned to look at Jon questioningly.

'Don't blame me,' he said. 'I called him but he didn't want to get up.' Frankly he had hoped that no one would have noticed and they could have left without him. 'Too much to hope for,' he thought.

'Well, he'll have to hurry and eat on the run or else go without. We cannot delay any longer,' Urim said with conviction and added, 'We will not go without him though; he may well prove invaluable to us.'

He addressed this last statement at Jon, who ducked his head trying to avoid it.

'I'll go and rouse him,' Braun offered.

'No, Jon will do it. It is his responsibility, seeing as they shared the room.'

Urim looked at Jon in a way that he knew arguing would achieve nothing, so reluctantly he climbed the stairs to get Hamill out of bed. A few moments later he returned.

'He's up now. He'll be down shortly.'

Sure enough, a few minutes later, Hamill came down the stairs apologising for having kept them waiting.

'We cannot spare the time to wait while you have breakfast; you'll have to grab some fruit and bread and eat it as we go,' Urim chided him softly. He had a twinkle in his eye as he spoke and a smile played at the corner of his mouth. He obviously had a liking for Hamill despite his annoying ways. They left Green Lodge tavern to take up the next leg of their journey towards the Ward a little later than planned. It was still going to take two days to get there, providing the weather held. The country was not difficult to traverse though and the scenery pleasant enough to make the walk an enjoyable one.

The dwarves took the lead again, setting the pace, followed by Jon and Anna then Braun and Urim. Hamill tagged along at the back, having left the guest house last and was struggling to put his backpack on while juggling a piece of toast and an apple.

Having consumed them he licked his fingers and, catching up with Urim, asked, 'Just as a matter of curiosity; when are you planning to stop for lunch?'

The smile played around Urim's mouth again and without breaking his stride or looking at Hamill he answered, 'We will probably be stopping at around midday for some refreshments, all being well.'

'Oh! Will we be stopping for a rest before then?'

'I expect we will but that will be up to the dwarves. It is they who are in charge of this march; not I.'

'Oh!'

Hamill fell silent and hurried to catch up to Jon and Anna.

'Morning; how are you both today? How's that arm of yours, Anna?'

A little painful but otherwise I'm fine, thank you, she signed as best she could and Jon translated.

'Urim said we should make good time today and have a rest mid morning,' Hamill ventured, trying to make conversation.

'No thanks to you,' Jon whispered under his breath.

Anna heard him though and gave him a playful dig in the ribs that made him wince.

'Are you OK, Jon?' Hamill enquired.

'Yes, yes, I'm fine; no problem.'

He rubbed at his bruised ribs where Anna had just poked him; inwardly he was saying, 'Go away, Hamill.'

Anna walked closer to Jon and threaded her arm through his, clinging tightly with affection.

He was feeling rather sullen this morning and she knew it. She also was aware of why he was feeling this way and was delighted that he was jealous of Hamill's attentions to her. It gave her new confidence in his feelings for her and she welcomed it but decided that she needed to do something to put Jon's mind at rest.

Feeling Anna so close to him lifted his spirits. He had a funny feeling in the pit of his stomach that was not unpleasant and he smiled broadly for the first time in a couple of days. The further they walked together arm in arm, the better he felt. She was like a breath of fresh air to his moodiness and it sent a clear message to Hamill where her affections lay. She was telling him that he need have no fear of Hamill, that her smiles to him were purely those of friendship. Jon could see that now because when she looked at him as she was doing now, he knew that she loved him.

He wanted to kiss her but lacked the courage to do so; he simply smiled foolishly back at her, squeezing her hand. His animosity towards Hamill melted away like the frost before the morning sun. He breathed deeply and felt great.

Hamill on the other hand saw the connection between them and lowered his head for a while then picked up his pace and began to whistle. A cloud seemed to lift from off the little band of travellers and pretty soon they were all smiling and chatting as they walked. When they met the occasional travellers going in the other direction, they would exchange news. There was talk of strange things happening in the land, of creatures prowling the land at night and folk not wanting to be out after dark.

At around midday, the dwarves called a halt for lunch, much to Hamill's relief. They had had a short break a couple of hours ago but he was in need of a longer rest before starting up again.

It was a pleasant spot on a gently rising slope near a copse of trees. The dwarves knew the road fairly well and said that they should reach the next town later that afternoon. The Fox and Hounds was almost as good an inn as the Spotted Cow; they had stayed there on their way to Foundry Smelt.

The warmth of the late summer sun was comforting and quite sleep inducing but they could not spare the time to take advantage of it.

Urim fidgeted about, becoming more and more restless.

'Something is not right here; I can sense it.'

Suddenly he turned and yelled. 'Quick. Get to the trees; hurry before it's too late.'

They all ran for cover, all except Hamill that is.

'What's the matter? What's all the fuss about?'

He looked around bemused but then froze. Looking to the sky he paled and scrambled to his feet. He reached the trees before Jon and Anna who were puffing away and gasping for breath. His elfish half must be his legs for they were quick as the wind.

'What is the matter, seer?' Javelin enquired of Urim.

'Listen.'

They all stood still, hardly daring to move. Gradually they began to feel it. They felt a subtle vibration in the ground; rhythmic and growing stronger.

'What is it?' Jon whispered to Tracker who stood nearby.

'Gnomes; hundreds of them are headed this way if my guess is right,' he hissed in reply through gritted teeth.

'That's not all. There are things in the sky too. Hopefully they didn't see us.'

They made their way through the trees, taking care to stay hidden in the shadows, towards the top of the rise. There in the valley below them they saw a solid black mass of gnomes; the largest army amassed that they had ever seen. The ground shook at their passing. The head of the army had just entered the valley from the north and was sweeping down towards them. Column after column; clanking and stomping its way across the country-side like some huge millipede. There was no end in sight; before long the whole valley floor was filled with them. Shadows swept over the grassland either side of the swarming gnomes. Huge birds circled like vultures high up in the sky; swooping down every now and again, then catching the thermals and rising back again. One of them swooped down close to the copse of trees surveying the area closely, before catching a thermal and rising high back into the air. Jon and Anna gasped in amazement.

They were not ordinary birds; they were kite-folk; half bird of prey, half human. What were they doing here? Both the gnomes and the kite-folk were out of place. The gnomes had not been seen in this number ever before, certainly not this side of the Eastern Mountains. The kite-folk had never been seen outside of their domain around the Hand Lakes and were almost thought of as the product of a fertile imagination, but here they were, large as life. For the two races to be together, here and in such numbers spelled trouble.

They stayed hidden in the shadows for a long time, amazed by the sheer size of the army passing before them.

Braun asked the question that everyone was thinking. 'Where do you think they are going?'

'I don't know. What I'd really like to know is where have they come from, and how they got past our borders.' Javelin answered with a worried look towards the other dwarves.

The dwarves looked questioningly at one another, concern etched into their faces.

'Something is most definitely amiss,' Trapper said, uneasy about the appearance of the gnomes.

'Ebon has had a hand in this, I'm sure of it. As to where they came from or where they are going to, it is indeed a mystery. One thing is for certain, they are bold and confident to be marching through here in broad daylight,' Urim pondered aloud.

'If we could capture one of them we would soon find out,' Trapper offered a suggestion.

'No, no; it is too risky. There are far too many of them and the kite-folk watch from the sky. There would be very little chance of success; you would only alert them to our presence,' Javelin countered quickly.

It took almost two hours for the army of gnomes to pass and for the sky to be clear, yet Urim was cautious.

'Javelin, might I suggest that a scout be sent out to confirm that the way is clear and it is safe for us to proceed.'

'Agreed; Tracker, do your best not to be seen.'

Tracker looked at him with a hurt expression, as if his remark had slighted his ability but Javelin simply smiled and winked at him, having full confidence in him; he was just being playful with the young but experienced and able dwarf.

They waited nervously for his return. Jon looked down into the valley. Where once it had been lush and verdant grassland, it was now a raw scar in the landscape. It would not take an expert to follow them.

After what seemed an age, Tracker returned, saying, 'It is all clear, we can carry on now but I suggest we hurry if we are to make the inn before nightfall.'

They travelled as quickly as they could, Braun keeping a lookout to their rear for any signs of the gnomes or the kite-folk. They reached the inn just as the sun was setting and decided to go in as separate parties, just in case they were being sought after by Ebon's spies; they did not want to arouse too much suspicion. The dwarves went in first and after giving the pre-arranged signal that all was well, Jon, Anna and Hamill also went in. Braun and Urim waited a few moments before they entered the inn. They secured rooms for the night and ate their meals as three separate parties, not daring to be seen to be together. The locals were used to seeing strangers passing through, although Braun caused something of a stir when he approached the bar. They gave him a wide berth though, having heard of the volatile nature of a Foundry man when away from his beloved smelt.

They retired to their rooms, the dwarves again discreetly standing as guards, keeping a watch for any danger. Jon and Hamill discussed the day's events until too tired to stay awake any longer.

*

Jon awoke with a start from a troubled dream; he looked around him sleepily and it took him a while to recognize where he was. He realised that he was bursting to go to the toilet and thought, 'I shouldn't have had that last drink.' Fumbling under the cot for a chamber pot and not finding one, he was annoyed that he would have to use the washrooms; he quietly tiptoed out of the room so as not to disturb Hamill.

The night light cast a warm glow along the landing and down the stairs, leaving some of the recesses in darkness. The washroom was downstairs and he had considered waiting until morning but his need was too great. As he rounded the corner to go down the stairs he caught a movement in the shadows of a recess and jumped as a cloaked figure emerged into the light.

'Archer, don't do that; you half scared me to death.'

Archer laughed quietly, and then asked earnestly, as he became his more serious self, 'Is all well with you, young Jon?'

'Yes, yes, I'm fine, I just need the toilet that's all.'

The washroom was dimly lit and a little scary being there all alone in the semi darkness. He hurried as it was also quite cold and he relished the thought of climbing back into a soft, warm cot. The stairs creaked as he went up, which he had not noticed on the way down. It reminded him of the other night when Ebon had come for them and he became concerned. He hesitated on the stairs and peered round the corner into the recess where Archer had been. He could just make him out in the dark and felt immediate relief. Jon skipped quickly along the landing past the recess, whispering to Archer as he went past, 'I'm glad you're looking out for us, Archer; thanks for doing that, it's much appreciated.' He turned to go into his room when he heard a swishing noise that made his blood run cold. He had heard that sound before; in the forest that night with Urim when the gnomes had tried to kill him. It was the sound of an arrow whizzing past him. A split second later there was a muffled thud from behind him, as it buried itself in something.

He heard a short gasp and then a loud thud like a sack of potatoes being dropped onto the floor.

Just ahead of him he could see movement in the shadows and a cloaked figure emerged slowly into the light; an arrow cocked in readiness to let fly pointed in his direction.

'Archer! What? Who?'

He turned in puzzlement and saw a gnome, sprawled on his back with an arrow embedded in his chest; he held his blade in his hand, glinting in the flickering light.

Archer crept forward and whispered, 'Be careful, Jon, he may still be dangerous; I don't think I killed him and there may be more of them.'

Archer approached carefully, keeping his bow taught, ready to release its deadly missile at the slightest move from the gnome.

The other dwarves were out of their room in seconds, blades at the ready. Braun and Urim also arrived and in hushed voices asked what had happened.

A light flooded the lower landing and a man's voice whispered hoarsely, 'What do you think you're doing up there? My wife and I are trying to sleep.'

They stood as statues for a second or two, and then Javelin whispered back, 'We're very sorry to have disturbed you. My friend had a bit too much to drink and he fell over. We won't disturb you again.'

'I hope not.'

With that he went back into his room grumbling under his breath about folk not being able to handle their drink and the light disappeared as he shut the door.

The dwarves carefully disarmed the gnome and carried him into their room whilst Archer resumed his guard duty.

Braun decided that he would stand watch for a while as well.

'As Archer has said, there may be more of them.'

Urim suggested that Jon go back to sleep.

'There's nothing you can do here; you might as well make use of the remaining hours until daybreak to get what sleep you can. It will be a long, hard day tomorrow. I shall assist the dwarves in finding out what we can from this assassin, if he's still alive. My methods are more effective and less painful, which I am sure will be a disappointment to the dwarves.'

Urim went in with them and Jon reluctantly went back to his cot, but did not immediately get back to sleep. He mulled over in his mind the narrow escape he had had, yet again. This was proving to be an interesting journey he had undertaken; he wondered whether he would live to see it completed.

*

102

The next morning he awoke early and got ready in a hurry, he wanted to know what had happened last night with the gnome. Braun and Urim sat eating their breakfast but there was no sight of the dwarves. He was itching to sit with them and discover the news but they had agreed not to be seen together so he restrained his eagerness and went back upstairs to wake Hamill and Anna.

It took a while to rouse Hamill but he eventually succeeded and he quickly told him about the events of last night. He left Hamill to dress and went to Anna's room and knocked on the door; she must have been ready to come out as it opened almost immediately. He stepped into the room, pushing her gently back and closed the door behind him.

She looked at him with a surprised look on her face that she changed to one of playful scolding, wagging her finger at him.

Holding her in front of him he recounted what had happened:

'Anna, we had a visitor last night. A gnome tried to kill me out on the landing but Archer got him before he could do any harm.'

She looked incredulously at him at first, but when she saw that he was serious she signed, *Are you OK? What happened?*

Jon told her all that he knew and that Urim and Braun were already at breakfast but he had not seen the dwarves. They were not in their room; the door was open and the room empty; all their things had gone.

The three of them went down for breakfast, sitting a couple of tables away from the others. Jon ventured to ask the landlord as he approached them.

'What was all the noise about last night?'

'Were you disturbed too, sir? I'm sorry about that. The other gentleman told me that the dwarves who stayed here last night got drunk and were making a noise, though they didn't appear drunk to me; didn't hear a thing myself. Anyhow, they left early this morning. Will you three be staying over?'

'No, thank you, we are just about to leave ourselves. Do we owe you any more for the lodgings and food?'

'No, sir. You paid in full last night, but thanks for asking all the same. Will you require a packed lunch each? It's usually half a florin for two but I'll put in the extra seeing as there's three of you.'

'That will be great. Thanks.' Hamill accepted the offer too quickly for the other two to have a say in the matter.

'They'll be ready shortly.'

Urim and Braun left with packed lunches of their own; Urim discreetly signalled for them to follow.

The lunches seemed to take an age in being prepared as they were keen to get going and find out what was happening. Once they had them and handed over the half florin, they paid their respects and hurried out the door.

Urim said in a loud voice so that others could hear.

'Good morning to you. Which way do you travel my fine young friends?'

'Oh, well, we are headed east.' Jon tried to sound casual.

'We are also going that way; would you care to join us as we travel?'

'We would be only too pleased to travel with you.'

They set off along the track making small talk until they were sure that they were safe from any eavesdropping.

'What's going on? Where are the dwarves? What happened to the gnome?'

Jon and Hamill were firing questions quicker than Urim could answer them.

He laughed and signalled for them to slow down a little.

'Give me a chance; the dwarves have been burying the gnome; unfortunately he died from his wound before we could glean anything useful from him. We shall join up with Javelin and the others shortly. For now, we must be alert and take extra care if we are to reach the Ward safely today.'

The last couple of days walking had begun to take their toll on Hamill. He was starting to limp and screwed his face up in discomfort every now and again. He did not like walking, he decided, as they rested by the side of a stream and refreshed their flasks. He sat himself down on a rock slab at the water's edge and, removing his boots, dangled his feet in the cool running water; he immediately felt better and smiled contentedly. He had already done as much walking as he had cared to do but realised that it would take them at least another four to five hours before they reached the Ward. He was not looking forward to the walk, but he was looking forward to being in familiar surroundings again, knowing that he would not have to do any more walking for a while.

'I'm sure my feet are worn flat,' he said, hoping to receive some words of sympathy from the others. All he got was a reprimand from Javelin, telling him to put his boots back on before his feet swelled.

Hamill liked the dwarves; even when they told you off they did it cheerfully, without any malice. The weather was good for the time of year and made for pleasant walking, it was just that he was not used to it. He would far rather take the coach anywhere and was beginning to wish that he had waited for the next mail coach back at Foundry Smelt. The dwarves were setting a hard pace and were used to forced marches. He was not; even though he was half elf he was suffering under the strain and made sure everyone knew about it.

Why I wanted to come with this lot I don't know. Then he remembered that Anna had smiled so nicely at him when Urim invited him to join them; that coupled with the coach being full and the next one not going for another two days had confirmed his decision to travel with them. He liked Jon and Anna and thought that they could become friends; he also liked the dwarves and if he were to travel anywhere on foot, then he would definitely choose to do it in their company.

He did not know too much about the metal masters and was a little intimidated by them when he first arrived in the smelt but once he had got to know them, they were really quite amicable. Urim was a different matter. Although he was friendly towards the elf (so Hamill preferred to be known, rather than a halfer) Hamill was not sure how to take him. He had never met a seer before and was surprised when he had been told that he was Urim of the Council of the Sight. He had thought him to be a friar of some sort, albeit a bit strange. The group were seeing a different side to Hamill today. He was moody and complained a lot about his feet and how they hurt, so much so that they were all getting a bit irritated with him. Javelin chided him on.

'Come on, Hamill. We haven't got all day. I should have thought you'd be glad to be almost back at the Ward.'

Hamill felt reluctant to put his boots back on just yet; he was enjoying the cool, soothing water.

'Yes, hurry up, Hamill. We must get started again. With or without you we must reach the Ward today. It's your choice.' Braun was beginning to lose his temper with him and was eager to get going.

'I am afraid we will have to hurry you, Hamill,' Urim joined in before Hamill could reply. 'There is but a little further to travel, then you will be home and we can all rest.'

Hamill grumbled discontentedly into his chest as he struggled to put his boots back on, annoyed that he really had no choice but to continue, as he did not want to be left behind. He laced up the boots and heaved himself wearily onto his feet. He had only gone a few steps when he knew that he would regret having taken them off in the first place. His little toes rubbed against the inside of his boots and he knew that he would have blisters before the day was done.

The others had already forged ahead quite a distance, the dwarves setting the pace again; he would need to hurry if he were to keep up with them.

After what seemed an age of trudging up hill and down dale, they finally rested for lunch. They were well into the Plains of Uniah now, rolling grassland punctuated occasionally by small communities of mobile herders who followed the migration of their livestock across the plains.

They kept a lookout for any that might be in their path as they did not want to be seen; they all kept an eye on the sky looking out for any kite-folk that may be spying on the land. As they topped a rise, Javelin stopped abruptly and dropped to a crouch, signalling the others to stay back. He signalled for Tracker to join him and they peered out into the dale ahead, conversing in whispers. Jon and the others in the group were curious to know what Javelin and Tracker had seen.

They were feeling very nervous, following their previous day's encounter with the army of gnomes.

The two dwarves stayed quietly intent on what lay just ahead of them and eventually Javelin worked his way back down to them and spoke to Urim.

'There is a herder's group a hundred lengths from here but something is not quite right. There is no movement and no smoke coming from the chimney, which is most unusual. There is no sign of them or their animals. I don't like it.'

Javelin was nervous.

Braun suggested an idea to Javelin. 'Perhaps we can skirt around them unobserved.

'We could. However, it would take us time to do so and I'd rather discover what is amiss than have unsolved questions at our backs. I want to know that we are secure,' Javelin replied with an edge of concern to his voice.

They looked to Urim for a decision.

'I agree with Javelin. We must be secure in our movements. Can Tracker discover anything about the situation?'

Javelin reported back on what the situation was at present.

'We have been observing for some time and I believe that we four can approach and find out if all is well. We can signal you from there.'

Having agreed this course of action the four dwarves cautiously approached the bivouac they had been observing; Braun kept a lookout for the signal, which came not long after the dwarves had gone.

They all descended into the encampment. The dwarves were sheathing their weapons and standing easily so Jon guessed that there was nothing to be concerned about.

'Do not go into the shelters and do not touch anything. We must move on quickly,' Javelin ordered curtly and stomped off up the trail in ill humour. The other dwarves were equally dejected and ushered the others of the group past. As Urim caught the eye of Tracker, the dwarf shook his head, jerking it back towards the shelter nearest him.

Urim sighed and bowed his head, walking heavily on.

Jon caught up with Archer and asked, 'What did you find, Archer?'

He looked sadly back at Jon and, clearly moved, said, 'The gnomes have been here.'

He did not need to say any more. Jon realised the cause of their reaction and respected their silence but asked inquisitively, 'Shouldn't we have buried them rather than leave them for the wild animals to find?'

'Yes, we should, and we all would have liked to have given them a decent burial but that would have given away the fact that we had been here, as well as delaying our arrival at the Ward.'

Archer was clearly uncomfortable about leaving them but knew that they could not afford to take the risk of stopping.

Nothing was said for quite some while by anyone. A solemn mood had fallen on them and the leagues went by without conversation. The mood only lifted when they came in sight of the Ward. The twin watch-towers stood out like bronze pillars as the waning sun reflected off the redwood timber structures; within an hour they would be safely inside its stockade.

Chapter VII

The Ward

They heard the alarm being sounded and a flurry of activity behind the closed gates of the Ward as they drew near. Hamill was surprised that the gates were not open and said to the others, 'That's strange; they don't normally have the gates closed until after sunset.'

'Maybe they heard you were coming back,' Javelin joked with Hamill and gave him a smile and a wink.

'No, seriously, there must be a reason for it. I wonder what the matter could be.'

'Halt. Who goes there?' demanded a sentry from the top of one of the towers, as they drew within hailing distance. Several others were on the other tower and along the ramparts of the wooden stockade; they levelled crossbows in their direction and seemed ready to defend the Ward from them should they prove to be hostile.

'This is not the sort of welcome I would expect from my kinsmen,' Hamill shouted back at them. 'It's certainly not the kind of treatment afforded visitors when I left not a month ago.'

'A lot can happen in a month.'

The captain of the guard strode forward to inspect them from the tower.

'Hello, Hamill, good to see you. I take it that these others are with you and can be vouched for?'

'Hello, Captain Quentin. Yes indeed, I can vouch for them; these are my friends. We have travelled from Foundry Smelt and have some news that would be of interest to you. What's all the alarm about?'

Urim quickly stopped Hamill from saying any more.

'Captain, I am Urim of the Council of the Sight. My friend here is indeed correct in that there is something you may find of great importance. Perhaps it would be better for us to discuss it inside?'

Captain Quentin hesitated momentarily, as if weighing up the situation, then gave the order to let them into the compound. A contingent of soldiers met them inside and Captain Quentin emerged from the stairway of the tower.

'You will forgive our caution, Hamill. We cannot afford to be casual when visitors arrive these days. Come. I will conduct you to the reception hall where we can more comfortably discuss things.'

The guards led off across the courtyard through another set of high gates and made their way across an inner courtyard to a large thatched building that served as the common place for eating. There were many elves going about their business and the sight of such a strange group of visitors aroused quite a bit of interest. Word had spread quickly that a seer had arrived and that Hamill was with him along with a small group of dwarves and a metal master.

Inside the refectory it was brightly lit by lanterns and felt warm and inviting. The elves in the kitchen were busy getting the evening meal ready and there was a great deal of clattering of dishes going on the other side of a dividing screen.

They went to the far end away from the noise where they were ushered into a smaller room. Captain Quentin dismissed the four elf guards who returned to their duties. He stood facing them, arms crossed, feet firmly planted.

'Now then, what is this news that you feel is of such importance?'

Urim nodded to Javelin who then related the events of their journey and their encounter with the army of gnomes, along with the gnome assassin and their discovery of the herders bivouac.

Urim added his own story concerning the seers and Ebon; of his need to discover a way to release them. He stated that they were on their way to Ffridd-Uch-Ddu with the dwarves and must leave the next day but would be grateful for any assistance that they might be able to provide.

Captain Quentin listened without interruption or any display of emotion. When they had recounted their stories, the captain relaxed his manner and sat down with them at the head of the table.

'It appears that you were fortunate indeed. Now let me tell you of what has been going on while you have been away Hamill.'

He told them of strange reports coming in of creatures moving about in the forests; of people and livestock going missing and that about a week ago another seer had arrived along with two badly wounded dwarves.

'One of them had died but the other one we had managed to treat and had made an astounding recovery; so much so that they had left two days later. It was shortly after their departure that we discovered the body of one of our orderlies who had been missing from his duties. His throat had been cut and he had bled to death.'

'Did you say dwarves, captain? You're sure that they were dwarves?' Urim and Javelin exchanged glances.

'Yes quite sure. We buried one of them in the cemetery and the other left with the seer soon afterwards. Ebon was the name that the seer called himself. So you see it is with interest that I hear your account and had it not been for Hamill being with you, then your arrival here would have proved a little less welcoming than it was. We were told a slightly different story you see by the other seer; he warned us of the plight of the seers and that he was in pursuit of another who had perpetrated the act. The things you have told me would explain a great deal.'

He continued by relating the more recent reports of farmers losing cattle and sheep; of disturbing sounds in the night, sightings of strange creatures, even of the murder of a farmer from the south.

Ebon's appearance in the midst of all this caused considerable concern to all at the Ward. So they were taking no chances when anyone came along; his priority, as captain of the guard, was the safety of the Ward and its occupants.

Urim pondered on what he had been told then asked, 'Is there anything else that you can tell me about Ebon? Did he give you any indication of what he was about?'

'Not that I can think of, other than that he asked to see the maps we have here of the area leading into the Eastern Mountains. Come to think of it he was rather interested in Crystal Falls; he said that he had a message to deliver to the Sprite Queen from the Sight.'

Urim chewed nervously at his lower lip then thanked the captain for his help.

'Well, if there's anything else I can help you with I would be pleased to assist.'

'I thank you, captain. We would be grateful for a meal and somewhere to rest for the night.'

'Of course; I will send the concierge to you. In the meantime, dinner is almost ready, please help yourselves. Hamill will no doubt be able to assist you. He always was the first in line when food was about.'

The captain smiled at Hamill's protestations and they all laughed.

Dinner over and having been assigned rooms for the night, Urim suggested that they all get a good night's sleep. He also suggested to Javelin that he and the other dwarves do 'a bit of digging around' to see what they could discover about the two dwarves who had been treated here. Javelin replied that he had already decided to do just that. There was no need for them to stand guard tonight; the elves were capable enough.

Hamill insisted on seeing to Anna and Jon's ailments now that they had arrived at the Ward. The bruising to Jon's side was fading and was not as sore as it had been so Hamill was satisfied with him. Anna, however, was still in discomfort, with her elbow inflamed. Hamill had called upon another physician who, having inspected it, recommended complete rest with only gentle finger exercises to help with the healing process. That did not include signing, at least not for a couple of days.

'Sorry, Anna, but you will have to follow orders if you want that arm to heal properly,' Hamill soothed. Then he had some treatment himself for his tortured feet; a footbath of hot mineral water would soon ease the discomfort. Jon and Anna left him to receive his treatment and went to their rooms for a well earned and much longed for night's sleep.

'Good night, Anna. Sleep well.'

She blew him a kiss and went into her room. It seemed to him that he floated along the corridor to his room, a smile spread full across his face; actually it was more like a stupid grin.

Morning came with the sound of birds chirping to greet the new day. Jon stretched and yawned, the smile still upon his lips; he wondered whether he had slept that way all night. He washed and dressed then made his way to the food hall where he found Hamill already tucking into a large helping of scrambled eggs.

'So it's true what the captain said yesterday, you are first in the queue.'

He teased Hamill and held up his hands as he laughed, indicating that it was only a joke.

Hamill choked on his mouthful of food in protest but saw the funny side of his remark and laughed all the same. They both felt better today, free from the strains of the road, and a sense of well-being settled upon them.

'This is a fabulous place, Hamill.'

Jon felt comfortable and relaxed as he breathed in deeply of the atmosphere that pervaded everywhere.

'Indeed it is. There is no better place in the land for healing and making you feel great. Apparently it is due to the confluence of two magnetic fields that generate a healing process. That is why the Ward is where it is.'

'Well, whatever it is, I like it. I wonder you can bear to leave it.'

'It is hard to do so at times, but it is necessary to offer our skills to those who are in need throughout the land. Someday I will be called upon to leave here and practise my skills at Winters Hold. I am assigned to be their court physician once I have qualified. My father is currently the physician there and I suppose that has had some bearing on my appointment; something in the fact that they trust him and they are comfortable with keeping a family connection.'

Jon whistled softly in admiration.

'Wow, that's some position. So do you think that it's because of your dad? Not that you aren't able of course,' he added hastily, not wanting to cause offence.

'It is because I am half human as well as half elf. Apparently they feel more comfortable than with a full-blooded elf.'

'Phew. How do you feel about that?'

'I'm OK. I am quite fortunate really. It is a prestigious position and I'm quite looking forward to it.' Anna joined them at the table, her arm secured in a sling that offered more support than the one Hamill had given her at the Spotted Cow in Foundry Smelt. Consequently she found it difficult to sign to them but she did manage the words *good morning* and sat down next to Jon.

'Can I get you anything for breakfast?' they said almost at the same time and laughed; Jon no longer minded Hamill's attention to Anna, he felt happy enough with where her feelings lay.

Hamill got the breakfast for her as he had finished his and Jon was still eating, returning with a tray full of choices. Fruit, cereal, milk, toast, jams, butter, a selection of pastries and some juice; all balanced precariously on the tray he carried. There was more than enough for Anna so they all tucked in and cleared the lot.

Feeling satisfied, Jon sat back in his chair and sighed contentedly. He could quite happily stay here forever.

Urim entered the food hall and, seeing them, came across with a determined stride. His expression was serious.

'Come with me all of you, there are some matters that need to be discussed.'

Curious as to what could be the matter, they rose from the table and followed Urim out into the morning air. It felt damp with a fine mist hanging in the air so they were glad to get inside again. They found themselves in the office of the coordinator, Janine Tanner. She was there along with Captain Quentin.

Urim closed the door and said gravely, 'I am afraid I have some disturbing news for you. The dwarves you treated who were with Ebon, the other seer, were not, as I had suspected, dwarves; they were in fact gnomes.'

Captain Quentin reacted with disbelief and exclaimed, 'Impossible. We know the difference between a dwarf and a gnome and I can assure you they were indeed dwarves.'

'I am afraid you were tricked into thinking so. Javelin and the other dwarves have assured me that the body in the grave is that of a gnome, not a dwarf.'

'How do they know that?'

'Because they exhumed the body last night, you may examine it if you wish before they re-inter it.'

The coordinator nodded to the captain who disappeared out of the door. He returned within a couple of minutes ashen faced and nodded to Coordinator Tanner that it was as Urim had said.

'This is a disturbing discovery, seer, and does you no favours. How can we tell that you are who you say you are and that we are not being fooled again?'

Hamill interjected at this point. 'I can vouch for them, Coordinator Tanner; I am absolutely certain that these folk are completely genuine. I would trust them with my life, in fact I have done and they are true to what they say.'

Urim breathed a little easier and, placing a hand on Hamill's shoulder, thanked him for his support.

'Very well then; it is perhaps fortunate for you that Hamill was with you. I believe you. How can we be of assistance?'

'I would like permission to inspect the maps that Ebon looked at when he was here and request that we may impose upon your hospitality for one more day?'

'Of course; anything that you need, Captain Quentin is at your disposal.'

She looked at him and he came to attention.

'Yes, Coordinator.'

Turning to Hamill, she said, 'I would ask that you refrain from any duties here and see to the needs of our young guests.'

Hamill nodded, happy to undertake the task. Urim went off with the captain while Jon, Anna and Hamill decided how best to spend their day, now that they knew they were going to be there a little longer.

The weather closed in for the rest of the day, which meant that they were confined to the stockade and spent most of their time around the various buildings that comprised the Ward. It was interesting enough to start with, but once you have seen one section then you have seen them all. They whiled away the hours by discussing what they thought they would do next about the situation with Ebon and the seers and tried to outdo each other with the most outlandish suggestions. Jon imagined the colossi returning from their long absence and defeating Ebon's forces. Anna imagined Urim conjuring up a great storm that would ravage through Ebon's army and Hamill thought of the elves creating a sickness that would infect only the gnomes and others who fought with them. They all agreed that Hamill's suggestion was the most far-fetched; he won the contest and they treated him to candy bought from the store at the Ward.

Braun contented himself by visiting the blacksmith shop, discussing the art of metal working with the elves. No one had seen the dwarves; their kind came and went so frequently here that they hardly noticed them. However, since the discovery that it was a gnome and not a dwarf treated here, they had been watched a little more attentively, which is probably why they had made themselves scarce.

Urim had closeted himself away, poring over the maps of the area, concentrating his power on the ones Ebon had been using. Urim was able to exercise his own talisman: a small book made of gold, it being a replica of the much larger Golden Tome over which he was guardian.

He placed the talisman in the palm of his hand and brought up the power from his staff with the words of command. The room began to spin around him and figures flashed in and out of the room in quick succession; soon he clasped his hand tightly around the golden book and he became a watcher of events that had transpired there days ago. He saw Captain Quentin give Ebon the maps that he had requested and begin to pore over them. Urim watched as he traced his finger across the page, first from the forest where Urim had met with Jon and rescued him from Ebon's clutches, then to the Ward; from there he moved his finger to the Eastern Mountains and to where Crystal Falls was situated; here he stopped and tapped his finger on its location before rolling the parchment up and returning it to Captain Quentin. Urim sighed heavily as if weary and opened his hand slowly; speaking words that none other than a seer would know, he brought his vision back to the present, placed the talisman back into his pouch and left the room; he knew what he had to do.

The dwarves appeared again in time for the evening meal; they had been out scouting the area looking for any signs that would indicate the presence of gnomes. They had found some tracks in the wood at the top of the rise not half a league away and had also found the tracks of much larger creatures; possibly marsh-mogs.

Urim considered the reports and stated, 'That makes sense; Ebon had headed in this direction from the forest; he must have come through here and sought aid from the elves to heal his two gnomes. Not wanting to arouse suspicion, he obviously tricked the elves into thinking that they were dwarves. He has travelled fast, my friends. I suspect that he has discovered the use of one of the talismans that he stole from Seers' Tower.'

Curious as ever, Jon asked, 'What's that, Urim?'

He answered softly and a hush fell over them.

'He has the ability to travel like the wind. I suspected as much from what you told me of how Ebon escaped from Braun's forge shop.'

'What are we going to do now?' Braun asked, eager to do something constructive.

'I think we ought to find out where those gnomes were going,' Tracker suggested, following his instincts.

Javelin interjected with some passion, 'No. We must find out where they came from and why they got past our army at the border, I fear that all is not well with them.'

Urim said nothing for a few moments, and then, looking up from his feet at Jon, asked, 'What do you suggest, Jon?'

Jon was so amazed that anyone would ask for his opinion, let alone Urim, of all people, that he was stumped for words. He looked around at the others, doubting that they would be interested in his opinion but they all wanted to hear what he had to say.

'Well, I don't really know. I suppose we should carry on with our plan of going to Ffridd-Uch-Ddu. Whatever has happened does not change the need for us to go there. Possibly along the way we can determine what has happened at the border with the dwarves and maybe also discover where the gnome army came from.'

They all looked at him, pondering his logic; slowly he saw heads nodding in agreement and Urim smiled knowingly.

'That is precisely what we must do, Jon. Well done, your thinking is sound and what you suggest will serve all our purposes.'

Urim turned to the others and asked, 'What say you my friends? Shall we continue with our original plan?'

They all responded with an approval of Jon's suggestion.

'Anna,' Urim said softly and looked her in the eye, saying gently and with feeling, 'This time you really must not come with us.'

Before she could offer any resistance to this statement, Urim raised a calming hand and continued. 'You have shown much courage and dedication up till now and, I suspect, will have much more to contribute to our quest. However, you have an injured arm, which, I have been told by a reliable source, you are in need of resting so that you may make a better recovery.'

She spun around to glare at Hamill who raised his hands in surrender, acknowledging that it was indeed his recommendation.

'We will be gone but a few days, a week at the most, all being well; and we will return here before we go any further. I give you my promise that we shall come back for you.'

She wanted to sign her discontent and argue her case but the sling kept her arm firmly secured to her side. That way it gave her the maximum support, and she found it impossible to sign adequately.

Hamill stepped forward and urged her to remain; the dwarves and Braun echoed their concerns for her well-being and emphasised the importance of getting her arm back in proper working order.

Braun teased that she would not be able to tell them off properly until her arm had healed; that softened her mood and made her smile. Hamill then turned to Jon for moral support with this; he agreed with the suggestion but knew how badly it would hurt Anna by not going. He put his arm around her and took her to one side, saying, 'Anna, you can see how we all love you and want you to be better. I really believe that it would be the best thing to do. As Urim said, we will be back in about a week; and no following after us this time.'

He wagged his finger at her in mock admonishment and smiled.

Reluctantly Anna agreed. She could see the sense of what they were saying and nodded her head but pouted sulkily all the same.

Urim then did something that took her by surprise. He stepped forward and gently rested his hand upon her shoulder, looked her in the eye and said, 'Anna, I know now that I was wrong to try and prevent you from coming with us; I see that you are equally important to the success of our quest as Jon is and I swear to you that we shall return for you. In the meantime, rest that arm of yours; it will play a vital part in our welfare in times to come.'

She looked at him in amazement and felt the power of what the seer had said. His eyes had moistened and she believed in him wholeheartedly. She would never doubt him again; there was something in his eyes that reminded her of Jon; she believed that Urim really was kinsman to him and that he would take care of him.

She smiled up at the seer and gave him a peck on the cheek.

Urim swallowed hard and turned his head away. Quickly he strode towards the door and in a trembling voice urged the others to get an early night so as to be ready for the journey to Ffridd-Uch-Ddu.

Bright and early the next morning, the strange alliance of seer, dwarves, metal master, half-elf and Jon set off on its way towards Ffridd-Uch-Ddu; they would need to cross the mountains and the best way from here was via the pass at Deadline Crack. It would take a day's journey just to get to the base of the pass; then possibly another day to reach the top and the packers' lodge, a purpose built refuge for travellers to rest in should there be the need. From then on it was another day to get to the dwarves' capital.

Anna stood on one of the towers waving goodbye to them with her good arm. A tear rolled down her cheek, not so much for being unable to go with them, as for not being with Jon. They had drawn much closer this past week and she did not want to lose that. They all turned to wave and, with the dwarves in the lead setting the pace again, walked off briskly.

She could not help smiling as Hamill's voice drifted up to her complaining at the speed of the march, saying that he thought his legs might break if this continued. Poor Hamill; he really did not want to go with them this time and had tried to convince the coordinator to let him stay. She had insisted that he go, saying that it was necessary for the party to have someone with them who was capable of treating any injuries that may occur along the way. The Ward is honour bound to send someone when travellers go through the pass and as he knew these travellers, he was ideally suited; besides, she had told him as an aside, the seer had requested that it be Hamill to accompany them.

That surprised him and he felt flattered by the request, so he had somewhat reluctantly agreed. Anna thought that inside he would have been disappointed had someone else gone instead of him.

Chapter VIII

Deadline Crack

They made good time on their journey; the terrain was not difficult, which meant that Hamill found the going quite easy and did not complain too much. The mountain range drew closer and looked a formidable challenge to Jon, and he wondered why they had to use this route in getting to Ffridd-Uch-Ddu. The dwarves would rather have gone through the lower passes that were protected by their border guard. For reasons of his own Urim had insisted that they travel through the high pass at Deadline Crack and was unwilling to discuss it further with the dwarves. One thing was clear: he was determined on this course and you do not argue with a seer.

Late afternoon saw them at the foot of the mountains, at the last village before crossing the range. It was a regular stop for those using the pass and a comfortable place to rest for the night before setting off on the long climb up the track.

The tavern was not very busy other than for the locals having a social drink with one another; there were few travellers at this time of year as the snows were due to start in the high pass. They enjoyed a good meal and slept well, the dwarves resuming their rota of night watches, although there had been no signs of gnomes to give them any concern; they just felt it prudent to keep guard and Jon slept better because of it.

They exchanged the comfort of the tavern for the rugged terrain that lay ahead of them. Jon noticed that the dwarves exchanged glances with each other before they set off and were obviously unhappy with Urim's choice of routes. Nonetheless they had agreed to follow Urim's decision even though he would not explain why; he simply said for them to wait and see.

They set off for Deadline Crack; it was visible even at this distance on the mountainside like a great scar running through the rock. As the crow flies it would take them only a matter of hours to get there, but they had to traverse the foothills and several smaller gorges before they got to the pass itself.

The weather seemed pleasant enough; there was a cool breeze blowing through the dale that was very refreshing. Jon breathed in deeply. It reminded him of his trips to the forest before the time he met with Urim. It all seemed so long ago now but it was just over a week since that night in the forest glade. How it had changed his life!

The dwarves were busy checking their packs. Braun shouldered his own with the ease expected of a big man; his pack was as big as one of the dwarves, but he swung it across his shoulders as if it were naught but feathers. Hamill stumbled out of the door, looking as if he had just gotten up from his cot; that was not far from the truth. Jon had had to shake him several times to rouse him from his slumber.

'Go away, it's too early,' he had muttered from under his goose-down quilt. Well, he had had to get up eventually in order to have his breakfast, which he had demolished in double-quick time.

At last the group was ready to leave and, without any further ado, Urim strode off after the dwarves. He was a solitary figure; they all admired and respected him but they were also a little unsure of how to behave towards him. At times he would be cheery and friendly, then there were times he would withdraw deep into himself and it was as if there was a curtain drawn between him and them. He was, if nothing else, a person of mystery; a mystery Jon felt compelled to resolve.

Doubts had tormented Jon about who Urim really was after Ebon's disclosure. If not his uncle, then who was he? Pieces of the puzzle were too fragmentary at the moment; he had his ideas, but he dared not hope at this stage of his search for the truth; he could not face the disappointment of raising his hopes, only to have them dashed.

The dwarves travelled easily along the trail; they were used to hiking and despite their size could outpace a grown man on a long walk. Jon and Hamill chatted about nothing really, just the odd comment or observation of things that caught their attention from time to time. Braun ambled along behind them like a rearguard, his long legs striding gracefully as if in slow motion.

122

They stopped for lunch near a tumbledown stone shelter being utilised as a pigsty; several of the beasts were resting inside away from the glare of the midday sun. The travellers did not appear to bother them; they were too intent on getting an afternoon nap. After a short rest to eat a light meal of fruits, bread and some cheese, they continued on their way. The road became steeper now as it narrowed into a gorge with a small stream tumbling through it over rocks borne there by springtime floods.

It would have been a pleasant experience walking amongst the shrubs had it not been for Hamill constantly complaining that his feet were hurting and could they stop for a while. They had heard it all before, no one seemed to take any notice of him and continued walking on, which only made him whine the louder. Eventually they did stop, but only for a while, and they would not let him take off his boots. Braun was rapidly losing patience with him and stomped off in disgust rather than lose his temper.

The sides of the gorge grew narrower and narrower as they continued on until they could touch both sides of the rock cliffs with outstretched arms. A boulder, which had fallen from the side of the mountain, had become wedged between the two sides just above their heads. Braun had to duck slightly to avoid banging his head. Eventually it broadened out again as they emerged, after a bit of a climb, and could see the trail snaking its way above them through to Deadline Crack; they would not reach it much before evening.

Jon noticed the dwarves exchange glances but they said nothing.

It was a wearisome trek up the sloping trail; the temperature was dropping rapidly as they climbed. They had still not passed through the Crack and there was no shelter nearby in which to spend the night that was closing down on them.

They rounded a bend and stopped. Ahead of them, just before the mouth of the Crack, there was a rockfall that totally blocked any further progress. To their right was a sheer rock face and to their left the trail fell away sharply for a good hundred lengths or so into a canyon. They could just make out a white-water rapid running along the bottom. The trail was fairly broad here but afforded them no respite from the bitter wind that was now blowing in their faces.

There was no snow as yet at this level of the mountains but it would not be long before the snows came. The temperature was dropping rapidly and the threat of it was in the air. Yellow tinged storm clouds were gathering overhead and there was a distant roll of thunder that boomed and echoed through the mountain passes.

Jon looked off into the distance the way they had come. Squinting against the wind, he could just make out the small village where they had stayed last night. He wished for the warmth and comfort of the tavern now and would have given anything for a mug of mulled wine and a nice warm fire to toast his feet.

It had taken them all this time to climb the trail and reach the Crack where it cut through the mountainside connecting the folk of the Yield with the Eastern Mountain people. Not many travellers used the pass at this time of year though; it was too risky. Rockfalls and snow storms had claimed many a victim before now; Jon hoped that they would not be the mountain's next casualties.

He searched the darkness past the rockfall but could only see the sheer walls of the gorge as it cut through the solid rock; it was an awesome sight. If anyone had wanted to spring a trap upon someone else, then this would be as good a place as any, he thought to himself gloomily. He started to get a bad feeling about this; the dwarves were also apprehensive, though they tried to hide their feelings from the others. Jon could tell they were nervous because they had taken their packs off and had unsheathed their weapons.

Urim hunched over his staff and surveyed the situation; he did not seem perturbed by this turn of events at all, almost as if he had expected it. He was examining the rock wall at the side of the trail intently and seemed to be looking for something, moving his hands across the rock face at various places, without success it appeared, as he would mutter to himself in frustration every now and again.

Whatever it was that he was searching for, it was eluding him. Jon braced himself, back bent against the icy cold blast that whistled and howled through the fissure of Deadline Crack. By now the others of the group were huddled into whatever cover or shelter they could find, which was not much.

Fighting to keep from being blown over the precipitous edge

and keeping as much distance away from it as he could for fear of stumbling and falling, Jon tried to keep what little warmth he had inside his cloak but the wind just snatched it away. He thought it ironic that Urim called himself a seer yet had not foreseen this. The dwarves had argued to go through the Eastern Mountains a different way but Urim had been adamant that this was the right way to go. Jon could not help thinking that this time the dwarves were right and Urim wrong. Whatever the rights or wrongs of it, none of them wanted to be stuck here, barring Urim, but they were here and couldn't do anything about it.

They were clearly in need of shelter for the night or suffer the effects of the biting cold and suffer from frostbite; but there was none to be found situated where they were on the trail at this point in time.

The little group was in a desperate plight: if they did not get off the mountain and out of this predicament soon, they would all suffer the consequences of Urim's stubbornness. Thank goodness they had persuaded Anna to rest up in the Ward before undertaking this ill-fated expedition.

Hamill staggered against the biting wind past Jon towards the seer, causing Jon to groan inwardly and wonder what he was going to say now; sometimes he could happily gag him. He could not hear what they were saying, only snatches of words from which Jon gathered he was not happy with the seer's decision to come this way. From the expression on his face he could tell that he was not mincing his words. He was either stupid or lacking in any tact, then he realised that it was probably both.

Urim turned slowly to make eye contact; Jon saw that he was struggling to contain his anger. He wished he could hear what they were saying. He watched Hamill intently, noticing the change that came over his features as Urim delivered his rebuke – word by word – like body blows; he flinched away from Urim but the seer secured him in a vicelike grip by his heavy travel coat.

Hamill was there for the duration of the lecture.

Jon smiled smugly to himself at first, and then began to feel sorry for him; he just could not help interfering; it was in his nature. He was not a bad chap really; you just had to understand him and be patient, as you were with a little child.

Eventually Urim released his grip, smoothed down his lapel and gave him a playful slap on the shoulder. He then jerked his head back towards the rest of the group indicating for him to return to where he should be.

A fatherly smile played across his face as he watched him shuffle back down the trail, 'tail between his legs', trying to get deeper into his coat for warmth, or to hide his embarrassment. He gave a furtive glance at Jon as he passed, hoping against hope that no one had witnessed his humiliation.

Jon smiled back, not at Hamill's embarrassment but as a token of support and friendship.

Hamill tried to become invisible against the cleft of rock he had been sheltering in, but was far too prominent by his actions to do so. Tracker offered him a sip of relk to revive his spirit and combat the cold, which he accepted with relish. It was not often the dwarves offered it to anyone other than their own kind, it being a very strong beverage. Hamill knew it was, so only took the merest sip; even that made him wheeze as it cut across his taste buds like fire. Jon could see tears in his eyes and they all laughed; even Hamill saw the funny side of it and the mood lightened a little.

All day, since leaving the tavern, Hamill had been complaining and whining at being chosen to accompany them but mostly of how his feet hurt. It was about time someone had told him to grow up; he had probably got more than he bargained for from Urim.

Hamill's head jerked up; being half elf, his ears had caught a sound on the wind that the others would have missed.

'What's up?' Tracker asked, alert and ready for action. The other dwarves were also up and scanned the track listening out for what Hamill had heard. They trusted him; elves were renowned for their good sense of hearing, even half elves.

Keen eyes pierced the gathering gloom trying to spot any movement but discerned nothing through the fine flurry of snow that had started to fall.

'Great; that's all we need,' Jon moaned silently to himself.

They all stood perfectly still, eyes darting to and fro nervously looking for any tell-tale sign of danger. The wind gusted and shrieked then died to nothing before howling again. Each blast clawed at them with icy fingers, dragging at their clothing.

126

Hamill leaned his head to one side, pointing back the way they had come.

'There, down there I heard a howl.'

'Are you sure it weren't the wind?' Braun asked; he still felt annoyed at Hamill for his earlier antics.

'*No*, no, I'm certain. There was a howl, I'm positive.'

'If the halfer thinks he heard a howl, I believe him,' Archer said, defending what Hamill had said.

Hamill momentarily showed exasperation at the dwarf's comments. A back-handed compliment if ever there was one; halfer, indeed, he was proud of his ancestry and hated being referred to as a 'halfer', but this was not the time to enter into a debate about it.

Braun snorted his disgust but respected the dwarf and bowed his head to acknowledge Archer's comments.

Urim now joined the group.

'What's amiss?'

'Hamill here thinks he heard a noise from down there,' nodding his head back down the trail, in the direction that Hamill had said he had heard the noise. All four dwarves stood poised and ready for action: Archer, legs astride with an arrow already notched in his bow; Javelin, spear at the ready; Tracker crouched, with his two long knives before him, razor sharp. Trapper, who faced down the trail ready for any oncoming threat, offered the twin blades of his axe to all who would dare to try and get past him. For a dwarf he was little, the shortest of them all, but Jon would not want to be against him. He was a ferocious and fiery adversary who showed no fear to anyone, be they short or tall.

Just then a howl that chilled them more than the night carried on the wind as it blew first one way and then the other; it lasted but a second or two before the wind snatched it away.

'Then he heard well. We must prepare for a fight I'm afraid. Archer, Braun, you know how best to handle this. I'll try to scare them off as best I can but I fear I will not be much help to you at this time.'

They nodded smartly and engaged in a hasty conference as to who was to do what. Jon and Hamill found themselves ushered back towards the landslide that blocked their path. Trapper proceeded to take up position a little way in front of them, checking on them from time to time to see that they stayed out of the way.

127

Trapper told them, specifically, that they were not to become involved as they would be more of a liability than a help; there was enough to think about without worrying about them. Jon caught Trapper's attention.

'Go and join the others, we'll be fine, they will probably need you.'

The dwarf looked towards the others then back at Jon and Hamill.

'If I'm needed I will go, but for the moment, I will stay.'

Another howl penetrated the wind, this time closer, followed by countless yelps and snarls. They were close. A cold hand beyond the cold of the mountain seemed to grab hold of Jon's stomach.

'What was that?'

Urim murmured in response, half to himself, 'Something you don't want to meet up here in the mountains but which you may not have a choice about.'

They all waited nervously for the first sight of their adversary. Again the howling and yelping drifted on the wind, coming and going with a ghostlike quality. The suspense was palpable. This time deep throated growls of hatred accompanied the other sounds. It seemed as though they were right on top of them, but it was just the wind carrying their cries.

This was not an ideal situation to be in, Jon fretted inwardly. Things did not stack up well in their favour at all, despite the presence of the seer. 'At best he could only scare them off,' were his words to the dwarf.

Jon felt useless; he knew the dwarves were right about Hamill and him being more of a liability. He, they, would probably not be much help at all as neither of them was experienced in this kind of fighting, unlike the dwarves, who were always involved in some sort of dispute or another. It was who they were, that was how they lived their lives, going from one confrontation to another, usually against the gnomes.

The other dwarves had gone down the trail a little way to see what was happening and to spy out their adversary.

Braun stood like a mountain; his broadsword held drawn and ready to be brought into play at an instant. He held his hand up to protect his eyes against the intermittent gusts of wind that flung the dry, powdery snow at him, as if it were trying to drive him back.

One look at his massive bulk barring the way would be enough to frighten anyone, but Jon sensed that these attackers were not just anyone.

Jon looked around him to assess their situation; it was bad. The rockfall not fifty paces behind them, solid rock face to their left as he looked down the trail, and a precipitous drop twenty paces off to their right. There was nowhere to go; a perfect trap and they had walked right into it.

The three other dwarves came running up around the bend in the trail, gasping for breath; they gestured several times down the trail as they reported in to Urim. He quickly ushered them further up the trail while he occupied himself with inspecting the rough rock face. Jon saw him reach into his pouch and place something in a crevice just above head height then crouch down against the rock ten paces further back up the trail and draw his cloak around him. To the casual glance he looked for the entire world like a rock that had tumbled to the track and ended up against the wall of the pass; he wondered what it was that he was doing.

The dwarves and Braun had begun to gather many loose rocks and boulders to build a defence across the trail at a narrow point some forty paces from where they were; they worked feverishly.

'Can we help?' Jon yelled, cupping his hands around his mouth.

'No, we work better this way. Stay where you are,' Javelin shouted in reply.

Jon looked at Hamill who just shrugged his shoulders in submission. He had looked scared after Urim had told him off, but now he was shaking with fear; either that or he was suffering from the cold.

Javelin was probably right, he thought, but it did not make him feel any better. He did not have time for any further reflection on the matter because at that moment all hell seemed to break loose. A clamour of shrieks and howls rent the air as a wave of white fur seemed to flood up the trail towards them. They were almost upon Urim when he sprang up in front of them causing panic and alarm along the first few lines of the attacking horde. Some of the creatures were very close to the edge of the precipice and were shouldered over the side by the startled creatures, their cries echoing into the gathering gloom.

The surge from behind forced the vanguard onwards towards Urim as he stood arms akimbo, staff in hand. He dropped his right hand sharply and a bright light shattered the night. For a moment Jon could not see what was happening.

All he could hear was screams of fear and pain from the massed creatures followed by a loud thunderbolt that rocked the mountain. He heard the sound of falling rocks and through the darkness saw a cloud of dust billowing up the trail. He could taste the dust as it caked his mouth; he quickly covered his face with his cloak, coughing with the irritation that the dust caused. After what seemed an age it settled and he saw that the dwarves and Braun were getting to their feet; they dusted themselves down and checked for injuries; there were none, fortunately.

Urim lay prone on the trail not far from where they had last seen him, rocks and debris scattered all around. Jon's heart skipped a beat.

'Urim,' He shouted but was not sure whether he had actually spoken the words or just thought them. There was no sign of the creatures, other than those who also lay prone further down the trail; they had not fared well from the blast. There were a dozen or so of them, twisted and broken by the rockfall; the others had obviously been scared off for now, but for how long? They all rushed to where he lay, Trapper getting to him first, closely followed by Braun, the other dwarves and then Hamill and Jon.

Hamill bent over the seer, gently rolling him onto his side, examining him carefully for any sign of injury. He responded to the situation, caring, as trained to do so from his time at the Ward, for those who were unconscious and possibly injured.

'How is he?' Braun asked, concerned for the seer.

'I can't tell yet. Give me some room will you, you big lump.'

Usually Braun would take offence at any one talking to him in that manner and would have given them short shrift; under the circumstances, he let it go.

Hamill checked Urim from top to toe but reported that he could ascertain no external injuries other than a bump that was growing on the seer's temple. A groan escaped Urim's lips and he began to raise his head from Hamill's supporting hands before wishing he had not done so and raising his hand to his head.

They all breathed a sigh of relief. The dwarves were quick to encourage them to make haste and to regroup further up the trail away from the bend in the trail. They helped the seer to his feet and supported him as they returned to where Jon and Hamill had been sheltering. It had stopped snowing now, which brought some relief for the group but it was still bitterly cold.

Hamill insisted that Urim sit on a boulder nearby so that he could finish his examination. He held three fingers up to Urim's face.

'How many do you see?'

'Five. Three of course, you fool, let me up, I must be with the others.'

'You're not going anywhere just yet, old man; not until I'm satisfied that you are able to stand and that there is no permanent damage to your head or vision.'

Hamill was quite insistent, so Urim acquiesced in his demands; he knew the physician was right to finish his examination. The dwarves had been busy meanwhile in forming the new rockfall into some form of barrier to hinder further attacks. None too quickly as it transpired: no sooner were they finished than the onslaught commenced again.

It was just as Urim had feared; all he had done was frighten them away for a while. A terrible howling rose into the air followed by deep resonating coughs.

The blood drained from Hamill's face. 'What was that? I know something I don't want to meet!' he answered for Urim who looked up at him in mock despair. He then gently pulled himself up off the boulder, shaking his head carefully, checking to see that he was not suffering from any lingering effects.

The metal master stood close to them allowing the dwarves to take their positions by the small barrier they had erected earlier; it was not much but it would help. Braun's eyes darted back and forth between them and the trail; he knew the dwarves could fend for themselves but he had taken it upon himself to protect Jon and Hamill.

The muscles in his powerful forearms twitched nervously under the short tunic he was wearing. Only the thick, black bearskin draped across his massive upper body and tied at the waist by a thick leather belt provided him with any warmth. He did not seem affected by the cold, which was surprising seeing as he had been used to the heat of the furnaces at Foundry Smelt. His breath came out in great clouds of steam that gathered on his big red beard. His barrel of a chest heaved unevenly and he coughed nervously to clear his throat. So the great Braun was not unaffected by all this excitement, despite any protestations that he might give to the contrary.

Urim sprang to his feet, almost knocking Hamill off balance, upon hearing the new sounds from the creatures.

'Enough, physician; I must find a way out of here or we all die.'

He rushed, unsteadily at first, but then with more confidence, over to the rock wall not far from the blocked trail. He clawed desperately at the surface, shouting out to the night.

'I know you're here somewhere, you must be; but where?'

They watched him aghast; they had not seen him act like this before; the bump he had received to his head was worse than they had thought.

Another shriek from below them turned their attention to the barrier. Another of those strange coughing sounds and a cry of alarm from the dwarves made Urim's expression fall into desperation and despair.

It frightened Jon that Urim should be like this.

Urim bowed his head between his outstretched arms as he leaned against the rock face, and then when he looked up again, appeared to be in full control and back to his old self. He grabbed his staff and rushed towards the barrier to aid the dwarves who, along with the metal master, had begun to fend off the vanguard of creatures. There were wolves and white bears by the score and hundreds of the smaller, more agile snow foxes. They were usually shy creatures who ran from the likes of human beings, but here they were snarling and nipping at the dwarves. Why they were acting this way was unknown, it was as if they were driven on by some maddening rage, snapping and pawing at the dwarves. Jon could only guess that somehow Ebon had a hand in this.

The dwarves looked like mere children in comparison to the great snow bears; there were wolvets, a hybrid creature somewhat akin to a hyena, that stood as high as the dwarves' waists. Yet they held their ground and inflicted gruesome wounds to those who came at them and to some came death.

132

They could not keep this up for long though; it was too much to ask of them. As if their situation was not bad enough, there came such a shriek from below the barrier that it would chill the resolve of even the hardiest and bravest of individuals. Below them, striding through the ranks of lesser animals were huge, white, shaggy coated ape-like creatures. Smargs. Even the creatures gathered against the little band of travellers quailed at the sound, and it was not *them* that the smargs were after.

They all guessed who *they* were after. It sent a chill to the pit of Jon's stomach. Jon had heard tales of them but had believed them to be just creatures of fantasy, made up by persons who had had one too many drinks, yet here they were amongst the attackers. His shoulders slumped in dejection, he all but lost hope of seeing the next day in one piece, if at all. 'So this is why so few people return from these mountains,' he thought.

The dwarves, however, determined not to give in and renewed their battle with the ferocious beasts before them.

Braun rushed forward to help the dwarves stave off the attack. He reached them just in time. His huge broadsword swung in great arcs severing heads and limbs of all who fell within his reach.

He was careful not to harm the dwarves, however, and but for the seriousness of their dilemma he would have been a sight to see.

Jon and Hamill looked at each other in awe and then back at the carnage being wrought. Lunging forward, one of the massive smargs, all teeth and claws under a mass of white fur, swept one of the dwarves aside as if he was no more than a rag doll. Archer smashed into the rock wall with a sickening crunch where he sprawled and lay still on the cold, hard ground littered with the dead and dying. A frenzied wolvet, eyes burning red, sprang upon his back. Another of the dwarves – Jon could not see who – caught it behind the ear with a hand axe and felled it with a second blow to the head that must have shattered its skull. It was dead before it hit the ground.

A scream of pain rent the air as Braun's sword sliced into a smarg; a deep crimson gash ran the length of its torso.

It was incredible that it had survived such a blow. Maddened to the extreme, it tumbled past him and came lurching on towards where they crouched. A dark shadow leaped past Jon and Hamill towards the staggering smarg. Urim had seen the danger and hurried to their aid. He thrust his staff up into the wound, the staff crackled and sizzled, there was a flash of blue light from the tip and the creature was flung backwards through the air. It did not have time to cry out because it had died the instant Urim's staff had sent its lethal charge through it. An occasional twitch ran over its body as it lay spread-eagled, a smouldering heap of fur. The stench of singed hair filled his lungs making him cough and gag.

Urim had carried on without even a falter to his stride, confident that he did not need a second dose of his staff to halt the smarg; his black robe and cloak billowed out around him as he ran towards the band of battling dwarves.

Something had to give.

One of the dwarves went down under an avalanche of fur; a wolvet sank razor sharp teeth deep into his arm. Another dwarf close by had seen it and turned to help; with a sweep of his short sword at full stretch he decapitated it before it could do any further harm. By doing so he had left himself wide open to attack and two of the creatures pounced. He was in danger of going down himself under the sheer weight of the creatures but some- how he mustered the strength to shrug them off and threw them, howling, over the abyss.

The little dwarves glanced over their shoulders towards Urim with plaintive looks as the battle faltered. Urim had stopped dead in his tracks; quickly, he fumbled at the thongs on the pouch at his side.

'Curse my foolishness,' he yelled into the wind in frustration. He managed to get into his pouch and yanked out a clenched fist, then strode purposefully towards the barrier and the affray. He threw his hand up towards the dark sky. A moment later there was a blinding flash of light so bright that Jon could see the ghost of it from behind closed eyelids. A split second later there followed a crack of thunder that reverberated through the hills and deep into his chest. He felt he was going to burst apart.

When he opened his eyes again, he saw that the battle at the barrier had ended. Yelps of fear came from the escaping crea- tures as they retreated back down the slopes of the mountain in disarray, seeking the shelter of the hollows and shadows; scared off by the thunderflash that Urim had thrown into the air; there to hide from the sting of the defenders' cold steel and to lick their wounds – literally.

'Next time you do that, can you give us some warning, like shouting "duck" so that we know what's going to happen, my ears still hurt,' Braun suggested, holding his hands over his ears.

Hamill had sprung to action upon seeing the battle was over, his healer's instincts spurring him forward. He rushed to give aid to the dwarves and made a beeline towards Archer who was still lying senseless on the ground; fortunately he hadn't been badly hurt, just concussion with a few bruises. His pride hurt him more than anything else. The dwarves were renowned for their ability in battle so the fact that he had lain helpless while his comrades were fighting on would smart more than any injury he could ever have sustained.

Javelin had fared the best of the dwarves, suffering only minor cuts to his lower legs, despite wearing the traditional leather leggings, bound in place with cords cross-style around his shins and knotted just below the knee.

He had kept the attackers from reaching him by exchanging his pike for more effective weapons in close combat. Double headed battle axes, one in each hand, were best in a hand-to-hand fight. When swung in synchronisation they were the most deadly force any creature could face. They had come at him thick and fast; the thicker they came, the faster they fell. He had probably single-handedly accounted for a quarter of the body count without serious injury. He would be singing long and loud about that if they got out of this alive.

Braun was resting from the exertion of his struggles and leaned on the hilt of his broadsword, the blade darkened with the blood of the smarg and wolvets. He breathed raggedly in huge gulps, followed by great clouds of steam as he exhaled; apart from his fatigue he was none the worse for wear physically.

Urim stood surveying the carnage, carrying out a head count; he was looking concerned.

Jon asked him, 'What's the matter?'

Urim replied anxiously, doing another quick head count, 'We're missing two dwarves!'

Everyone became as concerned as Urim for the twins, Tracker and Trapper. Jon had seen one of them receive a bad bite to his arm and the other kill the culprit. Then Urim had lit up the sky with a thunderflash and he had not seen them again. The battle had been frantic and he had lost track of who was where.

Forgetting their own worries, they began a hurried but careful search for them amongst the bodies of the creatures that littered the ground. It was quite slick in places so they had to be careful with their footing; the smell was rather unpleasant: they probably did not smell very good when they were alive, but combined with the blood and gore, it did not make a good combination.

Speedily they moved amongst the corpses. Braun was searching down near the barrier and he called to Urim, 'I've found them.'

Jon expected the worst and hurried over with the others converging from different areas. They were all mightily relieved when Braun gently removed first one, and then the other dwarf from under a pile of rock and debris. Caught by the repercussions of the thunderflash Urim had set off above them, they had been buried by a small rockfall but had been shielded from serious injury by the creatures that had been on top of them; they had been killed but had unwittingly saved the dwarves. The battle had progressed around and over them without any further injuries being sustained. Tracker's arm, however, was showing signs of infection from the wolvet's bite. Deep lacerations ran from his elbow down to his wrist and it was in need of more attention than could be given to it in their present circumstances. The young dwarf was in terrible pain; Javelin proffered him a slug of relk, which he took gratefully.

Hamill did what he could by putting a salve and bindings on it, but it was clearly in need of hospital treatment. If he were to keep his arm it would have to be attended to, and quickly. Hamill looked helplessly at Jon and shook his head slightly, concern etched on his face as he tended to him. Trapper stood nearby, worried by the injury to his brother and concerned for his well-being. Dust and dirt caked them both, their eyes bloodshot and sore from the irritation. Jon set Trapper down on a rock and gently washed his eyes, helping him to recover from his ordeal. Several swallows from his relk bottle soon had him feeling better.

While the others were engrossed with the dwarves, Urim had been checking the trail and beyond for any signs of the creatures massing another attack.

136

'That won't keep them away for long. They've tasted blood and will be back in earnest next time.'

'Weren't they in earnest this time?'

Jon thought they were.

'The gods protect us if that wasn't an earnest attack,' he whispered under his breath and he crossed his fingers in the token of fending off bad luck. Jon looked around them. Everything had happened so fast, yet it had all appeared to have been in slow motion; he had not had time to think let alone act. He felt useless; all he had was his hunting knife, not much use against a wolvet. How would he have fared against a hulk of frenzied madness such as the smarg, intent on wiping him from the mountainside? Not too well, Jon supposed.

Hamill was now tending to Archer again and was bandaging his head, a trickle of blood from his temple the only sign of anything amiss. Apart from his dazed look, he was shaken but was otherwise fine. Jon watched Hamill work and felt appreciation for the care with which he was attending to the dwarves. They were in a sorry state and it was well that he was here. There was no question but that the dwarves had saved the rest of them from certain injury; even Braun could not have kept the mountain creatures at bay for long. There were too many of them. They had been frightened away by Urim's intervening as he had, but they would be back.

The wind was easing a little, making it feel less cold but Jon did not relish the idea of spending the night out here exposed to the elements; besides, they were not rid of the smarg and the other creatures yet. Jon thought of the smargs and wondered at them, what terrifying creatures they were; at least eight feet tall with long, shaggy white fur or hair, he could not tell which. They had a relatively small head but no neck that he could discern. He had got a pretty good look at the one that had made a run towards him and Hamill. It had looked rather bizarre as its mouth seemed to be at the top of its chest below a blue bulbous nose; deep-set black eyes with red pupils accentuating its wild and ferocious look.

The injured dwarves were tended to and made as comfortable as possible. Hamill kept a watchful eye on Tracker especially; he had lost consciousness and appeared to be in a delirium. His arm had begun to swell alarmingly, turning an angry red, the veins in his arm clearly visible as they tried to burst from beneath his skin. Hamill had used snow to cool the wound and try to keep the swelling down; sweat ran from the dwarf's brow and his eyes rolled in their sockets, his face contorted in pain and whimpering moans escaping through clenched teeth. It was apparent that the wolvet had inflicted more than just a bite; there was some kind of venom. Jon and Hamill looked on helplessly; everyone felt concern for Tracker but were powerless to do anything more than that which had already been done. They desperately needed to get him to a medical centre. The Ward was not too far away; but how could they get him there in his condition?

As if reading their thoughts, Braun, with Javelin's help, was trying to make a stretcher of sorts on which to carry him. He had cut down two small saplings that had been tenaciously clinging to the rocky slope in order to make an A frame on which to carry him. Urim and Archer were deep in a hushed conversation. He could sense that he was the subject of their conversation as occasionally Archer would look in his direction and either nod or shake his head. They finished conversing and Urim approached Jon. He put an arm around his shoulder and drew him to one side. Well, Jon thought, this makes a change; I finally get to be in on something.

'Jon, the dwarf is in bad shape, the wolvet has infected him with a poison, possibly the Rage – it's too early to tell. I believe it to be more serious for the symptoms are strange. I have seen it before, many years ago, but I cannot for the present recall what it is. Anyway, his life is in the balance unless we do something, his ailment goes far beyond that which Hamill can attend to here.'

A look of deep sorrow mixed with anguish was in the seer's eyes, as if he blamed himself for what had happened. He had a fondness for the dwarves. Well, he probably was to blame in a way because it was on his insistence that they all were here.

'What do you want me to do?' Jon ventured to ask. He was desperate to do something useful. He had felt as useless as a hen without an egg to sit on during this latest crisis.

'We must move the dwarf away from here to safety as quickly as we can, the trail ahead is impassable and the only way back, unthinkable, yet the only choice we have. The creatures have been scared off for a while, but not for long. What I need you to do is to take my pouch.'

He handed Jon a small satchel; Jon buckled it to his belt, a quizzical look on his face. The seer placed his hand lightly on his shoulder, his green flecked eyes, just like his own, soft with encouragement.

'Be of good cheer.' He paused as if struggling for the right words to say, then smiled to himself and finished by saying, 'You must be strong. The capsules that are in the pouch will create the thunderflashes and will ward of any attack by the smarg or any other creature. They are sensitive to the light and the noise frightens them. It is imperative that Hamill get the dwarf to the Ward where they can attend to him.'

Jon felt overwhelmed and started to protest his lack of strength or experience, saying that Braun or the dwarves would do better than he.

'No. The lot has fallen to you; they have other tasks to attend to if we are to succeed in locating that which we have come to find. You and Hamill must hurry if you are to save Tracker. Trapper will accompany you; we wouldn't be able to prevent him from coming with you anyway.'

Just as he was about to say something else a shout from Archer at the barrier cut him short. They both started and spun around to see what was amiss. It was quite dark by now, the clouds that had gathered obscured any moonlight that would have illuminated the mountainside. The dwarves had produced small hand-held stick torches, which spluttered into life with a touch from Javelin's tinder-box. They illuminated the trail, making their shadows dance against the rock face.

Braun, after completing the stretcher, had gone a little way down the trail to keep a watchful eye on things and to give warning of any further activity from the creatures. It was well that he had but it was almost his undoing.

'Fight for your lives, lads,' he shouted as he sprang nimbly over the barrier. Two wolvets followed close behind, illuminated in the torchlight as they sprang into the air after Braun. They did not make the ground alive as two arrows from Archer's bow dispatched them in mid-air. They crunched to the floor and lay still.

'I'm afraid it's too late now, Jon; we must stand or perish.'

He rushed to help in case any others attacked, brandishing his staff and yelling over his shoulder, 'Quick, throw up a thunder-flash towards the barrier.'

Panic gripped him. He fumbled at the drawstrings, all fingers and thumbs, mostly thumbs if his dexterity was anything to go by.

He could see that Braun had stumbled as he landed, this side of the barrier. One of the dead creatures from the previous attacks caught his foot as he landed sending him sprawling in the dust. A large wolvet had made it over the barrier and pounced onto his back, sinking sharp yellow teeth into the bearskin that he wore. It saved him from receiving any injury but the mad-dened creature was intent on a kill. Thwack. A spear impaled it through the ribs, knocking it off his back. It struggled for a foot-ing and hampered by its wound, with the spear still deeply embedded in its side, it slipped over the edge into the dark; its yelps of fear and pain were lost in the abyss. Braun scrambled to his feet and acknowledged Javelin's assistance by nodding to the dwarf in appreciation.

Other wolvets bounded over the barrier eager to taste blood. Archer was ten paces away and accounted for one with a well aimed arrow; Trapper quickly turned around on his heel, letting a beast go past but turned and whipped up his hand-axe, slicing deeply into its side and mortally wounding it; another wolvet made for Javelin.

Jon watched it all unfold as if in slow motion. The beast lunged forward towards the stocky dwarf, confident in obtaining its purpose. Jon could only stand and stare, the outcome was inevi-table; there was no escaping his fate, or so he thought. Javelin froze and waited, then at the last minute, dropped to one knee, planting his other spear, still attached to the sapling in a makeshift stretcher, into the ground by his side, holding it in steady hands, its blade glinting in the torchlight. Determination and concen-tration engraved into his features as he faced the oncoming beast. The wolvet had no chance to avoid its death. It had committed itself to a powerful leap just before Javelin had made his move, the momentum of which carried it onto the tip of the spear. Jon heard its sternum snap with a sickening crunch. The dwarf held fast to the spear and rolled over backwards with the beast impaled

140

on it, ducking under the creature before it landed with a heavy thud on the frozen ground.

This was but the start of the attack; many more could be heard rushing towards their position. There arose such a cacophony of shrieks and howls, which carried up the slope in the wind, as they had not heard before; there seemed to be hundreds of red eyes blinking at them in the dark beyond the barrier. Urim had been right when he said that they would be back.

Braun was standing at the barrier with Urim. They turned and faced the creatures; Urim, cloak flapping against his legs in the wind; Braun, broadsword in hand. They prepared to meet the inevitable rush as the smarg drove the wolvets on with greater urgency, lashing out at them if they failed to respond.

Javelin, Trapper and Archer rallied to the metal master to consolidate their defence; hand-axes and short swords, arrows and broadsword, they were hardly in a position of strength but they were a formidable combination.

Archer let fly a couple of arrows into the dark and smiled with satisfaction upon hearing yelps and coughs as they found their mark. With the creatures so tightly packed together on the trail below them, he could not fail to hit something, which he did time and again. He kept on letting loose into the darkness until he had run out of arrows. He lay his beloved bow aside and picked up Tracker's swords, determined to fight to the end alongside his comrades-in-arms.

Hamill squatted by Tracker, protecting him as best he could from the elements. Jon stood frozen to the spot. He sensed, rather than heard, movement behind him; he felt sick with fear. A thousand thoughts went through his mind; all of them ended with being surrounded by smarg. Being faced by the creatures below the barrier who were massing, howls and coughs and yelps rising in pitch as the bloodlust built within their ranks. They were more respectful now of the blades and skills of the dwarves and the metal master and still wary of Urim and the thunderflashes.

The thunderflashes; he had forgotten them. Urim had given him the pouch. He slowly felt towards the drawstrings. He feared the creatures had worked their way around behind them and caught them in a pincer movement. He dared not look around. Rock ground against rock; they are coming over the rockfall, he thought.

His fist closed around something small and round like a pebble, a thunderflash; if only he could summon the courage to turn and fling it at them. He had to do it.

'I am going to turn and throw it now,' he thought resolutely, but still he did not move. The grinding rock grew louder with great thumps that he could feel reverberate through the ground. He saw in his mind's eye the smargs and other creatures falling on them from the rear; the brave little dwarves overrun. Braun downed by three of the largest smargs and Urim lost in a sea of white fur.

He could hardly breathe, his heart was pounding within his chest, feeling like it was in his throat.

'Blast it,' he yelled silently in his mind. 'Why must I always be so useless?'

He forced himself to action. Pivoting on his heel he spun himself to face the other way and whipped out his hand to throw the blast. As he did so, it caught on the straps, undoing the fastenings and flinging the pouch away into the air behind him. Tears of frustration welled in his eyes as he remonstrated within himself at his ineptitude. Because of his fumbling his friends would die; it cut like a knife. All these thoughts took only seconds to run through his mind; what he felt now was that the momentum of his swing was taking him off balance and he felt himself falling to the ground, tripping over his own feet. He did not hit the ground. A cold iron-like grip took hold on his arm and he was jerked back onto his feet. He gulped in astonishment.

He could hardly believe his eyes. Staring down at him was a mountain of a man, twelve feet tall. Then he realised that it was not a man at all, more like a statue carved from the rock, but this one moved; it was alive.

Chapter IX

The Colossi

Fine chiselled features gazed upon him from a weathered face of pale grey stone, grey eyes fixed his in a gentle embrace; his long shoulder-length hair was secured by a headband around his forehead, just like carved, polished stone. Indeed, other than for his clothing, everything about this being was of the appearance of stone. He wore a short-sleeved tunic belted at the waist and leggings secured in the traditional fashion with thongs around his lower legs. He wore open-toed sandals, the only items that he wore that appeared to be of stone, and a huge leather scabbard secured to his belt. The hilt of the sword was larger even than the one Braun carried but it looked small in comparison to the giant figure.

Beyond the stone giant Jon could see two more just like him, striding with graceful movements down the trail towards them. The ground trembled at each footfall as stone ground against stone.

'Stay here, little man.'

The colossus spoke in a voice like gravel but his tone was gentle and kind.

Jon gulped in awe at what he was witnessing; he felt faint; a feeling of nausea came over him and he felt dizzy. He fell against the side of the rock wall and slumped to the ground where he hugged his knees to stop them from trembling. He watched, mesmerised, as the three stone giants made their way down the trail towards the mêlée.

Urim had only just reached the others at the barricade having, seconds earlier, dispatched a wolvet as it had leaped towards Braun. He had levelled his black staff at it, faltering only momentarily in his stride, as it emitted a ball of energy towards the creature. The wolvet incinerated in a flash of blue light and a shower of ashes fell to the ground amid a cloud of smoke that drifted away into the night air; all that remained of the creature was a memory. Other wolvets lay dead or dying around the beleaguered group on the slippery ground; it was becoming increasingly difficult to keep their footing as they met the maddened beasts that were driven on over the barricade at the defenders by the smargs.

One of the smargs had challenged the battle skills and strength of the metal master and had paid the price for its foolishness. Braun had caught it with a sweeping arc from his broadsword, almost cutting it in half; it now lay at his feet amidst the others struggling in its death throes, then lay still. The stench of death was thick in the air.

Warning shouts of alarm from the dwarves mixed with the grunts and groans from their efforts to combat the hordes as the creatures launched themselves in a suicidal bid to dislodge them from the trail. Shrieks of frustration and pain echoed down the mountain as time and again they thwarted them in their aim. The smargs dared not approach, having witnessed the speedy dispatch of one of their fellows; they now had a healthy respect for the steel and the man who wielded it.

Jon could not see exactly what was transpiring as the torches, thrust into cracks in the rock, were fading; giving off very little light now. The moon gave a cold, eerie light from out of the cloudless sky that reflected from the snow of the mountain ranges around them. It looked a pretty desperate battle; one that they seemed doomed to lose before too long, due to the mass of creatures that were assailed against them.

Hamill was crouching over Tracker trying to offer some protection from further injury, though what exactly he could have done if confronted by a wolvet or any other of the creatures he did not know. Strange, Jon thought, how he can be so irksome and difficult to be around at times yet how dedicated and loyal he was to them, especially the injured dwarves. Hamill must have caught a movement in his peripheral vision for he jerked his head around to face whatever was coming. His face was a picture of astonishment; he came slowly to his feet, mouth agape, and lowered the knife he was holding to his side. Were it not such a serious situation that they were in, Jon would have laughed at his reaction; yet he was as astounded as Hamill. They watched, nonplussed, as the giant stone men walked past without even an acknowledgement that Hamill was there.

They neared the barrier and the attack began to falter as the creatures became aware of the approaching giants. Howls and yelps and awful cries went up from them as they backed slowly and fearfully away from the beleaguered little band.

Braun and the dwarves were near to exhaustion and welcomed the lull in the onslaught, though as yet they were unaware of the cause. Urim stood to the side letting the stone men pass; they hardly acknowledged him either. Jon noticed that Urim was not displaying any surprise at their appearance; rather it was as if he had been expecting them. Relief showed visibly on his face, his shoulders drooped from released tension and a broad smile stretched across his gaunt face. His head bowed and his lips moved as if in silent prayer. When Urim looked up again Jon could see that tears stained his cheeks and he quickly wiped them away with his sleeve.

The dwarves and Braun must have felt the tremors in the ground because they looked at their feet, then at each other and then back, up the slope towards the advancing stone men. The dwarves bowed their heads towards them in acknowledgement but Braun, clearly taken unawares, almost stumbled as he stepped back in his surprise.

At twelve feet high, they overshadowed the dwarves, being only five feet high themselves; even Braun, who stood nearly seven foot, was as a dwarf in comparison.

They continued on up and over the barrier, driving the cowering masses back down the trail. A few paces from the barrier they stopped. They had no weapons other than the huge sword that was still hanging in its sheath at the first giant's side. He raised his hand towards the creatures trembling before them, cowering in submission. His great booming voice sounded out and reverberated down the trail.

'Disperse from here. Leave these travellers in peace. Return to your lairs and dens and you may live; stay and you shall surely die.'

They all stood still. Hardly a sound came from the creatures massed ahead of them; a large number of the massed creatures turned tail and ran, whimpering from the scene. Those that remained gradually began to whine and yelp and snarl, the sound

145

building as guttural coughs and growls followed by barks and shrieks were aimed at the three stone giants.

The noise was frightening; clearly they were not going to go without a fight.

Suddenly, from a ledge on the rock face, a large wolvet launched itself, snarling in hatred, at the nearest giant. He caught it by the throat in mid air and allowed its momentum to carry it on. With a fluid, easy flick of his wrist he snapped the creature's neck with a sickening crack; it went limp and fell at his feet. This action only seemed to incense the creatures even more and several more wolvets sprang forward. The other giants dispatched them as quickly and as effortlessly as the first.

Four of the smargs pounced on the three of them; they were either very brave or stupid; Jon did not know which. Their long, sharp claws ripped at the giants causing only their clothing to be torn. Being made of stone they were unaffected by the damage that the creatures were trying to inflict; the sound of their claws rasped across their stone bodies.

The contest did not last long. One of the stone men lifted a smarg in both hands high over his head, as if it were a rag doll, and flung it, screaming in terror, over the precipice. Another two had their necks broken in quick succession and lay lifeless on the frozen ground. The fourth backed away snarling defiance but decided that it was no match for the three of them. It made a hasty retreat into the dark, following the fleeing hordes that had seen enough and were scattering every way they could to get away.

Slowly and deliberately the stone giants turned and faced the exhausted dwarves who were leaning on their weapons or crouching on the ground, weary from the prolonged exertions of the battle with the creatures.

They truly were a pitiful sight: caked in grime and blood; wounded and dishevelled, but thanks mainly to the skills and determination of the valiant dwarves and the strength and courage of the metal master, they were still alive to tell the tale. Urim had played his part too, but Jon felt rather self-conscious at his not having done a thing to assist. Hamill at least was able to offer his skills as a physician and had accounted himself well. Jon felt only guilt at not having done anything useful; even when he had had a chance to do so, he had failed. It was only good fortune

146

that it was the stone men who had been there as opposed to more smargs; otherwise they would have been lost.

Urim approached them, lifting his right hand in the gesture of peace and greeting, saluting them for their timely aid.

'We extend greetings to you, my friends. We are most grateful for your assistance.'

There was no response so Urim continued.

'I am Urim, a seer from the Council of the Sight. My companions and I are on our way to Ffridd-Uch-Ddu, beyond the pass, home to these dwarves. Master Braun is accompanying us as are Jon of Ashbrooke and Hamill of the Ward.'

Still no communication was forthcoming from the stone beings; Urim was getting a little agitated by the lack of response and tried again.

'Is there somewhere we could shelter from the cold? We would be grateful for your hospitality; we are not as able as you appear to be at withstanding the conditions here.'

The stone men just stared back at Urim unmoved; then the one who had spoken to Jon and the creatures looked past Urim towards Braun and said, 'Hail Braun of Foundry Smelt, master of metal, and forger of the sword. We recognise you amongst us. I am Bearer, leader of the colossi. My brothers are named Petros and Holdhard. You and your companions are welcome to our home. Come.'

With that he turned and with the others strode up the trail towards the rockfall. Urim stood open-mouthed and looked to Braun for an explanation. Braun just shrugged his shoulders and shook his head, signifying that he knew nothing.

The giants were a little ahead now so Urim urged everyone to follow on as quickly as they could. Trapper and Hamill helped carry Tracker up the slope followed by Jon and the other dwarves. They looked questioningly at each other but were only too glad to be relieved from the onslaught of the creatures and were happy to ask questions later. Urim and Braun brought up the rear, whispering questions to one another that neither could answer.

Just before the rockfall the leading giant reached up and touched a protruding stone, whereupon a section of the rock face ground aside to reveal a large tunnel.

'So that is what Urim was doing,' Jon thought to himself. He turned to Urim, saying, 'Is that what you were doing earlier?

Looking for the entrance to this tunnel? You knew didn't you? You knew this was here?'

'Yes. I knew; it was why we had to come this way. These colossi are the reason we are here. I, we, need them in order to defeat Ebon.'

Urim showed visible relief.

As they passed through the entrance they heard a whirring along with the sound of rock moving against rock. A huge stone slab slid into place behind them, locking out the wind and the cold from Deadline Crack. There was a sharp whistle of rushing air as the slab slid into place then was silent.

Immediately the air felt warmer; it must have been a good ten degrees warmer than out on the mountainside; it felt as if they had entered a furnace in comparison, but it was very welcome; very welcome indeed.

They had entered a large tunnel lit by luminescent stones from niches in the walls; although not bright, it was enough for them to be able to see where they were going. The dishevelled and exhausted group followed Bearer and his brothers along the tunnel as it bore into the rock; their footsteps echoed ahead of them. The air was dry and fresh to breathe, not at all as one would have expected. Jon's recollection of caving was that it was always cold and damp so this was a pleasant surprise.

As his eyes adjusted he noticed a myriad colours reflected off the walls by the light from the stones. The rock was rich with minerals and they twinkled and danced as they passed by: red, green, purple, so many colours; it was beautiful. They followed in silence, awed by the spectacle before them.

The tunnel wound its way down and to the left in a wide spiral deeper into the mountain. It felt a little warmer as they descended and the light grew stronger with each turn of the spiral.

Without warning the ground levelled out and they found themselves coming to the end of the tunnel; it was a welcome relief as Jon's calf muscles were aching, not that the slope had been a steep one, just long. Ahead of them the tunnel opened out into a cavern from which there could be seen the outlines of three other tunnels that afforded exits to other parts of the mountain city.

Jon noticed carved figures to either side of each entrance; they looked just like the colossi but these were not alive, these really were statues, cracked and damaged by time. There were tables and other such household furnishings, sufficient to accommodate a score or so of the stone men. A yellowish glow emanated from a shaft set into the wall from which heat wafted into the cavern they had entered as well as being the source of heat and light to other levels within the city.

Bearer turned and signalled for them to rest here, which they were very glad to do; none of them could have gone much further without rest.

Petros and Holdhard stood to one side, arms crossed, facing the group as if on guard duty. Bearer sat on a chair nearby that looked more like a throne, which enabled him to look the metal master in the eye on level terms.

'Make good ease, metal master, Braun of Foundry Smelt and your companions too; repair here for the time of darkening and renew your strength. We have no food to offer as it is not needed for ourselves but you may rest and be warmed.'

Bearer invited them to sit, though the stools and chairs were far too big for any of them other than Braun, but even he struggled to sit comfortably on one of the big chairs. The dwarves did not have a hope of reaching a stool; let alone sit on one. They all sat on their bundles or straight on to the floor, which was only a little dusty but warm.

'We became aware of your plight and decided to offer aid. We would normally not have interfered but for the fact that you, metal master, maker of the Token were amongst those being assailed. We have noticed a change come over the creatures hereabouts and are intrigued by this. Have you an explanation for this?'

Braun looked to Urim for help but he just encouraged him on, as it was Braun they were addressing and not him. The fact that he was a seer did not seem to impress them very much; that it was Braun who was receiving all the attention was interesting and intriguing for Urim.

Braun squared his shoulders, coughed to clear his throat, and in his best manner spoke to the stone giants.

'May we offer our greetings, your honours? We thank thee for your timely assistance and for the offer of hospitality.'

Braun looked to Urim again for help but he only signalled for him to continue.

'We would be glad of the time to rest and shelter from the cold.'

Urim nodded in agreement and pointed Braun's attention to the injured dwarf.

'However, we are all rather concerned for the welfare of one of our small companions. Would you be able to assist in some way?'

Bearer looked across at the injured dwarf then signalled to one of the giants. Holdhard came across to Bearer; they exchanged a few words together in a low rumble after which Holdhard nodded and stood to the side as before, arms crossed.

Bearer turned back to the group and said, 'There is no healing amongst us that would be of any use to your form. However, we do know of a place where he can obtain the necessary treatment. It is but a day's journey from here through the tunnels and out onto the Plains of Uniah, as you fleshers call it.

'It is named the Ward I believe, it is on the western bank of the River Nune and is run by the elves; although you have one amongst you if I am not mistaking the features of the one who tends the dwarf. Is he not able to heal him?'

'He is not; the dwarf is in need of more intense treatment than can be given by him alone,' Braun replied with urgency in his voice.

Hamill stepped forward unable to stop himself; pulling himself to his full height and risking insulting the colossi by doing so he said defiantly, 'It is true, sir, that I am an elf, or at least half an elf, from the Ward in the Plains of Uniah; however, it is imperative that I get Tracker to the Ward as quickly as possible or else he may die.'

Having been so bold in making his statement and surprising everyone at his outburst, Hamill said apologetically, 'Your pardon, sir, I mean no disrespect but I am fearful for the well-being of my friend and it is that which concerns me most.'

Bearer stared at Hamill for a while, unflinching. The others held their breath hoping that he had not caused offence to the colossus. A broad smile spread across Bearer's face and he gave a chuckle of amusement that rumbled around the cavern.

'It has been a very long while since I have been spoken to in that manner; I applaud your conscientiousness to duty, little elf.'

They all let out a sigh of relief but Urim cast a scolding look in his direction.

Bearer continued.

'Fear not, little healer. I have already arranged for Holdhard here to carry your friend to the Ward as soon as you are ready to go. I assume that you wish to attend him there?'

'Indeed I do; thank you, sir.'

Hamill beamed in delight and rushed to get his things together; he felt tired, they all did, but nothing would prevent him from going with the giant and Tracker.

Trapper also prepared to go with them; he did not want to be parted from his brother in his present condition. Urim had a word with Javelin who then talked to Trapper. He did not look very happy and was clearly intent on going with them but finally agreed to stay behind.

He went to his brother and bade him farewell then sat alone whilst they readied themselves to leave.

Jon gave Hamill a hug and said, 'Look after yourself, my friend; we'll catch up with you as soon as we can. Say hello to Anna for me and tell her to save some of that sweet root for me.'

'It rots your teeth you know, see you soon,' Hamill teased Jon.

Holdhard gathered the injured dwarf gently into a sling he had fashioned from a large piece of cloth that they probably used to cover the tables; this he placed around his neck and shoulders, securing the dwarf in front of him so that he might travel more comfortably.

Trapper came forward and offered Hamill his flask of relk.

'Here, healer; take this. It might be useful.'

'Thank you, Trapper. I am sorry you're not coming with us. Why did they not let you come?'

Trapper tried his best not to look disappointed but failed as he answered with a slight tremor to his voice. 'It was considered advisable that I remain with the others in order to permit you to make better progress. The seer has requested my skills for when they leave here on the morrow. Javelin is my leader and has requested it; I obey his command.'

'Come, little healer,' Holdhard said as softly as the colossus could. 'Let us be going or we will not make the Ward before dark of the day next.'

'I'm ready,' Hamill replied and took his leave of Trapper, promising to look after his brother. He picked up his things and followed Holdhard into one of the tunnels almost at a run in order to keep up with him; the giant took long strides and covered a lot of ground with each step. As they disappeared into the gloom and around the bend in the tunnel, Hamill shouted back to them, 'I'll have a good hearty meal prepared, ready and waiting for you all. See you in a couple of days.'

Their footsteps echoed into silence.

Something nagged at Jon; it troubled him because he felt it was important and had significance to what was happening. If only he could remember what it was that was teasing at the back of his mind? Something to do with the light from the stones in the tunnels had triggered the thought, but it was too tenuous a thought to grab hold of and identify.

'What is it?' Jon scolded himself.

It seemed that the harder he tried to recall the matter, the more distant it became. It was almost like being alone in the darkness and seeing a spark brightly light up a room, only for it to fall back into darkness before he could take it all in; it was so frustrating.

He was shattered, physically, from the stresses and strains of the day, particularly the encounter with the creatures outside on the trail. This trek he had undertaken with Urim was certainly no Sunday afternoon stroll; he used to enjoy his walks into the forest but they were nothing compared to this.

He sat on one of the smaller stools, which was probably only a footrest for the giant stone men, but to him it served as a good seat. While the others sat near the shaft in order to warm themselves and drive out the cold of the Deadline Crack.

Jon did not feel like being with them so settled down a little distance away, but not so far away as to appear rude. He thought that he should sleep but found that he could not, the events of the past weeks until now crowded into his head and he found himself reliving those walks into the forest. He could almost feel the warmth of the summer sun on his face and the rich fragrance of pine cones; he could smell it now, wafting on the breeze.

He recalled how people would refer to him as a dreamer, they did not understand his need for solitude; he wasn't comfortable with people. He often thought that it was his lot to be alone; that

152

he was destined to achieve some great purpose; mere fancy of course, nothing more than an idle dream.

'Maybe this was it,' he thought to himself – being involved in a great quest that would benefit the whole of the land and encompass all men, dwarves, elves and sprites. Delivering them from the great danger that hung over them, though many were unaware of it; living in ignorance of it, as had he, until now.

He dreamed of restoring peace to the land and striding side by side with Urim into Seers' Tower, having defeated Ebon and released the other seers from their enforced imprisonment, of the adulation he would receive along with the others; maybe he would even be remembered as part of a saga or a song. He was not sure how he felt about that; he was never comfortable about being the centre of attention.

Cold reality would not let him stray for long; he became distracted from his reverie before he even had a chance to enjoy being the all conquering hero. As things go when day-dreaming dark shadows creep onto the stage of one's mind and take over. He recalled the stories being told of late in Ashbrooke; of robbers abroad in the lowlands. Stories reached them from the travelling merchants of strange goings on in the south. Rumours of large footprints found in the mud and sightings of strange beasts; of cattle being disturbed and heard to be lowing anxiously; some even said that whole flocks of sheep had disappeared overnight.

There were fewer strangers of late as folk would tend to stay close to their homes and avoid travelling if they could. There were reports of people going outside in the dark to investigate noises they had heard and them not being seen again. Jon had wondered many times whether such a fate had overtaken his father, who had also disappeared without trace many years ago. It was hard for him to think of his father being killed; but it was preferable to thinking that he had abandoned them. His mother had said that he never knew that she was expecting his baby; it was only a few days after his disappearance that she knew, although she had suspected.

His mother's death earlier this year had left an emptiness inside of him that defied being eased. He tried not to think about it as the thought of being without her still hurt. He did not want to shed more tears over her, not here, not now.

The voices of the others impinged upon his senses and he

turned his attention, half in day-dream, to what was being said. As he did so the thought returned that he should have remembered something important. It tugged tantalisingly close to the edge of understanding yet eluded him still.

Jon shivered involuntarily. Feeling the need for warmth he wandered over to join the others near the shaft and sat with his back against the wall; it seemed no one could sleep. The dwarves had passed around a couple of flasks of relk, though wisely Urim and Braun had not taken up the offer since it was rather strong, so only the dwarves had been drinking.

Archer offered some to him but he likewise politely declined, he remembered the look on Hamill's face after he had taken a mouthful of the brew. No, not for him, he thought. Despite the spaciousness of the refectory (for that is what this place appeared to be) and it being inside the mountain, it was not cold, though it was more pleasant being closer to the shaft. Their faces, bathed in a soft amber glow, gave them a look of well-being. It was warm and comforting.

He had not meant to fall asleep; he had no idea of the time. It all seemed so timeless seconded away from the world and its woes. The shaft continued to flood the room with warmth and light, as he assumed it always did. The floor and the wall he rested against felt warm and comforting despite it being hard. He supposed that it was this warmth, coupled with his exhaustion, that had induced his sleep.

The others lay scattered around, heads resting upon their travel packs and their cloaks covering them as they slept, all except Urim. He sat on one of the giant chairs at a table. He was intent on examining something laid out on the table in front of him. His face was taught and tense, exaggerating the lines in his tanned skin. Jon watched him for a while, curious about this stranger who had come into his life. He could not make him out, was he friend or foe? So many things about Urim intrigued him, not least of all, his identity. Was he really his uncle as he had said? Ebon had said not, but then Ebon could not be trusted. Jon wanted to believe in Urim; he wanted to believe he was his uncle. He needed, more than ever, to know that he was not alone, without kin in this life.

His stomach growled. He tried to stifle the noise with his hands but to no avail.

'I trust you slept well.'

Urim spoke quietly without looking up from the scroll. He continued in a whisper, so as not to disturb the others.

'Are you feeling refreshed?'

'I guess so, thank you; but what about you, have you slept?' Jon whispered in return.

'A little; come, join me.'

He motioned for Jon to join him at the table.

Jon got up and made his way quietly, trying not to make any noise, between the sleeping dwarves and Braun, who had curled up on a bench near the shaft.

It was with some difficulty that he climbed into, rather than onto, one of the large stone chairs. Ideal for a colossus, but not the most suitable for a 'flesher', as the stone man Bearer had called them.

He looked around for them but they were nowhere in sight.

'They have returned to the mountainside. They had gone there to remove the rockfall so that the trail would be clear for travellers.'

Urim invited Jon to eat, passing him a bowl of dried fruit and a flask of ale that they had been carrying in their backpacks.

'It is not very much but it is nourishing.'

Urim clasped his hands together and leaned forward explaining to Jon what he had learned about the stone men while Jon had been sleeping.

'These colossi prefer to remain aloof from the affairs of the land and would not have interfered were it not for the metal master's presence. You may recall how, when we first encountered them, I tried to address them but I was ignored.'

Urim seemed a little uncomfortable with this but continued.

'It seems that long ago Braun's people and the colossi were of help to one another. The sword that Bearer carries was presented by the metal masters to them as a token between the two races. Because of that, they came to our assistance and offered us their services and hospitality. It was fortunate indeed for us that they did so or we would have had little chance of surviving the night.'

Jon took in the import of what Urim was saying. Thinking back on the events of the battle on the pass he remembered that when they first arrived at the rockfall, Urim had been searching for something on the rock face. Urim knew about the colossi. He knew they would appear and help them. Jon's mouth gaped wide. Looking at Urim, he realised that he knew Jon had discovered this fact and was smiling at his look of surprise.

Urim confessed.

'Yes, Jon, I knew they were here. I tried to open the doorway into their mountain home and avoid all that we have suffered but I could not discover the trigger to open the door. I am aware of some of the things that await us but I am unable to alter the outcome of my vision of them. Things must unravel as they are supposed to it seems.'

Urim sighed heavily and bowed his head then leaned back into the big chair. Jon digested all that Urim had told him then asked, 'So you can see into the future but you can't alter what happens; is that right?'

Urim responded wearily.

'That is a fair assessment of the situation; I am here for as long as it takes to retrieve the talismans that Ebon has stolen and ensure the release of the seers, I am on onlooker with very little ability to alter what happens. I can adjust things here and there and offer guidance and help where necessary, as I did out there on the pass. Otherwise my involvement has to remain limited.'

'Have you seen whether we succeed in defeating Ebon and releasing the other seers?' Jon asked, chewing nervously at his lower lip.

'That is unclear at this time. If we proceed carefully, I have confidence that we will,' Urim responded. He shuffled in his seat as if he were uncomfortable, and then asked, 'Do you happen to know what became of the pouch that I gave to you?'

Jon could have curled up and died at that precise moment in time.

'That's what it was,' he chided himself. That is what he had been trying to remember. It had been niggling at the back of his mind earlier; Urim's pouch of thunderflashes. He had dropped it out on the pass when the stone men appeared; he reddened, deeply ashamed at his clumsiness and that he had forgotten all about it.

Urim spoke softly and without recrimination.

'Do not berate yourself, Jon; it could happen to any one of us. No one can blame you at being so surprised by the appearance of the colossi. I alone knew that they would come to our aid. They have gone back to the pass and are looking for it; they will find it and return it, have no fear.'

'I'm really sorry, Urim. I know I should have said earlier but with all that's been going on and being so tired, I just forgot all about it; I knew there was something I needed to remember.'

'Think no more of it,' Urim said calmly and returned to examining the papers laid out before him. Jon could see now that they were maps of the colossi's mountain chambers and tunnels, with other maps of the surrounding area including the Plains of Uniah and the Ward.

'Where are we going from here, Urim?'

'We must continue on to Ffridd-Uch-Ddu and obtain the information that is contained in the scroll. Then we will join Anna and the others at the Ward.'

The room fell into silence, broken only by the rustle of parchment as Urim sifted through the maps, and the occasional snore from one or more of his sleeping travelling companions. Jon should have been sleepy too; he had no idea how long he had slept earlier, he guessed at a couple of hours, but he did not feel like sleeping right now.

He looked around at the hall he was in with abstract interest and noticed that the place appeared rather neglected. Although the room was bright, it had an air of melancholy silence; he felt sadness all around him. Shadows filled the farthest reaches of the room, giving it an eerie feel. There were tapestries hanging on the walls, though he could not make out what they were depicting as their colours had faded. It occurred to him that the colossi, being made of stone, had no need of nourishment, yet they were in what seemed to be a dining area, some sort of refectory. Why would they need it? Either they did at some time require food, or these caverns and tunnels had been made by and for someone else. It appeared that this was suited to the colossi, so perhaps there was a story to be told.

He looked at Urim again and considered him for a while. What was it about him that made others accept him as the leader of the group? It was more than just being a seer. There was something about him that was almost hypnotic and it drew people to him. Here he was, a seer of obvious ability and power, travelling the land in search of talismans and with the task of releasing the other seers. He was accompanied by a motley crew: the dwarves, the metal master, a half elf, Jon and Anna. Surely he would fare better without them. What was it that they could offer that would make the difference in Urim's tasks?

A rumble echoed through the tunnel that they had used earlier to enter the room from the mountainside and Jon guessed that the colossi were returning from the pass outside. He hoped that they had been able to find the pouch he had dropped; he sat waiting in nervous anticipation.

He heard the stone men approaching and hardly dared look. He had his back to the tunnel so he watched for any reaction from Urim. His heart thudded and he broke out into a cold sweat, sitting back nervously into the chair, biting at his lower lip.

A smile slowly spread across Urim's face, his eyes sparkled in the light from the shaft and he visibly relaxed.

Encouraged by this reaction, Jon dared to look for himself. Much to his relief he saw that Bearer held the pouch in his hand; a weight lifted from him as if it had been a millstone around his neck and he let out a sigh of relief.

Bearer approached them and placed the pouch on the table.

'We return your property to you, seer. It was where you said it would be, lying on the trail just below the rockfall. The pass is now clear so you and your companions can continue on your way as and when you wish to.'

'We thank you, Bearer, we shall continue on our way soon,' Urim responded courteously and, placing his hand on the maps, asked, 'May I prevail upon you to allow us to make our way along your tunnels through the mountain as it would make our journey much easier and quicker?'

'You have examined the maps to your satisfaction?' Bearer enquired.

'Indeed I have and I thank you. It has shown me that we can reach Ffridd-Uch-Ddu quicker but it is necessary for us to ask for your guidance. Would you help us please?'

'It would be our pleasure and honour to do so, seer. Those who are allied to the metal master we consider also allied to the colossi.'

Bearer nodded and strode off with Petros, leaving them to rest.

Jon suddenly felt very weary and settled down in the big chair to sleep. He could hardly keep himself from doing so and drifted off content now that the pouch was safely back in Urim's possession.

Chapter X

Double Quest

Jon awoke with a start; he had been dreaming of being pursued by the smarg and not being able to run; his feet seemed to sink into the ground while they pounced upon him in great leaping bounds. These thoughts clouded his mind; although just a dream, he felt deeply troubled by it. It took him a few moments to realise that it was only a dream, but it haunted him even though he was awake.

The others were also rousing themselves from sleep and stretching away the stiffness in their bodies. Water had been provided for them to wash with. What Jon really needed, apart from a wash, was some food. A hot meal would go down very well indeed. Unfortunately, as the colossus had said, they did not have any food to offer, so they had had to provide for themselves, that meant cold biscuits and fruit. 'Oh well,' Jon thought, 'at least it's warm and dry in here.'

The colossi were nowhere in sight and he wondered where they might be and whether they would lead them through the tunnels as promised.

Urim and Braun sat at the table, and were discussing what to do next. Urim asked if Braun would take the lead in the conversations with the giants, since they related more to him than Urim and asked, 'What connection is there between your people and them?'

'I am not sure. All I can remember is from legend. When long ago it is said that a race of immortal giants had been in need of the skills of those at Foundry Smelt and an alliance had been formed between them. As a token of their alliance, a sword had been made especially for the leader of the colossi; I had thought it to be a myth, but I am not so certain now.'

Urim agreed that it was not a myth as they had the evidence

of it before their own eyes; the one called Bearer obviously carried the sword that Braun referred to.

'Whatever the circumstances, it is fortunate for us that it is not a myth or we would probably have failed already,' Urim continued. 'They have agreed to guide us through the tunnels to Ffridd-Uch-Ddu. It is a much better route than the one we would have taken and will probably save us about half a day's travelling time.'

'When do we get started?' Braun asked, always eager to be on the move.

'We leave just as soon as everyone is packed and ready to go.'

Having eaten a nourishing but bland breakfast, the group were ready to set off. Bearer and Petros had returned and waited patiently for the group to shoulder their packs before leading the way into one of the tunnels. Bearer looked to Braun for the signal to go; Braun checked with Urim, who nodded that they were ready.

Braun then nodded to Bearer. Without a word spoken between them, they started into the labyrinth of passages that would take them through the mountain and bring them out close to the dwarves' capital, Ffridd-Uch-Ddu.

It was all rather strange, Jon thought, being taken through the city of the colossi. Here it had lain for hundreds maybe even thousands of years unbeknown to the outside world, a whole community that had been self-sufficient and made no communication with others for decades. He felt a thrill run through his body at the privilege of being here; of having met with the colossi. Would anyone believe him, after all these years of silence on the part of the stone giants? They wandered for many leagues along the passages and huge caverns within the mountain city of the giants. Wherever they went, the glow-stones in the niches illuminated the way. It was only in the larger caverns that dark shadows hung where the light could not reach. Bearer strode along easily, at the head of the line, followed by Braun, then the dwarves, followed by Urim, then Jon. Petros brought up the rear, so that no one got lost or separated from the main group. They said very little to each other, feeling the confinement of the rock around them despite the size of the tunnels. There were times when Jon felt the weight of the mountain bearing down on him

160

and involuntarily hunched forward as if the roof were to collapse at any moment.

After what seemed an age, Urim suggested that they rest for a while upon entering one of the caverns, asking Braun to communicate that fact to Bearer. They sat and ate some more fruit and biscuits washed down with clear, sweet water taken from a spring where they had replenished their flasks.

As he ate, Jon looked around him and noticed that the sides of the chamber had openings dotted around it at regular intervals.

'I wonder what those holes are for?'

He had not realised that he had vocalised his thought, so when Petros spoke to answer his question, it took him by surprise.

'Those are the doors and windows into the houses of our people,' he said softly and with a sense of sadness.

'They have stood empty for many of our years and perhaps hundreds of yours. Ever since they left the city and departed for the better land.'

He could not conceal his melancholy and sounded as if he were a very lonely giant.

Jon felt sorry for him but could not find any suitable words to say, so he said nothing; instead he concentrated on eating the last few mouthfuls of fruit.

They continued on their way for about an hour when they drew to a halt. Bearer held up a large lantern that he had just lit and instructed Petros to do the same. The way ahead seemed darker as Jon craned his neck to look. The glow-stones ended at this point so they needed an alternative light source and the lanterns afforded that light.

They pressed on, but this time in an upward spiral, much like the one they had used to enter the complex.

After a while, Jon thought that it was getting a bit lighter and sure enough, before long, he could see the end of the passage as they rounded the curve of the tunnel. It hurt his eyes, being used to the softer light from the lanterns, and he had to squint until his eyes had adjusted to the daylight. They stood at the top of a stairway, cut into the mountain but hidden from view in the valley below by a curtain wall. It wound down between rocky outcrops and crags, rising and falling until it eventually reached the valley floor behind a large boulder. Unless you knew the stairway was there, it would be almost invisible to anyone looking at the mountain from below.

Across from them, in the centre of a broad valley and surrounded by arable farmland was Ffridd-Uch-Ddu. It was a beautiful sight and upon seeing it the dwarves raised their hats and gave a cheer of delight. No wonder they spoke so highly of it. Jon could understand their joy at seeing it again; he had no words to describe its splendour. He could just make out the tiny homes that surrounded the central mass of buildings with towers and pinnacles, flags flying from every one; it brought a tear to his eye.

Archer turned and saw his reaction.

'We are pleased that you like our capital, Jon. It is a source of great pride to us.' He grinned from ear to ear.

The dwarves were keen to reach their home and hurried down the stone steps, beckoning the others to follow.

Bearer turned to Braun and said, 'This is as far as we take you, Master Braun, but should you require our assistance again, you need only ask and we shall be happy to aid you in whatever way we can. Please take this with you as a remembrance of your visit. It may be useful to you some day.'

He handed him a small glass pebble, a glow-stone.

'We thank you most heartily for your gift, Bearer, Petros. We are also much obliged for your timely assistance and hospitality. Is there anything that we might do for you?' Braun asked.

The giant slowly shook his head and offered his hand in a token of friendship to Braun and also to Urim. They responded, their hands swallowed in the gentle clasp of their new friends. With a smile and a nod towards Jon, they turned and strode back up the way they had come.

The three of them watched as the stone men disappeared back into the dark of the tunnel then set off after the dwarves who had run on ahead, eager to be home; they managed to catch up with the dwarves eventually, just before entering the city. It buzzed with activity and everywhere they went they met with smiles and polite greetings. Everything was on a smaller scale, to suit the needs of the dwarves; it must have appeared like a model village to Braun. Javelin urged them to follow him and to stay close; Archer and Trapper fell in behind Jon and Urim so that they would not become lost. Making their way through the crowds, Javelin led them towards the centre place and the university buildings to meet with the elders and tutors. He was as keen for news of the dwarves' border army and of any contact with the gnomes as he was for finding out about the writings on the scroll but opted for taking Urim to the scholars first.

The pathway was busy with dwarves of all kinds going about their business; some were intent on getting wherever they needed to be in as short a time as possible; others walked arm in arm ushering a clutch of smaller versions of themselves. Jon presumed them to be their children but he had never before seen children with beards. They were not as long as their parents' but nonetheless, any man would be proud to have one like theirs. What fascinated Jon more than anything else was the notion that a female would have a beard. It looked so odd but they were trimmed and decorated with pretty bows and clips, whereas the males just wore their beards as they grew.

There was a great deal of activity, it was obviously a busy time for the city and they found it heavy going through the crowds. It was not made any easier by many of the dwarves stopping to stare at the strange group of visitors. Jon felt quite exposed and became very self-conscious.

They gradually made progress along the streets, passing through a market square where traders were doing a brisk business selling all kinds of wares; the air was filled with their cries telling folk of the bargains that they could purchase; things that they never knew they needed until now. Jon was particularly amused by a stall that sold beard curling equipment, obviously designed with the fashion conscious female in mind.

'Here you are, madam, try it for yourself, now doesn't that look charming? Take a look in the glass; it's all the fashion in Winters Hold this season.'

They did not stop to see whether or not the female in question made a purchase but Jon rather thought that she would.

They continued on along a broad street lined with hanging baskets that trailed fragrant blooms over the sides of the bowls and along wires that connected them to one another forming long garlands of colour. A sweet scent filled the air and tickled at his nose; he was not certain as to whether he would sneeze or not; as it happened he did not.

After a bit of pushing and shoving through the crowd by Javelin and Archer, they reached the steps that led to the Acad-

163

emy of Antiquities, where they hoped to find someone who could interpret the writings on the scroll.

Javelin quickly explained their situation to the attendant who signalled for them to follow him. They dutifully did so along echoing corridors and through rooms filled with artefacts, up broad stone stairways and finally stopped outside a set of heavily varnished double doors.

He admitted them into a room with books stacked from floor to ceiling around the walls. A large wooden desk occupied the centre of the room and light streamed in through large windows on the opposite wall. The attendant had them stop where they were and approached the desk where he spoke to someone.

At least they assumed he did for they could not see anyone, just piles of books that covered the table and obscured from view whoever sat behind them. They heard muted whispering between two persons as the attendant bent close to the one seated behind the desk in a quiet exchange of words.

Over the books appeared a mop of white hair that looked wispy and sparse as the sunlight shone through from behind, followed by a pair of spectacles, behind which bright blue eyes peered at them from a pale, time-worn face.

The attendant signalled for them to approach, which they did and respectfully bowed in greeting to the learned dwarf.

The attendant introduced them. 'Senior Bridgeford, this is Urim of the Council of Seers. Seer, this is Senior Bridgeford, the one who is most likely to be able to assist you. Please be seated.'

They did so, Urim close by the desk, the others on benches and assorted chairs; Braun had a little difficulty finding somewhere suitable but finally settled himself on a bench. He looked rather amusing with his knees bent up to his chest due to the smallness of the furniture. Urim started with the formalities.

'Please accept our greetings, Senior Bridgeford; it is a matter of some importance that we learn what is written on the scroll that I carry on behalf of Terra Standfast of the Council of Seers. Are you able to translate its meaning?'

Urim handed him the scroll and the dwarf laid it on the table before him.

Senior Bridgeford reached into his coat pocket and pulled out a magnifying glass with which to examine the scroll better.

'Ah! Yes. I see.' He exclaimed excitedly as he moved the glass

164

over the scroll, turning it gently as he did so. 'You spoke the truth when you said it was from Terra Standfast for it has the mark of the Council of the Sight upon it. Where did you say you got it from?'

Urim quickly explained how it had come into his possession and that he believed the knowledge contained within it would help him find a way to release the seers from the Tower.

'Hmm!' Senior Bridgeman mused as he considered the facts.

'Yes. I can see how it might do just that, but the information it contains is too valuable, too dangerous for common knowledge. Indeed it must not be made known outside of those who need to know how to use said information. I will tell it to you, but no one else. After which you must take a vow of silence regarding what you have learned, as must I. Are those terms acceptable to you, Urim of the Council of Seers?'

'I agree wholeheartedly,' Urim responded with conviction.

'Well, that settles it; Samuel,' he said, calling for the attendant, 'escort our visitors to the accommodation centre where they can refresh themselves. No doubt you are all in need of food and lodging?'

'That would be most kind of you, sir,' Urim replied and asked Jon to book a room on his behalf so that he might study things later without disturbing anyone.

'Excellent. We will begin when we are alone. Your friend will join you in a couple of hours so I suggest you get some rest in the meantime,' Senior Bridgeman said to them as they left.

The doors closed gently behind them; they heard the key turn in the lock and a bolt slide into place, he obviously meant for them to remain undisturbed.

The accommodation centre catered for their varied needs; the only difficulty was that Braun's cot did not allow him to stretch out. His feet hung over the bottom of the mattress but it was the largest one they had, so he had to make do. His cot at the Ward had been perfect as the elves are prepared for all sizes of visitors.

Javelin, Archer and Trapper had left them to find out as much as they could about the movements of the gnomes. They returned soon after with worried looks on their faces.

'What's the matter?' Jon asked Archer.

'There is no news of any gnomes crossing our borders. They

say that the gnomes have been very quiet lately and have not had any trouble from them here. All the reports are that things have gone quiet,' Archer told him.

'So surely that's good news isn't it?' Jon queried.

'Not really. You're forgetting the gnome army that crossed our path on the way to the Ward. They must have come through the mountains some way. If not through our borders, then where and how did they do it without being noticed?'

They all fell silent, not having the answer to that question at this moment in time.

They washed and ate a good hot meal followed by a dark mulled wine that made Jon's head spin. He drank rather a lot of it as it tasted so good and before too long he realised that he was feeling rather drunk.

'They like their shtrong drink, these dwarvesh,' he slurred in a loud whisper to Braun, who just giggled in reply; it had obviously affected him too. They retired for the night without seeing Urim who had gone straight to his room and had had food taken to him there.

The next morning, Jon awoke and sat up; the room whirled around him and he was almost sick; he flopped down on to the pillow again holding a hand to his head and groaning loudly, saying, 'What did they put in that drink?'

There came a knock at the door, the sound of it reverberated around in his head. Archer popped his head into the room.

'I thought you might be awake by now, young Jon. I've brought you a tonic to help you recover from the effects of the wine. I assume you are in need of it?'

Archer's voice sounded like an echo in his head as it bounced around inside.

'Too right I do. I think I need a new head. What's in that drink I had last night anyway?' he murmured, not daring to speak too loudly as his head was thumping.

'Oh, nothing much; it's made up mostly from fruit juice with sweet chilli, mustard, ginger, horseradish and a tipple of relk,' Archer replied, laughing.

'Ouch! Well they ought to issue a public health warning. Where's that tonic?'

Jon reached out in the direction of Archer's voice, not wanting to open his eyes just yet. He drank deeply and spluttered as a result.

'My word; what's that? It's as bad as the wine.'

'Oh come on, Jon, it's not that bad. It's just what you might call "the hair of the dog"; it will have you up and about in no time at all.'

'Great. Thanks; next time I need a remedy I'll know where not to go.'

Archer opened the door to leave and said before going out, 'Come on. There's no time for lying in your cot.'

Whatever was in that tonic, it cleared his head and by the time he arrived in the canteen for his bacon and eggs, he felt much better.

Urim and Braun were already tucking in to theirs and the dwarves were not a lick behind.

'I hope you've left some for me?' Jon quipped.

A bread roll hit him in the back of the head as he made his way to the serving counter to help himself; some dwarves who saw it laughed. He turned to see who had thrown it but his travelling companions kept their heads low and concentrated on their food. He could swear he saw Javelin stifle a laugh and he ended up coughing as he almost choked on his drink. They all burst into laughter, including Jon, who tossed the roll back in their direction but missed and it landed on the floor.

'Get me another roll will you, Jon,' Archer asked, stifling a laugh. 'Mine seems to have disappeared.'

At this everyone burst out laughing and enjoyed the fun, they were all in a buoyant mood this morning and Jon could not remember feeling this good for a long time; it was great to feel like he belonged and was appreciated.

Breakfast over, without any more food fights, they gathered in a spare room at the academy buildings. Urim instructed the dwarves to make sure that they were safe from being overheard.

Satisfied that no one could, he outlined what he proposed needed to be done.

'Javelin and I have had discussions with the garrison commander; he has agreed to send out more scouting parties in an effort to discover how the gnomes got through onto the Plains of Uniah. They will return by tomorrow evening with whatever information they have been able to gather. What I propose to do, in order to make the most of the time available to us, is to split our group into two.'

That came as a surprise to Jon and Braun, who looked at Urim with open mouths. Braun could not see what would be gained and argued.

'Are you sure that's wise, Urim? What do you expect to achieve by dividing us up? Surely we would be better served staying together.'

Jon nodded in agreement with Braun but the dwarves remained emotionless, as if they had expected the announcement.

'Normally, I would agree with you.' Urim chewed at his bottom lip thoughtfully and explained. 'Unfortunately we are not in a normal situation and tough decisions need to be made; decisions that on the face of it seem irrational. There is, I fear, little time remaining to us in order to thwart Ebon's designs on ruling this land with an iron fist.'

He clenched his hands together and sighed.

'The march of the gnomes through our own backyard, as it were, is reason enough to know that Ebon is bold and confident enough to believe he has already won. There is much that needs to be done and we can achieve more by spreading our resources and separating.'

The dwarves nodded in agreement but Jon was still not convinced and was curious as to who would go with whom if they did split. He would have asked but Urim continued to explain his plan whilst looking at Jon, but addressing them all.

'I am unable to shed any light on what we should do next as my vision of things is hazy but I feel that I must go to Crystal Falls and seek the help of the sprites. I believe that there is much that can be learned to our advantage there. Captain Quentin said Ebon had made it clear that he intended to go there with a message for the Queen of Sprites and I am concerned about that, so I have decided that Braun and I will go to see the Sprite Queen together, setting off within the hour. You, Jon, in company with the dwarves will await the return of the scouts. Using whatever information they bring back, you should be able to better discover the means by which the gnomes are getting through the mountains, if they haven't found it themselves by then. Finding it may be decisive in our efforts to prevent any reinforcements being sent through; it will be deadly enough dealing with those who have already done so. The garrison commander has agreed that two of his scouts will accompany you, if the dwarves have failed to discover its whereabouts themselves; should you locate the pass that they are undoubtedly using, you are to follow it through to discover where it emerges on the other side. The scouts will then get the news back to him and he will gather his forces to stop the gnomes or any of their allies getting through.'

He paused to gauge their response, but no one spoke. His logic was sensible: no matter how much they would have liked to stay together, it made sense to do as Urim had suggested. 'Now, if there are no further questions? Braun, I recommend that we start immediately. Jon, we will meet up again at the Ward in a couple of days, all being well. Either you will have discovered the secret pass or the dwarves will have done. Either way we will see you back at the Ward. Take care and remember, you will be safe with the dwarves, of that I have no doubt.'

They clasped hands; Jon felt that a bond had built up between them since their meeting and was reticent to be parted from him, but recognized the sense in what Urim had decided.

'I will be careful and I believe I could be in no better company outside that of you and Braun. Watch out for yourself. See you back at the Ward.'

'Indeed you shall.'

Urim smiled and gathered his things together.

'Take good care of yourself, young Jon, and we shall meet at the Ward to share our stories.'

He nodded to Braun who nodded back and gave Jon a slap on the back, which almost sent him reeling. He slipped something round and hard like a stone into his hand and said his farewells to the dwarves before heading off to get his things. Jon opened his hand and discovered that Braun had given him the glow-stone that Bearer had presented him with when they had parted company. It looked for all the world like any other glass pebble, but Jon knew just how bright the light from one of these can be when in the dark.

Urim winked at him saying, 'Keep it safe, for you will have need of it and it will prove a valuable aid in a time of darkness.'

Jon put it into a pocket in his backpack and buckled it securely and watched after Urim and Braun as they left the city without any guides; Urim had insisted that it should be just the two of them that go and would not be moved by the protestations of the dwarves; he would take no one else.

Preparations were made and provisions supplied; enough to last them for a few days, at least until they reached the border where fresh supplies could be obtained from the dwarves who guarded the way. The garrison commander gave Urim a letter to give to the captain there who would offer them any assistance necessary.

Jon watched them leave with a heavy heart, he wanted to go with them but Urim had emphasised the importance of finding the way through the mountains that the gnomes were using and that Jon would have a key part to play in doing so.

Chapter XI

The Canyon

With nothing much to do until the scouts returned, Archer took it upon himself to give Jon a guided tour of the city, with its narrow winding streets and contrasting boulevards bedecked with late flowering blooms. There was a sense of well-being about the place that made any visitor feel relaxed and at home; the city was busy and Jon could feel the buzz of activity around them. With the autumn sun warm on his face, in such pleasant surroundings it was difficult to believe that there was conflict and strife brewing; he wished for it to be over. The scouts returned throughout the afternoon to the garrison reporting to their commander on the various areas that they had searched, but they had found very little to help. The only thing that was of curiosity was that a small river had appeared to have changed its course in one of the canyons, about a day's journey to the south, due to a landslide. These happened every now and again because of the nature of the rock, so it had gone unreported until now. Trapper assimilated all the reports but could not glean anything of value; they were stumped. There were not even any tracks or signs that an army had passed through and there most certainly would be if they had done so. Jon needed some fresh air after spending a couple of fruitless hours trying to figure things out with the dwarves so he sat on a bench in one of the many gardens. He sat absentmindedly watching the ducks as they waddled past and swam about on the small lake. They paddled about, quacking away contentedly when he noticed a movement at the centre of the lake. A beaver was trying to build a dam and had been gnawing away at a small tree on the bank. It crashed to the ground and lay across the mouth of the small stream that emptied into the lake. An idea formed in Jon's head; what if the gnomes had caused the landslide in order to conceal their movements? It seemed far-fetched, but what else did they have to go on? He rushed back in and outlined his idea to Trapper.

'It's a consideration, young Jon.' he responded with enthusiasm. 'I think you may just have hit on what we have been looking for. To think it was right under our noses all the time. Let's tell the others.'

They were also enthusiastic at Jon's idea and determined to go to the place and investigate further. They congratulated him heartily and he could not help grinning with delight at their praise. The two scouts who had reported the incident, Digger and Mason, studied geology at the academy and had been assigned to take Jon and the dwarves there early the next morning.

Jon got up early and was keen to get going; his idea had excited him and he wanted to find out whether he had guessed right about the landslide. He and the three dwarves met the scouts, Digger and Mason, after breakfast, having gathered their things together and packed ready for the journey. Pleasantries were exchanged and they set off at a brisk pace before the city became too busy, so as to avoid the crowds. Mason altered his stride allowing Jon to catch up with him.

He addressed Jon formally.

'I'm very pleased to be undertaking this journey with you, sir; I heard that it was you who came up with the idea of the gnomes disguising their route with the landslide. Very astute if I may say so.'

Jon blushed with embarrassment.

'Oh, I was lucky I guess; besides I may be wrong and all this will be for nothing. By the way, please call me Jon.'

'Thank you, sir, I mean Jon; my name is Mason.'

'Yes, I know. I understand that you and Digger were the ones who reported this?'

'That's right. We didn't see it ourselves though; some farmer told the local border patrol. We didn't think it that important at the time as these landslides happen quite frequently.'

Mason appeared to be friendly and Jon relaxed in his company; happy to talk as they walked; enjoying the scenery and the distraction from their task. This was a much more pleasant walk than those he had completed recently. Jon asked the dwarf about his work at the academy and what he hoped to do when he had qualified. As it turned out, Mason had hopes of undertaking an archaeological dig to the east in search of clues to the ancient history of the dwarves. There were stories of magnificent ruins deep in the mountains. So they continued chatting as they went, sharing episodes from their lives that appeared very dull to themselves but highly interesting to the other; the day passed quickly with Jon and Mason forging a strong friendship, one with another.

They made camp under the shadow of the mountain where the reported landslide had been discovered. It was only a few hundred lengths away but lack of light meant they would have to wait until morning to investigate. The dwarves quickly set up the cocoons that slept up to four people, three of them in each one. Jon shared with Digger and Mason whilst Javelin, Archer and Trapper had the other. Having spent a restless night – made even more difficult due to the snores coming from the other cocoon, keeping him awake – he went for an early morning stroll. As if he hadn't done enough walking, he mused. It was a dull morning and looked like it was going to rain soon; he did not look forward to that. He did not fancy spending the day huddled in a cocoon feeling miserable, though that would be preferable to walking around getting wet. He crouched by the bank of a small river that flowed lazily into a secluded canyon. Looking downstream he noticed the bend of the rivulet looked odd, in that it seemed unnatural. There was a sharp bend to the left where there was a large deposit of small rocks; what made it look strange to him was that the rock seemed out of place.

Everywhere else was covered in vegetation, all but for this place where the flow of the water had been diverted. Was this the landslide that the dwarves had mentioned? If so, then why had they not noticed its peculiarity? He ventured closer, wary of any dangers. His tracker instincts took over and he made his way along the bank of the stream with caution, keeping as close to the cover that the vegetation afforded.

Gingerly he climbed the face of the loose rocks, slipping once or twice. When he got to the top, he could scarcely believe his eyes. He had been right; this was not a natural deposit or a landslide. These rocks had been put here deliberately. Stretching away towards the mountains, through the trees was the old river bed; but what was more, there were clear signs of the passage of many people that came from the north under the cover of the trees and along the old river bed.

He returned to the others with news of his discovery and together they explored beyond the unnatural barrier of rock. Mason and Digger took the lead along the dry river bed, having scaled the rock barrier with Trapper close behind, followed by Jon, then Archer and Javelin. They had congratulated Jon on his discovery; Trapper went as far as to say that even Tracker would have been proud of him; praise indeed.

They followed the dried out river bed, which revealed obvious signs of many feet trampling past. They also found some half eaten fruit and a belt buckle. Trapper immediately identified it as being gnomish in design. They had found the hidden passage that the gnome army had used to cross the mountain, but where did it lead to and where did it emerge on the other side? That was what they had come to find out.

The walls of the canyon closed in on them until it was barely five lengths wide. At this point the ground had been well trodden, where the gnomes had had to squeeze through the confined gorge.

The land began to dip and an opening appeared in front of them, leading down into the ground; so that was it. The gnomes had diverted the river so as to use its underground course as a highway through the mountain.

The dwarves had come prepared for anything, producing torches and oil, which they lit before entering the cave. Carefully they made their way through, following the old course that the river had taken. Mason pointed out to them the marks on the walls, left by the gnomes to give guidance to the next group of gnomes presumably.

'What if we are still in here and another gnome army uses this route?' Jon asked tentatively.

'Then we make sure that we stay ahead of them,' Archer said in reply.

Jon did not ask anything else. He decided that not knowing was probably best and concentrated on following in Trapper's footsteps.

The sound of dripping water constantly echoed through the cave complex and the surfaces were still damp. They slipped and slid along the original watercourse; down, round and over boul-

174

ders, navigating the natural twists and turns of the mountain's innards.

For what seemed hours, they wound their way through, following the signs left by the gnomes.

It felt cold and was very wet; occasionally they would come across a body of water, still and clear as glass, that blocked their path, but there was always a way past, indicated by the markings.

As they ventured further in, water trickled along the floor and pretty soon it was more of a flow than a trickle. It increased in volume and they found themselves wading knee deep in freezing water. Jon had tried to remain calm but he was feeling rather nervous about this. He glanced over his shoulder at Archer who looked as nervous as he was; he tried to smile reassuringly back at Jon but his eyes betrayed his concern.

Mason shouted back to the others.

'We must try to find higher ground and get out of this water; I suspect it has rained and the water will rise even further. Stick close to me; I think I see somewhere ahead where we should be safe.'

Carefully they made their way to a shelf of rock above them, close to the roof, which they were able to clamber onto by pulling and shoving each other. They sat there exhausted by the exertion and the cold.

Digger asked how everyone was and they all nodded in turn to say they were fine: Cold and scared although no one said so, but happy to be out of the water flowing rapidly below where they perched. The level of water continued to rise; inch by inch it crept ever closer to their place of retreat. The noise was as a roar in Jon's ears.

'What if the ledge isn't high enough?' he shouted into Archer's ear in order to make himself heard.

'Pray that it is, young Jon; pray that it is,' Archer shouted back as he clung to the rock wall.

Jon closed his eyes and uttered a silent prayer. Not that he was particularly religious; it was just comforting to have a belief in something, which he did; he just didn't know what. Crossing his fingers superstitiously he gulped down his panic as the water reached the lip of the ledge and kept climbing. The icy cold water swirled around his ankles and leeched the warmth from his bones. Still the water rose, showing no signs of abating. Things looked bad. The water rushed into and through the cavern they were sheltering in, on the ledge, high up against the roof. There was nowhere for them to go. The torrent of water clawed at them as they clung as best they could to the rough rock wall with numb fingers. The torches failed and they were left in the inky darkness. Panic welled up within him as Jon held on for dear life. How were the others doing? Were they still clinging on as he was? He presumed so; they were hardy folk, these dwarves.

He could not hear anything but the water; he could not feel anything but his grip on the rock. If it was cutting into his flesh, he was unaware of it; such was the cold. The water covered his whole body now, only his head was clear and still the freezing water tried to pull him away from the safety of the ledge.

He did not know how long he clung there praying for a miracle, but the water did not get any higher; in fact it started to recede. Gradually at first and then faster as the flow of water eased. He gasped with the effort of breathing; his body wracked with the pain of the cold. The noise lessened and he heard Digger shout out to them through chattering teeth.

'Is everyone OK? Call out your name so that we know you're all right.'

One by one they weakly called out their names. Javelin; Archer; Jon; Trapper. Then there was silence. Mason did not answer.

'Can someone light up a torch? Do we have anything that will give us some light?'

'No, everything is saturated by the flood; there's nothing dry,' Javelin replied.

Then Jon remembered the glow-stone that Braun had given him. Gingerly he let go of his hold on the rock and slipped his pack off his back; fumbling with fingers that had no feeling, he drew out the glow-stone, holding it in the palm of his hand. Immediately there was a bright glow, which hurt their eyes momentarily. Getting used to the sudden change, in that they were able to see, the dwarves marvelled at the stone, temporarily forgetting why they wanted the light. Trapper was the first to hush them all by saying softly, then more loudly, 'Mason is gone.' They fell into silence, shocked at the loss of the dwarf who had such plans for the future; a future that would now never be realised.

Jon looked back towards Digger who held his head bowed, his shoulders heaving as he mourned the loss of his friend.

'Perhaps he is OK,' Jon offered hopefully.

'I am afraid there is little chance of that, young Jon,' Archer spoke quietly and placed a gentle hand on his shoulder. 'Thank you though, for trying to give hope.'

They sat there shivering from the effects of being covered by the freezing water in the light of the glow-stone, waiting for the water to subside sufficiently for them to continue. Before long they were able to get going again; only now they were short of a member of their group. Of the six who entered the passage, only five would make it through.

They followed the old course of the underground river as it continued to twist and turn through passages worn smooth by the flow of the water, the glow-stone giving them just enough light to illuminate the way. Ahead of them the dark was less intense, a shaft of soft moonlight was penetrating the side of the cavern they had entered, towards the top of a cascade of rocks. Jon could see that if they climbed these, they could be used to navigate their way up to where the moonlight was shining through. After slipping and grazing his shins, Jon and the others reached the point where a shaft big enough for them to climb up in single file took them out of the underground caverns; the light from the moon seemed as bright as day and he had to squint his eyes and hold his hand over his brow to shield them. When they finally emerged from the maze of caverns, they were sorely in need of a warm fire and a hot meal. They decided to risk lighting a fire and it soon crackled into life cheering their spirits; they kept a watchful eye open though in case there were gnomes around, guarding the way into the passages. They found some cover under a tree and spent a very sorrowful and uncomfortable night, it having taken them almost the whole day to make their way through.

When morning came they ate a sparse breakfast, saying very little to each other before taking stock of where they were. Javelin consulted the maps he carried after they had dried out and concluded that they had come out of the mountains just below Crystal Lake and were probably no more than a day's march from the Ward.

They tried to convince Digger to come with them but he

refused, saying that he had to return to Ffridd-Uch-Ddu and deliver his report. The dwarves had to try and seal off the entrance to the passage to prevent the gnomes from using it again.

They bid him a sorrowful goodbye, thanking him for his help and wished him luck as he went back into the passage to return to the dwarves' city; the light of his fresh torch disappeared into the blackness within.

Jon determined that when this was all over, he would return to Ffridd-Uch-Ddu himself and seek him out; he did not want to lose another friend.

Shouldering their packs, they started towards the Ward at a jog, wanting to get there as quickly as possible. Despite their sorrows, their spirits lifted with the physical exertion and the pumping of adrenalin around their bodies. The thought of a hot bath and a good meal with smooth, crisp sheets to snuggle into that night was a tonic to their nerves.

Chapter XII

Hamill's Journey

Hamill followed alongside the stone giant as best he could; he tried bravely to keep up with his long strides, having to skip and run at times to do so. The tunnel was much like the one by which they had entered the giants' complex, sloping down in a steady spiral, illuminated by the glowing stones in the rock niches giving off a subtle light that did not strain the eyes.

He looked up occasionally at the stone man, thinking to himself, 'Wow. So this is actually one of the stone men I have heard about in tales from the old days. A colossus; and here I am walking along side one of them.'

He was feeling heady and excited at being with him; Hamill was normally not one for adventures and was all for a quiet life, happy helping the sick and injured, either at the Ward or in other places around the land. He had not bargained for all that he had experienced this last week. 'If I had known then what I know now,' he thought to himself, 'I would not have joined with the others; yet I would not have missed this experience for anything.'

He thought of the look on their faces when he, Hamill the apprentice, walked into the Ward in the company of a colossus. He sported the biggest grin he had ever grinned at the prospect. For now though, his biggest concern was the speedy delivery of the dwarf to the specialist help that he required in order to save his arm and possibly his life.

Still the tunnels took them further down into the mountain, passing through gallery after gallery, their footsteps echoing into unknown depths. The place was huge, obviously created for a larger population than the three colossi but there was no sign of anyone else; no sound of industry and no sight of any other giant stone people.

'Are there others like you three, Holdhard?' he ventured to ask.

'Yes, there are others.'

Hamill waited for more from the giant but realised that that was all he was going to say. He tried again.

'Do the three of you live here by yourselves?'

'Yes.'

This was not going to be easy.

'So if there are others like you but there are only the three of you here, where are the others?'

'They have gone away.'

His curiosity aroused and frustrated at the lack of response, he tried a slightly different approach.

'Tell me about it?'

'It all happened long ago. We have been guardians over the pass and of the mountains for longer than I can remember; certainly longer than you and your kind have been in the lowlands. The elders received news of a place that was free from the interference of man and his kind. Several expeditions were sent. Finally one of them returned saying that they had found the place. We are the last three of five who remained.'

Hamill's interest was roused.

'You said there were five of you. What happened to the other two?'

'They became despondent and they petrified.'

'What do you mean, "they petrified"?'

'In your language it would be the same as saying they died.'

'Oh. I'm sorry to hear that. Pardon me for asking, and I apologise if I am being indiscreet, but I didn't know that you could die, being made of stone,' Hamill ventured tentatively.

'It is true that we live for far longer than you fleshers and although we have the appearance of stone, we are not. We are of a very durable mineral base, not like you, but we are not of the same material as the rock around us. For centuries we carved out our city in the rock, adding section by section as we expanded. Then we just stopped. The land was filling with your kind and we saw much bloodshed amongst you. Having discovered the other place we decided to relocate ourselves, away from the disharmony around us. That was many years ago; so long ago that I was but a child. I am but a young man now but in your years I would be about four hundred years old. We have been known to live for a thousand of your years.'

Hamill fell into silence as he felt a melancholy settle upon the stone man. They did not speak again for some time.

Holdhard stopped at the end of one of the tunnels, indicating a ledge upon which were several firebrands and a kettle of oil into which one dipped the firebrand. He said, 'We must hold torches from now on. The glow-stones do not continue past this point and you will need the light to see where you are going.'

Hamill obediently lit up a torch and tucked a spare one into his belt. It almost dragged along the ground it was so big.

'Are you going to have one?'

'Yes. I will carry one, though I have no need of it; I have walked these passages so many times that I know instinctively where I am going.'

With torches held high so as to provide the maximum effect, they left the soft glow of light behind them and immediately Hamill felt the chill of these lower levels bite into him. Their torches sent flickering shadows dancing around them; it was quite unnerving and Hamill proceeded with more than a little trepidation but took comfort from the presence of the giant. He stuck close to his side.

They traversed cavernous rooms, carved out of the mountain innards, probably by enlarging naturally formed caverns. Each linked by the ever descending tunnels that spiralled their way through the labyrinth of the underground city. From time to time they passed huge statues of colossi standing as silent sentinels, guardians of the rooms that Hamill followed the giant through. They were so lifelike and appeared to move as the flickering torch light played across them. He fancied that they watched him as he passed: this insignificant little being that dared to disturb their slumber. They seemed to be of a great age; many of them bore large cracks, while others had parts of their anatomy missing.

A hand or an arm had fallen to the ground and crumbled, lying amidst the dust that covered the floors at these lower levels. Clearly the colossi had not used this part of the city for many years, perhaps even centuries; he felt like an intruder.

After what seemed like leagues of endless tunnels and rooms

and the use of two firebrands, Hamill heard the sound of running water in the distance; the air started to take on a deeper chill and it was damp.

He realised then, at the sound of the running water, that he needed to pee. He did his best to hold it back; but the more he tried, the more desperate he became. As the sound of the water increased, so did his need to pee. Finally he could bear it no longer.

'You have to wait for a moment. I need to go,' Hamill announced.

'Go where?'

'No; I need to *go*.'

Then seeing the giant did not understand he stopped and propped the torch against the wall of the tunnel, turned his back and started to 'go'.

'Oh!' Holdhard said, as he realised what it was that Hamill had been telling him.

He could not remember the last time it had been such a pleasure to relieve himself. He stood there groaning at the relaxing of his bladder; the sheer joy of feeling the discomfort ebb away was almost indescribable. For a long time he stood there; it seemed like he was never going to stop, but eventually he did.

'That is so much better!' Hamill declared. Picking up the torch, he said, 'Right, I'm ready to go now.'

'But you've just been.'

'No, I don't mean that sort of "go". I mean I'm ready to "go", to move on.'

'Oh! Not much farther now.'

Hamill was glad to hear it; he did not know how much longer he could remain patient with the man of stone and his apparent inability to converse intelligently; besides, he had had enough of walking lately and was keen to get back to the Ward, particularly for the sake of poor Tracker so that he might have the treatment he needed.

Tracker had been asleep all this time, cradled in the sling around the giant's shoulders. Hamill checked him before starting off again to ensure he was OK. His arm had swollen to the shoulder and was an angry red; his pulse was weak and his temperature was up but he was still breathing without any problem. They had to get there soon, before his infection reached his lungs, or they would perhaps be too late to do anything for him.

Striding off down the slope, Hamill found it difficult to keep up with Holdhard but was determined to do so. He had to run so as not to be left behind, calling upon reserves that he never knew he had. No matter, it was vital that they got the dwarf to the elfin doctors as soon as possible, before he slipped further into unconsciousness and perhaps into a coma. It would be difficult for them then to rouse him from such a state.

Hamill liked the dwarves, he decided, and he did not want to lose this one; they were all relying on him, particularly Trapper, to deliver the dwarf safely to the Ward. The dwarves and his folk, the elves, had had their minor differences in the past; but for all that, he liked them. They were rugged, hard working, honest, dependable creatures. They just spoke plainly, that's all, and bore no nonsense; whereas the elves were a more tactful and gentle race.

The sound of the water grew louder and soon it became a deafening roar; the air was full of moisture that soaked him to the skin. Ahead of them the tunnel levelled out slightly and a massive curtain of water, cold, clear and refreshing, blocked their passage.

They had emerged from the tunnel behind a huge waterfall. Hamill tried to shout to the giant that there was no way around it and that they had better turn back.

'You must have taken a wrong turn back there.'

He tried to signal to the giant, but he dismissed his attempts by signalling for Hamill to remain where he was.

Before Hamill knew what was happening, the giant braced himself and leaned over to protect the dwarf, then disappeared through the cascade. The giant was gone for several minutes it seemed before he saw a shadow through the thundering waterfall and Holdhard strode through as if it were nothing more than a washroom shower. He was alone. He had obviously left Tracker the other side of the falls and returned for Hamill.

'If you think I'm going through there, you've got another think coming,' Hamill declared, backing away from the giant. He could not hear him of course and as it was the only way forward, Holdhard scooped him up, braced himself against the flow and stepped into the wall of water. He felt it slam into the giant. No ordinary man could have withstood it, not even Braun. Holdhard shielded Hamill from the rush of powerful water just as he had done for Tracker. The colossus was knee deep in the swirling white foam and before Hamill knew it, he had carried him safely through the torrent, hardly any wetter than before.

Out from under the falls, Hamill squinted against the brightness of the day. He saw a rainbow arched above them as the early morning sunlight caught each tiny drop of water. It split the white light into its separate colours, just as a prism would do.

The sound of the rushing water was not so bad this side of the falls, probably because the sound of the falls would have echoed along the tunnels magnifying its volume. The giant put him down on a grassy bank nearby, where he had laid the wounded dwarf.

His ears rang with the sound of the roaring water that emptied into the pool; cold and clear around the edges but midnight blue at the centre. The river then continued to flow south towards the Ward, leagues away to the south and beyond there through the Yield and eventually to the Great Salt Sea.

He recognized where he was now, this was Rock Falls, he had been here before; who would have guessed that there was a tunnel behind the cascading water that led to the mountain city of the colossi?

'What a thrill,' Hamill thought to himself now that he was safely on solid ground once more. 'I'd do that again.'

He grinned up at the giant who was totally unaffected by the experience, either physically, being made of stone, or emotionally it seemed.

'Thank you, Holdhard. That was neat.'

'Are you happy to continue, or do you require rest?'

'No I'm fine,' Hamill responded, the adrenalin rushing through his body, giving him the energy he needed. 'We had better get Tracker there as quickly as we can. Which way do we need to go?'

Holdhard carefully and gently placed the stricken dwarf into the sling again and headed off without a word.

'Hmm! Something I said, or just not talkative?' Hamill uttered under his breath; the colossi were not great conversationalists, so he put it down to that.

He followed the giant through a copse of fir trees. The scent from the pine cones refreshed him and he breathed deeply of its fragrance; it was a pleasant change to be in the fresh air again. The tunnels were an experience he would never forget, but were musty and dank in the lower levels. The fresh air and the sunshine revived and warmed him, making him feel glad of heart, all but forgetting why he was here and what had brought him to this point. Reality is never far away, however, and he soon came back to earth with a bump as his feet started to play him up. 'Well, nothing for it; I've just got to keep going, I'll worry about my feet later, once we have Tracker safely back at the Ward,' he thought, resigning himself to the task that lay ahead

Before them lay the rolling grasslands of the Plains of Uniah, which stretched away for leagues in all directions before them. To their right were the Northern Steppes and the Hand Lakes, home to the kite-folk. Before them for a hundred miles or more were the plains, moving like an ocean as the gentle breeze wafted across the tall grass. To their left, the River Nune snaked its way through the lowland. Somewhere near the river, hidden by the undulating land, was the Ward and the help that Tracker needed. Hamill guessed that they might get there before nightfall, if they pushed themselves; all they needed to do was follow the river downstream.

What they needed was a boat. Then looking at the stone giant, Hamill reconsidered, thinking that it would take rather a large boat to withstand Holdhard's weight. Besides, there were no boats this far north. Not until you reached Ashbrooke did it become more navigable where the River Nune and the Crystal River joined and became the River Bune. There were too many shallows until then to make it worthwhile. So, it meant walking. He was beginning to get used to it by now, though his feet still hurt from the walk from Foundry Smelt.

Passing through the mountain city of the colossi had saved them a great deal of time and effort; they had avoided having to clamber through the lower gorges of Deadline Crack. It had saved them a lot of time from the route that they had taken to get there. They set off at a goodly pace, Holdhard striding forth, swallowing up the land with his great thudding strides; Hamill had to jog alongside in order to keep up but found it easier on his feet somehow in doing so.

Hamill had his mind firmly fixed on getting the dwarf to the Ward as quickly as possible but he kept in mind what had happened on their journey up from the smelt and remained alert to any sound he might hear that would cause concern; even the panicked flight of a ground bird could be significant. Hamill instructed Holdhard to keep his eyes open for any sign of gnomes. If there were any kite-folk around, then he would hear them before they were spotted and could go to ground. Not that there was much cover in the grasses. They would have to trust to the gods; he crossed his fingers for luck; they needed all the help they could get.

Several times they had to slow their pace in order to let Hamill catch his breath; he worked off a stitch in his side and got into a steady gait that meant he was able to make better progress.

They had a short mid-morning break so that Hamill could tend to Tracker and for him to refresh himself. Stopping again at noon he found that Tracker was starting to become delirious. He mopped the dwarf's brow and placed a cold, moist cloth over his forehead to help bring the temperature down a little; they had to hurry, the poison in his arm was spreading and it would be too late to save him unless they hurried.

Nearing exhaustion, they came in sight of the Ward before the day reached its hottest. Fortunately for them, at this time of the year it did not become uncomfortable, even when at a run, but Hamill's energy was nearly spent; he could not remember the past few leagues and he stumbled from time to time, catching himself and grimacing against the pain that stabbed through the soles of his feet.

They approached the Ward from the north-east on the opposite side to the fortified gate but the lookouts were alert and he heard the alarm being given while they were still some way off. He could make out a flurry of activity on the towers followed by raised voices. The guard began to panic as they realised that the person approaching was of considerable size compared to the one running alongside.

A squad of soldiers bearing crossbows lined the rear stockade, ready to repel any hostile act; even at this distance, Hamill could see that they were rather nervous about the approaching figures. He waved to them as they drew nearer but did not have the ability to shout out, being too out of breath. He could make out a little of what was being relayed by the soldiers to others in the stockade. He could not help but wear a mighty grin when he heard his name called.

'Hamill, is that you? What on earth is going on?'

He signalled for them to open the gates; they ran straight past the amazed sentries, who stood open-mouthed at the sight of the stone giant. The guard backed away, unsure whether they should challenge him or not. None of them had seen a colossus before and were dumbfounded at the sight of one striding right into the Ward. There were stories from a thousand years ago of giant men of stone but they had become folklore and were considered the workings of a fanciful mind. Very few of the elves believed the stories any more. Cries of amazement and gasps of awe came from the gathering crowd, though they kept a respectable distance from the giant.

Hamill and Holdhard stopped within the outer courtyard and several attendants rushed forward; cautiously, they took the dwarf from the giant and hurried him away to receive attention. Hamill managed to convey to them that the dwarf had been bitten by a wolvet and been infected with some sort of venom, before everything went blank and he collapsed in a heap at the feet of the giant.

When he awoke, he found himself in a soft, cosy cot in one of the attendance rooms; his feet tingled and he was aware of them being bandaged; the bedding was kept off his legs by a support cage. He drifted off into a blissful sleep and dreamed of giants and dwarves.

When he awoke again sunlight streamed through the open window and birds chirped in the branches of the trees in the orchard. He caught the aroma of freshly cooked bacon and immediately his stomach rumbled.

'Oh, you're awake are you? There's someone who wants to see you.'

The orderly had come in to check on him and opened the window to let in the fresh air.

'You just sit tight and I'll have her bring you in a nice breakfast. How does that sound?'

'That sounds great,' he croaked in reply.

Minutes later there came a knock at the door.

'Come in.'

The door opened and in came Anna, beaming with delight, carrying a tray with his breakfast.

'Hello, Anna. How are you? I see that you no longer have your arm in a sling. Is it feeling better?'

She nodded and placed the tray on a table across his cot, then proceeded to help raise him up into a sitting position and propped him in place with a few pillows.

She took out a pencil and a writing pad and wrote asking him to tell her everything that had happened; especially about the stone giant who was standing, still as a statue, in the courtyard.

'Is he still here?' Hamill asked in surprise.

Yes, she nodded.

'Tracker; how's Tracker? Did we get him here in time? Is he going to be OK?' He fired off a string of questions and started to become agitated until Anna soothed him and nodded with a smile.

She wrote on a piece of paper and showed it to him.

Yes, he is going to be fine; you got him here just in time. Another day and they say he might not have made it; you are quite the hero of the day.

Hamill relaxed back against the pillows and sighed with relief then smiled contentedly at the thought of him being a hero.

She allowed him time to eat his food and waited patiently to hear his story. In the meantime she wrote the occasional question that he could nod or shake his head to; such as, *Is Jon OK?* and *Were any of the others hurt?*

Having completed his breakfast, he settled back and pretended to go to sleep; she pounced on him and beat him playfully on the chest to which he feigned injury and laughed.

'OK, OK, I surrender. I'll tell you what happened.'

He proceeded to tell her every detail about their experience and of their good fortune in having the colossi appear when they did. He finished by recounting his long and arduous journey back here with the colossus. Not that he embellished any of it at all; well, maybe a little.

She gave him a peck on the cheek and mimed that he should get some more sleep; before tucking him in and taking the tray. He did not even hear the door open; he was asleep before she got to it. He slept right through the rest of the day. Anna popped in on him occasionally to see how he was doing, careful not to

188

disturb him. They had administered a sleep inducing herb so that his body would have the rest it needed. He had pushed himself to the limit, far and above the normal call of duty, in order to save the dwarf. He was indeed a hero.

The days passed, during which time Tracker slowly recovered. They placed him in a private room, under constant supervision, the physicians and attendants working day and night to rescue him from death. His condition was so serious that they feared the worst and worked a system of four healers, each one taking a watch of six hours at a time to tend to him. They feared that he might not pull through or that they may need to remove his arm if the spread of the poison continued. The master herbalist applied a poultice that drew much of the venom from the wound but it was necessary to apply leeches to the upper arm to purify the blood. Such was the potency of the poison within the blood that the leeches became bloated with it and quickly succumbed, falling from his arm. More were applied, constantly being replaced until the time when they ceased to be affected by the bad blood. They had done their job and the poison extracted. He was out of danger. Shortly thereafter, his arm began to lose the angry red swelling and returned to normal. White scars ran along his forearm bearing testament to his close brush with death but, with his fever subdued and the delirium calmed, he was able to rest peacefully for the first time in days.

It was the afternoon of the sixth day since Hamill had set off from the mountain city with Holdhard and Tracker; he and Anna were visiting with the dwarf when a shout of alarm went out from the sentry on the tower.
  'Travellers are approaching. I think it's the dwarves: the ones who were here with Hamill before.'
  They rushed out into the courtyard where Holdhard stood, rooted to the ground. He had not moved during all this time. Hamill supposed that for someone who lived for a thousand years, a few days would appear as just a moment in time.
  'Where are they?' Hamill shouted up to the sentry.
  'They're coming from the east.'
  The guard pointed in the direction of the river.
  'How many do you see?'

'Four: three of them are dwarves and the other a man.'

Anna rushed ahead of Hamill and climbed the ladder to the lookout, straining her eyes to see. There was nothing; just the rolling of the grasses like the waves of the sea and the River Nune at the base of the mountain backdrop. Desperate to know about Jon, she clapped her hands to attract the sentry's attention and signalled for him to point out to her where they were.

She looked again in the direction he pointed and saw them appear over a rise in the ground several hundred lengths away. She jumped up and down with excitement, hugging Hamill and waving towards the approaching group; Jon waved back and started to run the rest of the way. If she could have screamed with delight, she would have done so and rushed down to greet him at the gate. She flung herself into his outstretched arms, nearly knocking him over, planting a kiss firmly on his lips.

He responded and held her there for some moments until a cough from Hamill reminded him where he was. Shyly, he placed Anna back onto her feet and reached to shake Hamill's hand. Jon and the dwarves looked as though they had seen hard times and were weary from their journey.

'Welcome back, Jon, Javelin.' Hamill nodded and smiled a greeting to the other dwarves.

'It's good to see you all. Where are Urim and Braun?' he asked, confused that they were not all together.

'Good to see you two as well; it's good to be here. I didn't think we were going to make it at one point,' Jon responded. Then looking concerned, he added more seriously, 'I don't know where they are; we separated and agreed to meet back here. He went to Crystal Falls to see the Sprite Queen. We had hoped that they would be here already; I take it that they are not?'

'No. We haven't heard from them or seen them since I left you to bring Tracker here. What's happened?'

'I'll tell you all I know over a hot meal and a mug of chicory. In the meantime, I need a nice hot bath,' he said as he sniffed at his clothes.

Anna nodded in agreement and held her nose in mock disgust then laughed her silent laugh, but she ushered him towards the washroom nonetheless.

Trapper was keen to know how his brother was faring and was

much relieved at the news that he was doing well, wishing to visit with him as soon as possible.

They sat together at dinner, the three of them, enjoying each other's company. The dwarves had excused themselves, following their meal, having refreshed themselves with a bath and change of clothes. They all wanted to visit with Tracker, so they hurried off in the direction of the infirmary; he had been moved there from the private room they had kept him in until he was out of danger.

Jon brought Anna and Hamill up to speed with his experiences, telling them of the loss of Mason in the flood, then asked to hear of Hamill's journey back. He reciprocated by telling Jon what he had done and of his being hailed a hero.

'Imagine that, me a hero,' he chuckled, feeling quite proud of what he had done.

'From what Anna and the others have informed me, it is quite true. I believe you *are* a hero. It is well deserved. Enjoy it.'

Secretly he was, but not in a big-headed way, at least he thought not.

Another day went past and still there was no sign of Urim or Braun. The routine of the Ward continued as a new arrival caused a bit of a stir for a while. A herder, badly gored by one of the bulls on his farmstead he had been trying to tether. They made him comfortable and fortunately for him he was not in any danger.

What was of interest though was his telling of a large section of his herd going missing and stories of strange creatures moving around the countryside. He assumed that his animals had been killed by these creatures for food; the poor bull was still very nervous and this is probably why he had gored him; it was spooked by the scent of something. The herder knew something was amiss because he saw the look of terror in the animal's eyes but could not get out of the way and avoid the incident. Whatever it was that lay behind the disappearance of the cattle, must remain a mystery for now, but they drew their own conclusions and exchanged knowing looks with each other.

Later into the evening the alarm sounded again, followed by

shouting and the scurrying of the guards to their positions. They established very quickly that there was no need for alarm; Captain Quentin recognised the approaching figures and gave the order to stand down. 'Well hello, seer, metal master. We wondered what had happened to you. Open the gates.'

Word reached the dwarves, Hamill, Jon and Anna, and they gathered in the assembly hall, adjacent to the food hall, where Urim announced, 'We must go to the First city, Northill, before it is too late; Ebon gathers his armies to make war on the people of the Yield; the people of Southill may already be lost. I only hope to heaven that they managed to make their escape through the passages in time. They need all the help they can get so I have requested of Captain Quentin that a contingent of elves, with their crossbows, be sent to their aid. He has agreed to send help and they will be leaving in a couple of days. Being fleet of foot, they should get there in about five days from now; it will take us nearly a week, so we should get there at about the same time if we leave immediately. Braun, we must request the assistance of the colossi, speak with Holdhard. Ask him to go back to Bearer and have them meet us at Northill. Better still, go with him; make sure that they come. Without them, the course of history could go either way; all being well we will meet with you there.'

Urim crossed his fingers in the traditional way to ward off bad luck, so did Jon.

Chapter XIII

Tri-Bune

They had been travelling for five days, avoiding contact with anyone else in the hope that Ebon would not be forewarned of their presence. He would know that Urim would not simply give up and go away so he would have sent his spies to search for them; this meant that they had to walk. If they had used the waterway of the River Bune from Ashbrooke, they would most certainly have been spotted and possibly been attacked. It also meant delaying their arrival at Northill but Urim reckoned that it was better to get there late than not at all.

Tracker and Trapper had been posted as advance scouts to ensure the way ahead was clear and safe to proceed. Cautiously, but with the best speed they could, they made their way south to the Yield, to the First city of the land and the centre of government for humans. Hoping against hope that they would get there before it was too late. Urim was confident that the defences of the city would withstand a prolonged attempt to breach them. He only hoped that as many as possible from Southill were able to escape to Northill, or some of the outlying villages. The seer was driven relentlessly by his desire to stop Ebon from succeeding in his purpose; what else Urim had in mind remained to be seen; Jon suspected that there was more to this than met the eye. Whatever it was, it remained as yet unknown. If Urim were to be true to form, only when it occurred would they know the reason.

The first three days out from the Ward, the group of travellers managed to make good headway. There was very little in the way of cover, other than the occasional spinney of woodland, though Urim said that it was unlikely that they were to encounter any problems until they got further south; still the dwarves were vigilant. Hamill too kept his ears open for any sound of approaching trouble.

It was towards the end of the third day that they had approached Ashbrooke. Jon and Anna would have loved to have visited their homes there and it had been tempting to them all to have rested overnight under a proper roof, instead of camping out. It was a long way to Northill and a long time before they could enjoy decent lodgings again. However, Urim had insisted that they must remain invisible to the eyes of the petulant seer and his spies, or they might fail in their task. One of the places Ebon expected them to turn up was at Jon's home; it would most certainly be watched, so they must avoid it, despite the comforts they were sacrificing.

It seemed that wherever Ebon went, Urim was bent on following. That night, when Jon had first met Urim in the forest and had warned him of Ebon's intention to kill him, saving his life; then he, with Jon and Anna, had gone to Foundry Smelt because Urim had said that was where Ebon would be; then the trek up to the Ward, where it turned out that Ebon had been just days before. Their discovery of the colossi at Deadline Crack, followed by Urim's quest to follow in Ebon's footsteps again by seeking out the Sprite Queen at Crystal Falls. Now they had set off after him again and were approaching Rainbow Lake and the Second city of the Yield, Tri-Bune, before heading on down to the First city of the Yield, Northill, where Urim said Ebon would be found.

He had known that Ebon and his army were bent on besieging Northill because the Sprite Queen had informed Urim that it was his intention to do so; she had relieved Ebon of the crystal he had stolen from one of the seers prior to his incarcerating them in the Tower. He had no ability to use the crystal himself and had planned to trick the Queen into revealing its power so that he could utilise it, along with all of the other seers' talismans for his own ends. He had thrown himself into a fury at her refusal to help him and at losing the crystal, but against her and the sprites he knew he could do nothing; for they are ethereal and live on the very edge of existence, between two worlds.

Urim had not disclosed what had transpired between him and the Queen there at Crystal Falls, the home of the sprites, to anyone else. He had taken Jon aside and in confidence told him that when all of this was over and the seers released, the crystal would be returned to its rightful owner. Until then it was to remain in the custody of the sprites. In anyone else's hands it was

194

simply another crystal, a piece of polished glass; but it was a powerful tool and could lead to great turmoil in the land if it were to fall into the wrong hands. Better to leave it with the Queen than risk tapping into its powers.

Urim was concerned for their well-being.

'So far things have turned out well for us but we enter a different stage of the game, the stakes have been upped and we must proceed with speed and caution. It will be difficult to maintain the balance but I believe we can succeed. We have been able to remove two of the talismans from Ebon's grasp – the scroll and the crystal – but there are another six that we must obtain if we are to deny him of any advantage over us.'

Back at the Ward, when asked by the others what had happened, Urim said firmly that he did not intend to say at this time. Always secretive and keeping his own counsel, Urim would not be drawn any further on what had transpired between him and the Sprite Queen. It was almost as if he was protecting them from something unpleasant or he was just being uncommunicative, as was his way at times.

They had asked Braun what had happened, before he set off with Holdhard back to the mountain city of the colossi, but he could shed no light on the matter as he had not been privy to the meeting. He had told them of the marvels he had seen and his eyes misted over as he went into an inward stare, reliving what he had witnessed and so many others were unable to.

All he said was that Urim had emerged from the meeting with a grave determination etched onto his countenance. What Urim had told him was that he now knew what Ebon intended to do and that they must stop him at Northill, or the Yield, and all lands known to them, would fall into a dark age of servitude and suffering.

Jon reflected on what Braun had told them of the sprite world and tried imagining what it would be like to be there; of the peace and tranquillity that existed just outside of their own world, protected for all time by the powers of the Sprite Queen. He also thought many times on what Urim had said as he lay at night, trying to sleep. Each time he closed his eyes he imagined all manner of troubles upon this land and people. The consequences of failure on their part, to stop Ebon, were too horrific to contemplate.

195

He stole a glance at Anna; he was glad she was with them again. He would have worried about her and he had missed her when they had gone to the dwarves' capital city; she would have loved seeing Ffridd-Uch-Ddu with its colourful markets and bustling streets. He was glad that she had stayed at the Ward though as they had been through some rough times; he felt relieved that she had not had to experience the flood in the caves and the loss of Mason. That hurt him almost as much as losing his mother; he had built such a bond with the dwarf even though he had known him for such a short time. He hoped and wished for Anna's safety in the coming days and weeks; he could not bear the thought of anything happening to her; that would be too much to bear.

This night as he lay staring up at the stars, he realised that his feelings for her had grown beyond those of a friend. A tear fell down his cheek as he looked at her face lying next to him, soft and delicate in the silver light of the moon.

Tomorrow, Tracker had told him, they would be within sight of the Second city of the Yield: Tri-Bune. So named because it is where the River Bune divides into three before entering Rainbow Lake, the largest body of fresh water in the land, renowned for the quality of fish found there, particularly the rainbow trout. Jon had never been there but had heard a lot about it from the traders who travelled all over the land. Their tales of far off lands and distant places had intrigued him; he had often dreamed of travelling himself but had never thought that he would be doing it in such a way as this. He went to sleep with conflicting images in his mind: of the sprite world, of the mysteries of the land and its peoples and of the threat that hung over them all now, thanks to the ambitions of the power hungry seer, Ebon.

The morning chorus roused them from their slumber; the air felt crisp and a chill encouraged them to greater speed in getting ready for the day. Autumn was encroaching throughout the land, bringing with it the beauty of so many variations of colour. The leaves on the trees had turned from their different shades of green into the splendours of glorious reds, browns and yellows.

This part of the journey afforded them more cover than before as the Plains of Uniah, above Ashbrooke, gave way to the Yield. It was the breadbasket of the land, dotted with farms and their fields of grains separated one from another by stretches of wood-land. It was through such a wood that they now made their way.

They approached the edge of the wood with care; they had been using it as cover while they travelled. Tracker and Trapper had returned from scouting ahead and were talking with Javelin and Urim in an animated fashion, pointing the way towards the city of Tri-Bune. Jon saw Urim hold his hand to his head and his shoulders drop. It was clearly not good news that they had brought to him.

He turned to look in their direction and slowly approached with measured steps, looking at the ground. He stopped just a few paces in front of them, leaning wearily on his staff and with a heavy sigh he said, with much sorrow in his voice, 'I am afraid we are too late for the people of Tri-Bune. The army of gnomes we saw has besieged the town and razed it to the ground.'

They were stunned. Anna started to cry. Tears welled up in her eyes as the impact of what Urim had just said hit home. Jon felt the blood drain from his face in shock and stood open-mouthed for a moment before finding his voice.

'What, the whole city? Surely you mean just a part of it? What about the people? There were thousands of people living in Tri-Bune; what of them?'

Urim was silent for a while, chewing his lower lip.

'Tracker has been able to find some signs of activity following the unprovoked attack, for such it was, but cannot tell how many survived. The damage to the ground with the passing of such a large body of gnomes makes it difficult to say for certain how many escaped.'

'Why, Urim? Why would they do this?' Hamill asked, incredulous that there could be such wanton destruction of life.

'I believe it is to serve as a message to the rest of our peoples. Ebon means to rule, at any cost, and will tolerate no opposition; he probably allowed people to escape so that they would tell others what happened and instil fear into their hearts.'

Urim became angry, the first time Jon had seen him really angry; he did not shout or stomp around, he bridled his anger, but it was plain for all to see how he felt.

'I will bring him down, I swear by all that is sacred, I will bring him down.'

197

They stopped in the woods for a few minutes, gathering their composure, waiting for Urim to tell them what to do next. They all looked to him as leader and respected his decisions. They had not always done so; some of his actions had been questionable and caused unease, but he had always been right. He was not called to be a seer without reason; Jon was learning a lot about how they worked. Although Urim may have known certain things about the future, he did not always know the exact outcome. What they did here and now, each day, could alter what happened tomorrow. It seemed that Urim could only second guess, at best. Urim gathered them together and said softly:

'I had not intended for us to pass close to the city. However, I believe that it would be better for everyone here to see what has happened, so that we may bear witness to the tragedy that has occurred.'

Javelin nodded gravely in agreement, saying, 'In a way, it will be like paying our respects to those who have died so needlessly.'

They left the cover of the trees and silently made their way towards the banks of Rainbow Lake and the Second city; all thoughts were on what would meet their eyes. Ahead of them, the sky was filled with circling birds: black ravens, cawing loudly.

They skirted a notable rise in the land known as Clee Hill that lay between them and the city of Tri-Bune; nothing could have prepared them for the shock: where once had stood a thriving, vibrant city that covered many square leagues, what sprawled before them was desolation. Wisps of smoke drifted lazily from charred and blackened ruins that had once been the dwellings, shops and schools of the citizens of Tri-Bune. It was as if a fireball had engulfed the city from end to end, leaving nothing but the ghost of what had once been a proud and industrious place. The only building still standing was the garrison and that was badly damaged; what had happened to the soldiers and where they were now was anybody's guess, for there was no sign of life other than the raucous birds. The stench of the place filled their nostrils; the birds would swoop down into the ruins whilst others climbed up into the sky to circle again in search of food. That food, they guessed, was the bodies of the dead and it was this that assailed their senses causing them to gag.

The land all around, as far as the eye could see, had been

ravaged and trampled underfoot by those who had no conscience for what they did. Where the gnome army had been encamped about the city, they had left the trappings of warfare that were no longer needed or usable. Outside of where the city gates lay in ruins, Jon saw a large blackened pit. Tracker saw him looking puzzled and explained that it was where the gnomes had cremated their dead.

Suddenly Hamill whirled around and looked up into the sky behind them, shielding his eyes with his hand.

'Kite-folk, I didn't hear them until now because of the noise the birds were making.'

They all turned to look in the direction that Hamill indicated and saw two kite-folk coming in from the south-west; there was nowhere for them to run, other than back into the wood, but the woods were too far away and the kite-folk had probably seen them already. Sure enough they had and were making towards them to investigate; no doubt wanting to discover whether they were the ones that Ebon desired news about.

'What shall we do, Urim?' Javelin asked, waiting to put into action whatever the seer suggested.

'Everyone gather together, quickly. They will need to get closer in order to see who we are.'

'I thought that was what we didn't want them to do,' Hamill queried but he complied anyway.

'I think I know what you want, Urim. Together like this, it is difficult to tell who we are so they will need to come closer in order to identify that we are the ones they are seeking. You want to draw them closer so that we can despatch them and prevent them from reporting our whereabouts to Ebon.'

Archer had second guessed what the seer intended

'Exactly; Archer, are you able to down one of them with an arrow when I give the word?'

'If they get close enough, yes; but if I miss I may not get another chance.'

'Better not miss,' Javelin said over his shoulder to Archer and winked mischievously.

'If this works and they do come closer, you take the one on the right and I'll take the one on the left, understood?' said Urim.

Archer nodded and made himself ready, notching an arrow in

his bowstring but keeping his bow hidden from sight so as not to alarm the kite-folk. They had keen sight, but Urim's plan might just bring them close enough so that they could bring them down.

'Archer, tell me when you think they are close enough for you to be sure of hitting your one then wait until I say "now" before you let loose your arrow; the rest of you hit the ground to give us a free shot.'

The kite-folk wavered, holding back and chattering to each other before coming closer; they were obviously wary, but if Urim was right and they were sent by Ebon to spy out the land in search for them, they would want to be certain. They hovered now, about fifty paces away. Their chattering could clearly be heard in the quiet that had descended on them all; the ravens had left the sky empty over Tri-Bune at the arrival of the kite-folk.

'Come on, just a little closer, just a little closer,' Urim urged quietly under his breath.

'I think I can get him from here, Urim,' Archer whispered.

'Very well then, Archer, NOW.'

The others all threw themselves on the ground while Urim pointed his staff towards one of them sending a blue ball of power sizzling through the air. Archer let loose his arrow, catching his target in the chest whereupon it fell to the ground landing with a thud. All that remained of the one that Urim had targeted was a puff of smoke and some grey ashes that fell to the ground like snow.

Tracker and Trapper sprang upon the downed creature, taking no chances that it had survived and wanting to get some information if it were still alive.

As the others approached, Trapper turned to Archer saying, 'Well, I guess we can confirm that you didn't miss. He's dead; your arrow went clean through his heart.'

'Wow, that was some shot.'

Hamill looked in amazement at Archer, who stood leaning nonchalantly on his bow as if it were nothing at all.

'Well done indeed.'

Urim and the others applauded in praise of his skill.

'Oh, I've seen him do better,' Javelin teased Archer, giving him a slap on the back and smiled at Archer's feigned look of hurt pride.

'We must hurry on; where these creatures fly, gnomes are not far behind them,' Trapper urged and encouraged them to make haste.

They quickly shouldered their packs and made towards the next grove of trees, wanting to make the most of any cover that was available to them. They had no time to spare to bury the body so left it where it lay for the ravens to pick clean, just as the gnomes had done to the people of Tri-Bune. They felt bad about not giving it a decent burial; every creature, no matter what they were, deserved to be buried and not left like some discarded item of rubbish; but they could not afford the delay.

Setting their backs to the ruins of Tri-Bune, they hastened away, heading parallel with the banks of the lake on their left. Tracker told them that they should reach Northill by mid-afternoon, provided there were no further delays and they hurried.

As if he had tempted fate and just as Tracker was about to take up his scouting position, Hamill stood still, lending his ear to the wind.

'What's the matter, Hamill?' Jon asked as he saw him respond to something he had heard.

'Shush; I thought I heard something from up ahead. It sounded like people running. There it is,' Hamill said; his face drained of colour and he looked as if he would break out into a run at any second.

'Gnomes; and they're coming this way.'

'The kite-folk must have alerted them to our presence before we dealt with them,' Urim said, half to himself. 'We must get under cover quickly before we are discovered.'

'Let's make for the wood,' Javelin urged and they started to run.

'No, wait,' yelled Urim as he slowed to a walk and then stopped, causing the rest of them to halt in their rush towards the woods. Urim looked puzzled and chewed at his lower lip.

'This does not feel right; we must go back.'

'What? Are you sure about this?' they queried as if on cue.

'Yes. We must go back; back to Clee Hill. We will have the advantage of height and there is cover in the clump of trees at the top; I am certain that is where we must be. Quickly, back the way we have come.'

They were not entirely convinced, but followed him anyway.

The chances of them being discovered seemed less by heading for the woods than being slowed down by climbing the hill in full view; it all depended on how close the gnomes were.

They made a dash for it. Hamill was by far the fastest and could have left them standing, but he stayed with them and encouraged Jon and Anna on. Huffing and puffing with the exertion of the climb up the grassy slope, they managed to make it to the wooded summit with barely a minute to spare before the gnomes came into site. There were about thirty of them travelling at a run, using the track along the lakeside with the woods on their left that were to have been the refuge of the little band of travellers.

They watched and waited as the gnomes drew closer to where they had been just minutes before. Were they coming in response to the kite-folk having somehow alerted them to their presence? Would they see the fallen creature?

Then they saw a kite-folk appear over the top of the trees in which they would have taken cover. Had Urim not insisted they come here to Clee Hill they may well have been spotted by it. There had obviously been three of them; this one must have flown off to alert the gnomes of the group of travellers before being identified by the other two as the ones Ebon was seeking.

It spotted its fallen comrade and shrieked out to the gnomes who headed in the direction of the furious creature. It landed next to the body then sent out a wailing shriek that carried to them on the hill half a league away. It jumped up into the air, gaining height quickly with powerful beats of its wings. It searched with keen eyes for any sign of the perpetrators but found nothing. Then it hovered over a point at the foot of the hill and sent out a call that had the gnomes charging towards them.

When they reached the place that the creature indicated to them they searched the ground, looking for what it had seen. One of the gnomes suddenly let out a cry of triumph and held up something in his hand; it glinted in the sunlight.

'Did any of us drop anything as we ran?' Urim questioned, searching himself for anything that might have come from him.

Hamill voiced quietly, 'Oh, oh. I think a buckle came off my boot; sorry.'

'No matter, it could have been any of us. It's just bad luck that's all.'

Urim crossed his fingers to ward off any more, almost at the same time that Jon did. Urim looked at him and smiled.

'Old habits die hard it seems.'

The gnomes were searching the ground for any further signs and very quickly one of them, probably Tracker's counterpart, found traces of their passage through the grass and pointed up the hill to where they were concealed.

'I think we may be in for a battle,' remarked Javelin, clasping one of his spears.

'I believe you are right, my friend. What do you suggest?' Urim knew that Javelin and the other dwarves were better suited to call the shots in this instance.

'We wait and see. What they will probably do is send a couple of scouts up the hill to ascertain whether we are still here. They will also send some of their number around the hill to approach us from different directions so dividing our forces. There will also be some kind of diversionary tactic but, as you said earlier, we have the advantage of height. What I would dearly like to do, is get rid of the threat of that kite-folk. We can't afford to let it fly off for reinforcements,' Javelin explained quickly, then, turning to Archer, asked, 'Is there any chance of you getting in a shot at it?'

'Not really,' Archer said, looking out of the trees that as well as giving them cover, also shielded the creature from his arrows.

'Nevertheless, keep a watchful eye on it; the moment you have a clear shot, take it, no matter what. It is a greater threat to us than these gnomes, we can handle them but that "thing" up there is another matter.'

Javelin jerked his head in the creature's direction.

They dared not move about too much or the gnomes would see them, though that was academic now really. They knew they were up there in the woods, the tracks told them that; it was just that they did not want the gnomes to know their exact location because they would know where to launch their attack; the longer they could remain concealed, the better. The kite-folk flew overhead searching through gaps in the treetops for any sign of them. That was its undoing; Archer had been tracking its movements constantly and needed only a window of opportunity to make his move. Several times he made to release his arrow only to hold back as the creature disappeared from view, obscured by the canopy of the trees; then he had an idea.

He told Trapper to make some movements near the edge of a small clearing in the woods where a mighty tree had fallen and smaller ones were competing for the space. What he wanted was to draw the creature's attention to where he could get off a clean shot. It worked: for a small moment it became exposed and that was all the chance that Archer needed.

Thwack! Without any hesitation he unloosed his deadly missile; as with the other one earlier, the arrow embedded itself into its chest and it fell from the sky like a stone, landing in a tangle of branches overhead.

The gnomes had no doubts now as to their position, but that was a small price to pay for getting rid of the threat of the kite-folk. A shout of fury went up from the gnomes as they saw what happened and several of them rushed up the slope towards them brandishing their weapons and carrying shields in front of them.

Javelin warned. 'Watch out, this is their diversionary tactic; let them come into the woods, we'll stand a better chance against them here. Jon, keep an eye on what the other gnomes do whilst we deal with these.'

The six gnomes, who had launched themselves up the hill, came on yelling and creating all manner of noise to distract them from seeing what was going on below. It did put fear into Jon's heart and momentarily he was distracted but remembered Javelin's command and kept watching the others.

Sure enough, just as the oncoming gnomes reached the edge of the trees, at the moment of greatest distraction, two groups of gnomes ran around the foot of the hill. They split in either direction, leaving about a dozen of them waiting below for the move to be completed before they would make their frontal assault. They were trying for a pincer movement.

True to his word, Javelin and the other dwarves were dealing with the ones attacking them now. With a precision that was chilling to watch they were despatched before they had come ten paces into the trees.

Javelin's spear took the leading gnome off his feet as he drove it right through his shield and into his gut. As he leant his whole strength against the struggling gnome he pinned him to the ground like a stuck pig. Whipping his short sword from its scabbard, he ran at another, rolling on to the ground in front of him, under his shield, and thrust his sword up between the legs of the unfortunate creature before he could have time to react; he crumpled in a heap.

In the time Javelin had taken to deal with these two, Archer had used a similar approach and sent an arrow at close quarters through his opponent's shield. It penetrated his leather body armour and sent him stumbling against a tree where Urim finished him off by driving a knife up through his throat, into his brain. Turning to Jon he quickly said, 'Remember, Jon; that is how to deal with a gnome. Show them no quarter because they will show you none.'

Archer then dealt quickly with his next victim by dodging to the side of a thrusting sword that would have impaled a slower person and swinging his own short sword around onto the back of the neck of the gnome as he fell forward having missed his target. He did not move again. Tracker and Trapper clothes-lined another, Tracker stopping to finish him off with a stab through the heart while Trapper sparred with the last one who was a little more adept than the others had been. Lunging at the gnome with his sword in his right hand, the gnome went to defend himself but Trapper switched his sword to his left hand at the last moment and drove it into the surprised gnome; he cursed the dwarf with his dying breath and collapsed onto the ground.

It was all over before it had had time to start; Jon marvelled at the dexterity and prowess displayed by the dwarves and he was glad that they were on his side.

'What happened to the gnomes, Jon, while we were dealing with these?' Javelin asked animatedly.

'They split into three groups, one remaining there at the bottom, the other two separating either side.'

'Well done, lad; did you notice how many separated from the main body?'

'Yes, six went that way and another six went the other way round the hill.' Jon indicated their directions.

'Excellent, good job; what we need to do now is pray for a miracle. If they catch us all at the same time, we don't stand much hope of escaping without casualties. What do you say, Urim?'

'I am afraid I agree. It may be that the best chance we have is to take the battle to them; that way we can deal with one group at a time and perhaps catch them off guard, they probably will not expect it.'

Anna produced a sling from her pack, having picked up some pebbles from the ground while the others had been discussing what to do. She signed furiously to Jon that she could help in the affray; she was a good shot and might be able to put one or two of them off.

'Fine idea, we need all the help we can get.'

Javelin then issued orders to the others.

'We will take the lead followed by Jon, Hamill and Anna; you will cover our rear, Urim, if you are in agreement.'

'Absolutely; I can keep a watchful eye on these three at the same time,' Urim added with a wry smile to Jon.

'I would use more thunderflashes except I don't think they would do much to harm these characters. What I will do is use my staff, though I hesitate to use it too much for it will eventually run out of power; I need to recharge from time to time in Seers' Tower, but that is unavailable at present.'

'Understood; use it only if you have to, we may have more pressing need for it later. Now, if everyone is ready we had better get on with it, any further delay could be costly.'

Javelin organised them with instructions as to when to break cover and to go when he gave the command.

'On my command, go.'

The dwarves burst from cover and all but flew down the grassy slope catching the gnomes by surprise, but they soon recovered; they were well trained and experienced fighters. This was a huge gamble they were taking and the dwarves were outnumbered three to one.

The gnomes organised themselves quickly by placing their shields in front of them, creating a wall through which they put their swords. It seemed that the dwarves would run headlong onto the blades but they split either side of the wall and went around the edges, catching the end gnomes as they sped past. Two down, ten to go. They dodged from side to side, managing to evade the attempts to cut them down and circled round again coming in on their rear. Jon, Hamill and Anna just kept on running, following the dwarves, stopping when the dwarves wheeled back into the attack. The gnomes were being assailed from front and rear because by this time Urim was charging like a madman, waving his arms and yelling for all he was worth.

Some of the gnomes became spooked and broke ranks, leaving only a handful of steadfast troops to face the oncoming seer. He bulldozed his way into them, scattering them like ninepins, wielding his staff around him like a whirlwind, catching anything that came within reach.

Anna unleashed a steady hail of pebbles at the gnomes and knocked two of them senseless, distracting others and keeping the dwarves from being harmed. They had teamed up into pairs the better to tackle the gnomes in their disarray, hacking them down in quick fashion until only two of the twelve gnomes remained alive; they fled to join up with the others who would soon be upon them seeking revenge for their being fooled and for the death of their comrades. Javelin had said that they needed a miracle; apparently they had received one for none of them had received serious injury. Yet they had caused the demise of a total of sixteen gnomes. Archer had been caught on the leg by a frantic sweep of a gnomish blade and Urim had a cut on the back of his hand. He was not sure how that had happened; otherwise all was well, other than being short of breath after their exertions.

Hamill speedily dressed Archer's leg and dabbed at Urim's hand.

'It's just a scratch, nothing to worry about. Keep this pressed against your hand for a while; it will stop the bleeding soon.'

'Is everyone all right?' Javelin asked, checking everyone to see that there were no further injuries.

He turned to Anna and bowed.

'Thank you, young Anna; we owe you a debt of gratitude for your assistance. I fear we would not have come out of this so well had it not been for your sling and shot.'

The other dwarves bowed towards her, causing her to blush with embarrassment, which deepened when Jon, Hamill and Urim also effused in their praise for her.

Before anything further could be said, Hamill warned of the approach of the other gnomes, who had been alerted to the situation by the two who had escaped along with the noise of the skirmish. They came at a run from both sides of the hill. This time there would be no taking them by surprise, they were ready for a scrap and it would not be a pleasant one.

'What do you suggest we do now? Stand and fight it out or beat a retreat to the woods behind us and try something different?'

Javelin looked to Urim for any kind of idea that would help save them from more serious injury or perhaps, death.

Weighing up the situation, Urim looked to Jon for ideas.

'What say you, Jon? What do you think we should do?'

Surprised to be asked for his opinion again and at such a dangerous time he simply said, 'I don't know what anyone else thinks, but I'd rather not wait to be cut down out here in the open. I think we ought to try for the woods so that we can use their cover to divide them up and possibly get some of them with Archer's arrows and Anna's sling before they get to us.'

He gulped nervously wanting to flee the field and escape what seemed inevitable. He would rather not see the dwarves cut down or have Anna or Hamill harmed in any way. Urim, he thought, was quite capable of saving himself if need be; perhaps he could make them all appear to vanish from their sight by using his powers. Whatever happened they needed to act fast as the gnomes were closing on them.

'Right then, to the woods as quickly as we can, we stand a better chance there than here,' Urim said as he led the way followed by Jon, Anna and Hamill with the dwarves acting as a rearguard. It was a long way to the woods but they managed to keep ahead of the incensed gnomes who, having seen what had happened to their comrades, were determined to wreak revenge.

They managed to reach the woods but had no time to discuss tactics as the gnomes were hot on their heels. Urim turned to face the gnomes and threw a thunderflash at them over the heads of the dwarves; it burst into incandescence and boomed out across the lake. It stopped them in their tracks, blinded by the light, and had them stumbling around in confusion for a moment. It gave the dwarves time to regroup and for Archer to send three of the gnomes crashing to the earth to rise no more; Anna too had sent a couple of well aimed stones and accounted for one more of the gnomes, hitting him full on the forehead, burying itself into his skull. The other one she hit would have a nasty headache when he regained consciousness, his helmet having saved him from more serious injury.

The gnomes regrouped quickly and formed together behind

their protective shield wall then began to advance on them, intent on the kill; it was because they were so intent on getting at the dwarves that they failed to observe what was happening behind them. All that the beleaguered group saw was the shield wall collapse in front of them like a wave that crashes onto the seashore; none of the gnomes moved for each one of them had two or three bolts from a crossbow in his back.

It was only then that the exhausted group saw the phalanx of elves in battle formation that had arrived from the Ward; the elves had seen what the situation was and despatched the attacking gnomes before they could reach them.

The little group sank to the ground in utter relief, smiling and waving to the elves that had appeared just in the nick of time; having despatched the gnomes, the elves made their way towards them.

'Captain Quentin, you have never been so welcome a sight as you are now,' Urim declared as he slapped a friendly hand on his shoulder.

'Thank you, I think,' he said with a wounded look on his face, which he quickly changed to a broad grin. 'I'm only glad you left some for us; that would have spoilt all the fun if you hadn't.'

'We didn't expect to see you until we got to Northill,' Javelin said, shaking Quentin's hand warmly.

'Well, we made good progress and when our scout reported a fight between gnomes and a mixed bag of travellers we guessed it could only be you so we doubled our pace and got here as smartly as we could. It seems just in time too. That thunderflash or whatever it was nearly caught us out though; we were just the other side of the rise so were lucky not to get the full impact. I assume that was your doing, Urim?'

'Indeed it was; I'm sorry if it caused you or your company any problems, we didn't know you were there, but I'm glad you were.'

'Not at all, but it did give us a fright, quite exhilarating really. It reminded me of our end of year celebrations,' Captain Quentin teased.

'What are your orders now?'

'We must reach Northill as soon as possible. I take it that you saw what had befallen Tri-Bune?' Urim asked the captain.

'Yes we did,' he answered soberly.

'It is a great tragedy; we are all shocked at such wanton destruction of life and property. I was personally acquainted with the garrison commander, Major O'Rourke, who I assume has perished along with the others. This is a sad day for us all and I mourn his loss.'

They stood in sombre silence for a moment, paying respect to those who had been massacred by the gnome army.

Javelin broke the silence first with a heavy sigh, saying, 'We must be going if we are to reach Northill by dusk; we have been delayed long enough because of having to deal with these gnomes, but we can't just leave them here like this.'

'I have already assigned a detail for burial duty; they will take care of them whilst the rest of us march on and will catch up with us when they have done,' Captain Quentin said.

'Excellent.' Urim commended the elf. 'Tell your men that they will find another six gnomes at the top of Clee Hill in the woods and to be on the alert for kite-folk; they will be missing three, which reminds me: there is a dead one in the trees up there as well.'

'My, but you have been busy.'

Quentin was impressed with the dwarves.

'I salute you, sirs.'

'Well, we wouldn't have been able to have done it without the sure aim of Anna and her sling; she accounted for a number of them herself,' Javelin explained to the elf.

Again he saluted smartly and bowed in respect towards Anna who acknowledged his actions with a shy smile.

'Hear, hear!' the others chipped in and again congratulated her for her actions.

'Let's get moving without any further delay,' Urim encouraged them. 'We must see just how Ebon means to overthrow the First city and find a way past his troops. We must make contact with the city guard and work together to stop Ebon and I think I know just how we can do it.'

Chapter XIV

Northill: Prelude to Conflict

Northill, the capital city of the land of humans and the seat of their government for as long as anyone could remember. It stood atop an old hill fort dating from the times of flint at the southern end of Rainbow Lake. Over the years the hill fort had been besieged and rebuilt, having been fortified on many occasions. Each time it had been rebuilt, bigger and stronger than before, learning from the mistakes of the past, until now it was considered to be impregnable. The rampart of a thick wall enclosed Northill and was defended by rounded towers every forty paces. At the foot of the hill, the ditch surrounding it had been deepened and an earth bank erected to inhibit access by any forces that gathered to besiege the city.

Outside of this to the south, enclosed within another thick wall of stone and earth, the town of Southill had been built to house the general populace. As the city had developed and grown, it had become necessary to expand even further, which meant that homes were also situated outside of the walls as the urbanisation of the lower Yield continued.

Connecting Northill and Southill, a funicular railway had been built into the hillside; powered by water and gravity. There were two gatehouses protecting access to the railway, one in Southill at the bottom and one built into the walls of Northill at the top, where the railway cars loaded and unloaded.

There was a secondary route linking the two: a service tunnel running in tandem with the funicular railway, giving access to the huge iron pipes that carried the water that powered the railway cars. This was accessed through the pumping station in Southill, emerging in Northill close to the cistern holding the water that powered the ascent and descent of the cars. Time and again throughout history many had come to admire the imposing

211

structure and to marvel at the funicular railway, unique throughout the land. A thriving tourist trade had developed, with guided tours along the walls and displays of the several stages in its development; a trade that was now an integral part of life in the capital. Boarding houses had been established throughout the city and below in Southill to accommodate the sightseers. Fortunately at this time of year there were relatively few who would be holidaying as the harvest would be in progress and the markets busy.

Jon and the others had followed in the trail of the gnome army, keeping alert for any more signs of scouting parties from the gnomes and a keen eye open for the kite-folk. They had made good progress after their skirmish with the troop of gnomes, not encountering any others to delay them. The elves had given a lift to the pace at which they travelled and they now stood at the point where Northill could be seen prominently sitting on the top of the old hill fort; its walls indeed appeared as though they would stand forever, indomitable.

Urim hoped that the onslaught of Northill had not yet begun, allowing them the opportunity to make better preparations and maybe allow for some of the citizens to escape. It appeared that his hopes might come to fruition, for the gnome army had not headed straight to the First city, but had deviated to the west, several leagues from the city. Their tracks, which were clearly visible, led away to the west and around the city as if to encircle it; probably so that they could gather their forces *en masse* at the entrance to the First city.

That the gnomes were gathering with no good intent would have been quite evident to the inhabitants as it was impossible for them to have passed so close and not been observed. Jon recalled the awful sight of them as he watched the army progress through the valley up in the Plains of Uniah. He knew the fear that would have been instilled within the hearts of the people.

As they surveyed the way ahead, there seemed to be nothing to prevent the group, with the elves, from walking right up to the walls of the city unmolested; at least that is what Ebon probably wanted them to think.

The sun was starting to sink towards the horizon, leaving little time for them to make any plans. They either had to take the chance of trying for the city in the hope that they were not running headlong into a trap; or wait out the night and review the situation in the morning. There were some farm buildings not far from them so Javelin suggested that they check them out; if they were clear, then they could at least discuss their options under cover and take advantage of the shelter if they were to wait until morning.

'Good suggestion, Javelin; send Tracker ahead to make sure it is safe for us to do so,' Urim instructed.

They waited as Tracker approached the buildings and saw him enter first one and then another, finally signalling to them that all was well and that they could join him there. Captain Quentin gave instructions for his company of elves to occupy the barn and to set up a watch over the buildings so that they would not be taken by surprise if anyone approached; he specifically instructed them to keep a lookout for the other elves who would be catching up with them after burying the gnomes and kite-folk. He then joined with the others so that they could discuss what to do next.

Safely inside the farmhouse they immediately felt a sense of relief; they had been living off their nerves these past few days and the encounter with the gnomes had drained the energies of the dwarves. They needed to rest, all of them. It was decided that, for the moment, they would rest a couple of hours at least and if they decided to continue on to Northill under cover of dark, then they would be awakened by the elves' duty officer on watch at the time. The dwarves gratefully found somewhere they could lie down out of the way and sank into a long deserved sleep. Hamill also curled himself up in a chair and was soon fast asleep.

Jon and Anna were too interested in knowing what decision would be made to sleep yet, tired though they were. Urim gathered them together, along with Captain Quentin, to share his thoughts with them so they were rather surprised when he told them that he must leave them here to follow another course.

'In order for us to succeed here and defeat Ebon, I must do something on my own. You will not suffer from my being absent and we will meet up again in four days time; that I promise you.'

They started to object, saying that they needed him, but he hushed their protests so as not to wake the others and patiently waited until they subsided into silence before assuring them that it was a necessary thing for him to do.

'If I were to stay with you now, we would fail and all would be lost. I have seen the way ahead and know what must be done. You will go under cover of dark and enter Northill by way of the service tunnel between the two gatehouses for the hillside railway. They will both be guarded: the one at the bottom by gnomes; the one at the top by the men of the First city. You must be careful when approaching them both, especially the lower one. There is a blind spot in my sight about it that concerns me. I have seen that you will succeed, but it may be at a cost. Do not take any chances and you may pass through unscathed.'

They took in his words and realised that he would not be moved from this course though Jon and Anna would have wished it to be otherwise. Jon recalled what had happened the last time Urim had left them, at the smelt, and gave Urim a sideways look of distrust at his decision to leave them again. Urim caught the expression and responded with quiet assurance that all would be well and that he would not leave if he thought that they would be in any danger.

'I will take my leave of you now and I want you all to make your way to the service tunnel in an hour from now. Captain Quentin, I ask that you follow the lead of the dwarves and assign your elves as you feel appropriate. Whatever happens, you must be within the walls of Northill before sunrise and ensure that the service tunnel is sealed. There will be no more friendly forces trying to enter that way once you have passed through. It is imperative that the way be secured, do you understand me?'

'You may rely upon me, seer,' Quentin replied, coming to attention and nodding in acceptance of this charge, then leaving to brief his officers and organise his company of elfin soldiers.

Urim drew Jon and Anna to one side so as not to disturb the dwarves and Hamill from their slumber.

'I must go now but I wanted to again reassure you that all will be well with you both so long as you stay close to the dwarves. There will not be a great deal that you can do to help once you are inside the gates other than to urge the garrison commander to hold his ground. If he tries to send for reinforcements, it will fail and those lives will be lost in a most terrible way. It can be avoided, Jon, and it is up to you both to convince him. The next few days will be hard on you all but I shall return; I promise. Remember, Jon, follow the light and keep to the left. Keep to the left and you will not fail.'

He held him at arm's length and secured him with a piercing stare as if to emphasize his point. They all three embraced and Urim slipped quietly out of the door into the night. Jon felt an emptiness inside that he had not felt before when parted from Urim and he felt concerned that he may not see him again, despite Urim's assurance that he would return in four days time.

Urim slipped away silently into the night without looking back and was lost to sight almost as soon as he left, his black cloak making him all but invisible.

An hour later and they were ready to leave; the other elves had joined them a short while ago. Javelin and the other dwarves had taken Urim's departure as a matter of fact; Hamill had been surprised and a little disturbed by the news. Captain Quentin had sent out scouts to search ahead and ensure that the way was clear. They returned stating that it was and that they could get into the lower city of Southill without being seen provided they were careful.

Stealing through the night like ghosts, they could see the great walls of the city towering over them like huge granite cliffs; lights burned within and through the narrow windows they caught glimpses of shadowy figures as they passed by. The walls of Southill had been extended right down to the water's edge with just a narrow track to navigate along the lake side. It was rather muddy and had been used recently by a large number of gnomes; their footprints were evident in the clay that clung to their boots; it was heavy going and slowed them considerably. Captain Quentin was concerned that they might be headed into a trap with gnome guards waiting at the end of the track so he sent scouts on ahead to ensure their safety. Hamill wanted to complain about the mud and how his feet hurt but decided that this was not the right time or place for raising any objections. They continued on in silence but for the occasional squelch as they laboured through the sticky clay that was the shoreline of Rainbow Lake.

They navigated the pathway without incident and found they were now walking on grass; they were glad to be able to rid their boots of the clay by wiping them on the stones that lay scattered around. Captain Quentin was relieved to find that there were no sentries posted by the gnomes and they continued on in silence towards the outer buildings making their way carefully through the maze of streets until they came to the defence wall and one of the gateways into the older parts of Southill. There were signs that a pitched battle had taken place here not too long ago; the walls were blackened from the fire that had eventually destroyed the gates that led into the lower city proper.

One of the elves from the Ward was leading the way in as he had visited the city some years earlier and knew where the lower gatehouse to the funicular railway was located. They approached with renewed caution, keeping in mind what Urim had said about there being an unseen danger. As silently as they could they put into action the plan they had agreed upon before setting out from the farmhouse.

They turned and twisted through the streets and alleyways in order to remain unnoticed; several times they ducked into dark doorways as patrols of gnomes passed by; otherwise their approach to the gateway was without event. The only sound they heard was the snoring of the gnomes as they slept in the captured houses, no doubt having ransacked them before doing so. The elves set up a perimeter defence by occupying the empty buildings around the gatehouse; they found several gnomes who were sleeping in one of the alehouses, having drunk so much of the ale that they had fallen into a stupor. They despatched them without a sound. Having been given the signal that all was secure, the elves mounted the steps at the front and entered the gatehouse with precision timing, checking each room as they went. The place was deserted; apparently the guards had decided that there was no threat to be faced from anybody at this time, so they had all gone to the alehouse to 'refresh themselves' with the free drink that was available, now that the lower city had been taken.

They could not believe their good fortune; this was going to be easier than they had expected. The dwarves signalled for Jon, Anna and Hamill to stay close to them and for the elves to act as a rearguard.

The gatehouse opened up into a large, bare, stone-built room; ahead of them, protected by heavy iron railings, was the funicular with a railway car at the platform; its windows smashed. In a corner of the room a flight of wooden steps led to the upper stories whilst in the centre of the room, a broad stone staircase had been cut into the floor that descended into the dark. Tracker led them down, holding aloft a flaming torch to light the way; at the base of the stairs they entered an antechamber with three doors in the wall in front of them. One of them would lead them to the upper city via the service tunnel; the other two were decoys in the event that intruders made it this far. They would be forced to waste time in discovering which one was the genuine one. Tracker lit the torches that were on the walls and, turning to Javelin, asked for any suggestions as to what they should do.

He looked thoughtful for a moment then shrugged his shoulders indicating his indecision and looked to the others for any suggestions.

'Are there any signs of more usage in one of the tunnels than the others?' Hamill queried. 'Perhaps that would indicate which one was the right one.'

'Good thinking, Hamill.' Javelin commended him on his suggestion.

They opened two of the doors, the one on the right and the one on the left. The centre one was locked tight. In the dim light of the torches they could make out that attempts had been made to open it without success. Obviously the gnomes had been trying to get it open, making them think that perhaps this was the one they needed.

The one on the left showed clear signs of recent use and disappeared into the dark straight ahead. The one on the right also showed signs of frequent usage but went down into the bedrock, possibly to another basement.

Captain Quentin became impatient with the delay.

'We waste time standing here. I shall send two of my elves, one into each tunnel, who can investigate and return with a report on their findings. They are quick of foot and can search out the tunnels far quicker than anyone else.'

'I agree with you, captain; send your elves quickly; I don't like being in these confined conditions with gnomes about; it makes me uneasy.'

Javelin was clearly concerned with the safety of everyone and would only feel better once they were secured behind the defences of the First city. The elves were despatched with flaming torches to search out the two tunnels to discover if they led to the top. In the meantime the dwarves tried to force the central door open by pitching their weight against it. No matter what they did, it would not shift. Hamill leaned against the wall on the

217

left, placing his arm to rest on one of the torch holders. It moved and a section of wall slid noiselessly aside revealing a hidden passageway. He stood for some moments in astonishment before saying to the dwarves, 'I think I might have found the tunnel you are looking for.'

They all turned to look and were equally surprised at Hamill's discovery.

Jon said with conviction, 'That must be it; it's got to be; when Urim left earlier he told me to follow the light and to stay to the left. I thought he meant something else but this must be what he was telling me. There's the light and there's the left. It's to the left of all the others. It's got to be the one.' Jon indicated the torch holder that Hamill had moved with his arm.

He had never felt more certain about anything in his life before and all but jumped up and down with conviction.

Just then one of the elves who had been sent to spy out the tunnels returned, coming out of the one on the left, almost at the same time as the other elf emerged from the one on the right. The elves reported back to Captain Quentin.

'The tunnels are the same, one going around in a loop; we have both ended up back here. We met in the middle as we were going round and realised that the tunnels were one and the same.'

'That settles it. We go through the one that Hamill discovered,' Javelin decided and proceeded to lead the way forward.

Captain Quentin issued the order for his elves to make a phased withdrawal from the surrounding buildings and to follow the dwarves and the others into the passageway. Most of them had gone through when a shout went up from an elf outside.

'Alarm! Alarm! We are discovered.'

A commotion broke out above in the reception area and sounds of fighting echoed into the basement chamber from the square outside. Captain Quentin and a few of his command flew up the stairway while ordering the elves to continue to go through the passageway and to pass the word forward for them to make haste.

Upon reaching the door of the gatehouse he saw that the gnomes had discovered them there and were massing to the call of battle. Horns were being blown furiously along with shouts and curses aimed at the intruders; sporadic fighting had broken out between the gnomes and elves. Several gnomes lay dead on the square outside and a number of elves were being assisted into the gatehouse having received wounds. The elves were making a controlled retreat with three levels of crossbows firing in order as they withdrew one line after the other, each line providing cover for the next. They were hopelessly outnumbered and despite the awful toll they were exacting upon the gnomes, it would not be long before they ran out of crossbow bolts and would be forced into hand to hand combat with them. This was something they did not want to do as they were not as strong or as proficient with fighting gnomes as were the dwarves; they were no match for the gnomes if that were to happen.

Just as they seemed to have made a successful retreat, a dull roar reverberated through the square. From out of the shadows in the main street, a troll strode forward, fully armoured and carrying a heavy cudgel; he would inflict heavy casualties if he were to catch the elves out in the open. Quentin sounded his whistle, giving the order to run for the cover of the gatehouse. Those who had already made the gatehouse provided covering fire but the thick armour of the troll meant that he was able to come forward unabated. He proceeded to swing his cudgel, catching several of the elves and sending them flying like chaff before the wind. Quentin urged the others to make haste and despite their fleetness of foot, several more of them were caught by the troll. At least the gnomes were kept at bay or they would have been swept aside as well as the cudgel was used indiscriminately, first this way then that. A group of gnomes decided that they wanted to get at the elves and timed their run at them; unfortunately for them they did not time it right and were caught with the next swing from the troll. They suffered the same fate as the elves they had sought to catch and were tossed aside to crash to the floor, bloody and broken. The last of the elves dashed through the doorway and it slammed shut behind them; it was secured with heavy iron bars that slid across into recessed notches where they locked into place.

Catching their breath, they made their way to the stone stairs and descended to the basement to join the others. They moved a little quicker, however, when the door shuddered on its hinges following a mighty blow from the troll's cudgel.

Down in the basement, Captain Quentin was the last to enter

into the passage that Hamill had discovered, closing the entrance behind him by pulling on a weighted lever as he heard the door to the gatehouse splinter from a shattering blow. The noise from outside fell into silence as the stone door slid easily back into place, locking out any who would follow. It would only be a matter of time, however, before the passage was discovered so they could afford no delay in obtaining the top of the service tunnel and Northill. The gnomes obviously knew about the decoy tunnels and had assumed, as had they, that the central door was the passage to Northill. Hopefully that would keep them busy for some time yet, unless they discovered the entrance in a similar manner to themselves.

Quentin looked around to see if there were a locking device; there was another lever, which he decided to try and he heard a whirring noise followed by a click. He hoped that that was indeed the lock; that way, no one could come in through that door unless someone from the inside wanted them to. The elf standing nearby held a torch aloft in what appeared to them to be a spacious tunnel.

In reality it was only just big enough for two grown humans to walk side by side; huge iron pipes ran along both walls before plunging into the ground, probably carrying the water that powered the funicular.

'Well, sergeant, that should keep them out. Now let's go and get some breakfast; I'm starved.'

The passage fell into darkness behind them as they climbed the deep cut steps, slipping every now and then on the places where it sloped and where it was covered in green algae. A flicker of light could be seen ahead of them where the others made their way up towards Northill and a well earned rest.

They climbed for what seemed like an hour. Quentin counted the steps absentmindedly: three hundred and twenty two; three hundred and twenty three; three hundred and twenty four. His counting was interrupted by a shout from up ahead requesting that he come up to the front. Despite his legs starting to burn from the effort of the climb, he doubled his pace, passing his elves who stood in a queue as the way ahead was blocked by the others. He soon arrived at a square chamber that had no exit or doorway other than the one through which they had come.

'What's the problem?' he started to ask, then realised that they needed to find the door.

There was no lever here as there had been with the lower chamber and no sign of anything that could remotely be identified as one. The large iron pipes had disappeared into the ceiling of the tunnel several lengths behind them, affording them more room to move.

'Perhaps Hamill should lean against the wall again,' Quentin joked with a wink in his direction.

'We've tried all that; there is nothing here that lends itself to anything that could be a handle or a trigger,' Hamill snapped back in irritation. 'I'm sorry, captain, please forgive my outburst; it is just so frustrating.'

'That's quite all right, Hamill, I'll make that allowance; but it's time for us to use our heads and not to be discouraged. The first thing I would suggest is for us to clear the chamber so that we can get a better look at things instead of standing in each other's way.'

Having cleared the room, Quentin began a thorough search of the walls; after several minutes he scratched his head, looking perplexed.

'I see what you mean, Hamill, it is rather annoying, but if there is nothing on the walls, then the next place to look is on the ceiling and the floor.'

He craned his neck in a detailed study of the roof of the chamber but could see nothing; a search of the floor was likewise fruitless.

He mused, stroking his chin. 'Ah, that is curious. Jon, did Urim say anything else to you that could be of assistance to us in locating the exit to this passage?'

'No, not that I can recall; he just told me to follow the light and keep to the left.'

'I wonder.'

Quentin thought for a while.

'Give me room out there. Sergeant, order our elves to extinguish the torches, all but the last one at the end of the queue.'

The order was passed down the line and the passage fell into darkness with only a dim glow from the last torch below. As their eyes grew accustomed to the dark, it became apparent that there was a soft luminescence from one of the stones in the wall a little way down the steps, back the way they had come.

'Soldier, push on that stone,' Quentin ordered. It gave under his touch and a doorway opened up in the wall where he stood, giving access to another chamber. The torches were relit and Quentin, the dwarves, Jon, Anna and Hamill all entered. They found they were in a chamber similar to the one they had just been in.

'This looks familiar,' Javelin said in a matter-of-fact tone. He was impressed by the work that had been put into these defences, but none too enamoured by their inability to find their way out.

'Patience my friend,' said Quentin, 'we'll get out, all in good time. There is a way out and we shall find it.' He called for more torches to be brought into the room, shedding more light into the recesses. Hidden away in one of the recesses was a square hole. It seemed to be blank but placing his hand over it he could feel a draught.

'Ah! Now we're getting somewhere,' he mumbled to himself. He hesitated from placing his hand inside but he was able to see that a duct led up from the hole; he stepped closer to it. He shouted into the duct, 'Hello. Is there anyone there? This is Captain Quentin from the Ward, of the first detachment of the elfin guard. Is there anybody there?'

Placing his ear to the hole he thought he heard noises as of voices whispering in the distance, though he could not be certain.

They waited for what seemed a long time, searching the walls, ceiling and floor for any other means of exiting the room before trying the 'voice hole' as Quentin called it, again.

'We have come here at the request of the seer, Urim, from the Council of the Sight.'

'Quentin? Is that you?'

The voice resonated down the duct but was unmistakable.

'Major O'Rourke? Yes it's me. I thought you were dead. How did you manage to get away?'

'Well, why don't you come on in and we can catch up with each other's news.'

An opening appeared in the wall at his side revealing a set of stone steps leading up to another level and more light spilled into the room. Leading the way, he led them up into a large reception area much like the one below in Southill. Major O'Rourke greeted Quentin warmly, pulling him to one side and ushering the company of elves past to be shown hospitality and quarters. The dwarves, Jon, Anna and Hamill hung back, waiting for Captain Quentin to introduce them, which he did almost immediately.

They listened as the two recounted their stories, Quentin telling Major O'Rourke about Ebon and Urim, the journey here with the dwarves and their encounter with the gnomes. O'Rourke told them that the gnomes had besieged the Second city of Tri-Bune for a whole week, gradually reducing it to a smouldering ruin, slaughtering the people who were unable to get to the safety of Northill. The garrison had been targeted and had been unable to aid the rest of the inhabitants; all they could do was fight for survival and watch as the gnomes and trolls trawled through the city. The worst of it was watching helplessly as trolls waded into the thick of the battle wreaking havoc and destruction with every step.

Many of the inhabitants of Tri-Bune had perished in the battle whilst others had been caught in the fire that swept through the city towards the end of the week. At that time he was unsure how many had escaped, but it seemed unlikely that they were great in number as they were attacked from every quarter, including fireballs catapulted into the quayside from boats on the water.

A fierce counter-attack had been mounted catching the gnomes off guard and the battle had been hard fought during which many gnomes had perished. It only delayed the inevitable and enraged them even more so that when any captives were taken they were tortured unmercifully in full sight of the garrison guard. A few of the guard could not stand the torment of watching their fellow citizens being treated in such a fashion and slipped out of the garrison in an effort to rescue them. All they succeeded in doing was providing the gnomes with more helpless victims and they all died horrible deaths.

Major O'Rourke concluded his report, saying, 'Finally, after the city had been drained of life, a man dressed in a black robe and carrying a staff stepped up to the gates of our compound and declared his intention to destroy us all unless we acceded to his demands. We were to deliver a message to the commander of the First city; he told us that he would do to Northill what he had done to Tri-Bune unless he was recognized as ruler and that we were to be his ambassadors in delivering his message; the army then withdrew, leaving us to fend for ourselves. From a city of some four thousand souls, less than a hundred walked away to tell the tale. We made for the only place we could, Northill, to warn them of what was to befall them.

'We have been here since then, planning ways of defending the city and our way of life. It has been determined that we will fight to the last rather than be in subjection to such a tyrant.'

It was a harrowing tale, one which moved the emotions like a pendulum, swinging first one way with anger, then another with anguish.

Major O'Rourke led them through the passages away from the ante-chamber, pointing out strategic positions as they worked their way into the heart of the upper funicular gate tower; up stairways and along echoing corridors until they reached a guarded door. After satisfying the guards that the new arrivals were no threat to anyone, they were admitted into an office where they were introduced to the commander of the city garrison, Colonel Dyer, an affable person of goodly proportions, with silver hair; he was a seasoned campaigner but with a mind that was keen and alert. He suggested that they get some rest and they would talk later. He placed them in the care of one of his junior officers, a Lieutenant Perkins, who escorted them to quarters where they could sleep.

It was getting light when Jon was awakened by Archer shaking him to consciousness.

'Come on, Jon. Time to get up; we're having a meeting with the colonel soon and I think you would want to be there.'

He made sure Jon was awake before going off to raise Hamill from his cot; Anna was already awake and getting ready for breakfast. Breakfast; that word alone gave him the impetus to get out of his cot; he felt famished. They had been shown the officers' mess hall yesterday and invited to have their meals there, so having washed and dressed he hurried to get there and sate his hunger. The smell of ham and eggs wafted up the staircase making his stomach rumble in anticipation. When he reached the food hall the dwarves were each tucking into a huge plateful of food. Anna was there ahead of him and had saved a place beside her.

The food was the best he had tasted for a long while; they had been on the road for almost a week without a decent hot breakfast and his taste buds reacted with pleasure to the textures and flavours that assailed them. Hamill joined them and also enjoyed the food; it is amazing how a good meal lifts the spirit and revitalises the senses.

They were summoned to a meeting with the colonel and escorted in a very military fashion by four guards and Lieutenant Perkins, who had been assigned to be their aide for the duration of their stay. Colonel Dyer asked to be brought up to date with all the information that they could of their encounters with the gnomes and the rogue seer. Captain Quentin had already appraised him of all that he knew and suggested that Jon and the others could give some insight into what was occurring.

The dwarves told their story up until their meeting with Urim, Jon and Anna; then Jon recounted the details of all he knew from the moment he had met with Urim in the forest. The colonel stated after listening intently to all that had been said, 'Well, that is quite some account, my friend; you say that this Urim will meet you here in four days time. Let us pray that we will still be here for him to return too if all that Major O'Rourke has told me is true.'

They fell silent, horrified at the thought of what he implied by that.

'Thank you all for your input, it is greatly appreciated. I would suggest that we consider our options. Jon, Anna and Hamill, would you mind leaving the rest of us to plan what can be done, if that's OK with you? I mean no offence but this is an area where I fear you cannot help, though if you should think of anything that might help, you have only to speak with Perkins.'

'Colonel, we'd be grateful if we could be shown around as we have not been here before and would be interested in learning more about the place.'

'I do not have a problem with that, in fact it may be useful for you to know your way around if things become difficult, shall we say. Perkins, see to it that these young people receive all the assistance they need.'

'Yes, sir.'

'Now if you will excuse us we have much to discuss. Perkins, I suggest a trip to the ramparts to show them the view would be in order. It would be well if they were made aware of the situation.'

Colonel Dyer turned his attention to the others and began discussing options for the defence of the city.

The panorama that stretched out before them as they viewed the Yield from the ramparts was sickening. For as far as they could see the land was covered with the encamped gnome army. Smoke drifted up from the thousands of camp fires fuelled by the felled trees of the once pleasant woodlands. The land that had been green and verdant was now a blackened wasteland and the smoke seemed to hang over the camp, refusing to be moved. It gave the whole area a doomed and forbidding feeling that weighed down on the senses. They could make out the route by which they had arrived at Southill, between the foot of the old hill fort that Northill sat atop and the banks of the lake where the land was narrow. The gnomes had not bothered to defend or guard it as they were only concerned with people escaping from the city, not anyone going in. As far as they were concerned, the more who entered the city, the more there were to torture when they finally captured it. They had been promised rich pickings here; far better than they had taken at Tri-Bune.

'They have been building in number over the past two days, ever since Major O'Rourke arrived with the survivors from Tri-Bune. When we heard what had befallen them there it was decided that the lower city of Southill should be evacuated, leaving only the wall guard to defend the outer wall and the funicular. We disabled it after our withdrawal from below, securing the upper car. The only way it can be used is if we allow it to be used and that will never happen while there is someone here to defend the place.'

The sound of breaking glass and furniture could be heard below them in the abandoned Southill as the gnomes ransacked the place, looting and generally taking out their frustration on the city. Sometimes they fought with each other as petty disputes broke out between them, which were usually followed by an agonised scream from the victim of a disgruntled individual. Hamill looked at the funicular and, seeing the track that ran all the way to the bottom, he asked, 'Wouldn't they be able to scale the hill by using the tracks?'

'A good observation, Hamill; normally that would be true if it were not for the defence posts situated at various points along the track, which are accessed from the top only. We have already repulsed several attempts to reach us by that route. You see this fortification has undergone many alterations and modifications over the years. Every possible way of attacking and breaching our defences has been considered and steps taken to counteract that event. So you see we are confident that we are safe here. There is plenty of water from the deep well and we have enough stores for the whole city to last a year. No, we are perfectly safe. The only thing that causes any concern is the kite-folk who keep a constant watch on our movements, but they don't come too close any more; not since we brought a few of them down with a ballista.'

'What's a ballista?' Jon asked.

'Basically it's a large crossbow mounted on a carriage for mobility. There is one just over there.'

He pointed across to show them the weapon; it was indeed a giant crossbow with a vicious looking spear, instead of a bolt, ready to be let loose. Three soldiers kept vigil nearby in the hope of claiming another hit.

They looked sideways at each other hoping that what Perkins said about being safe held true; Anna slipped her hand into Jon's and they exchanged a reassuring smile. They looked out over the expanse of Ebon's army, which covered the once fruitful Yield, awed and dismayed by the sheer size of it and the destruction that had been done. Jon felt the bile rise in his throat when he considered the damage and mindless rape that had been inflicted on the land; he wondered where Urim had gone, what he was doing now and how much more of this would be allowed to happen, not only to the Yield and the surrounding land, but to all the inhabitants of the free peoples of whatever race. This was the first day of his absence, there were three more to go until his return; Jon hoped that Urim's promise that they would be safe held true.

Chapter XV

Weathering the Storm

It was the morning of the second day; two more days to go until Urim had promised to return. The gnomes and trolls had been hammering at the defences of the hill ever since first light yesterday with very little success; the kite-folk had been employed in dropping rocks on to the defenders but it was nothing more than annoying because all the rocks did was keep people from going outdoors; if they had to go out then a careful eye was needed and the falling rocks could be avoided. The kite-folk dared not fly too low or too close to the city towers or they could be hit by the arrows sent up in volleys from the troops inside; the use of the ballista proved to be a real deterrent and the soldiers had managed to drive them off several times. One of the kite-folk had flown a little too close and had been winged, resulting in them abandoning any further attempts at dropping the rocks on to the fortress and its people; none had been seen since then.

Siege machines called 'slingers' had been set up by the trolls and they had tried to bombard the inhabitants inside the outer walls with showers of rocks and flints. These had been smashed into pieces to make them sharper so inflicting nasty wounds on anyone unfortunate enough to be caught by the barrage. Larger boulders were also used to hurl at the walls, with little or no success in either attempt. The missiles simply bounced off the stonework, hardly leaving a scratch. Some of them did not even manage to reach the walls, falling far short. The officers had reported to Colonel Dyer that there was no need for concern at this stage of the siege; the defences were standing up to the test. This kind of thing had been tried before and the city had remained safe then; there was no reason to believe that the results would be any different now.

Several more attempts were made by groups of gnomes

during the day, determined to storm the Northill gatehouse by climbing the rail track; the gnomes had formed their shields over and around them as a protective shell, which had deflected the bolts and arrows from the small arms of the defenders. Gradually the gnomes had inched their way forward but their shields were no defence from the spears from the ballista bows; one of them had been manoeuvred into position at the top of the railway in the gatehouse to defend against just such an attack; the doorway of the empty docking bay made a good firing position. Several heavy, barbed spearheads had torn through the gnomes' defences, killing and maiming many of them each time. Later in the day four heavily armoured trolls had also suffered the same fate as they endeavoured to storm the upper gateway via the funicular. Their broken bodies lay at the foot of the track bearing testimony to the futility of any further attempts being made.

At the foot of the old hill fort, the gnomes had been busy erecting shelters against the slope of the hill and there was plenty of coming and going. They were attempting to burrow into the hill but it had rained fitfully during the day, making the ground sodden and it was proving difficult to push barrow loads of soil, mud and stone away so heaps of excavated debris were being formed around the entrances where they were digging, giving them additional protection from the defending archers and spearmen. It seemed that they were intent on burrowing into the hill in an effort to gain entry to the city by means of tunnels; Colonel Dyer had wished them good luck while viewing their activities from the south tower of the perimeter wall.

He told Jon, 'It took our engineers five years to complete the service tunnel for the funicular. I do not believe they seriously intend to tunnel their way in; it must be a diversionary tactic.' He called for vigilance from the sentries on all sides of the city wall, however, just in case it was being used as a diversion away from another attack from a different source. The gnomes were concentrating their forces at the south of the city, opposite the gatehouse, using the lower city of Southill as cover when making their assaults. The other sides of Northill were left unmolested; although there had been one or two incursions against the defenders there as if to test the strength of the parties concerned, gnomes and humans. They did not appear to be serious attempts and were easily repulsed with no loss of life to the defenders who inflicted heavy losses on the assailants.

The day had drawn to a close with no let up from the gnomes in their efforts to excavate beneath them; they were using the strength and experience of the trolls to dig into the hill and, judging from the amount of debris that was now being carted away by a continuous fleet of heavy farm carts and horses, they were making good headway. Major O'Rourke had been given the task of assessing the likelihood of gnomes achieving the unthinkable and actually being able to tunnel their way into the city. He had assembled engineers on the ramparts to watch the movement of the soil and discover from the volume removed what their progress was. They had calculated that at their present rate it would take a year for them to reach the city walls; it was noted that the soil was being deposited into the ditch surrounding the hill at a point just west of the boundary wall of Southill. Major O'Rourke reported his concerns to Colonel Dyer that he thought it possible an assault could be made across this area once it had been levelled sufficiently to afford easier access to the hill fort, allowing the attackers a better approach to the walls.

A faint, regular reverberation was felt throughout the city, which grew a little stronger with each hour that passed; Jon wondered whether the colonel's confidence in the defences of Northill being unassailable was not being overestimated. The city had been taken many times in the past; on each occasion the defenders had boasted of the city being impregnable, only for it to fall and be ransacked. However, the last time Northill had been successfully taken was two centuries ago though it had been assailed many times since; all had failed in their attempts. So it was no wonder that confidence was high, that on this occasion, the attackers would meet with as much success as the previous attempts had. The one thing that they had not taken into account was that the funicular was a fairly recent addition, replacing the ropes and pulleys that had operated here before.

The mood in the mess that evening was subdued and very little conversation passed between them as they sat at two adjoining tables: Jon, Anna and Hamill on one; the dwarves on the other. They had been 'snooping around' as Hamill had called it, much to the chagrin of the dwarves who denied any deviousness, stating that they were merely being cautious and wanting to be prepared for any eventuality.

'They've been "snooping".' Hamill repeated with a wink towards the dwarves as they bristled in mock indignation and they all laughed, dispelling the depressive mood in the room momentarily until the reverberations from the tunnelling beneath them impinged upon their senses once more. Nerves were becoming taut as the regular thumping in the ground beneath their feet began to wear away at the people's nerves within the First city.

That night, Jon had fallen into a fitful sleep, filled with unpleasant dreams of being trapped in the tunnels under the city; being unable to run from the gnomes and trolls because his feet seemed to be stuck to the ground and moved in slow motion, while his pursuers flew at him with winged feet. He had had similar dreams before and was troubled by them. He had woken up in a cold sweat and had not been able to rest easily afterwards; the constant thumping of the mining trolls beneath the hill kept him from sleep.

The next day was unusually dark with black clouds gathering from the east casting a grey gloom over everything; the rumble of thunder promised more rain. Lightning played around the edges of the storm as it rolled relentlessly towards them and a chill wind blew through Jon's hair. The meagre warmth of the autumn sun disappeared with the shadow of the cloud as it swept across the land, but it was more than the wind and the shadows that chilled him through. He felt alone, even though he was surrounded by friends and their conversations were lively; yet he felt isolated. He missed Urim and felt an affinity towards him; but the same old questions kept coming back. Who was he really? Ebon had said that Urim had lied to him about being his uncle; what would he have to gain by telling him that? Jon felt himself drawing closer and closer to asking outright just who Urim was in relation to himself. Their resemblance to one another and the familiar habits of biting his lip or crossing his fingers when concerned: they all pointed to them being closely related. Dare he hope that in reality Urim was in fact his father? Ridiculous, he thought, to even consider that he was the son of a seer. He could not consider it with any seriousness at this time; he had to concentrate on the day to day routine of survival, but one day, when this was all over, he would discover the truth of who Urim was in connection to himself. Not that there was anything certain about their surviving through these perilous times, standing as they were between their fight for freedom on the one hand and servitude under Ebon on the other.

Urim had promised to return but Jon had no idea how he was going to do that seeing as the service tunnel was sealed. The only other way into Northill was via the funicular and that was out of service although it was still capable of being used should the defenders wish to; the bodies of the trolls that had fallen to the bottom of the railway track had been removed during the night along with those of the gnomes who had perished, giving them clear access up and down; it was just too great a risk to allow it to be used.

He stood leaning against the battlements wrapped snugly in a greatcoat that Perkins had acquired for him; it helped keep out the wind but the chill was from inside; no matter what he tried to do, he just could not get warm.

He looked out over the Yield. Once so alive and fresh, it had now become a place of desolation; it looked so different to how it had been described to him by Perkins. There had been orchards, lush pasture and clean water; now the ground resembled a quagmire after the persistent rainfall of the past twenty-four hours. Gazing out at the gnome encampment made him feel depressed; the ground had been churned up by the movement of the gnomes and trolls. Orchards no longer flourished and it was difficult to imagine it before the gnomes had arrived to put their mark on it. The army below had swollen in number since Jon had arrived with the others; it now stretched further round the base of the city and deeper into the lower Yield. Marsh-mogs had gathered at the perimeter of the camp. When the wind blew from that direction, their foul stench was almost overpowering. He did not know how those who were nearest to them could put up with the smell, but then the gnomes were none too healthy from being encamped for so long without the use of effective sanitation. For such a large army to be maintained they must be using enormous resources and were probably taking cattle and sheep from miles around in order to cater for their needs.

The darkness of the day threw a heavy weight upon his mind;

he was not the only one to feel it: Anna and Hamill also felt it, in fact everyone went about with their shoulders drooped as if carrying a heavy load, with an air of despondency about them.

It started to rain, a few drops, then with more force until it had built into a deluge; he ducked into the cover of the tower and watched the activity below from an open window.

'Great,' Jon thought, 'even the heavens conspire to add to our misery.' At least he was dry, sheltering from the rain in the stone tower; the army below was exposed to the elements and, were things different, he would feel sorry for them. He did not like the rain very much, he hated getting wet; Anna had teased him about it on many an occasion as they had walked together in the past and been caught out by a sudden downpour.

Anna had been looking for Jon and found him in the tower after trying his room and the mess. She made him jump as she threaded her arm through his; with the noise of the wind in his ears he had not heard her approach. He laughed involuntarily at being caught unawares, which lightened his mood.

Why are you up here on your own in the cold?

'I just needed some space; somewhere to think and to blow the cobwebs from my mind.'

Jon started to sink back into his depression.

Well, now that you've done that, come on inside and we'll have a game of sticks; Hamill and I are bored.

He smiled weakly with a far away look in his eye and would have preferred to stay where he was; however, as always, she won him over by the look she gave him.

He said, 'All right; I guess it will pass the time more easily at that.'

They descended from the upper room of the tower via the spiral staircase and immediately the air felt warmer; it was amazing how cold that wind felt. The three of them had explored the city and marvelled at the buildings, but the thing that impressed itself upon them most was the dark mood that had settled on the inhabitants. People walked around in virtual silence and very few smiled; the quiet intensity of it was heavy in the air. Perkins had shown them round the main parts of the city defences and it had taken them over an hour to walk the perimeter wall; the place filled Jon's mind with awe: no wonder they considered themselves safe here. Anna led Jon by the hand, trying to hurry him as he dawdled along the corridors, eventually finding Hamill in a rest area waiting eagerly for them to join him in a game of sticks.

'Ah! There you are; I told you he'd be up there,' Hamill beamed, delighted to see them.

'Who wants to throw the dice to see who goes first? If you don't mind I think I will.'

Hamill eagerly sent the dice tumbling along the table; he was a keen player and, they had discovered, a bad loser.

'Come on; roll to see if you can get a higher number than me.'

He encouraged Jon and Anna but secretly hoped that they did not. As it turned out, they did not and Hamill rubbed his hands together with glee. The idea of the game was to throw as high a number as possible to determine who went first then, when the game got under way, they sought for the lowest number possible by a throw of the dice to signify how many sticks they had to remove on their turn without disturbing any others. The game was started by holding a bunch of sticks together in a clenched hand, then letting them go to fall wherever gravity dictated; the first person to go removed from the fallen sticks the number that the dice indicated. The fewer you had to remove at each turn, the less chance there was of disturbing another stick. It was quite an absorbing and skilful game, spoilt only on occasion when some-one took it more seriously than it deserved. Hamill had that quality but the other two had come to accept this about him and now found it to be an endearing part of his character.

Today, however, Jon was in no mood for games; he played along for the sake of the others but his heart and mind were not in it. He was too concerned over the situation they faced with the gnome army encamped outside their front door, so to speak, and was mindful that Urim was out there somewhere. He appreciated what they were trying to do by distracting him from his dark mood, but thoughts of Urim were never far from his mind.

Lieutenant Perkins came into the room to spend some time relaxing before resuming his duties. Seeing the three of them playing, he came over to them to watch while he sipped from his cup of chicory. Jon looked up at him and they exchanged nods and a smile while Anna took her turn at the sticks, watched closely by Hamill.

'What's the latest on our situation?' Jon asked absentmindedly of Perkins.

'Not a lot has changed since yesterday; the gnomes are still hammering away at the hill, as you can no doubt feel.'

He stopped and cocked his head to one side and they all listened for the now familiar feel of the reverberations coming from deep underground; they were a little louder, but not by much.

'The sentries reported that no more gnomes have arrived since yesterday but a large group of creatures have been seen on the rim of the camp; they could not see clearly as it was dusk when they arrived. It was reported that they had been pulling a large siege machine and Colonel Dyer has asked for some volunteers to make up a scouting party – to "seek and destroy" were his words. They left under cover of darkness and slipped out the rear of the city, being let down from the walls by ropes; no doubt they will come back in the same way. They had to be very quiet and extremely careful; that is why he asked for volunteers.'

Jon jumped up from his seat almost upsetting the table and disturbing the sticks.

'Hey, be careful; you'll ruin the game,' Hamill complained as he tried to steady the table and the sticks.

'Shut up, Hamill; this is no game we're playing here.'

Then, turning to a startled Perkins, he asked animatedly, 'When did this happen?'

'This morning; they left in the early hours of this morning,' Perkins replied, surprised by Jon's sudden outburst.

'Fool; I warned him against this. How could he be so stupid as to do this? Where is the colonel now?'

'The colonel's in his office awaiting any news of their return.'

'Of all the idiotic things; why did he have to go and do it?' Jon fumed and he rushed out of the door, heading for the colonel's office, leaving the others behind him, bewildered.

'What's rattled his cage?' Perkins asked in astonishment.

'You have to ask?' Hamill shot a questioning glance at him.

'Come on, Anna, let's see what's going on; this should be very interesting.'

They followed hot on his heels, anxious to see what he proposed to do and to restrain him if need be from upsetting things here.

235

Anna was as shocked as the others; she had known Jon longer than anyone else but had never seen him so angry.

The colonel was being briefed by his advisors on the latest situation with the gnomes and reviewing any possibilities of attack, so that they would be ready for them, when the door was flung open and a madman burst in on them.

'Why did you send men out when I'd told you what Urim had said?' he demanded in a fury.

Colonel Dyer bristled with indignation at being interrupted in his meeting and was especially offended with the manner of the interruption let alone the content of the question, which accused him of being incompetent. He jumped to his feet, reddening with anger himself and shouted Jon down.

'How dare you come in here like this and hurl unfounded accusations at me in that manner. Do you realise who you are addressing? If you were a military man I would have you tried for insubordination.'

Jon did not flinch in his stance and ground his teeth together in sheer frustration, banging his fist on the desk.

The others in the room were shocked at this display from an outsider, one who had been shown nothing but friendship and hospitality.

Hamill grabbed Jon by the arm to drag him away from embarrassing himself and them any further but he shrugged himself free.

'Why did you do it?' he asked again; this time with emotion as he sank down on to a chair and held his head in his hands.

A sergeant at arms with four men appeared at the door, responding to the commotion, but he was waved away by the colonel and they retreated to the guard room nearby.

'Let me tell you, young man that . . .'

'Pardon me, sir.' A young officer entering the room interrupted the colonel.

'. . . I have weighed up the situation and . . .'

'Sir . . .' The officer became more insistent.

'Not now, Ashton.'

'But, sir, I have been sent to have you come to the south tower immediately.'

Reluctantly Colonel Dyer turned his attention to the young

man, sensing that something was amiss or he would not have dared to interrupt him.

'Very well, Ashton, you have my attention; what's the urgency?'

'You should come and see it, it's . . . it's huge.'

'What is? What are you babbling on about, man; make some sense.'

'The creatures that came last night; they're at the earthworks and they have set up a slinger, the size of which I've never seen before.'

They snatched their coats to protect against the cold and rushed to the tower; the scene that greeted them was one that put fear into the hearts of all who saw it. A huge slinger had been erected at the foot of the hill by the earthwork and ditch that surrounded the hill fort.

'Do you think that it could breach our outer defence wall, colonel?' the young officer asked shakily.

'I believe we are about to find out.'

The deliverer (the pouch that carried whatever it was to be flung at its target) was being wound slowly back into place on the slinger and it strained to be let loose. On the word of one of the gnome commanders, it was released and the whole thing juddered as it was freed of its constraints. The deliverer, secured at the end of a thick rope, threw its contents towards the city, watched by all with bated breath. The stones it threw did not look as if they would do any damage as they were far too small and sailed over the wall to land harmlessly in the streets behind.

'Well if that's all they've got, I don't think we're going to have much to worry about.' Colonel Dyer breathed out in relief.

'Wait a moment.' Major O'Rourke went white in the face and pointed back out to the slinger. 'It's him: the seer, Ebon. He's the one who was at Tri-Bune.'

They all turned to look in the direction he had pointed and sure enough there was Ebon: standing theatrically on the slinger with a gnome at his side and Khan sitting on his haunches nearby. His voice rang out in the stillness following the slingshot's action.

'I return to you something that you are missing; pretty soon you will all be grovelling at my feet begging for mercy. Was not what happened at Tri-Bune warning enough for you? Surrender and you shall be spared. Defy me and you will all die.'

'If we all die who will there be left to rule over, Ebon?' Jon shouted back at him before he could be stopped.

'Is that you, Jon? So we meet again; where's that uncle of yours?' Ebon asked, mockingly.

'Doesn't he want to play any more? Too frightened to come out is he or has he abandoned you to your fate?'

Jon was constrained by Major O'Rourke so as not to say anything else.

'Say nothing more; everything you say gives him a little more knowledge about us and boosts his ego. Ignore him; he can achieve nothing with his taunts. It's that machine we have to worry about.'

A messenger appeared from the stairs breathless from his climb from below.

'Sir, the scouts you sent out . . .'

'Ah! They've returned, excellent. You see, lad, I knew they could do it,' turning sideways and addressing his remarks to Jon.

'No, sir, you don't understand . . .'

'Well, have they come back or not?' the colonel asked irritated by the messenger's prevarication.

'In a manner of speaking sir; yes they have.'

'Well, I want to see them immediately, where are they?'

'They're all over town, sir.'

'You're not making sense, man; now report: where are the scouting party?'

'That's what I've been trying to tell you, sir. The slinger: it returned them to us; they'd been cut into pieces, put in the slinger and fired at us. Their body parts are spread all over the square.' He grabbed hold of the handrail in order to steady himself and looked like he was going to be sick.

Colonel Dyer's face fell and he appeared to age ten years, stumbling at the shock the news had been to him. Clasping a hand to his chest, he winced in pain. As the officers lent a steadying hand, he brushed them aside, stating that he was fine and regained his composure; he slipped a small pill into his mouth from a container that he had in a pocket and swallowed. He drew a couple of deep breaths before turning to look at Jon. He was a man who believed in accomplishing what he set out to achieve and this was the worst kind of news he could have received. All around them fell into a deathly silence and tried not to look at the colonel, casting their eyes to the ground as he put his hand to his forehead and said in a broken voice:

'It would appear, young man, that you were right and I was wrong. For what it's worth I offer my apologies. I sent six good men to their deaths; it is never an easy thing to come to terms with.'

He turned and silently descended the staircase to return to his office; the junior officers followed in stunned silence.

Jon did not feel smug about his being right about this; far from it, he would have gladly been proven wrong and the colonel right if it would have brought back the men whose lives had been lost so unnecessarily. A dark mood had settled upon everyone following the return of the six men in such a fashion; the reality of Ebon's cruelty being forced home in such a way came as a shock to all who witnessed it, all that is except Major O'Rourke.

The gnomes had roared their approval at the grisly deed and were now gathering ammunition for the slinger in readiness to unleash its mighty power against the walls of the city. The reverberations from beneath the hill continued incessantly, generating unease and edginess amongst those in the city.

'Remember what happened at Tri-Bune.'

Jon caught the whisper from one of the guards talking to another as he passed, thinking that Jon had not heard.

It seemed that Ebon had planned for the attack to be mounted on two fronts: from the slinger, delivering a pummelling to the walls; and from below. Though how they hoped to tunnel their way through all the way up to the city with any hope of getting through in a reasonable time, he did not know. Then he considered what Colonel Dyer had said about it taking five years to complete the service tunnel. Maybe they had no intention of tunnelling through; maybe it was, as he had told them; a diversionary tactic to disguise their real intent. Why dig a new tunnel when there was a perfectly good one already there. All they had to do was find the entrance. The service tunnel; that was it, they were trying to access the service tunnel. He rushed after the colonel and the other officers to tell them of his fears.

A thunderous boom echoed through the bastion and he felt

the floor quake. 'What on earth!' he thought to himself as he checked himself and doubled back to the rampart with Anna and Hamill not a whit behind him. Dust was settling from a cloud that had been raised by the impact of a huge boulder that had slammed into the wall, disintegrating on contact. Several soldiers were peering over the edge to inspect for any damage; fortunately, none could be discerned, other than some marks in the stone where it had hit. The officers arrived just in time to witness another attack as a boulder was launched by the slinger; they watched in awe as it arced up into the air towards the wall where it smashed into little pieces and another dust cloud settled around them. Coughing and spluttering, the soldiers again inspected the wall; as before there appeared to be very little damage and a cheer went up from the defenders, restoring some of the confidence that had been seeping away over the past few days.

The colonel and his officers had also returned to the ramparts to see what was going on and witnessed the second boulder smash against the outer wall. Jon turned to him saying, 'Colonel, sir.' Jon addressed the colonel more politely than he had before. 'I apologise for my rudeness earlier, I should not have spoken to you in such a manner, especially not in front of your men, so I wish you would accept my apology.'

'I wish for you to accept mine, young Jon. It is I who must apologise for not heeding your warning. Had I done so, then none of this would have happened.'

He came to attention and bowed his head acknowledging his error.

'If there is any other advice that you feel you would wish to render to a stubborn old man I will gladly hear it. For now I must return to the task of eliminating the threat of that machine. The wall has held for now, but if this continues, which it will, it most assuredly will fall.'

'Well, actually I was just on my way to see you and share a thought I had about the tunnelling.'

Jon went on to explain his theory and that he believed the colonel was right about the digging by the gnomes and trolls being a diversion away from their true intent: the service tunnel.

'Good Lord, of course; that's it. Now why hadn't we thought of that?'

'I expect that with everything else going on and with your

faith in the tunnel being locked that it had escaped your mind,' Jon offered.

'No doubt, no doubt. Officer Marshall, get some men into the antechamber and check on the security of the tunnel. The gnomes must by no means be allowed to find the entrance or to use the tunnel to get to the city; if they do gain access then you know what to do.'

Marshall looked at the colonel for a moment then nodded curtly before turning to carry out his orders.

Anna tapped Jon on the shoulder and signed to him.

'Anna asks whether the tunnel can be flooded in the event of it being breached or sealed in any other way.'

Colonel Dyer called to Marshall as he was leaving the tower.

'Marshall, you heard him, see to it that what the young lady has suggested be carried out in the event of the tunnel being broken into. Don't flood it though, unless it is your last option; it can only be done once; then we must wait for the cistern to refill, which would take several days. I suggest you try our other option first.'

Marshall hastened off and he could be heard barking orders as he went for soldiers to follow him to the gatehouse. Turning back to the three of them Colonel Dyer smiled and invited them to share lunch with him.

'It is the very least I can do and perhaps we could discuss any other ideas you have.'

They accepted the offer and had an enjoyable meal albeit the conversation was stilted due to recent events.

The bombardment continued throughout the afternoon. Several attempts were made to destroy the machine but it was too far away, even for the ballista weapons to reach with their barbed spears. Still the wall held fast, despite the constant barrage it received. The reverberations from below continued to drill into the senses, unnerving all within the besieged fortress.

A careful search of the service tunnel revealed that it was still secure but attempts were being made to find it from within the antechamber of the Southill gatehouse. The juddering of the masonry there confirmed to them that Ebon was intent on its discovery and would not give up until it was found. Once they discovered that the central door of the three in the antechamber was a decoy like the other two doors and that the tunnel beyond that middle door was filled with traps, the gnomes would start tearing the lower gatehouse apart in order to reveal the secret entrance.

A guard was organised in pairs on a four hour shift basis to keep a careful watch on things; at the first sign of the hidden door being discovered, the guards were to return up the tunnel at all speed to report to the duty officer of the watch. A decision would then be made as to when the tunnel would be flooded; but there was a secret that only the top rank officers were aware of. It would not be flooded with water; there was one more option open to them: to release a toxic gas that had been discovered in the salt marshes and bottled for use in just an event such as this. The whole tunnel would have to be sealed at the top to prevent any leakage at this end or the ones who had released it would also be among those to feel its effects. As it was a heavy gas, it would sink to the lower stages of the passage so there was little chance of anyone at the top suffering any ill effects. The decision to use it had been discussed in secrecy at the highest level and approval given to the officers in charge to proceed should the gnomes gain access to the tunnel.

The day lengthened out towards evening with the barrage continuing unabated; at a regular interval the thud, crash and shudder of the boulders disintegrating against the wall could be felt. The reverberations from the ground beneath them also increased but the message was noised abroad throughout the city that it was not a threat; that it was simply a ploy on the part of the gnomes to undermine their confidence and not the hill. This news was well received by all and lifted the mood a little for a while, but the incessant vibrations and noises from both sources dulled their senses and they all fell under its spell again very quickly.

They ate their evening meal without a word being said to each other. The whole mess hall was depressed by the onslaught and rumours circulated around that the gnomes would break into the upper bastion within days. After dinner, Hamill said he had heard some of the soldiers talking of trying to escape by going over the wall in the night; they went to see Lieutenant Perkins and reported what Hamill had heard; he said that he would deal with it.

'I need some air; how about you, Anna? Do you fancy coming up to the rampart?'

Jon squeezed her hand in affection.

She nodded her consent and grabbed her coat from the back of her chair. Hamill made to come with them but Jon coughed and winked at him, shaking his head quickly as Anna's back was turned. Hamill took the hint and made his excuses, saying that he was tired and wanted an early night so would meet them for breakfast in the morning.

Darkness covered the land, made even darker by the lowering cloud cover; it had stopped raining but the threat of it remained in the air. Thunder rumbled away in the east and flashes of lightning split the night with incandescence just as it had on the first night. The view before them on any other occasion would have been marvellous to behold. A myriad tiny fires, sparkling like stars, outlined the extent of the army encamped before them. Gnomes, trolls, marsh-mogs and kite-folk were all arrayed before them, eager to be tearing at the structure of the fortress and to sate their bloodlust on the inhabitants within the city.

Jon and Anna stood close to each other, his arm around her waist, as she leaned her head on his shoulder. He quickly became lost in an inward stare, thinking of more pleasant times and imagining them together after all this was over and living in peace.

The slinger had ceased to discharge its boulders for the day but the tunnelling continued unabated; it would be difficult to sleep with that going on throughout the night.

Anna lifted her head from his shoulder and shielded her face from her hair, which blew into her eyes; she stiffened and he looked at her to see what was wrong. She shook his shoulder to get his attention and pointed away to their right. He followed the direction of her pointing finger but could not see what she wanted him to look at; then he noticed flashes at the edge of the gnome encampment. 'It's just more lightning I think,' he said but was unconvinced; as he looked closer he noticed that the flashes were coming from the ground and rising up into the air, not the other way around. The colour was wrong too: the flashes were coloured green and blue. The display lasted for about a half a minute before it ceased. It was too far away for any sound to be heard but there was certainly something going on to alarm the gnomes and others in the camp below them. Little spots of light from hundreds of torches gathered to the point where the flashes had been seen so that it looked like a spectacular show of fireflies concentrating towards one place.

The wind suddenly stilled then shifted direction and gathered strength, whistling in from the west through the battlements with a fury, just as a lamb might flee from a lion. It felt unnatural in its intensity and they could hardly hear each other for the screeching in their ears. Jon and Anna had to cling to each other and duck behind a wall to prevent them from being blown over. Several of the sentries tried to battle against it in the fulfilment of their sentry duties but were blown off their feet and bowled over backwards to crash against a wall. Trying to gain their feet unsuccessfully, they retreated into the tower and descended to report on the change in the weather.

Jon and Anna crouched behind the protective wall of the rampart, not daring to move from the safety of the spot for fear of losing their footing. The night stars appeared above them as the dark, storm-laden clouds were driven back towards the Eastern Mountains, boiling amid the battle of forces at play.

A few minutes later, Hamill appeared at the door of the south tower not ten paces away, with Lieutenant Perkins, Captain Quentin and the dwarves. Everyone had heard the wind beating against the walls and whistling through open windows and when the sentries had reported that Jon and Anna were still up on the ramparts, they had come to see if they were in need of help. They were, if they were to make it safely to the tower and not be blown over the edge by the force of the wind.

Hamill cupped his hands to his mouth and shouted something to them but Jon could not hear as his words were snatched from his lips as he spoke them. Jon shook his head and put his hand to his ear signifying that he could not hear what Hamill was saying. Anna waved to Hamill that he should take his hands away from his mouth and she would then be able to lip read. He did as she had signalled and repeated what he had said; she nodded that she understood and signed to Jon what they had in mind to do; he in turn nodded that he too understood.

Lieutenant Perkins held a rope and he tried to throw a coil of it to them but the wind was so strong that it blew it right back at him. He tried several more times without success before abandoning the attempt. The dwarves linked themselves together with the rope passing between them and tried to make their way across to them; the strength of their short, stocky bodies was tested to the limit as they bent into the wind but they too failed to get anywhere near them. Trapper, being the stoutest, held the rope in support of the others and had to strain to keep his footing when Archer slipped and was swept sideways, dragging the other two with him. Frantic attempts were made by them all to stop being blown off the city wall and only succeeded because Tracker managed to get the point of his axe in one of the joints between a couple of flagstones and held on with gritty determination. With Trapper standing firm and with assistance from the others in the tower, they were able to rescue the dwarves and haul them back into the shelter of the tower.

Lieutenant Perkins signalled for Jon and Anna to stay where they were and tied the rope around his waist; he was going to try to reach them. He lay flat to the ground and inched his way forward, out of the shelter of the tower and into the flow of the wind that grabbed at him with invisible hands, trying to snatch him from the stone walkway. As well as the rope that he had secured around him, he also carried a second one coiled over his shoulder. Gradually making his way towards them, he held a knife in each hand and used them to slide into the crevices between the flagstones for grip; it took several minutes for him to reach them and by the time he had, he was exhausted. Struggling for breath, he sat with his back against the wall that Jon and Anna were also using for shelter, and rested a moment.

He handed them the other rope and shouted into Jon's ear to tie one end around Anna's waist, leaving a bit of slack so that it did not cut into her. He then undid the rope that was around his waist and threaded it through the loop of the rope Jon had tied around Anna; she was now securely tied with both ropes. He signalled for her to lie as flat on the floor as she could then explained that he wanted her to start to crawl back the way he had come to where Hamill and the others were waiting holding the other end of the rope. She turned and gave Jon a kiss for luck; he kissed her back and smiled encouragingly. Between them they fed out the rope as she inched her way over to the shelter of the tower where Hamill and the others were pulling in the slack from the other rope that Perkins had had tied around him. With Jon's help at keeping the rope taut, they managed to get her across the floor and to safety. Quentin knotted the two ropes together, after releasing Anna from them, and fed it back to Perkins and Jon who pulled it in ready for Jon to go. Perkins secured one end of their rope around the castellated rampart before tying the other end around Jon's waist. The other rope was secured as before so that the others could pull in the slack with Perkins taking the strain on the other. Jon also managed to crawl his way back, slipping only once as a particularly strong gust of wind almost took him up into the air. Perkins gritted his teeth and dug his heels in to the cracks of the stones that offered a little leverage and strained to hold him, whilst the others did the same at the other end of the ropes; between them they managed to save him from being blown away.

Jon was heartily received by Hamill into the shelter of the tower and reunited with Anna, shaking hands with everyone in gratitude for their help. The ropes were tied together again and Perkins hauled them in, tying the one that was secured to the battlement around his waist and the other he attached securely to the first, enabling Hamill and the others to keep him secure should he slip. He edged backwards along the flagstones towards the tower, keeping as close to the cold stone as he could; with the wind lashing into him it made it difficult for him to grip the knives or to gain any kind of handhold. He was only a few feet from the tower's entrance when a gust of wind caught him. The power of the wind pulling at him caused the blades of his knives to snap off in the cracks of the flagstones; the wind seemed to pick him up and carry him away beyond the doorway. They tried to grab him as he went past but without success and the rope that was secured to the wall went taught, straining against the force and snaking up and down as the weight of his body dragged at the other end. The rope the others had hold of was slack so they carefully drew it in until resistance was felt, then hauled with all their might to reel Perkins in. Several agonising minutes later, with their arms burning from the strain, he appeared by the doorway and they managed to drag him in to the shelter of the tower, away from the howling fury of the clutching wind.

He was unconscious and badly battered about the head and body; Hamill examined him to ensure that he was safe to move and fortunately could find no broken bones. The dwarves removed the ropes that had saved him from certain injury or even death; he was lucky to be alive. Carefully cradling his limp form between them they followed Hamill's guidance in handling him and took him down the stairway and across to the infirmary for a more detailed examination and treatment. Hamill insisted that both Jon and Anna come with them so that they could also be checked over, just to be on the safe side.

They were both feeling shaken by their experience and agreed to do so if only to appease Hamill, otherwise they would have got no peace. He would have persisted until they had finally acquiesced to his demand.

There was a flurry of activity along the corridors and passageways with soldiers moving items hurriedly from one place to another amid a tumult of orders and counter orders from the officers. The howl of the wind could be heard above them as it battered against the defences of the city as if to pluck it apart, bit by bit. Here in the shelter of the fortress, they were indeed warm and secure from any threat of harm, although Jon swore that he could feel the stone of the defences being pummelled as the storm grew in intensity.

Colonel Dyer appeared ahead of them looking concerned and then relieved as he spotted them.

'Thank goodness you are all right; I was just informed of your situation.'

His look of concern returned as he noticed Lieutenant Perkins being carried into the infirmary.

'What happened? Is Perkins OK?'

'Yes, he's fine; concussed and bruised but otherwise he's going to make a good recovery,' Hamill answered him with an assured look.

'He saved our lives and deserves a medal,' Jon stated, hoping that his suggestion would not fall on deaf ears.

'Indeed?' Colonel Dyer commented with raised eyebrows. 'Well, I think that can be arranged. I think we can even do better than that; how about we promote him to captain, eh, Jon?'

'That would be great; I mean, if that's what he wants.'

Jon looked excitedly at Anna who also beamed with delight.

'I can assure you that it would please him no end to be promoted to captain,' the colonel stated.

'And I should add, it is a little overdue. His devotion to duty and his selfless efforts to secure your safety at the risk of his own life demonstrates a high degree of bravery. It merits rewarding.'

Inside the infirmary the attendants were now tending to the care of Perkins and made him comfortable whilst others tended to the scratches and grazes that Jon and Anna had sustained.

They were advised to get a good night's sleep; this was a suggestion that they readily accepted due to their exhausting experience. Colonel Dyer assured them that they had nothing to worry about all the time this wind blew as it did. At least they were safe and warm behind the solid stone walls; Ebon's army must be suffering untold damage out in the open Yield. Even the scant shelter they might have taken in the trees was gone now that they had chopped them down to build the siege machines and supply their fires.

Jon and Anna went to their respective rooms feeling the effects of their struggle with the elements up on the ramparts. Jon could not even imagine what it must be like being exposed to these conditions as the gnome army was. He would be interested to see what had become of them tomorrow and considered the events of the evening, especially the strange lightning and the storm that had erupted shortly after, wondering if they were connected in some way; he went to sleep thinking of Urim and his anticipated return tomorrow.

Chapter XVI

Northill: The Siege

Jon was awakened by Tracker who shook him into consciousness; it was still dark and the wind whistled past his window throwing rain against the glass with such force that it was a wonder the glass did not shatter.

'Jon, get dressed quickly, we have need of your help; I'll wait outside.'

Within a minute he was standing out in the corridor with Tracker; Trapper was also there and they signalled for Jon to be quiet. He was led through the corridors and down into the lower levels of the gatehouse; they kept to the quieter passages avoiding any contact with the night sentries and emerged in the anteroom of the upper gatehouse where they had entered Northill for the first time. The other dwarves were there with Captain Quentin and a troop of elves equipped for hiking; they had their crossbows across their backs and were also girded with swords.

'What is going on?' Jon asked, hoping someone would explain.

Javelin told him that they had been busy 'snooping' around, as Hamill had put it, asking questions and had, with the assistance of some who were not entirely convinced of the colonel's ability to make the right decisions, been able to obtain the plans for the service tunnel; it showed them every stage of its construction, including a secret exit from the service conduit that they had been unaware of before. It wound through a series of tunnels to the rear of the hill fort where it emerged some distance away through a trapdoor into an old building to the north of here. This needed investigating because it could prove vital to them in the event of an evacuation, or if the gnomes discovered it, as another means of infiltrating their defences. There were numerous other chambers and storage rooms higher up, which were marked as

249

restricted; they had managed to discover some disturbing information concerning them.

'We have reason to believe that the colonel means to use a poison gas to flood the tunnel in the event of the gnomes finding the entrance. We cannot allow that to happen,' Captain Quentin told him. 'Whatever their nature, we will not stand by and see this crime being perpetrated. We want you to shut the door after us and not open it again unless you hear me or one of the dwarves asking you to do so; do you understand what I am saying, Jon?'

'Yes, but why ask me, why not have one of your elves do it?'

'We cannot risk raising any suspicions; if one of my elves was left here they certainly would do that, whereas you have been seen to wander anywhere at will and you also have the ear of the colonel; you will not be challenged,' Captain Quentin explained hurriedly.

'Just tell them that we have gone into the tunnel to check it out and ensure it is secure.'

'I thought they were doing that anyway,' Jon said, trying to think of every circumstance that could occur.

Captain Quentin assured him he would be fine and said, 'Not any more; they are too busy with affairs up there to worry about something that they believe to be impregnable. If they should come in here just tell them that we have taken over responsibility for the tunnel and they can go about other business. They probably will not even bother you. Are you ready?'

Jon nodded and Archer showed him how to operate the secret door, which opened smoothly to admit them down the steps and into the chamber where the voice conduit was; they filed in following the dwarves and when they had all entered, Jon closed the door.

'Jon, can you hear me?'

He heard Quentin's voice from the aperture in the wall next to the door.

'Yes I can hear you.'

'If we are not back within three hours, report to Major O'Rourke what our intentions were; he will know what to do. Hopefully we will be back before then. In the meantime, no one else should come in after us; stay alert, because we may need to be let out in a hurry.'

'I will; good luck to you and be careful.'

Jon heard them open the outer door into the service tunnel and after they had all gone through, the door closed after them and the place fell into silence.

Jon wondered how he would know when the three hours were up and looked around for a time counter; he saw one on the table over by the entrance into the room and set it for three hours' time; even if he fell asleep he would be able to know when it was time for them to return. He made himself as comfortable as he could, determined not to fall asleep, but he was so tired, he could not help himself and was soon breathing heavily, his eyelids fluttering in a vain attempt to remain conscious.

After the door had slid into place behind them, the dwarves went down the slope towards the bottom entrance to investigate any ingress into the tunnel on the part of the gnomes and trolls; the torches flickered in the waft of air caused by their movements as both parties turned away from each other and headed in different directions. Captain Quentin led his elves up the slope of the tunnel towards the room that they had searched for an exit when they had first come to Northill. The dwarves carefully navigated the slippery surface of the floor speckled with patches of moss that was growing due to the moisture that trickled from the top of the tunnel. It made their descent down the stairway quite treacherous and at times they slipped, having to hold on to the brackets supporting the great iron pipes that carried the water that was pumped from the bottom cistern back to the top one, following the use of the funicular. The darkness was only illuminated by the torches that each of them carried, casting large shadows of each dwarf onto the circular, stone-lined tube of the service tunnel as they walked. They travelled as silently as they could so as not to give away their presence to any who might be listening for movement.

The darkness loomed before them like a wall that edged away from them, daring them to come further, holding the unknown within its gloom; the light from their torches only illuminated a few feet in front of them. The faint lights of the elves' torches could be seen what seemed like a long way away behind and above them; they too were being as quiet as they could and when elves wanted to be quiet, they were.

251

Captain Quentin and his sergeant led his four squads of elves into the stone-lined chamber at the top of the tunnel and had them stand in the centre of the room; he searched the walls more thoroughly than he had before. This time he knew what he was looking for: twelve square stones set around a large one in the middle of the wall. He pressed them in the sequence memorised from the plans he had seen and an opening appeared as the stones of one of the walls slid back revealing a passageway.

'Quinn, I want you to take one squad with you and see what the situation is regarding the gas containers; I shall be shutting you in there for as long as it takes for us to investigate the other tunnel; we may be some time,' Quentin explained to his sergeant at arms.

'Should we not return before the three hours are up then you need to open the door from inside, using the lever I told you about, then seal it again after you and return to the gatehouse, with or without the dwarves, and report to Major O'Rourke; is that understood?'

'Yes, sir, good luck to you, sir,' Quinn replied.

Quentin nodded in response and closed the door after Quinn had selected his elves and entered into the dark passageway that lay beyond the doorway.

Quentin then pressed the stones in a different sequence and another entrance opened up in the wall opposite the one they had all come in through.

'Right then; follow me through to the tunnel one by one and keep in sight of each other; I don't want anyone getting lost or injured and no one knowing about it. Be careful not to lean on these stones as you cross the floor, or you might trigger the door and it could close on someone.'

Single file and with an air of anticipation, they filed through the entrance past Captain Quentin into the rough hewn tunnel beyond; once everyone was through Quentin closed the doorway by using the lever situated inside; it closed with a swish of escaping air.

'Now remember that to the best of my knowledge, this passage has not been used for a long time and there could be rockfalls and other obstructions in our way so we must proceed with caution. Zefin, I want you to lead the way, seeing as you have the most experience in this kind of thing; everyone is to be on their guard for any possibility of traps or snares, even the most innocent of things could be significant.' Quentin urged his troops to take care.

They proceeded to descend into the heart of the hill, following the uneven track as it meandered through the rock following seams and crevices; occasionally there were steps cut into the ground to facilitate a better passage in the steeper parts. Zefin would stop every now and then to inspect a bulge in the roof of the tunnel and test its soundness before reassuring the others and moving on. Water could be heard trickling down the slope and drops of water splashed into small pools that the trail skirted around. Stalactites and stalagmites formed strange and beautiful shapes in the larger caverns that they traversed; sometimes these joined together and formed huge columns that looked like marble. At one point they had to cross a small bridge that spanned a deep chasm; the bridge was made from cedar and although it looked like it had been there for many years, it appeared to be solid. One of the elves was detailed to test it out but a rope was secured around him prior to him setting foot on the old timber; much to the relief of everyone it held under his weight and they were able to proceed without any difficulty, marking the trail as they went.

They were brought to an abrupt halt shortly afterwards when they were going through another tunnel between caverns and came across a blockage from a collapsed roof; Zefin inspected the fall carefully and started to remove some of the smaller rocks, which created a shift in the rockfall. Larger rocks above were unsettled by the disturbance and dust swirled around them choking those at the front, causing them to cough and splutter but it soon settled. Several of the elves, under Zefin's direction, removed the debris with care and gradually cleared away the loose rocks, passing them back along the line to be lain aside out of the way.

The flow of air increased and a dim light could be seen ahead of them down the tunnel; two of the elves scrambled through to the other side of the fall to investigate the source of the airflow and light whilst the blockage was being completely cleared. They returned shortly afterwards and reported that the tunnel ended a short way ahead and steps led up through a trapdoor.

They could not see where it came out and had not lifted the door as a light was burning in a room above, which filtered through tiny cracks in the wood; voices could be heard so they assumed that the tunnel emerged into a building of some kind.

Captain Quentin ordered everyone to be vigilant and continue along the passage as quietly as they could, which for elves meant silently; some of them unsheathed their short swords whilst others readied their crossbows. Gathering at the foot of the steps that led up into the building they remained silent, listening to the voices above; it was really quite difficult to hear what was being said and no words could be deciphered other than a rumble of sound, presumably their speech being baffled by the trapdoor. It was opened by means of two metal bars that were attached to the frame of the door and secured to retainers either side of the steps; the securing pins were removed and two elves on both sides took hold of the bars waiting for the signal from Quentin to raise the door, whereupon he would lead the others into the open and secure it by catching those above off guard. At the foot of the steps Quentin readied his elves and tested the door, it gave slightly and dust fell onto the first step; he signalled for the elves holding the bars to shove with their might and dashed up the steps into the room above, followed by the others.

It was difficult to judge who was the most surprised, the elves or those in the barn into which they had sprung; as Quentin burst up from below followed by his elves, the trapdoor was flung open with such force it crashed onto the floor. Three huge figures stood like sentinels watching over a sleeping form on a couple of straw bales; Quentin's jaw dropped open and he almost dropped his sword in amazement. The sleeping figure awoke upon the noise of the trapdoor falling to the floor and he sprang to his feet groggily shaking his head to arouse his faculties; he too stood in stupefied amazement at the sight of the elves that had appeared as if from nowhere.

'Braun! Holdhard!' Quentin exclaimed in bewilderment.

Captain Quentin; what are you doing here?' Braun asked, still trying to gather his senses from being awakened from a deep sleep.

'How did *you* get here?' Quentin asked. 'Never mind; I can see that you were successful in bringing the colossi. Holdhard, it is a great honour to meet with you again.'

Quentin bowed his head and ordered his elves to lower their weapons and to secure the area. A few of them slipped out of the barn doors battling with the elements as the wind tried to tear the doors from their hinges. They moved like shadows to scout around and ensure that they were safe from any form of attack or disturbance; others went down into the tunnel to report their discovery to those who had stayed to guard their rear.

Holdhard acknowledged his greeting and indicated Bearer and Petros who each bowed their heads in turn as they were introduced.

Braun clasped Quentin's hand in his, being careful not to press too hard as his hand was several times bigger than Quentin's and he could easily have broken every bone if he had not taken care.

'It's good to see you, my friend, but tell me: how did *you* get here and how are the others?'

Braun was obviously curious as he had thought that the way in and out of Northill to be inaccessible now with Ebon's army laying siege.

Quentin quickly brought him up to speed with all that had happened; that Urim had not been seen for three days, and how he and the dwarves had discovered the secret tunnel leading away from the First city, and had decided that it needed to be investigated; he also told him of the gas and Colonel Dyer's plans to use it on the gnomes if necessary. Quentin reckoned that they had a little time yet before they were due back at the gatehouse entrance where Jon was waiting to let them in; as the tunnel was not large enough to permit the colossi to enter, it was decided that the colossi would remain here and secure the tunnel from being discovered. Braun would go through the tunnel with the elves; they would take him as far as the chamber where he would continue on and join Jon in the gatehouse. Once the gas had been rendered unusable Quentin and the others would catch up with the dwarves in the service tunnel and ensure all was secure before returning through the antechamber into the fortification.

The colossi settled to the task of keeping the entrance to the secret tunnel secure and extinguished the light after the elves and Braun had departed, covering the trapdoor over again with an old blanket and dirt from the floor with some straw added on for good measure. Should there be a need to use the tunnel as an escape route in the eventuality of a retreat, they would be there to render whatever assistance was necessary. The place fell into silence as the dark of the early hours shrouded the three colossi who stood like statues in the large barn, their heads almost touching the rafters of the hay loft; all the while the storm raged outside and beat against the doors incessantly.

Braun had to duck his head a number of times as he navigated his way along the trail through the hillside, entering large caverns and narrow tunnels as they made their way back up to the antechamber. When they arrived at the place where the elves had separated, Braun carried on into the room with the voice box and whispered into it.

'Jon, open the door.'

Jon dreamed of Braun coming to the rescue of the besieged city and of Urim riding in on the wind like some spectral being.

'Jon, are you there? Open the door.'

The voice was becoming more insistent and he became aware of his surroundings. He had slumped across the table and had dribbled on to his arm; wiping the sleep from his eyes and the saliva from his face he came alert with a start.

'Jon, it is I, Braun; can you hear me?'

The voice came from the aperture in the wall, from the voice conduit. He jumped to his feet and stumbled over to the wall.

'Braun, is that you?'

'At last; yes, Jon it is I. I thought something was wrong when I couldn't hear a reply. Captain Quentin told me he had left you guarding the door.'

Braun's voice sounded strange through the conduit, but it was unmistakably he.

Jon threw the lever, which operated the secret door, and a few moments later Braun emerged from the gloom into the well lit chamber. Jon gave him a hug, which the big man returned.

'Am I glad to see you; but how did you get here?'

Jon felt a surge of friendship rise within his bosom and he could not stop from smiling, shaking his head in disbelief.

'I too am relieved to see that you are well, Captain Quentin told me that the three of you were being of considerable help to the commander here.'

Braun's remarks embarrassed Jon and took him a little by surprise but he was more interested in what had happened to Braun since they had last seen each other. Jon looked back down the steps.

'Is anyone with you? Where are the colossi? What has happened to the others?'

Braun laughed and calmed him down, saying, 'All is well; the others are still investigating the tunnels. Captain Quentin and his elves discovered the colossi and me sheltering from the storm in an old stone barn some distance yet from the city when we were taken quite by surprise and were surrounded by a troop of elves with levelled crossbows pointing at us. It didn't take long though to realise who was who and we were all very much relieved to have met with each other. The elves guided me back here through the tunnel but the colossi were too large to be accommodated within, and seeing as the weather did not much affect them, they were happy to wait there until they were needed. It worked out quite well actually as they are securing the secret entrance from any unwanted intrusions.'

'You must be in need of some food and rest but I do not want to draw attention to the fact that we have accessed the tunnel; can you wait until the others have returned?' Jon was torn between having Braun attended to and keeping their purpose undiscovered until it was deemed necessary.

'I'm fine for the moment, though I don't deny that a hot meal and a strong drink would be welcome right now. We shall wait for the others to return and in the meantime you can tell me what has happened. I understand that Urim is not here?'

'No, he left us several days ago before we got in to Northill; the service tunnel has been sealed since then and we have been waiting for Urim to return. He promised that he would be back today, though how he was to get in was puzzling me until the discovery of the secret tunnel; a lot has happened these past few days. Tell me your news and I'll tell you everything I know.'

Braun related his story of returning to the mountain city with Holdhard via the way that Hamill had been led out, through the falls, and of his discussions with Bearer, Petros and Holdhard. He had explained the need for their help in defending the whole land from the designs of Ebon and the gnomes. They had argued their neutrality and of their long held belief that they should not interfere in the lives of fleshers. Braun had fretted over a way in which he could sway the colossi to go with him to Northill to meet up with Urim; to help defend the people of the whole land from ultimate destruction. He had tried every persuasion he could think of but each time the same argument came up of non-interference. Finally he had asked them how they had come to have the sword that Bearer had strapped to his side. They had said that it was a token between them and the metal masters from ages past but its meaning had been lost, other than a service had been done. Braun called upon that token stating that if they had been of service to each other before that they could be so again. After some deliberation between the three stone men, it was agreed that they would accompany Braun and if it was found that their services were required then they would help. The journey had been undertaken and they had arrived near to Northill just as the high wind had broken over the Yield preventing him from going any further, so the colossi had stayed with him as he sheltered in the building where the elves had discovered them.

Jon in his turn told Braun of all that had occurred from the time they had parted back at the Ward over a week ago. It seemed more like a month, so much had happened to them; they sat in silence for a while each taking in the news the other had related.

The dwarves watched as the lights from the elves' torches were extinguished by the door of the secret tunnel as it closed after them; it seemed that they were all alone as the silence of the tunnel settled upon them. The way ahead stretched on into blackness as the floor of the passage fell away in front of them in long steps; they continued on with care.

Javelin led the way forward with Archer bringing up the rear, placing Trapper and Tracker in between them. They stood still every now and again listening for any sound that would indicate to them that the tunnel had been compromised. All they heard was the regular thump of the trolls' excavations as they continued to dig into the hillside in their attempt to find the service tunnel, having discovered the others to be decoys. That discovery had not diminished their efforts in respect of finding the tunnel and it stood testimony to the engineering prowess of the builders of the service tunnel in that they had not discovered it or been able to break through the concealed stone doorway.

The walls of the tunnel vibrated with each shock as the trolls hammered away at the rock; tiny granules of the roof fell like grains of sand from cracks that had opened up in the lining of the tunnel; evidencing the determination and desperation of the trolls to find the tunnel at all costs. The dwarves wondered just how close the trolls were to finding the tunnel and breaking through, enabling them to force an attack on the defenders of the city from the one place they least expected it. Colonel Dyer and his commanders had absolute confidence in the tunnel remaining undiscovered, and even if it was, then the secret rooms and entrances would deter even the hardiest of assailants; besides, as they had found out, the colonel had his ace card up his sleeve of the gas, which could be released into the tunnel and kill whoever was in it. They had been appalled by the discovery of the lethal gas that was stored at the top of the complex of passages. It was placed there in order to maximise the effect of being able to flood through any of the tunnels that were discovered by unwelcome visitors. It was so dense that it was almost a liquid and could snuff out a flaming torch in seconds; the individual carrying it would have died just as quickly. The only way of surviving its effect was, if you were aware of its presence, you could hold your breath until you were clear of it; the trouble is that you never knew when that was. The gas was contained in giant vats with tubes at the bottom of each one controlled by valves that were regulated by a mechanism attached to a system of rods and pulleys that disappeared into a conduit in the roof of the chamber. According to the plans that they had seen the system was controlled by a set of levers secreted in the office of the garrison commander.

The dwarves were somewhat unnerved by the fact that they were descending lower into the tunnel system and therefore further past the point of no return; if the gas were to be released while they were still in the tunnel, they would stand little chance of surviving. The plans revealed no other way out than the one at the bottom of the slope where they were heading and the one at the top where they had separated from the elves. After some considerable time, they reached the end of the tunnel and found the lever that opened the secret door. It was still locked shut and no evidence could be seen to have them believe that there was any danger of the gnomes and trolls finding their way through; the door was still firmly in place.

*

Having sent Braun on to Jon, escorted by two of his elves who were to guard the secret door into the gatehouse until he returned with the other elves, Captain Quentin and the rest of his troops closed the escape tunnel and entered the passageway that led to the room where the gas was stored. It was a huge cavern created naturally in the rock formation; its true size was difficult to gauge as the massive vats of gas almost filled the entire space; they felt like ants scurrying around its base. Sergeant Quinn's task was to assess what the situation was and to make the vats safe if at all possible but without endangering the rest of the elves or dwarves. He had managed to do so by sealing the vents where the gas would be released with the exception of one of the vats; the valve at the base was being rather stubborn. Whilst the others had been disconnected from the system of rods and pulleys without any problems, the one nearest the doorway had become frozen by years of leaking water from the ceiling, which had been running down the sides of the vat and over the valve.

Carefully they tried to loosen the connecting rods that triggered the release of the gas from the huge vat; several of the elves had received bad cold burns, their hands showing signs of frostbite following them touching the freezing cold metal. It was so cold that one of the elves' swords had shattered while he was trying to use it as a lever.

They were just about to give up the attempt to remove the trigger rods when they heard a snap and a fine crack appeared just above the valve; panic welled up in the elves as they realised that there was no way of stopping any gas leak from that position and watched in horror as the crack grew larger and spread around the collar of the connection. Quentin snapped the order to vacate the room and return to the antechamber but not quick enough to get out of the chamber without feeling the effects of the escaping gas. It hissed menacingly and the fracture could be seen to grow bigger until it burst open and the contents of the vat gushed out; an unseen but cold and deadly killer. A couple of the elves tripped in their rush to evacuate the room and were immediately overcome by the gas as it rolled over them; you could almost see it, like a heat haze, rushing to find its level; being heavier than the air they breathed it washed around their legs but was rising rapidly. They needed to get out quickly if they were to survive this. There was no time to warn the dwarves, any attempt to do so would be signing their own death warrants. They rushed through the open doorway, where the two elves were keeping watch and into the anteroom; they stopped the flow of the gas from coming in with them by closing the door quickly behind them; their action prevented all but a small amount from doing so; they could feel it swirling around their ankles.

The dwarves began a detailed inspection of the walls and ceiling, trying to find any evidence of cracking to the stonework that formed the core of the tunnel; the vibrations from the trolls' quarrying could be felt more intensely at this lower level. A shock wave rippled through the ground each time the heavy blows fell to dislodge more of the rock as they continued to burrow their way in. The dwarves stopped every now and again in order to determine where the noise of the tunnelling trolls came from. Prior to entering the service tunnel, the dwarves had looked out over the ground from the top of the ramparts, down on the mine entrances the trolls had started in the hillside. It gave Javelin a good idea as to the direction the trolls had taken but not how far in they had managed to dig.

For a long period of time they just stood patiently listening to the reverberations and also for any hint of there being any ingress from the antechamber into the tunnel from the south gate; it was the most obvious way in, providing that Ebon's gnomes could discover the doorway. Trolls were far too big to fit in the service tunnel and would only be employed in the heavier task of demolishing and removing stonework or for digging; the gnomes would be the ones to enter the tunnel, if ever that moment came.

Javelin was rather curious to know why the gnomes had not yet discovered the entrance; they had surely discovered by now that the three doors were decoys and that there must therefore be another, hidden, doorway into which they had disappeared upon first arriving at Southill, entering the gatehouse at the foot of the hill fort. Whatever the reasons, they were grateful that the door still stood intact.

Tracker turned and peered up the tunnel into the gloom; he thought he had seen a glimmer of light away up at the other end and heard some sort of commotion going on but it was too far away to make anything from it. Frowning in bemusement he turned his attention back to inspecting a hairline crack between the joints of some stonework he had discovered a little way up from the bottom. The others were about twenty lengths away further down the slope getting ready to make the return journey, packing the equipment they had brought with them. He felt something cold run over his feet and swirl around his ankles; he jumped, startled and looked down to see what had caused it. He could see nothing but the cold still flowed past his legs rising and falling as if coming in waves: GAS!

He paused momentarily, stunned, then shouted to the others.

'Javelin, the gas has been let loose; it's freezing my legs and filling the tunnel.'

Javelin thought furiously as to what to do; should they try to escape it by running back up the tunnel? Impossible; it would overtake them in its swift rise up the tunnel and they would die in the attempt. If they stayed here then they would likewise perish; they could go down to the bottom of the tunnel in an attempt to reach it before the well of the stairs filled with gas, open the door to let the gas out and allow it to flow into the anteroom of the south gate, but that would open it up for the gnomes to discover and get through to the others in Northill.

The gas was rising rapidly and chilled them to the bone; unable to decide for them all, Javelin put it to a vote: should they run up the tunnel and die in the attempt? Should they go to the foot of the stairway and open the door to save themselves but expose the others to danger? Or should they take their farewells of each other and sacrifice themselves for the greater good? They looked sadly at one another. Standing in a circle they laid their hands on each others' shoulders in a final gesture of friendship; Archer grabbed hold of one of the torches and gently lowered it towards the ground. It went out when he got to waist height; they could feel the cold grip of death creeping up their bodies. The bottom of the tunnel would be flooded by now, soon it would cover them and they would fall to the ground to rise no more.

Jon and Braun were disturbed by two of Major O'Rourke's men who had been sent to check on the tunnel having secured the fortified city from any damage or harm that the strong winds could have inflicted. They were taken unawares by the presence of Jon and particularly that of the metal master, and drawing their swords queried where he had come from. Jon jumped up and tried to calm them saying that Braun was one of their original party and had brought help with him; the guards were not entirely convinced and sent another soldier to fetch the major. They waited calmly for the major to arrive although the soldiers did not relax their stance and kept their swords drawn, distrustful at the sudden appearance of Braun.

Major O'Rourke arrived minutes later with a company of soldiers and demanded to know what was going on; he did not seem to be in any mood for mysteries or intrigues, standing glowering at them with hands on hips.

Jon was a little way through explaining who Braun was and how he had got in to the city when a cry was heard from the voice box.

'Jon, let us in quickly; hurry, man.'

It was Captain Quentin.

Major O'Rourke signalled to one of the soldiers to open the entrance to the tunnel. Quentin struggled up the steps coughing and looking ill, half carrying, half dragging one of his elfin soldiers; he was followed by three more supporting their comrades between them. They were in like manner looking as if they were about to fall to their knees; several of them appeared to be suffering from frostbite. When the elves had all passed through the door Quentin shouted at the guard to close the entrance; he did so quickly.

'Quentin, would you kindly tell me what is going on here and why you have been in the tunnel?' O'Rourke demanded.

'Where are the dwarves?' Jon asked, concerned.

Captain Quentin shook his head and gasped out bitterly between coughs.

'They've had it. They were in the lower parts of the tunnel when the gas escaped.'

'Sergeant, I want this room cleared of your men and I need these elves taken to the infirmary right now; jump to it, man.' the major snapped when he was slow to obey.

When the room was clear of the major's soldiers he helped Quentin to his feet and sat him at the table, giving him a drink from the flagon of water.

'Now then; what's all this about gas and the dwarves?'

Gulping and spluttering on his drink, Quentin explained.

'We found out that the colonel intended to use gas against the gnomes and went in to disable it in some way; we succeeded in blocking the vents where the gas would be released and dismantled the control valves with all but the last tank, which fractured as we tried to make it safe but the gas escaped. Four of my soldiers dropped to the floor like sacks of grain and we only just managed to make it to the anteroom without succumbing ourselves.'

He turned to Jon and continued.

'I'm sorry, Jon, but there was no way for us to stop the gas from going down the tunnel to where the dwarves were. I don't think they knew anything about it.'

His fit of coughing subsided and he breathed more easily. Jon and Braun were stunned and could not believe that the dwarves were dead; Jon ran towards the door to the tunnel and made to open it but Braun held him back saying that it was too late by now; Jon cried out in anguish and sorrow. The others sat with lowered heads and remained still, reflecting on the passing of the valiant dwarves. No one wanted to believe that they were gone but they had to accept the inevitable.

Quentin and O'Rourke went to report to the colonel while Jon and Braun made their way up the many stairways to the small refreshment room where they had played sticks yesterday. It was almost time for breakfast and Braun suggested that they have some brought to them from the mess hall, enough for them, Anna and Hamill. One of the elves had said that he would order up breakfast for them whilst another said he would rouse the other two and say that Jon needed to see them; he would then direct Anna and Hamill to them without saying anything. Jon thanked him and slouched heavily into a large chair in a depressed mood. What a terrible way for the dwarves to go; they would not have wanted to die in that manner; the way of death for a dwarf was in battle, his blade in his hand followed by a warrior's burial. Well at least he could do that for them; as soon as the tunnel was clear, he would arrange for the retrieval of their bodies and for their burial.

Anna and Hamill sat with tears in their eyes at the news Jon had broken regarding the dwarves. The initial jubilation of seeing Braun was now tempered by the death of their friends; it was hard to believe and it felt surreal to imagine being without them. Breakfast had been delivered with quiet reverence as the tale of the dwarves' demise had spread throughout the city. Not much had been eaten but a toast had been offered by Braun to the memory of the brave little soldiers, which they all stood up to do, draining their cups and fidgeting nervously. The officer named Marshall appeared at the door, knocking gently on the door post and with a gentle cough he asked respectfully that they come with him to see the colonel. They arose slowly and followed Marshall who walked at a respectful pace, not hurrying them.

'My dear friends, I have heard of the unfortunate events that have led to the deaths of your friends and wish to offer my condolences.'

He rose from behind his desk and walked around to place his hands on their shoulders.

'You must be Braun; welcome metal master; your assistance here will be invaluable to us.' He grasped the big man's hand in his and bowed his head slightly in respect.

'Captain Quentin has given me a full account of his actions and takes full responsibility for what has happened. It remains to be seen what will happen as a result of this and, were it not for the fact that we need all the help we can get, he would be facing disciplinary action. What would you suggest we do, Jon?'

Jon studied the floor for a moment before looking up through reddened eyes.

'I would promote him for his actions, colonel, because what he has done may well serve to save us all. When were you going to tell us about the other way out from here through the secret tunnel, colonel?'

'By the very words you have said yourself, Jon, about it being secret, you must realise that if it were common knowledge then it would not be a means of escape for us all if the need arose,' Colonel Dyer answered, aware of Jon's hurt and ignoring the sting in the question.

'And what of the gas? When would that have been used, colonel? I believe Captain Quentin to be a man of honour who would not consider the use of such a thing against even his vilest enemy.'

The colonel bowed his head to duck the intended slur but it hit home nonetheless and he shuffled his feet awkwardly.

'It is true that I had intended to use it if the time had come, but I stand by my decision to do so as a defence from barbarous animals that have no sense of fair play or conscience regarding other life. Major O'Rourke gave me a rather harrowing report of what happened at Tri-Bune and I would have no hesitation in using it against them rather than see my people butchered in the same way as the scouts were.'

His voice grew louder with the strength of his conviction and he looked defiantly towards them, daring them to challenge his beliefs.

None of them did.

Braun spoke on behalf of them all, saying, 'Colonel, I want to say that I can see why you would believe what you do; ordinarily it would be considered criminal to act in such a way. Just as that which Captain Quentin did in following his conscience. Even though it cost the lives of some of the elves and our friends the dwarves, we believe it was the right thing to do.'

'You make your point well, metal master and I see that Quentin did only what he thought to be right. Order must be maintained, however, or we will have everyone doing what they want as opposed to following orders. I will remove the incident from my report and release Quentin from house arrest. Now if you will excuse me I have things to tend to. At least we do not have to worry about the service tunnel as the heavy gas, which lies at the bottom, will deal with any intruders and give us advance warning of any breach in the defences. Feel free to make yourselves at home, and, Jon, I really am sorry about the dwarves, they were valiant and faithful friends to us all.'

Jon and the others nodded their appreciation and filed out back towards the rest area but they did not reach it as a cry went up from the top of the ramparts; the wind had ceased and the gnomes were preparing another attack.

They rushed to the battlements and were astonished at the destruction wrought on the encampment below. The whole land before them was unrecognizable; the tents and temporary structures had been blown away and the slingers smashed to pieces. Splinters of timber had been carried before the wind and torn into the cowering forces, decimating their ranks. A considerable proportion of the army had been killed overnight and with the coming of the day, as the wind had subsided, Ebon had rallied his troops of gnomes, trolls and marsh-mogs for a massed attack on the defences of the First city.

They were swarming across the levelled ditch where spoil from the excavations had been tipped. Large ladders were being raised against the walls and grappling hooks thrown up to the battlements; they were as numerous as ants and they covered the ground like a black carpet that heaved and swayed this way and that.

The soldiers atop the rampart fought ferociously to throw anything that would dislodge the assailants from the ladders and ropes; hacking with axes to cut the ropes and using poles to push the ladders away. For every one they dislodged, another two were put in place. Reserves were drawn up from around the city but there was only so much space on the battlements to repulse the attack without getting in each other's way.

The ballistae from each tower kept a steady rain of spears concentrated on them that gouged great scars through their ranks only to be filled as they surged forward. Kite-folk joined in the battle, flying in from the east and dropping rocks onto the crowded battlements, each one causing casualties amongst the defenders. They were becoming hard pressed to cope with the pressure and some of the gnomes had succeeded in gaining a foothold on one of the smaller towers. The black tide of Ebon's army was rolling relentlessly on; their gaining the battlements had encouraged them to greater efforts; the city would be lost unless something changed.

Captain Quentin had sped to the battlements following his release where he and his elfin company stood firm at the forefront of the defence and sent the gnomes back along the wall as swathe after swathe of them fell to the bolts from the elves' crossbows. The top of the walls were becoming difficult to navigate as the bodies of both sides piled up so that they had to be thrown over the top to allow better movement. Two armoured trolls had managed to reach the top of the tower that had fallen to the attacking hordes and were making headway along the wall, sweeping into the elves that had to retreat before their advance. Major O'Rourke directed the ballistae to open fire on the trolls and one of them was killed with several spears through its body. Captain Quentin led a charge forward to dislodge the other troll and was caught by the return sweep of the troll's barbed club; along with several other elves, he was brushed aside and fell to the stone courtyard below inside the city walls where he lay still like a broken doll.

Braun ran forward, broadsword in hand, and, dodging the troll's attempts to flatten him, managed to disable it by cutting into its leg, severing tendons so that it collapsed on to one knee; a well directed thrust of his sword up into the beast brought an end to its life. A cheer went up from the defenders who increased their efforts to repulse the attack, which faltered in its step.

A flash of green lightning exploded close to Braun and he went down amidst a handful of other soldiers who were fighting with gnomes intent on reaching Braun; all had been caught by the flash, friend and foe alike; they lay in a heap, singed and smoking.

This time it was the gnomes who cheered and rushed forward with renewed vigour, flashes of green lightning sending the soldiers of the First city back in retreat.

A huge mass of grey was spreading over the decimated land from the west as more came to join the onslaught; reinforcements from the marsh-mogs of the delta region were apparently coming in their droves, giving a huge lift for the gnomes and trolls. The troubled defenders, greatly outnumbered, began to give way before the onslaught. They prepared to make their stand at the tower above the gatehouse, unwilling to give any more ground, but it was inevitable that they would have to retreat into the tower and close the doors in the face of the pressing gnomes.

More lightning erupted onto the battlements but it landed amongst the gnomes, flinging them from the wall as chaff before the wind, causing mayhem and confusion. Three more times the flashes erupted, bright and intense in their blueness. This was different from that which had been levelled at the defenders; this time it was the assailants that were the target.

There was a pause in the forward movement of the attack, which faltered then crumbled as panic set in amongst the assailing forces. A whirlwind appeared above them and descended into their midst, sending them in all directions; blue lightning erupted from it and cleared the top of the wall where it settled and the wind diminished in intensity. From the core of the whirlwind Urim stepped forward, staff in hand, cloaked in blue light; bending down and reaching amongst the tangle of prone bodies, he straightened and lifted Braun from amongst the charred remains of the gnomes. He was still alive and had escaped serious injury as he had been shielded from the flash by the gnomes who had taken the brunt of the blast that had erupted around them. He had a blackened face and his hair had been singed. Smoke still rose from his clothes as a result of the heat that had hit him; but he was alive

Pointing out over the land towards the west, Urim shouted above the din of battle.

'Take courage, soldiers of Northill; behold, help is at hand.'

It was just as Jon had dreamed it would be with Urim's return, coming as he did out of the wind with the appearance of an angel clothed in blue power from his staff.

Away to the west, the grey mass that approached and had been thought to be reinforcements for Ebon's army, tore into the rear ranks; on closer inspection it was clear that they were not marsh-mogs at all. Realisation turned to amazement as the besieged defenders saw that the advancing troops were giant stone people; they were colossi come to give aid to the people of the Yield.

The soldiers of the First city rallied to the call of Major O'Rourke as he ran forward to challenge the retreating army of gnomes, trolls, marsh-mogs and kite-folk who quailed at the sight of the colossi coming upon their rear. The rush forward from the Major and his men put them to flight; so desperate were they that in the crush they even resorted to jumping off the wall to escape the wrath of men who sought revenge for the deaths of friends and family butchered at Tri-Bune.

The army of colossi scythed into the ranks of Ebon's army, tossing them aside like so many rag dolls; the destruction on both fronts was sickening to behold and the gnome army soon lost the stomach for fighting and fled before the irresistible surge that overwhelmed them. Only too keen to shed the blood of others and inflict untold horrors, when it came to their own, well that was a different matter.

The battle ended quickly with very little loss to those who fought for freedom under the banner of the First city as they forced their advantage, while almost on every hand the enemy fell before them. The gnome army had shown no quarter during their campaign; they were shown none now. They ran in all directions, getting in each other's way in their efforts to escape the retribution being handed out by Major O'Rourke and his soldiers who stopped only when they became too weary to pursue them any further, unable to raise their swords to inflict another deadly blow.

Chapter XVII

Gassed

Silence descended upon the battlefield where the dead and dying lay; those who had survived the onslaught rested on weapons covered in the blood of the vanquished. An occasional moan would escape an injured individual as they lay amidst the carnage; if they were friend they were taken care of and treated for their wounds. If they were foe, they were speedily despatched, no prisoners were to be taken with the exception of Ebon but he could not be found; no matter how they searched he was not to be seen and had obviously escaped during the confusion of the battle.

A terrible toll had been exacted by the defenders on Ebon's army and the battlefield was littered with their bodies. Sadly, amongst them were many of the bodies of the soldiers from the First city and of Tri-Bune. Around and along the city walls of Northill lay a goodly number of Quentin's elfin troops who had bravely stood in defiance of Ebon and all that he represented; Quentin himself was a casualty of the battle. His body was respectfully recovered and buried alongside his fallen comrades. a special memorial service was scheduled for the coming Sunday in honour of those who had given their lives.

A marker had been placed aside from the others bearing the names of the four dwarves whose bodies could not yet be recovered because of the gas-filled tunnel. It would have to be made safe before anyone could enter to reclaim them.

Perhaps one of the saddest things of all was the death of Colonel Dyer, not from any wound he had received in battle, but from heart failure. The stresses and the strains over these past few days had stretched this old man's reserves too far and at the height of battle he could bear the strain no longer; he had crumpled to the floor by the gatehouse tower clutching at his chest. His orderlies had carried him to the infirmary but upon examining him they found he was past any help that they could give him. Hamill and Anna had volunteered their help in the infirmary as soon as the battle commenced and witnessed the event. It was they who covered him and laid him in a side room awaiting preparation for burial. There had been no time then to mourn his passing, the wounded were in need of their attention as more and more arrived from the battle raging above them on the battlements. Reports kept coming in of the battle and how it swayed one way and then another; when it had been reported that a seer had come in a cloud, with blue lightning sweeping the gnomes from the wall, a cheer went up from the soldiers who lay around the room. Hamill and Anna grinned in excitement and jumped up and down with relief, guessing that it was Urim who had returned.

What was their amazement when it was voiced abroad that an army of stone men had arrived from the west to aid them and were at that very moment spreading death and destruction amongst the gnome army and that the kite-folk had fled! From that time on, very few arrived in the infirmary needing attention and soon afterward the chief orderly told Hamill and Anna that they could go and watch the final stages of the battle if they wanted to. They did not need telling twice and sprang for the door, headed up the stairs dodging the soldiers who were going up and down. Upon reaching the top, a scene of utter devastation greeted them. The gnome army had been rooted out and were in full flight pursued by Major O'Rourke and his men; from the west the grey ranks of the colossi cut deep into the black swarm of the mixed number of gnomes, trolls and marsh-mogs; the kite-folk were nowhere to be seen. None that were left alive that is; many of their bodies could be seen littering the battlefield as they had fallen victim to the arrows of the archers and the spears from the ballistae.

Jon and Urim were watching the events unfold with a dishevelled and bemused Braun who, apart from his blackened appearance, was none the worse for his experience; no sign of the blue power was evident around Urim any more and he looked drained by the exertions it must have caused him.

Soldiers from the First city could be seen preparing the funicular for use, clearing away any obstructions and bodies that would impede its progress. A signaller sent a message to Major O'Rourke of the death of Colonel Dyer and for him to return to the city immediately to assume command.

The colossi had reached the outer walls of Southill having dispersed any remaining opposition with swiftness. From the advantage point of the walls, the gnome army could be seen scattering in all directions in disarray; leaving their weapons and armour abandoned on the battlefield in order to make good their escape.

Jon broke the news to Urim of the dwarves' demise. Urim looked astonished, saying, 'I cannot believe that they are gone; I refuse to believe it; this ought not to be.'

He walked away saddened by the news and headed for the funicular. He stopped and invited them to come with him to greet the colossi and to thank them for their timely intervention.

'How on earth did they know that we were in need of help? It can't be just a coincidence with them turning up like this after all these years?' Hamill queried, confused by the situation as were the others.

'Did you manage to get a message to them, Braun?'

'No, I know nothing of this,' Braun replied. 'It took me nearly all my time to convince Bearer and the other two to come with me; they are still guarding the secret tunnel as far as I am aware and know nothing of this. It will be as much of a surprise to them as it was to us.'

Speculation continued, but Urim kept quiet as they entered the funicular and descended in the undamaged car to the bottom of the track and the lower gatehouse.

Halfway down the track, the damaged car that had been at the bottom of the slope passed them and they could see now just how much damage it had sustained; it would take more than just repairs to get it serviceable. A scene of utter destruction greeted them as they disembarked; the trolls had literally torn the place apart in their efforts to locate the entrance to the service tunnel. The engineers, who had built the hidden door of stone that had slid into place after them when they had entered, had done their job well; especially with the decoy doors and passageways that had led the assailants astray. When time allowed, they would investigate the centre passageway that had eventually had the door forced open; it was designed with traps and pits to delay progress and encourage any intruders into thinking that it was the real entrance on the basis that if it was not the way in, why protect it in such a way? In reality it ended at a sudden drop into blackness that descended for a long way into the ground; no one had been able to measure exactly how far. They had given up after recording two hundred lengths; there were no ropes long enough to go any deeper. Engineers from Northill were busy putting support scaffolding up around the ruins of the gatehouse as it was deemed to be unsafe. Jon was amazed at how quickly people were getting to the task of repairing and rebuilding so soon after the battle was over. He found out later that it was the legacy of Colonel Dyer; he had put in place a plan for this eventuality and organised who would do what and when; not by name of individuals but by virtue of the office that was held at the time of the plan being put into action. With the loss of the colonel, his role now fell upon Major O'Rourke, who by common consent had received the field promotion to the rank of colonel.

Several of the colossi had made their way into the ruins of Southill to meet with whoever was in charge whilst the others stayed outside and helped with the burying of the dead from the city and the burning of those of Ebon's army who had fallen. The leader of the colossi approached them and bowed his head respectfully towards Urim and then to Braun.

'It is as you had said, seer: the metal masters had need of us once more; the prophets were correct and we have returned as requested to renew our lives in the old lands.'

The rumble of his voice reverberated deep in Jon's chest and he marvelled anew at the stone creatures. He looked towards Urim, as did the others, confused by what the colossus had said.

'He knows you?' Jon asked incredulously.

Urim bowed in turn to the colossus and, indicating the others, addressed him, saying, 'Well met, Amorphous, I had feared that you and your people may have arrived too late in order to help us but you did not fail in your agreement, for which I am forever grateful. These are my friends and this is the metal master who has rekindled the bond between stone and flesh; his name is Braun.'

He caught hold of Braun's arm and guided him forward to meet with Amorphous; he was introduced to eleven other colossi, including four females. They all showed signs of respect towards him, which embarrassed him a little as they bowed their heads and greeted him, sharing their own names with him. He bowed in return and tried to look dignified, a difficult task when you have just been through a major battle.

The group were joined by the newly promoted Colonel O'Rourke and his loyal soldiers from Tri-Bune who formed a bodyguard around him; they were taking no chances that the odd gnome or two may be hiding and could still be a threat to him. It was well known for senior officers to be attacked following the end of battle from these gnome assassins as they played dead.

Pleasantries were exchanged and hospitality offered to the colossi but it was kindly declined as there was nothing that could be given them that would be of use. Instead Amorphous, after consulting with the other leaders, offered their further help in rebuilding the city of Southill as they were experienced in stone craft. This offer was gratefully received by the surprised Colonel O'Rourke who again stated that if there were anything that he could supply them with, they would be more than welcome to it. The colossi thanked him and went about their tasks in assisting the engineers to begin rebuilding while they all returned to Northill via the funicular. They heard the flush of water as the tank beneath the car emptied allowing the heavier one at the top of the track to descend and pull theirs up.

So the fight against Ebon had gone their way and the invading army had been practically annihilated; progress was being made on rebuilding the shattered buildings of Southill and everyone could breathe a little easier. Urim knew that the fight was not over yet though; Ebon had to be found and dealt with or all of this will have been in vain. He must be stopped at all costs, before he had the chance to build another army and cause further senseless bloodshed. For now it was time to heal their wounds and to rest their frayed nerves; to renew their strength, in preparation for the next phase of this deadly game of cat and mouse. They had won this battle, but the war was still being waged and had to be concluded by the release of the seers from their Tower.

Progress had been made but at a heavy cost; among those who had fallen were Captain Quentin of the elfin guard; Colonel Dyer, commander of Northill; Lieutenant Marshall, who had given his life in the defence of the small tower that had been overrun by the rush of gnomes and trolls. Many others had died in the defence of their city and the cause of freedom, willing to sacrifice themselves so that others might be free.

Leading the way into a new era of rebuilding – not just of stone and brick but of the people as a nation – were the recently promoted, Colonel O'Rourke and Captain Perkins, who had a huge task to fulfil. The latter was still in the infirmary, recovering from the injuries he had sustained while rescuing Jon from the battlements.

As for Urim and those who had travelled with him thus far, it remained for them to find Ebon and prevent him from ever trying to enslave the people and folk of the land again. For them the battle continued in their efforts to free the seers and finally bring Ebon to justice. The sadness of it was the loss of the dwarves; it still had not registered that they were gone and journeying on without them seemed wrong. Urim was particularly devastated that this should have occurred and found it difficult to accept their passing; he would not leave without establishing beyond all doubt that they had not survived.

So it was that under the orders of the new commander-in-chief, Colonel O'Rourke, the service tunnel was opened from Northill gatehouse and a search party recruited to ascertain the state of affairs. They were to proceed cautiously; a caged bird would be taken with them to detect any lingering gas, then if possible they were to open the concealed entrance at the bottom of the tunnel and allow the fresh air to clear it through. Volunteers were requested to sign up with the sergeant of the guard, Kristopher Beal; Jon immediately stepped forward but was held back by Urim stating that it would be well to let the soldiers of Northill carry out the task. Jon could wait with him and the others at the Southill gatehouse for the entrance to be opened, as he was confident that it would be.

Four volunteers to accompany Sergeant Beal were selected from among twenty who had put their names forward; they nervously entered the tunnel system, following the sergeant down the steps into the anteroom; the doors were left open to allow the air to flow through so that in the event of there being any gas still in the tunnel it would sink to the lower levels, being heavier than the air. Providing that they were able to reach it, the lower entrance would be unlocked and any vestiges of the gas would be allowed to escape into the open. There was a risk that if they carried torches, the heavy, inert gas would extinguish the flames and they would be left in the dark; so Jon had loaned them the glow-stone that Braun had in turn loaned to him and watched as they filed down the stairway into the outer chamber. The steady light of the glow-stone was just sufficient to allow them to make their way forward in the dark confines of the tunnel with safety. Sergeant Beal led the volunteers down the slope of the service tunnel, holding a lantern that had been modified hastily to accommodate the glow-stone; he also carried the caged bird low to the ground so as to be alerted to the first signs of the gas. Carefully they descended with just enough light to find their way; stepping with care so as not to lose their footing.

A nervous hush had fallen over the city as all were aware of what was happening and waited expectantly for the news that they were all dreading. Jon and Anna waited with Hamill and Urim outside the gatehouse in Southill, having used the funicular to descend the hill again. Braun had not wished to stay and had set off to meet up with Bearer, Petros and Holdhard who, it was presumed, were still guarding the secret entrance some distance away. He had taken with him Amorphous and two others in order that he could guide them to the long lost friends for what they expected to be a happy reunion.

It had indeed been a joyous reunion between the colossi and much hugging and loud exchanges were made between them; Braun had remained at a respectful distance to allow them the moment together. Petros particularly had been heartened by the arrival of the absent colossi and walked with a more noticeable spring in his step; the joy the three of them radiated was clear to be seen at being reunited with the others, especially when they were told that they were to stay and re-establish the commune at the mountain city.

He returned to Southill with the colossi moments before the secret door opened and a rush of stale air whistled through the tunnel out into the courtyard where they stood waiting with knots in their stomachs. Tension mounted as Sergeant Beal emerged into the daylight blinking against the brightness of the day, carrying before him the lantern with the glow-stone and the birdcage with the creature still alive and chirping animatedly.

One by one the others stumbled through the doorway carrying a small limp form, wrapped in their travel cloaks; they counted them as they came into the light one, two, three and four. Their bodies were laid on the ground amongst the ruins of the ante-chamber. Anna burst into tears and Jon gulped back his own tears as he comforted her while Hamill laid a consoling hand on his shoulder. They could hardly bear to look at them: where they had been so full of life and strength, they now lay like discarded rag dolls covered by their cloaks, lifeless amidst the carnage left by the retreating gnomes and trolls. Urim walked forward to look at the dwarves and confirm what everyone already knew: that they were dead.

*   *   *

Earlier, the three colossi had been alerted to the presence of gnomes heading for the shelter of the barn by their loud bragging to others they had just met while scouting; they boasted of torturing and dismembering six men from the First city whom they had caught yesterday and were laughing about it. There was little need for caution on their part as they supposed, seeing as all of the surrounding countryside was held by Ebon's army and the city besieged, so they were not expecting to be greeted by anyone other than gnomes, trolls or maybe even a kite-folk, although the latter would not be likely to be seen in a barn. The large doors were flung open by the unsuspecting gnomes revealing the three stone giants standing in the centre of the enclosure, heads lost in the gloom of the rafters. To say that the gnomes were taken by surprise was an understatement; the look on their faces was enough to show their shock at encountering them here. They stood frozen to the spot, outlined in the frame of the door, wet, bedraggled and confused; they were unsure what to do and looked at each other from the corners of their eyes, waiting for one of them to make the first move. It was only a few seconds that they stood immobilised by their surprise but it must have seemed much longer to them, when one of the gnomes turned on his heel and ran shouting loudly and waving his arms around like a person possessed; the others likewise turned tail and ran, colliding with each other as they tried to flee from the giants. It would not be long before they were back but in greater number, giving them more confidence and courage in the face of the colossi, possibly even bringing along a troll or two for moral support. There was no way that the stone men would be allowed to stay there without some vigorous attempts made to move them on or destroy them; maybe they even thought that they could be captured. Whatever it was that the gnomes decided to do, it meant that the three stone men had to do something to defend themselves, as well as the others, from the gnomes gaining entrance to the tunnel beneath them. The gnomes probably did not even know of its existence otherwise they would surely have tried to get in before now.

Bearer, Petros and Holdhard waited expectantly for their return and presently their waiting came to an end as the doors of the barn were torn off their hinges and two trolls, heavily armoured and with great spiked clubs, lumbered inside.

Any other being would have quailed at the sight of them in their war garments and helmets but the colossi simply moved aside at their attempts to hit them with a swing of their clubs. The space in the barn was not large when empty so with three colossi and two trolls milling around inside it was nigh on impossible to have a battle between the giants.

Knowing that the trolls would not give up in their attempts to evict the colossi from the barn meant that they had to be dealt with; reluctantly Bearer and Petros did so as quickly as they could so as to minimise any suffering. Catching the trolls as they attempted to club them and missing making contact by a matter of inches, the three colossi held the poor creatures in vice-like grips and snapped their necks by a twisting, jerking movement as they held them immobile between them; their lifeless bodies crumpled to the floor. When the gnomes saw how the colossi were unaffected by the trolls' attack and with what ease they despatched them, they again retreated to a place of safety to consider their next move.

The gnomes decided that so long as the stone men were not doing anything against them but were simply standing their ground, they would leave them alone but keep a watchful eye on them. Should the colossi decide to make a move it was not known what the gnomes would do, other than to run away; so the gnomes watched and waited nervously, sheltering as best they could from the storm under canvas sheets that the wind threatened to rip out of their hands at any moment. They made a sorry looking sight and were they anyone other than who they were one might have had pity on them. So it was that the time went by and the dawn broke with neither party moving until suddenly the storm abated and shortly afterwards the cries of battle could be heard coming from the other side of Northill. Not knowing quite what to do and seeing that even if the giants did move they would not be able to do anything to stop them, the gnomes scurried off to join in the battle, leaving a small group to watch the colossi. Lightning played along the top of the First city ramparts, first green then blue. A short time later they saw hundreds of kite-folk fleeing the area away from the city, chattering in fear as they winged their way as speedily as they could and headed north. Soon afterwards they saw gnomes, trolls and a few marsh-mogs running away from the city as well; as some of them passed nearby they asked what the panic was all about and they were told that the battle was over. A spirit had descended onto the city and killed hundreds of them with blue fire. Then giants made from stone had attacked their rear and decimated the army and they were getting as far away from here as they could.

'You'd better do the same yourself if you know what's good for you, unless you want to die.' They did not need any further encouragement than to see three more stone giants headed towards them led by a large, red bearded man, who would have been considered a giant himself were it not for the colossi. They decided that discretion was the better part of valour; in other words they said to each other, 'I'm not staying around here any more, I'm scarpering.'

So Braun arrived to introduce Amorphous and others of his kind to Bearer, Petros and Holdhard who were simply stunned to see their own kind again after so many years apart; there were tears of joy and none could speak because of the emotions that ran through them as they hugged each other, patting each other on the back with affection.

And what of the dwarves? What had truly been their terrible fate as the battle raged? Shudders had gone through the tunnel as loud thumps were heard against the door; the dwarves had become alert to the danger and readied themselves for an imminent attack should the door give way. They had retreated up the steps out of the cold of the gas so that it could be felt only around their legs as it continued to find its way to the lowest level. As it rose higher, so they had stepped further back up the stairway. They were at about the position that Tracker was when he first felt the gas and the thumps from the blows that jarred at the stone triggered the safety catch loose from its clip over the lever that controlled the door. The next mighty blow came and almost shook them from off their feet but they held fast and saw the lever jump from the shut position to open, whereupon the door slid open and the gas rushed out to fill the anteroom below.

With the opening of the door, the noise of the storm that had been raging outside could be heard battering at the gatehouse; cautiously, the dwarves descended, ready to defend the tunnel and themselves, but nothing could be heard and no one entered. Slowly they made their way down and had almost reached the bottom when two gnomes poked their heads around the corner of the door, bobbing in and out as they assessed the situation; they wore makeshift masks made from their cloaks, which they held over their mouths. When they were satisfied that there were only four dwarves inside, six gnomes rushed in to try and overpower them. A short battle ensued and the dwarves fought them back down the stairs; the cold of the gas could still be felt as they neared the bottom of the steps so the dwarves shoved the gnomes off balance so that they tumbled down the last few steps, knocking each other over.

They hit the floor hard and within moments had succumbed to the gas; two of them tumbling out of the door and into the outer chamber.

Archer had had an idea and suggested that they exchange cloaks with the four gnomes, then conceal their bodies in the tunnel and venture out to see if they could find anything useful to do. They were all feeling cooped up in the fortress and yearned for some real action against gnomes; this little battle had whetted their appetite and they all agreed that they should do what Archer had suggested.

The anteroom was dark and the light that was cast by the three remaining torches revealed a sad scene. The gas that had rushed out of the tunnel when they had triggered the door release had robbed the trolls and gnomes of air and they had collapsed where they stood. Two trolls with sledgehammers still gripped in their hands and a score of gnomes were dead on the floor of the anteroom. The gnomes who had made it into the tunnel must have come down the steps from the entrance room above when they saw what was happening; it appeared that Colonel Dyer had achieved his aim in defending the tunnel and the dwarves had helped him to do so, even though it was unintentional; still they were glad that it had enabled them to triumph and to live to fight another day. The air was cool but clean and breathable as the gas had settled and was falling away through an outlet built into the base of the wall. It flowed along conduits that had been installed just for the purpose of draining the room of water should the tunnel have been flooded, only this time it was gas that had flooded the room, not water. They could still feel it swirling around the lower parts of their bodies as it drained slowly away.

They quickly donned the cloaks of the gnomes who had made it into the tunnel and laid the bodies just inside the doorway covered by the dwarves' own cloaks; they then stepped out and closed the door by using the lantern fitting that Hamill had discovered, which operated the door from the outside. The stone door slid back into place, concealing once again the entrance to the service tunnel. Stepping over the bodies that lay strewn across the floor they climbed the steps up out of the room into the ruins of the gatehouse; it was a mess and was hardly recognisable as the place they had been in just a few days ago. The trolls had all but demolished the building in their attempts to find any secret passages in the walls that would lead them to the doorway and the service tunnel, then ultimately to the city above.

Creeping out of the gatehouse, battling against the wind that whistled through the streets, they hurried into the square below, hugging the shadows and trying to remain unobserved as far as possible. They heard snatches of conversations from sheltering gnomes as they passed through the city ruins with mixed feelings on how the siege was going. Some of the gnomes were angry with the soldiers above for killing their comrades in the abortive attempts to rush the defences up the funicular; some were losing faith in Ebon and would argue amongst themselves, sometimes coming to blows with those who held different views.

The dwarves decided that it would be better for them to find shelter themselves if they could and wait for the storm to abate before trying to do anything in the way of fighting or causing disruption to Ebon's army. They found shelter in a small house that showed signs of recent occupation. With luck they could stay here without them returning; taking turns to keep watch, they slept after having eaten a sparse meal from remains of food rations they had found in a cupboard.

Trapper, who stood watch at the time, roused them with the news that the wind had subsided and they could start to infiltrate deeper into the enemy camp and see if they could find a way of destroying the large slinger that Colonel Dyer said was a threat to them. Keeping their cloaks wrapped tightly around them and their hoods up to conceal their faces, they made their way unmolested through what used to be the encampment of Ebon's army but it had been devastated by the high winds. They were relieved to find that the storm had accomplished their task for them and destroyed not just the large slinger but all of the siege machines; they lay scattered across the field, splintered and almost unrecognisable amongst the debris following the storm.

With the cessation of the high wind the gnomes emerged from their shelter and the army gathered together with the officers, reorganising them into an attacking unit with armoured trolls; kite-folk were positioned at the forefront to fly high over the ramparts of the thick walls in order to cause the maximum disturbance possible to the defenders. Ebon appeared and spurred his army on, encouraging them with the promise of the looting and murder that they would be left free to indulge in once inside the city. A roar of approval sent a chill through the dwarves who decided that the best thing they could do was to keep a low profile and wait for an opportunity to do something without giving themselves away; it would be senseless to try and fight in these circumstances; they would be cut down in an instant.

Working their way back to the house they had sheltered in they saw the advance of the army as it swarmed across the infill of the ditch and the fall of the small tower. A groan escaped Trapper as he saw the advance and heard the cheer that went up as the gnomes and trolls gained the ramparts. Several gnomes looked closely at them as they passed, suspicious of them as they headed away from the fighting; Archer noticed that one of the gnomes had broken off from a group and was following them. They were attracting more and more attention the further they went so they decided to change direction and look as if they were waiting their turn to join the ranks. They stopped at a fire that had been left unattended to warm their hands; the curious gnome came forward trying to peer under their hoods. It was obvious that he would realise his suspicions soon so Javelin quickly grabbed him and drew him into the circle around the fire between himself and Tracker; a knife thrust up under his rib cage caught the unfortunate gnome off guard and he whimpered as he drew his last breath then slumped lifeless as the dwarves held him up. They all sat around the fire propping the body up in position as if he were asleep, trying not to bring further attention to themselves; waiting just a few moments, they arose and moved off towards Southill and the relative safety of the house. An explosion of green light on the ramparts made them stop and stare for a while and they watched as a roar of approval rent the air encouraging the assailants on only to be hushed as they saw a funnel of wind descend upon the ramparts and blue lightning erupt from it, scattering the attackers and driving them back along the wall.

The tide of battle changed as the attackers became the subject of a renewed counter-attack, which drove them from the city walls. A shout went up warning that they were under attack from the west and panic started to well up amongst the confused army; the kite-folk could be seen flying away from the scene in disarray, shrieking in fear. Cries of alarm that they were being overrun by giants and that statues had come to life and were sweeping them aside carried through the ranks like wildfire, causing them to break off their attack and to flee any way they could; any way of escape that was headed away from the west and impending death that awaited them if they remained where they were. The noise of the destruction as the gnomes died before the onslaught of the colossi made the rest of them turn tail and run, leaving their weapons behind them. The whole scene was one of panic and confusion, enabling the dwarves to pass unnoticed amongst them; occasionally a gnome would run into them in blind panic but as they parted he would fall to the ground, his blood mingling with that of the mud and mire of the churned soil.

Javelin decided that it would be a good opportunity to locate Ebon and press home their advantage amidst the mêlée by catching him and delivering him to Urim; it was worth a try. Pressing forward against the flow of the retreating gnomes, they had only gone but a few paces before they realised that it would be an impossible task so turned aside and, trying to stay as close to each other as they could, they went with the flow.

Archer found himself tripping over his cloak. He had stood on the hem and it ripped from his shoulders revealing his beard for all to see; a gnome who was fleeing along side him looked and had to take a second glance as, stunned, he realised that the gnome he had been running alongside was not a gnome at all but a dwarf. They turned to each other and laughed in surprise before the gnome ran straight into probably the only tent pole left standing in the field of combat, which flattened him on the spot. Pausing only to take the cloak from his prostrate body, Archer covered himself with it. He pushed through the crowd to catch up with the others, and they edged their way closer to the buildings of outer Southill, the four dwarves managing to keep together and reach the cover of the first house where they watched as the army of gnomes took flight.

A group of black-cloaked gnomes passing by attracted their attention. Jostled along in the midst of them was a bound figure; trotting along behind this group was a large grey wolfhound that stopped momentarily to sniff the air before cocking his leg against a fallen gnome who had been trampled in the rush to flee the field of battle. The dwarves turned to each other in surprise; Jon had spoken of a dog such as this belonging to Ebon. If this were the same dog then the person being held by the gnomes would be of interest not only to Ebon but could be of importance to Urim. They could not make out who it was but decided that as it was a captive of the gnomes it deserved to be rescued if possible. Slipping from the cover of the buildings, they followed as closely as they felt comfortable with, waiting for the opportunity to strike without the captive being harmed.

The dwarves noted that they had taken a turn east towards the lake and hurried their pace to try and rescue the prisoner as soon as possible, before the crowds thinned too much to shield their actions and cover their escape.

They decided that they could delay no longer and hastened to overtake them when out of the corner of his eye Trapper caught a flash of grey coming at him from the side. Ducking instinctively, he just managed to evade the snapping jaws of Khan as he launched himself at the dwarf. The great hound landed heavily on all fours, having missed his mark, but rallied quickly to pounce again.

'Trapper, watch out,' Tracker shouted a warning to his brother that unfortunately also alerted the gnomes ahead of them that something was amiss and several of them turned to fight off any who would try to interfere with their task.

'Go on, I'll deal with the hound, you save the prisoner.'

Hesitating but knowing that Trapper was more than capable of taking care of himself, Tracker and the other dwarves rushed forward, casting aside their cloaks, all attempts to hide their identity abandoned, so as to move more freely.

These gnomes were not to be discounted so lightly as those they had come across previously. One of them sidestepped a decoyed thrust of the sword from Javelin who had to react instinctively to avoid a side swipe at his ribs as he tumbled past. He rolled onto the ground, springing up in a flash to avoid a follow up strike and hurried on after the gnomes who had whisked the captive away, leaving the other two to deal with the gnomes who had challenged them.

Tracker and Archer were locked in battle with three of the gnomes, managing to seriously wound one of them before facing the others one on one. They squared up to one another; Archer feinted to his right and made a surprise attack on the gnome who had expected to challenge Tracker, felling him with a slash across his throat. Tracker in the meantime had spun around to face the bewildered gnome who had expected to face Archer only to receive a thrust through the gut that was followed up with a knife to the neck, giving the gnome no chance at all. With hardly any halt in their strides, they gave chase after Javelin to aid him in releasing whoever it was the gnomes held.

Trapper meanwhile was having a hard time in dealing with the wolfhound who dodged and sprang at him with bared fangs, managing each time to stay out of reach of the dwarf's sharp knives, one in each hand, one in thrusting position, the other ready to stab at the creature should it get close enough. As if facing the snarling dog was not enough to deal with, a gnome decided that he would have a go at the dwarf as he ran away from the colossi. Trapper nearly didn't see him as the gnome swung his spiked machete at his head but managed to duck beneath the blow, which unbalanced the gnome, causing him to fall to the ground. Seeing an advantage, the hound pounced forward at Trapper who, wrong footed, summoned all his agility and strength. He hurled himself into a backwards somersault and curled over the snapping teeth of Khan; landing on his feet, Trapper spun around to see the gnome struggling amidst the mud in front of the frustrated hound. Khan vented his anger on the nearest thing to hand by tearing into the gnome, leaving him a bloody mess, shaking him as he would a rat and breaking his neck. Still with the gnome in his mouth, the dog glared at Trapper and with a low throated growl dropped the limp form and started to circle the dwarf, baring his teeth and barking between growls. The dog was clever, feinting attacks on Trapper a couple of times before digging his rear paws into the ground and launching himself at the dwarf.

Trapper was ready for him and he spun aside, dropping to his knees, as the hound went past only inches away. He thrust his knives up into the creature, tearing into his abdomen and virtually disembowelling Khan in mid air.

The big dog howled in pain and lay writhing on the ground; unable to let the poor creature suffer, Trapper despatched him by wrapping his arms around his neck and jerking upwards, snapping his spine. Gently and respectfully, Trapper laid the lifeless dog on the ground; he had no qualms about killing gnomes or trolls, but he did not relish the death of a faithful hound that was only doing what his master had told him to do. The dwarf could not afford to linger so he checked around him and saw Tracker and Archer running after Javelin, having despatched two gnomes and critically wounded another; Trapper leaped forward in pursuit, he did not want to miss out on a good fight with a more worthy victim of his knives.

Javelin was hot on the heels of the troop of gnomes, dodging between the hordes that were fleeing the battlefield, when four of the guard stopped to face him, shields in front of them with hand pikes poking through. Undaunted, he made to launch himself over their heads only to drop into a forward roll at the last moment, duck underneath their shields and drive his short swords up into the lower abdomens of the two middle gnomes, just as he had the other day to the gnome at Clee Hill. It was a well practised and executed manoeuvre; the two remaining gnomes would have cut him down then had not Archer picked up a bow and arrow, sending the shaft through the eye of one of them, flinging him backwards. At once Tracker threw his hand-axe, which buried itself in the forehead of the other, causing him to collapse in a heap without uttering a sound.

Amazed at the loss of their comrades, the other gnomes turned to face the dwarves, meaning to teach them a lesson; one of them held on to their prisoner, who could now be seen to be a soldier from Northill. Grabbing a terrified gnome who had run into him, Javelin thrust forward, keeping his captive unbalanced and used him as a shield to force his way into the midst of the guard. Slashing out with his sword, he parried the blows that were aimed at him but felt a slash of cold steel tear into his side. He threw the now lifeless gnome he had used as protection on to the stumbling guard. He did not stop to think any more of his wound and let his momentum carry him through and on towards the frightened gnome who held on to the prisoner. He backed away, fear in his eyes as he saw the dwarf, like a demon, charge towards him.

Archer, Tracker and Trapper tore into the confused gnomes, using the same tactic that Javelin had done; catching hold of a fleeing gnome and dancing them into the midst of the guard, which enabled them to bring their deadly knives and swords into play at close quarters, discarding their 'shields' the moment they were no longer of use. They were a sight to be seen; gnomes were renowned for being unparalleled in the art of assassination, but these dwarves were more than a match for a gnome in any close quarter fighting. Before any of the gnomes could rally themselves to face the dwarves, the three of them had accounted for most of the guard, leaving only five to face them.

They were not so confident now and formed themselves into a tight circle to avoid being out manoeuvred and edged away into the flow of gnomes that charged past at that moment, enabling them to escape to tell the tale. Javelin meanwhile had relieved the prisoner of his bonds, having scared off the gnome who had been holding him. All he did was roar at the top of his lungs as he ran towards him, but this was all too much for the cowardly gnome; he had seen enough to know that he was outclassed and had turned tail and disappeared into the tide of fleeing gnomes.

Only now did Javelin look to his wound to discover a nasty

gash along his side that had opened up the flesh and was bleeding badly. One of the hand pikes had penetrated the leather jerkin he was wearing and sliced into him; it was a wonder that he had not been cut in half. Had it been an axe that had caught him, he would not be standing here now. Trapper quickly applied a temporary dressing from a backpack he found nearby and counselled Javelin to get the attendants at Northill to see to him as soon as possible, like now.

Javelin nodded, wincing now as the pain hit him and he collapsed into the arms of Tracker who bore him up; between them the dwarves made a makeshift stretcher and headed back to Northill.

The soldier, whose name was Jack, thanked them for their help, telling them that he and several others had been caught by the gnomes the day before; he had been kept alive to watch as his friends were mutilated in front of his eyes and flung over the city wall by the slinger; he did not know why they had spared him but he was certainly grateful for the dwarves' intervention and assisted them in carrying the stretcher with the unconscious Javelin laying on it; the field of battle had thinned now and no one stopped to interfere with them on their return journey.

* * *

Back at Northill Urim stepped up close to the first of the prone figures. Bending down, he tentatively pulled back the cloak to see who it was.

He exclaimed loudly, 'Hah! I knew it; come here everyone and see.'

He rolled one of them over and pulled back the cloak to expose his face and showed them that they were not the dwarves at all, but gnomes.

They were all shocked and bemused but relieved that they were not the dwarves but the question went begging: where were they, and how did the gnomes get inside the tunnel?

* * *

'Hi, lend a hand there; we've got an injured dwarf here in need of urgent help,' Archer shouted out to them, not knowing that the others had all thought them dead until this very moment.

'Archer, Tracker, Trapper, you're alive; where have you been, we thought you had died? What's happened to Javelin and who's this?'

Question after question was fired at them to explain what had happened but Hamill interrupted them all with a loud voice to plead the speedy removal of Javelin up the funicular to the infirmary in Northill. He went with him as the dwarves handed their charge over to Hamill and some of the soldiers. There was much backslapping and mock reprimanding for giving them the scare of their lives. Anna could not stop sobbing with tears of joy and relief that the dwarves were safe; Jon also wiped away a tear as did Urim, though he tried to hide it from them.

Jack was welcomed back with as much joy and disbelief by the soldiers of Northill; they all thought him dead, hacked to pieces by the bloodthirsty gnomes. They were mightily relieved to be reunited with him but he begged to be excused so that he could go to his wife, who still thought him dead. There was going to be one very surprised lady who would be overjoyed at his return.

He was taken up in the funicular with Javelin, Hamill and two soldiers, who took charge of the stretcher bearing from the dwarves.

Back safely in the fortress with Javelin undergoing emergency surgery and set to make a full recovery with plenty of bed rest, Urim felt prompted to call on the home of Jack and his wife. He knocked at the door and was met by a young woman crying into a cloth with which she dabbed at her eyes.

'Your pardon, madam, I'm seeking your husband Jack; is he here?' Urim enquired tenderly.

'Yes, he's here; I take it that you want to see him?' she replied somewhat matter-of-factly.

'Yes, if you don't mind?' Urim asked politely.

'Not at all, follow me, he's in here.'

She led him through a narrow corridor into a back room; there on a trestle lay a wooden box; he looked at the woman, non-plussed, a feeling of trepidation rising within him.

'That was all they could find of him after those gnomes had cut him and his friends to pieces.'

She sobbed, crying into her cloth, which she clutched to her face, tears streaming down her cheeks. Urim stiffened in alarm and strode quickly over to the box; laid inside was the battered and bruised head, torso and some limbs of her husband Jack. Urim's head spun and he gripped his staff tightly.

If this is Jack and he was amongst those dismembered who were sent over the ramparts by the slinger then who was it that had been rescued by the dwarves?

Ebon! he cursed under his breath. He thanked the woman and excused himself as quickly and courteously as he could before running full tilt to the office of Colonel O'Rourke.

Chapter XVIII

Ebon's Challenge

Colonel O'Rourke jumped to his feet in a fury; he knew what Ebon was capable of; he remembered what he had done at Tri-Bune, addressing the garrison so imperiously, mocking them before the embattled men following the utter devastation of the city and the slaughter of its inhabitants. He recalled Ebon's callous treatment of the survivors, promising to do the same to Northill if they refused to submit to his rule.

'Ebon; here in the fortress, are you sure about that?'

He was dumbfounded and angry at Urim's news that Ebon had tricked his way into the First city.

'Blast that man! If only I could get my hands on him; I'd tear him apart.'

He meant it too and it took a lot of self-discipline to control his feelings and meet the challenge of finding him with a calm head on his shoulders.

'What do you suggest we do, Urim? He's one of your own; you probably know how best to apprehend him.'

Urim was thinking on his feet, clasping the edge of the colonel's desk, his knuckles turned white with the force of his grip. He knew that finding Ebon would be a virtually impossible task what with his ability to appear as anyone he chose. Urim, by comparison, could not transform himself, all he could do was cast his appearance onto another for a short period of time, and with great effort. Ebon was capable of doing much more, at will. He suggested that the colonel organise his men to start a citywide sweep with the soldiers acting in groups of four, in order to avoid Ebon being able to conceal himself as another soldier.

'There must be an immediate census of everyone in the city to report into their line officer; each person must be accounted for and verified as being who they say they are. Sniffer dogs must be used to check every room in the city; they will not be fooled by his disguises and will soon let their handlers know if someone is not who they make themselves out to be. In the meantime I will search through the fortress. Now I know he's here I can use my staff to seek him out but he must be kept off guard and the commotion of the search will give me the distraction I need.'

'Very well, seer, but if I find him first, do I have your approval to dispose of him?' O'Rourke was passionate about finding him and meant what he said.

Urim looked him in the eye with a cold, hard stare and said emphatically, 'No; under no circumstances must he be harmed. It is vital for the freedom of the seers that he is kept alive. I am uncertain as to what his role is but I am absolutely positive that if he dies, then all of this – all the death and suffering that has been inflicted upon your men, the soldiers and citizens of this city and those of Tri-Bune – will have been for nothing. Do I make myself clear?'

Urim fixed the colonel with an almost hypnotic stare, which sent a tremor of fear through him, almost as if the seer had reached into his very soul and held his life cord in his hands.

Colonel O'Rourke swallowed hard and nodded. He knew now what it meant to be in the presence of a seer and to have his full attention focused on you; he quailed at the thought, not wishing to ever again feel what he had just felt. He shook involuntarily, as if a blast of cold air had hit him full on. 'Thank goodness Urim was on their side,' he thought to himself, he would not relish the thought of coming up against him as an adversary.

'Now then, Colonel, let's get this thorn in our side before he can do any harm.'

Still shaking from his experience with the seer, he wholeheartedly agreed and sent the orders for the registration and search to be undertaken with immediate effect.

The fortress city heaved with activity as everyone, it seemed, was rushing from one place to another, intent on their particular business. It was going to be a difficult task to track Ebon down, especially if he were to keep changing his appearance. The power and strength needed to maintain any form that he had chosen was truly exhausting and it was quite possible that he was simply resting somewhere in the fortress, gathering his strength. Without the lodestone he carried, after which he was named, he was just an ordinary man. With it he had a power for good in helping people but something had changed him somewhere along the line. He no longer had the care of the people at heart; quite the opposite in fact; it was almost as if he had totally reversed his role as protector and become a one man destructive force; he had to be stopped.

The registration was organised and squads of soldiers were detailed to work their way through the city under martial law, instructing everyone to return to their quarters immediately so that the census could take place. Speculation was rife about what this was all about and many worried that the gnomes had returned or that a disease had broken out and they had to confine everyone in order to contain it. None of the theorising was correct of course but the idea of an epidemic was encouraged as the last thing that Urim and the colonel wanted was for the truth to get out. If people knew that there was someone amongst them who could assume the appearance of someone else, mad hysteria would break out with people panicking and accidents happening with fatal results. No, the idea of a disease suited their purposes; it was quite a reasonable story to spread, what with the battle just ending; quite often after a big battle has taken place, some sort of sickness goes round the camps, so it was a believable subterfuge to use. Most importantly it should also serve to lull Ebon into a false sense of security and draw him out of hiding. With so many citizens confined to quarters and the army in control, it would only be a matter of time before he made a mistake and revealed himself for who he really was.

In the infirmary there was a flurry of activity and the corporal who had arrived to deliver the colonel's order was left to understand, in no uncertain terms, that the attendants had no intention of leaving the sick and the wounded. Orderlies ushered him out of the operating room and out through the administration area back into the corridor whereupon they locked the door on the guards and refused to either admit anyone who was not in need of medical assistance, or to come out themselves. The corporal was at a loss as to what to do so he left two of his men guarding the door and returned with the other soldier to report the situation and receive new orders.

Inside the operating room, Hamill and the attendants were

furiously trying to quench the internal bleeding in Javelin's wound, finally settling for stemming the flow from the tear in a blood vessel by sealing it with a hot poker. It worked and they could relax a little; they had possibly saved his life. Though he had lost a lot of blood he was a strong dwarf and of a good constitution; with time and rest he should pull through. The attendant surgeon thanked all who had assisted her and handed over to the house attendant to complete the cleaning up of the wound and closing it up with stitches. He would have a scar to be proud of and Hamill smiled to himself at the thought of Javelin sitting around a camp fire with other dwarves and lifting his shirt to reveal his scar, almost as a trophy, from his encounter with the gnomes. A whole new tale would be told of their confrontation with Ebon's army in the battle of Northill, which would pass on down through the generations. For a dwarf, it was a thing to be proud of; the story of how he got it would be told and retold a thousand times over, each time with a little more embellishment, encouraged by the intake of his favourite drink, relk. For now though, he must concentrate on recovering from the experience before he could start to enjoy the reputation.

Urim searched throughout the fortress, passing like a shadow from one floor to another starting in the lower levels; he meticulously searched every possible place that could conceal the man he was looking for. Occasionally he would stop people as they passed and examined them by means of the power in his staff to see if it were Ebon in disguise but none of them were and no one had seen or heard anything suspicious. He finally ended up on the ramparts of the gatehouse tower having been unable to locate the rogue seer. He was hiding himself well: even with the aid of his staff Urim had been unsuccessful in detecting him. It was so frustrating: he knew that Ebon was here; he just knew it, but where?

The gentle breeze of the late afternoon was a welcome treat as it wafted across the land; the angry clouds had been dispersed and peace had come to the Yield. It was not much to look at, now that Ebon's army had fled: the whole countryside lay before him, barren and empty, devoid of the many fruit orchards that had once graced the rolling landscape; mud and splintered timbers covered the once green and fertile ground now. Groups of colossi were gathering in the dead who had been left unceremoniously on the battlefield and were piling them into heaps ready for cremating; he would not want to be downwind from the fires when they started and took in a deep breath of the sweet air before it was defiled by the smoke of the burning. As he took a moment to survey the carnage left behind by this last week of conflict, he sighed deeply at the waste of life and effort on both sides. It was ever the way among the folk of this land that there would be a period of peace and prosperity followed by the turmoil created by someone's desire to rule over it all, and now because of one man's ambition and greed in wanting to subject others to his will the land of men had been ravaged by this latest warfare.

Progress was being made in bringing things back to as near normal as possible; the colossi were being of tremendous help to the engineers in the stabilising and restoration of the twin cities of Northill and Southill. The latter, almost in ruins, would take a lot longer to repair; it was almost a case of 'demolish and build anew'. Some of the buildings were in a poor state and were dangerous; many of them had already been pulled down. The city had never known such a time as this; with the help of the colossi they would have the city of Southill completely rebuilt within six months, whereas it would have taken a year at least without them. The land also would recover soon and, come the spring, would bloom again; the only absence would be the trees, although they could be brought in from other areas and replanted here. Urim believed that if anyone were to visit this place a year from now, they would scarcely believe that it had all but been destroyed.

Captain Perkins had signed himself out of the infirmary, against the advice of the attendants. He had taken up his new commission: supervising the repairs to the funicular railway, especially the car that had been so badly damaged by the gnomes and trolls. He had also been assigned to consider new ways of defending the cities from future attack, especially Southill, which had suffered the worst from this conflict.

Urim glanced over to the funicular and saw him standing by the track, his arm in a sling and his head still bandaged under his hat, giving orders to the four colossi who had volunteered their help; a team of men from the city were also hard at work hoisting a beam back into place over the entrance to the south gate. A messenger ran up to Perkins and saluted, then handed over a piece of paper to the captain. Reading the message quickly, Perkins began to remonstrate with the messenger, waving his hand, still clutching the message, in the direction of the work-force, then waving the paper angrily in the air at the poor man who had only been obeying orders. Urim saw him shaking his head then reach out and place his hand on the messenger's shoulder and smile. Then he nodded resignedly and waved at his men to stop working; he issued some orders. Urim could not hear what, but presumed that it was to return to their homes so as to participate in the registration that was being undertaken. They broke off from their task and began to assemble at the lower platform ready to ride the funicular up to Northill.

From here he could see all of the plain before him and by turning his head to his right, could see the buildings of the city, safe within the outer walls. Urim put his staff against the wall next to him then leaned forward and rested his hands on the parapet; he relaxed a little, allowing the stresses of the day to drain from him; his shoulders ached from the tension he had been holding himself under. He needed a rest; but that was not to be, not until he had found and secured Ebon.

The search continued throughout the afternoon as the fortress slowly came to a halt; with everyone returning to their homes, work ceased and the previously busy corridors and workplaces took on the appearance of a ghost town. The only movement was by the soldiers of the watch and those who were still tracking down small pockets of individuals who had not yet heard of the requirement for registration. Once they had been informed that there was an epidemic sweeping the place, they were only too glad to return to their homes as quickly as possible. The person upon whom all this attention was centred was sleeping soundly not that far from where Urim stood, frustrated and weary from the fruitless search he had undertaken throughout the fortress. Ebon smiled contentedly to himself while he dreamed. Despite having lost the battle he still believed that he would win the war; he had a trick or two left, which he was ready to play, when the time was right.

*

In the home of one of the guards, the soldier's wife and baby were at home waiting for his return; their pet dog was curled up on a rug next to the fire. The door opened and in walked a soldier, obviously the man of the house as he gave his wife a hug and a kiss; the dog looked up with heavy eyes, yawned and stretched then went back to sleep.

'You're home early; I thought you'd be hours yet, not that I'm complaining mind.' she responded with a giggle and wrapped her arms around his neck planting a kiss on him before rubbing her flour-covered hands into his face with another giggle.

'Ruby, you've made me a mess; look at me. How am I supposed to go back on duty like this?' the soldier moaned with a smile on his lips.

'Well then, Corporal Adams, don't go; stay here with me and Cory,' Ruby teased, pulling at the cords that tied his shirt at the neck.

'Tempting, I admit, but the sergeant would have me doing lavatory duties with a toothbrush for a week if I didn't turn up. I just popped in to tell you that I'd be later than expected; there's some sort of special duty that we've been assigned to; see you later, love.'

He bent down and kissed her then tickled Cory before grabbing a fresh scone from off the table and heading out the door.

'Come on, Patch, time you had your run out in the yard.'

The corporal encouraged Patch with a slap on his thigh but the dog did not even stir and continued to sleep soundly.

'Never mind about him, the lazy thing, I'll let him out later; try not to be too late.'

The door closed and the dog opened one eye, then both of them and slowly raised his head off his front paws. He raised himself up onto all fours and crept silently towards the cradle where Cory had fallen asleep. Ruby had her back to the room being busy at the sink washing her hands. Turning to reach for the towel, she saw the dog almost at the cradle. He stopped in his tracks and sniffed at the air.

Startled by Patch being awake and standing so close to the baby, she jumped and said, 'Oh you gave me a scare, Patch. Hungry are you, boy? Yes I expect you are after all that sleeping you've been doing; I don't know what's come over you today. No

298

you can't have any of my scones, but you can have a dollop of the mixture I've got left over; here you are.' She scooped up a spoonful of the mixture and tapped it into his bowl, placing it at his feet. The dog just sniffed at it then gave her the strangest of looks and walked away towards the door, pawing at it to be let out.

'Oh, so my cooking's not good enough for you eh? Want to go out now do you? All right then, at least it will get you out from under my feet.'

She opened the door and he trotted out into the front yard. She saw him sniff around a little before cocking his leg against a post. Ruby raised her gaze, as she always did when standing on the threshold, and looked towards the great outer wall of the fortress city and the huge tower that encompassed the gatehouse where her husband was stationed. She always looked, just in case she saw him but all she could see was one solitary figure up on the ramparts, leaning against the parapet and staring out over Southill, which lay the other side of the wall. She turned to go back inside, calling Patch to come, but he was nowhere to be seen.

Jon, Anna, Braun and the three dwarves were waiting for news of Javelin from Hamill; he had gone with the injured dwarf to the infirmary and was assisting with dressing the wound and making him comfortable. They waited for what seemed a very long time in the rest room, fidgeting impatiently. Each time someone came in to get a cup of hot chicory, they sprang to their feet hoping it was Hamill returning with news of Javelin's situation; eventually he did return and was set upon by them for news of the dwarf.

'Hold on, hold on,' he said, signalling for them to give him a chance. He sat down and wiped his brow then grinned at the dwarves.

'He's going to be all right, but it will be a while until he can move without any pain or difficulty. He has been badly injured but fortunately the wound is a clean one and the attendants have done a first-class job of sewing him up; he was fortunate indeed that the spear missed vital organs and only sliced through his flesh; that leather jerkin he was wearing undoubtedly saved his life.'

'When can we see him?' they asked, almost as one.

'Not until tomorrow,' Hamill said, holding up his hands at their protestations.

'I appreciate that you are concerned, as am I, but he has just undergone major surgery and he needs to rest. I can assure you that he is in the very best of hands. The senior surgeon is known to me; she taught a seminar at the Ward last season and has a good reputation for this sort of thing, so try not to worry, you don't have to.'

They all reluctantly accepted what Hamill had said as being wise counsel and were relieved to hear that Javelin was out of danger and the surgeon who attended him was the best there could be.

A squad of soldiers, each carrying a spear, the last two also carrying torches, entered the room and demanded that they register their names and account for each other. The corporal in charge saluted Jon. He was looking rather anxious and Jon noticed that he had a smear of flour on his collar.

'Sorry about this, sir, orders from the colonel; everyone must register and retire to their rooms until further notice. My men and I will accompany you to your quarters.'

'What's going on?' Jon enquired.

'Don't know, sir, just following orders; if you would just return to your quarters all of you.'

Disgruntled at the way they were being shepherded around, they reluctantly did as they were asked and agreed to meet up for dinner. They were all feeling pretty tired by now anyway, it had been a long day but it was far from over yet.

'We'll follow you to your room if that's all the same with you, sir,' the corporal said. He did not look like he would have taken no for an answer so Jon just shrugged and headed off to his room, followed by the squad of soldiers. The dwarves' rooms were in the opposite direction and they headed off along with Braun, who had been assigned a room not far from theirs. Anna and Hamill went with Jon and the soldiers to their rooms and were ushered into them as they came to them; first Hamill and then Anna, Jon's being the furthest away down another corridor.

They turned into the passage leading to Jon's room. The wall lanterns were not lit and the passage was dark. The light from the torches carried by the last two guards cast their light only a few yards ahead. The corporal gave the command to halt; Jon assumed that he was going to light the torches in the passage and looked over his shoulder. He was amazed to see him turn to face his men and thrust his spear into the belly of the first guard then continue in a powerful thrust to impale the other two as well. A green light passed through the guards and they crumpled to the floor, dropping the two torches, making things even darker than before, though they remained alight.

Jon was stunned, then horrified at what he had witnessed; fear and alarm flooded his whole being as he backed away into the darkness down the corridor towards his room. The corporal picked up the torches and placed them in brackets on the wall, designed for that purpose, and, placing his boot against the first soldier, withdrew his spear from the three bodies. Then, turning around, he stared at Jan with an evil grin on his face.

'So, young Jon, nothing to say? You're not so quick with your wit this time?'

This was impossible, he thought; this could not be, and he shook his head in disbelief. The voice that spoke to him was not that of the corporal, but Ebon. As he approached Jon he dispensed with his disguise as he stepped through the shadows and became Ebon, complete with cloak and staff.

'What's the matter, Jon? Aren't you pleased to see me?' he asked coldly and sarcastically as he moved towards him.

'Oh come now, that's no way for old friends to behave, or maybe you're not my friend at all.'

Ebon's voice changed from cold sarcasm to that of pure hatred.

'That's absolutely right, my dear Ebon; we are not your friend at all.'

The voice came from close behind him and made Jon jump, holding himself with his back against the wall.

Urim stepped forward into the gloom, placing himself between Jon and Ebon, then faced the rogue seer.

'This time you will not escape.'

Two squads of soldiers appeared as if from nowhere behind Ebon, cutting off his way of retreat.

Ebon's face was etched with fury at the trap he had allowed himself to be drawn into but he would not go without a fight. He thrust his staff forward at Urim and Jon but before he could send any burst of power at them, Urim had used his own staff to place a blue shield of energy before them and Ebon's green lightning simply crackled harmlessly against it and fizzled into nothing, discharging into the stone walls. He looked as if he would explode with frustration and levelled his staff at them again with renewed intensity but with no better effect than before, other than a few pops and bangs to accompany the fizzle. He howled in rage and turned to blast his way out past the soldiers behind him but they ducked behind their shields, which erupted into an intense blue when his green lightning struck them and simply evaporated into the walls, just as it had against Urim's energy shield.

'It's no use, Ebon, I've charged their shields with my power. There is nowhere for you to go and no one to help you. Put up your staff.'

'I'll never give in to you, you deceiver,' he screamed back at Urim and thrust his hand into the pocket of his cloak. Two things happened: Ebon started to transform right before their eyes into a colossus, the one being that would be immune to a seer's staff. Urim sent a ball of blue light that surrounded Ebon as he was transforming, causing him to lose hold on the stone, dropping it to the ground and stopping the transformation from occurring. Lightning flashed within the ball, concentrating on Ebon, sending him into contortions. Moments later the ball of light faded and went out. Ebon fell limply to the floor, unconscious but alive and still very much a threat to them all.

'Bind him quickly, and ensure that the manacles are good and tight; he's a slippery customer,' Urim charged the soldiers. He stepped forward and picked up the lodestone that belonged to Ebon, saying, 'This is one talisman that you will never use again, my friend.'

Straightening up, he placed it in the pouch he carried at his side. He then picked up Ebon's staff. 'I know just the person to look after this.'

He stepped towards Jon, holding Ebon's staff as well as his own, asking if he was all right.

'Yes, I'm fine, thanks to you. Do you want me to have the staff?' Jon asked tentatively, eyeing it with a mixture of fear and longing.

'Goodness me no; I am afraid that you are not yet ready for such a task. I have someone else in mind for that. Get some rest while you can; we leave for Seers' Tower on the morrow.'

With that he turned and left with the soldiers carrying the securely fastened Ebon between them, to be placed under lock and key.

Jon did not get much sleep during the night and when he did drop off it was to the vision of the men being impaled by Ebon on his spear. He felt a sense of excitement now that Ebon had been captured; it meant that their quest may well be nearing an end and that the seers would soon be freed from their enforced imprisonment. He was already up and dressed when Braun knocked on his door to rouse him.

'Oh you're up already, good; Urim has asked us all to meet him in the colonel's office.'

'Fine, I'm ready; I don't expect that Hamill's up yet though.'

'No, we've had to send the dwarves in to get him out of bed.' Braun laughed with a good-natured smile.

'Are we having breakfast first or has everybody eaten already?'

'Urim said that he wanted everyone to meet him in the office, there was no mention of breakfast but I haven't had mine yet and I'm so hungry I could eat a troll,' Braun replied and his stomach rumbled to confirm what he had just said.

When they got to the office, the door was closed and guarded but the sergeant of the guard admitted them with a nod of his head to the sentries, who opened the door to let them in. Colonel O'Rourke sat behind the desk that used to be Colonel Dyer's and was now his; Urim stood alongside his chair, dark and brooding. Anna and Archer were also there so it just remained for Hamill to be prised from his slumbers by Trapper and Tracker for the group to be complete. Jon sat next to Anna and she reached out to hold his hand; he mouthed the question.

'What's going on?'

But she just shrugged her shoulders and cuddled in closer to him. Jon felt a new strength within him now that he was sure of Anna's feelings for him; he was more confident and always had a smile on his lips when he was around her. (It was actually all the time though he did not realise it.) Braun stood against the side wall where the door opened on to it; he made the room look small, with his head almost touching the ceiling. No one spoke but they waited silently for the others to arrive. Braun's stomach rumbled and he looked embarrassed, holding his large hands over his middle to try and stop the noise. Urim eyed Braun with a look of disapproval then tried to hide a smile as if he had just remembered something amusing.

Moments later the door opened and the two dwarves entered followed by a bedraggled looking Hamill who had obviously just woken up and was bleary eyed. He stifled a yawn. 'Morning everyone; what's up?'

Urim looked at him and reproached him gently for being such a sleepy head and keeping them all waiting, but his eyes were full of endearment and a smile played at the corners of his mouth.

'Can we now all get down to business? Good; I did not tell you last night because I saw no reason to, but you need to know now that we have captured Ebon.'

He waited for the import of what he had said to register. There was stunned silence apart from Jon as he knew already and had assumed that everyone else did too. He was surprised that they did not know. Urim continued.

'He has been put under armed guard and his staff and talisman have been confiscated by me and are safe. All the time he is without them he is harmless, but should he get hold of either one of them then we had better watch out. He is like a caged animal and is resenting being held; he will try anything to escape and exact his revenge on us. If you thought he was dangerous before, mark my words, he will kill you as soon as look at you and will seek every opportunity to do so.'

Urim knew that the import of his message had hit home by the look on their faces. Braun's stomach growled and everyone turned to look at him.

'Sorry about that, I have not had my breakfast yet,' he apologised and drew his jerkin closer around him, folding his arms tightly across his belly.

'We will eat soon enough, my friend,' Urim reassured him and continued. 'We must take him with us to Seers' Tower and compel him to remove the barrier he has put in place; once it is free, the Council of the Sight will decide how best to deal with him. Now we must get there as soon as possible; even *I* do not relish the prospect of hanging on to Ebon any longer than is necessary. Now that Javelin has been incapacitated I realise that you dwarves may not wish to continue with us and we recognize the service that you have given already. We understand your need to stay with him until he has recovered.'

Archer spoke for the three of them.

'It has been decided before we came to the meeting that I would stay here with Javelin whilst Trapper and Tracker continue on with you, if you will have them to be part of your company again that is?'

They all assured Archer that nothing would give them greater pleasure than to have the two dwarves accompany them and would have been saddened if none of them had gone with them. They all wished Archer to convey their good wishes and thanks on to Javelin with the hope of a speedy recovery.

Urim settled everyone down and added his own best wishes then continued.

'What I propose to do is . . .'

Braun's stomach began to rumble angrily and could not be silenced; he shrugged his shoulders in resignation. Anna laughed in her own silent way; she was the only one of them that could do so and not have to hold back, but it set Jon going as well, then Hamill joined in with a snigger followed by a guffaw. The colonel had sat listening calmly in his seat all this time but even he succumbed to the laughter and spluttered out a loud bellow that he had been holding back. Poor Braun just stood where he was, grinning through his big red beard, and his stomach growled again.

Urim could see that there was no sense in continuing with the meeting until after breakfast had been eaten and Braun's belly had been filled; besides, they were all pretty hungry and what he had to say could wait. That apart, with the way things were, he was not going to get a serious conversation going for some time; better to let things settle down before recommencing. After all, Ebon was not going anywhere; he hoped.

Breakfast was eaten in high spirits. The battle with the gnomes had been won and Ebon taken captive. Pretty soon the task that was undertaken, to release the seers, would be realised and everything could get back to normal, at least as normal as it could be; no one was ever going to be the same again after this experience. Their good humour, however, was tinged with sadness as they remembered those whom they had come to call friends but who were now dead. They held an impromptu minute's silence in memory of them; each making a silent promise that their deaths would not have been in vain. They also offered a toast to the dwarves, especially for Javelin's return to good health and strength.

Hunger satisfied, Urim called them all together again to expound his plan to them for the journey to Seers' Tower deep in the Hammerhead Heights, a journey that would take them over a week if they were to walk or three days by coach.

'So which is it to be, do you walk or take the coach?' he asked, knowing full well what their answer would be.

Hamill was the first to vote for the coach; he had done more than enough walking for his liking, thank you very much.

Remembering how Hamill had moaned and groaned about his feet all the time on their journeying from the moment they had left Foundry Smelt, it did not take long for the others to also vote for the coach, rather than be subjected to his constant complaining. Besides, if there was a choice between walking and travelling in the relative comfort of a coach, then there really was no contest. Braun was the only one to be hesitant about it due to his size; he was not comfortable with the thought of being squashed up in a cramped coach for three days.

'However, if it means that I don't have to listen to Hamill complaining about his feet, then I'll go by coach, but I reserve the open seat next to the driver, if nobody objects that is.'

No one did, but Hamill expressed his hurt at the insinuation that he had been constantly complaining. They all shouted him down in a friendly way, teasing him about his moaning. He sat in his chair sulking for a while, red faced, but the friendly banter between them all made him smile and finally accept that maybe he had complained, once or twice, about his feet. This caused great amusement amongst them and they teased him all the more.

'All right, you win; I apologise for being a pain in the neck.'

'Some people would go so far as to say that they have a lower opinion of you!' Tracker teased, causing a ripple of laughter.

'All right, everyone, you've proved your point,' Urim intervened with a smile on his face and a wink towards Hamill. 'Let's not make him feel any more uncomfortable than he is already. I think that it has been agreed that the coach would be the better choice for you to take.'

He let the laughter settle and waited until he had everyone's attention.

'I am also happy with the decision for you to travel by coach; I'm sure that we can all agree with Hamill that you have done enough walking for a while.'

They all nodded in agreement, apart from the three dwarves – they were used to walking and did not mind the prospect of a brisk walk, though they appreciated that not everyone thought as a dwarf did.

Urim straightened from leaning on the desk and looked at them all, one by one. They sensed that he had something else to add to this discussion and that perhaps he had already decided what was going to happen, but was leading them towards agreement with his decision. He continued.

'Now then, my friends, what are we going to do about Ebon? How are we going to ensure that he stays compliant over the next three days or more to satisfy our desire to go to the Tower and release the seers?'

The room went silent. Urim seemed to be looking towards Hamill who fidgeted in his chair feeling uncomfortable at the seer's gaze. No one offered any suggestions. Urim lowered his eyes to the desk in front of him and ran his finger across it as if drawing out a pattern on the leather-bound top.

'There is a way in which it can be done to ensure that Ebon causes you no problems on the way; that is to administer a sleeping potion of some sort so that he can be kept unconscious of his surroundings and therefore not be a threat.'

They all got the drift of Urim's remarks and turned to look at Hamill; he was aware of their glances and crossed his arms across his chest, sitting with his legs straight out in front of him with ankles crossed. He was closed to any suggestion that he should administer a drug to Ebon.

'I will not do it. I don't care who it is, I will not drug someone into submission; it goes against all my principles to do so.'

'I understand, Hamill, and I appreciate your position on this.'

Urim seemed embarrassed to ask and looked as uncomfortable with the task as Hamill was in being asked.

'I must ask it of you, however, for the safety of not just your friends around you, but for the sake of all the peoples of this land and possibly even the lands beyond. Unless we can transport Ebon securely, I believe that we will fail and he will have no one to prevent him from obtaining his desire in enslaving the land and in killing you all.'

Jon had picked up on something that Urim had said a couple of times that none of the others seemed to have noticed and he confronted Urim with a question.

'Urim, I have noticed that a couple of times you have not included yourself in our actions; does that mean that you are not coming with us?'

The others all looked at Jon, then to Urim in surprise.

Urim smiled at Jon, saying, 'That was very astute of you, Jon, yes it does mean that I will not be accompanying you on your journey; there is another matter that I must deal with, but I shall meet with you at the Tower in three days time, have no fear.'

There followed a general clamour of alarm and concern from all but Hamill. He sat deep in thought at what Urim had said and amidst the uproar said, 'All right I'll do it.'

Gradually his remark registered with the others and they fell into silence.

'If you are not coming with us and what you say is true, then I have no choice but to act for the greater good. I will administer to Ebon so that he will remain unaware of what is happening for the duration of our journey, but no longer, so you had better be there to help us.'

The others were amazed at his last comment but Urim smiled and nodded, assuring Hamill that indeed he would.

'I have taken the liberty of sending Bearer and Petros on ahead of you; Holdhard will stay here with the main body of colossi and guide them back to the mountain city for repatriation. They have as much of a task there as here to make their city habitable again. I suspect that they will require the assistance of the metal masters of the smelt in doing so.'

'Then they shall have it, gladly,' Braun responded with conviction.

'All that remains then is for us to make our final preparations to depart. Colonel O'Rourke, we thank you for your help, we ask just one thing more of you before we go: that is the use of two coaches with teams of horses, which will be returned to you just as soon as our task is completed.'

'Of course, and anything else that you may require; I shall order the transport along with drivers to facilitate a speedy journey; I shall also ensure that ample provisions are placed on board. Please do not concern yourself with returning them before your need for them is finished; the drivers will stay with you as long as is required.'

'Thank you, colonel, we are indebted to you.'

'Not at all, seer, it is we who are indebted to you and your friends; for what it is worth, I bestow upon you all the freedom of the city, you may come and go as you will and receive the protection of its walls.'

They all thanked him and accepted a small parchment each that had been prepared for them earlier, stating their free access throughout the twin cities of Southill and Northill.

Urim took Hamill with him to administer the sleeping tonic to Ebon whilst the others prepared for their journey, agreeing to meet at the funicular in an hour.

Chapter XIX

Friend or Foe

Satisfied that Ebon was not faking his state of unconsciousness, Urim accompanied Ebon to the funicular. Ebon was borne there by several of the colonel's men. Hamill went back to his room to collect his things. He still was not very happy with administering the drug to Ebon but realised that what Urim had said made sense and that no matter how he tried to convince himself otherwise because of his oath to heal the sick, he knew it was the right thing to do. Back at the funicular, Colonel O'Rourke waited to see them off; he told the two dwarves that Urim was waiting for them with the coaches, making sure that Ebon was secured and comfortable.

Taking their farewell of the colonel, they boarded the car and heard the flush of water enter the tank below them and before long it descended the steep gradient to Southill, passing the other car coming up as they were halfway down; it was still in a state of disrepair but efforts were well under way to restore it. Reaching the bottom, they disembarked and looked up at the tower where the gatehouse was situated in Northill; even at this distance it was an imposing structure that loomed over them and the lower city.

The gatehouse in Southill was unrecognizable, almost demolished by the trolls and gnomes in their efforts to find the service tunnel; but the colossi and the teams of workers under the direction of Captain Perkins had made good progress in rebuilding it, having almost completed the ground-floor level. It was he who greeted them as they exited the car, saluting smartly and shaking Jon's hand warmly.

'It is a pleasure to see you all well and unharmed, sir.' He fairly beamed at Jon and the others, shaking their hands in turn. 'I am sorry to see you go, I did volunteer to go with you but they would not let me as they need me here apparently, but Fredericks and

Barker here will see you safely to your destination; they are good men.'

'In that case, we are indeed in good hands. I am also pleased to see you well; I'd like to thank you for saving Anna and me the other day. We really don't know how to thank you enough and we were so worried about you after sustaining your injuries,' Jon replied, taking his hand in both of his. Anna planted a kiss on the shy captain; he said that if his wife saw that, he'd be in for a telling off.

'But seeing as she didn't and she is not here may I take the liberty?'

He took off his hat and returned her kiss, one on each cheek, then donned his cap self-consciously. They both gave the young captain a big hug and he helped load their packs onto the coaches, although he was not able to do too much due to his arm being in a sling. Hamill and the two dwarves got in with Ebon, whilst Anna and Jon shared the other coach. Braun climbed on top to sit next to the driver who had the habit of chewing tobacco and spitting every now and again. Braun did look odd perched on the bench, head and shoulders above the driver, who was quite a small man anyway but next to Braun he looked like a dwarf. The driver watched in awe as he sat next to him, forgetting to spit and swallowing nervously at being so close to the big man. He regretted it immediately and showed his displeasure in his facial expression at the taste, then spat, grimacing.

'We promise you that we'll come back soon to see you; you'd better have all this done by the time we do,' Jon joked with Perkins, indicating the ruined buildings, as they waved goodbye and set off to rendezvous with Urim at Seers' Tower.

'You won't recognize the place, not when I'm finished with it,' Perkins shouted after them with a smile.

They headed off cross-country along a well used track; it had been reinforced with large stones to make the going easier, but after a while they gave way to a dirt track, which turned to mud in the wet season; that was not too far from starting so they hoped that it would stay dry for the duration of their journey. Jon crossed his fingers for good luck and chewed on his lower lip nervously.

The ride was certainly much quicker than walking but not always so comfortable. They were tossed around and thrown off the seat several times as the wheels either went over stones or down holes. It was pretty uncomfortable actually and Jon wondered whether they had made the right decision after all. They stopped for lunch at an inn to allow the horses to rest and receive food and water. Jon felt that they needed it as much as the horses and was glad to sit on something that was not moving. How anyone could enjoy such a mode of travel he did not know but Hamill seemed happy enough. Given the choice of sore feet from a day's walking or a sore backside from sitting in a coach, Jan knew which he would rather have and grimaced as he tried to sit on one buttock at a time to take the ache out of his behind. Anna was amused by his discomfort and appeared to have taken the journey better than he had. From his seat by the window in the tavern, Jon saw the dwarves disembark, showing that they were of like opinion: they stretched upon reaching the ground then hobbled across to the inn and a steady seat; Jon had to admit that they were a funny sight and guessed that he had looked just as funny to others. Braun seemed to have worn the journey well and Jon noticed that the driver's bench had a pair of iron springs attached to it that gave it more flexibility, affording them an easier ride; he had not envied Braun his seat on the top before, being out in the open, but he did now.

Hamill stayed with Ebon, so the dwarves took some food out to him and gave him a break to allow him to make himself more comfortable when he said that he needed to 'go'. He hurried off to relieve himself, glad to be able to stretch his legs for a while. They attracted a great deal of attention: tales of the appearance of the colossi and of the gnomes' defeat had travelled quickly. And wasn't there a seer who had helped defeat the army by descending in a cloud and sweeping the walls clear of the gnomes? Questions were asked of them whether they knew anything of this, but they had been warned by Urim not to draw attention to themselves. They responded by saying that they saw very little of the battle and were interrupted in their journey to the sea by the conflict, which was not untrue.

Back on the coaches and making good headway Jon wished for the day to be over so that he could have a hot bath and soak away his aches and pains. He tried not to complain. He knew how they had reacted to Hamill when he complained about his feet, so he mostly suffered in silence. He had pulled out his overcoat from his pack before starting off from the inn and was sitting on it to give him a little more padding but the driver still managed to find every pothole in the road; he swore he was doing it on purpose.

They completed the first leg of their journey by reaching Ebb-Lune, a town on a bend in the river Lune and the highest tidal point before it became a freshwater river at the weir and locks. They had had their fair share of conflict here as soldiers of the local garrison had contended with fierce creatures from the marshes further east. A large number of them had got through and headed north several weeks ago but since then things had been peaceful; Jon believed that they were the ones that he and Urim saw in the forest near Ashbrooke when they had first met.

At their chosen night stop, Ebon was assisted to a room that he would share with Braun and the dwarves. They said that he was feeling unwell from the journey and would take a little broth in his room if the landlord would allow it.

'Of course, sirs, no problem; I do hope that the gentleman feels better soon. This sickness he has, not serious is it?'

They assured him that it was not but said that they would appreciate some privacy, so Trapper would collect the broth from the kitchen when it was ready. Jon and Anna saw no more of them other than when Hamill came down for dinner and told them that Ebon had been fed, having regained consciousness for long enough to eat, before being induced to sleep again. The others were taking it in turn to watch him and would eat separately so as not to draw too much attention from the towns-folk who were obviously curious about them. The two drivers, Tom and Harry, declined to join them, but thanked them, none-theless explaining that they needed to care for the horses and would be sleeping close to them as a safety precaution. Captain Perkins had specifically ordered their diligence in this matter and they would not wish to disobey orders, especially if something did go wrong. They wished them all a good night and went to tend the horses, having had a meal in the drovers' section of the inn where they got a better rate for their meals.

Jon and Hamill shared a room across from Braun and the others, whilst Anna had a small room adjacent to theirs with an interconnecting door; this they left open so as to be able to access each other's room should the need arise. The night passed without incident. Jon made his way down for breakfast, leaving Hamill to come around in his own time. He had tried to rouse him without success. Jon met Anna on the landing and asked her if she had slept well and she shook her head, signing:

Not very well, I couldn't sleep for the sound of you two snoring.

'Oh, sorry about that, we'll close the door between us at the next stop if we have the same arrangements,' Jon promised with a sheepish grin, before dodging a playful blow to his side, which was much better now and did not hurt at all; obviously Anna's arm was fully healed too. At the bottom of the stairs they met the drivers who were on their way to get the coaches and horses ready, having just had their breakfasts. The one driving Hamill's coach was very amiable and polite but the one driving their coach was a bit standoffish and was constantly chewing on his tobacco, which had stained his teeth. They wished the drivers good morning and they responded, one with a cheerful wave of his hand, the other with a cursory nod of the head. Hamill stumbled down the stairs behind them, wishing that his head was still in his pillow because he was far from being awake and mumbled something about breakfast. He rubbed his face with his hand and brushed at his hair; it really needed a comb passing through it rather than his fingers. They made their way into the food hall and the boys enjoyed a cooked breakfast whilst Anna preferred fruit and sweetbread. They saw no sign of the others but decided to get their belongings, which they had packed earlier, and head out to the coaches. Hamill went to check on Ebon while they opened the door to their room. Jon caught sight of someone rushing out of the window and jumping to the ground below. He hurried over to see who it was but they had disappeared from sight by the time he got there; the only people he saw were the drivers who were busy harnessing the horses. When he asked them if they had seen anything, neither of them had. Clothes and personal belongings were strewn all over the floor and the mattresses lay askew on the cots; someone had been looking for something, but what and why? They ran across the corridor and knocked on the door to the others' room. Braun answered and asked what had happened when he saw their troubled faces. Jon quickly explained and Braun went to their room to have a look, leaving the dwarves and Hamill with Ebon. He studied the room in amazement.

'Whoever it was, they meant it; did you see anyone?'

Anna shook her head.

'No! We did see a figure leap out of the window, but by the time we got there, they were nowhere in sight and the drivers didn't see anyone either as they were busy with the horses.'

'Well, there's not much we can do about it, have you checked to see if anything is missing?'

They quickly gathered their things together but could not see that anything had been taken.

'It must have been a sneak thief who noticed we were at breakfast and decided to take the opportunity to rob us, not that he got what he wanted because I have my money belt with me,' Jon said, patting his midriff with both hands.

'Better get packed; I'll meet you downstairs in the coach after I've helped put Ebon in the other one with the dwarves; see you in a few minutes.'

Braun went back to his room and left them to pack their bags again.

They got underway, still mystified and somewhat aggrieved by the attempted robbery; it gnawed at Jon that someone had rummaged through their belongings and felt as if he had been stripped bare.

'How could people do that sort of thing?' he had asked the landlord when leaving. The landlord had apologised profusely for the inconvenience and distress it had caused and assured them that this sort of thing did not happen here usually. He offered Jon a reduction on the room rate as compensation but Jon said that that would not be necessary, though he thanked him for the offer. Hamill berated him for not accepting it when Jon told him about it as they were getting into their carriages; Jon simply shrugged his shoulders, saying:

'I don't see how that would change what has happened; it's not as if the landlord was the culprit, he was still down in the food hall at the time.'

Jon had his principles and did not think it right for someone to pay for something that was not their fault.

*

315

The weather closed in on them that day and rumblings of thunder could be heard away in the distant hills; rain could be seen descending in big black curtains over the highest points but the lowlands they were travelling through escaped the worst of it and only a few spots of rain fell. They were all glad of that, especially Braun and the two drivers who were atop the coaches; any slight shower and they would be drenched. Besides, the rain would have turned the dirt track into a quagmire and impeded their progress.

Jon had an uneasy feeling; he sensed that someone was following them and remembered feeling this way when he was in the forest the night that he first met Urim and again when he had been deceived by Ebon and followed him to the forge at Foundry Smelt. He then remembered that Urim had told him that it was he who had followed him and Anna that night. He relaxed a little then, thinking that it was probably Urim keeping an eye on them without wanting to be seen.

Despite the movement of the coach with its juddering along the uneven track, Jon managed to go to sleep and only awoke when it stopped at a village market where they bought food for their lunch. He was still quite dopey and stayed in the coach whilst the drivers collected what was needed. He was observing the traders selling their wares amid the hustle and bustle of the crowds when he noticed a black-cloaked rider across the square from them who had stopped to water his horse. Jon only noticed him because he was not a tall person and kept looking in their direction; he ducked back into the shadows of the coach so as not to alert the rider that he had noticed him. Jon signalled to Anna to look and caught her eye but when he looked back, the rider had gone; opening the small hatch in the roof of the coach, he spoke to Braun, asking him if he could see the rider. After a few moments of searching among the crowd, Braun peered back down at him to say that he could not see anyone that answered that description. More than a little unsettled by the experience, Jon could not help but wonder whether the rider was the same person who had rifled through their possessions back at the inn. If he was, then why was he following them? One thing was for certain, he would not be sleeping so comfortably tonight.

*

They stopped in the early evening at a town called Diggerton, which was situated on the edge of a natural formation known as Digger's Ditch; it had been formed by a shift in the ground, leaving a broad valley that stretched from Seaview in the south, all the way up to Pierhead in the north. Beyond the ditch was the peninsula known as Hammerhead Heights, named as such because of the shape of the land. The range of mountains dominated the whole area where Seers' Tower was located amongst the heathland. Traces of ancient civilizations could be found at various places here, including the magnificent stone circle known as 'Standing Stones' that inspired respect for the ingenuity of its builders.

They managed, with the help of the drivers, to secure rooms for the night that overlooked the valley and the track that they would be taking in the morning. Being tired, none of them felt like talking or staying up for too long, especially Jon. Despite his sleep in the coach earlier, he felt exhausted and retired to the room that he was to share with Hamill. Even though he had wanted to stay alert, there was no way that he could keep his eyes open for any longer than it took him to climb into his cot and pull the covers over him. Before going upstairs Jon had spoken to Trapper about his concerns; the dwarf had assured him that he and Tracker would take turns to keep watch through the night so that he need not be worried.

Trapper was right, the night passed peacefully enough and they got away at a good hour, although Hamill had complained at having to get up so early, for which he was sorely ribbed by everyone else. It was colder today, noticeably so; Anna had put on a thicker top and an extra pair of socks before putting on her boots, to help keep out the cold and prevent her feet from turning blue. Only Braun seemed unaware of the change in the weather, even though you could see his breath as it condensed in the air. They planned to make it to Landfall, the next big town closest to Seers' Tower, before the end of the day, and wanted to make sure of it by getting the early start. Ebon had been kept sedated for the last two days, being revived only sufficiently for him to take nourishment and to see to his daily needs. Hamill was looking forward to the time when he could stop drugging him; it went against his nature and left a bitter taste in his mouth, even though

317

he kept reminding himself that it was for their safety and that of the land.

The 'ditch' took most of the morning to traverse but the scenery was dramatic, with the high rise of each side visible for miles. They went north along the green valley floor for a long time before heading west and climbing up the side of the rift. They lurched up a steep track that the horses struggled with and had to rest them at a water station at the top. Whilst they waited everyone got out to stretch their legs and were awed at the sight of the Hammerhead Heights in the distance, topped by white snowcaps that dazzled in the sunlight. Away to their left they could see the Great Salt Waters and far to the north was the Grey Water Bay. The land dipped away before them, affording a panoramic view of the whole area. Somewhere before them, out of sight at present, was their destination for tonight, Landfall.

Anna signed to Jon to ask when they would get to the Standing Stones as she had never seen them and was keen to do so; Jon also had a hankering to see them so he asked Tom, the young driver of Hamill's coach, how far the stones were from where they were right now.

'Ah yes, the stones; quite a sight I can tell you. Well, we should pass close by them in about three hours or so. Enough time to enjoy the good weather, even though it's turned a bit nippy,' Tom answered cheerfully, before climbing on to his seat at the front of the coach and preparing to get going again. The horses, fresh from their rest and watering, bounded forward, as if keen to reach the inn and their feed that evening.

The stones were truly magnificent, standing at the centre of a shallow depression, in what appeared to be a perfect circle; everyone was struck by the magnitude of the task it must have been to erect such a structure and, like countless others before them, they wondered at its purpose. The drivers encouraged them not to loiter too long as the sun set earlier this far north and they needed to get to Landfall before dusk. As soon as they had completed once around the massive stone circle they clambered on board, stunned into silence by the great stones.

*

At the inn, they sat at a table near the log fire and ate together but Braun and the dwarves took turns in watching Ebon in their room. Tom and Harry, the drivers, preferred to keep their own company in the drivers' section as they mixed with others who were travelling through the area. It was a busy town, being the base for a thriving fishing industry, as well as a port where people embarked for a speedier journey to the south. The peninsula was heavily populated and rich in farming, especially that of sheep-herding. Seers' Tower acted like a magnet for trade and the folk of several villages surrounding it jealously guarded their employ-ment within its walls; it was situated just thirty leagues to the north at the base of the Hammerhead Heights.

Jon could sense that they were close now to fulfilling their task, waiting only to meet up with Urim to complete their mission. The others were engaged in lighthearted conversation: Anna was teaching Hamill her sign language and it must be admitted that he was doing very well at picking it up; occasionally he would make a mistake and they would laugh together. Jon didn't worry about Hamill and Anna any more, he felt secure at last in their relationship and was happy to see them enjoying the evening. His thoughts were a long way from here and he heard and saw things through a sort of fog, being distant from those around him. He wondered whether that was how Urim felt at times: being part of the group yet separate; never really being one of them. Was that what it meant to be a seer, alone and distant from everyone else? It seemed a high price to pay for the responsibility he shouldered; he could sort of understand it though. Were it not for Anna, he would probably feel the same himself; even though he was surrounded by those he now called friends, he would feel lonely. It is amazing what a difference she had made to his life, from the encouragement and companionship of early childhood through to the determined and confident young woman with a strong spirit but a soft and warm heart. She had come to mean more to him over these past weeks than life itself; he loved her, he knew that now and was glad of it. When this was all over ... he left the thought unfinished as their laughter impinged upon his thoughts and he was brought to an awareness that Hamill had been speaking to him.

'. . . Jon, are you listening to me?'

'Sorry, Hamill, I was thinking of something else; what did you say?'

'I said that I envy you this girl; she's one in a million and if you don't watch out I'll come and take her away from you.'

He grinned mischievously but Jon thought that deep inside he really meant it. A few weeks ago he would have taken offence at a remark like that, but they had all grown so close to each other now that it was almost as if they were family. Anna squeezed Jon's hand in reassurance that she was right there beside him and had no intention of going away. He leaned over and kissed her gently, smiling warmly with a twinkle in his eye.

'I say, chap, don't mind us will you,' Hamill teased, and they all laughed. Even Braun, who was normally so serious, broke into a broad grin and gave Jon what was intended to be a playful shove, but ended up unbalancing him as he perched on his stool and he landed on his backside on the floor at Anna's feet, which caused them even more mirth. As the laughter died down they made their excuses and bid each other good-night, arranging to meet early in the morning for breakfast.

With so many people staying at the inn it was considered prudent by the dwarves to maintain a watch, so they, along with Braun, arranged between them to take turns. Jon heard their plans and offered to take the first watch. He wasn't tired and would be happy to take his turn and help out. Trapper and Tracker exchanged surprised looks with Braun but they readily agreed for him to take the first watch and to wake Braun in two hours time. A round of hot drinks appeared in front of them, which the landlord brought out from the kitchen. Whilst the others took theirs upstairs, he made himself comfortable at a small table that had a good view of the rooms along the balcony above the tavern. He drank his cup of chicory and amused himself with watching the patrons as they continued their revelling until it was time to close the doors; his eyes grew heavy and despite his best efforts, he fell asleep.

He came too, groggily, by the efforts of the landlord shaking him and saying that he ought to go to bed. Jon shook his head to try and clear the fog from his mind but it persisted and he struggled to get to his feet.

'What hour is it?' he asked, barely able to stay on his feet; he felt so tired but could not understand why. The thought struck him that perhaps he had been drugged and that the others were in danger.

'It's nearly midnight,' the landlord replied and helped him stagger to the stairs.

'Had a bit too much to drink did you, sir? Drinking chicory isn't going to help you stay awake you know; what you need is a good night's sleep; can you manage the stairs or do you need assistance?'

'I can manage thank you.'

Jon grabbed a hold of the banister rail and dragged himself one step at a time towards Braun's room. His legs didn't want to work and the room swayed first one way and then another; the way he was reacting it made it look to everyone else like he had indeed had too much to drink. He knew he had not; he had not had a strong drink since his last night in Ffridd-Uch-Ddu, so he must have been drugged. Clawing his way up the stairs he stumbled through the doorway into the room where Ebon was being watched by Braun and the dwarves. Light spilled into the room to reveal a shadowy figure bent over Ebon. The dwarves and Braun were fast asleep in their beds.

'No, stop, who are you? Braun, help, someone's trying to free Ebon.'

His yells went unheeded and they slept on; they had likewise been administered a sleeping agent.

Jon grabbed a chair and flung it at Braun who stirred, and as Jon had done, came to his senses slowly and with difficulty. The figure pounced towards Jon but fortunately one of the dwarves, awakened by the disturbance, threw a pillow at him. Now, though a pillow is not a very good weapon to use, it was sufficient to take the figure by surprise and make him miss his strike at Jon, who fell sideways as he dodged the attack. Recovering quickly, the figure pounced back into the fray against the three stumbling friends.

'Gnome! Watch out, he's got a knife,' Tracker warned them.

Braun lunged forward and knocked Jon aside in his efforts to get at the gnome but he was too quick for the drowsy giant and slashed at him leaving a nasty cut across Braun's cheek. They danced around the room swaying this way and that, all the time getting stronger as the three of them fought off the effects of the

321

drug; seeing this and knowing that he would be no match for the hardy dwarf and swarthy giant once they had regained their composure, the gnome made a dash for the door, waving his blade in front of him, but Jon managed to trip him and he slammed against the doorpost, stunning him momentarily. Infuriated by Jon's intervention he launched himself towards him screaming in hatred; he never reached him. Braun's huge sword flew like an arrow, impaling the gnome and knocking him back to lay coughing and spluttering on the floor. Braun staggered across to the gnome and said:

'That's for burning my forge down.'

The gnome laughed and coughed, gasping out, 'You thought I'd done that; well, given the chance I would have done but it was already alight when I got there. So whoever it was, you're blaming the wrong one.'

With that he breathed his last with a cough.

Braun and Jon were stunned by this piece of news. If the gnome was telling the truth, and he might be, if it was not him, then who was it? They looked at each other in stunned silence.

'No, it can't be him, I refuse to believe it, the gnome's a liar.'

'But who else could it have been? He was the last one out,' Braun stated, shocked to think that it could have been Urim who had burned his forge to the ground. Trapper snored, undisturbed by the commotion; all three looked at each other and shook their heads in disbelief. They let him sleep on and Braun, shaking the effects of the sleep agent off, hid the gnome's body outside in an alley, then took over the watch from Jon who stumbled to his cot and fell onto it; he was asleep before his head even touched the pillow.

Everyone woke up with a headache resulting from the sleeping agent that had somehow been administered to them. They were grateful that it was only a sleeping draft and not poison that they had drunk. It must have been in the last round of drinks that the landlord brought over; they hadn't thought anything of it at the time, everyone had assumed that one of the others had placed the order so they just accepted it at that. Thinking about it now, they realised that none of them had ordered it so it must have been sent, with the drug in it, by the gnome or an accomplice of his. This told them that they could not be too careful and must watch their every move; thank goodness that they were almost at the end of their journey. Hamill took a look at Braun's cut. Fortunately it did not require any stitches and he assured him that it would not spoil his good looks to which Braun grunted and mumbled under his breath.

Braun was very morose today; a big black cloud seemed to hang over him and he refused to be drawn by the others as to the reason for it, saying simply that he had to think something through.

Climbing into the coaches for their last leg of the trek towards the Tower, they wished for it to be all over so that they could relax and go about their normal routines; Jon wondered whether anything would be normal after all that had happened and tried to imagine himself at home in Ashbrooke, sitting beside a roaring fire sipping at a nice hot cup of chicory. It did not help very much; rather it made him all the more discontented with what he and Anna had been subjected to. Hiking their way all over the land, being almost run down by a carriage and being abducted by Ebon at dead of night; then hiking again and almost getting themselves killed in the mountains; thank goodness for the colossi coming to their rescue.

Passing through the mountains and visiting with the dwarves at Ffridd-Uch-Ddu and finding the passage through the mountains that the gnomes had been using. He thought of the dwarf, Mason, who had been lost in the flood that had all but overwhelmed them on their way through the passage; the hike down to Tri-Bune and their skirmish with the gnome scouting party and then all that had occurred at Northill. His eyes misted over when he recalled those whom he had come to know and respect who were no longer with them, realising that he really had no room for complaint.

The coaches swayed and jerked their way along the track towards Seers' Tower and their final task. Harry, the driver, had said that they would be there before midday and the weather looked to be fine, though the weather around the Tower, being at the base of the Heights, as it was, was never predictable. Jon felt the palms of his hands sweat and his shoulders tense; he tried to relax them and made a conscious effort to do so. The trouble was that he tensed up again almost as soon as he had relaxed.

'You'll see the Tower on your left through the trees in a

minute,' the driver shouted down through the hatch, spitting to his right before recommencing his chewing. Both Jon and Anna craned their necks to be the first to see the Tower; she pointed excitedly as they cleared a clump of trees and there, not a league away, on a rocky knoll of an island, stood Seers' Tower. A huge bubble of energy covered the tower; it shimmered before their eyes as if a gossamer veil were drawn across it that swayed in a gentle breeze. Jon thought that it must be the barrier that Ebon had created to imprison the seers inside and keep others out.

Just a few minutes later they drew up not far from a jetty where a platform ferry was secured, linking the Tower to the rest of the land, across from them was the impressive gateway that led into the Tower. The ferry did not look like it had been used for a while; no wonder if the barrier had prevented anyone from getting to it. The shimmering field of power surrounded not just the Tower but the still, black water and a large area of land, in from the water's edge. It was stunning to behold and in its own way a thing of beauty; its energy could be felt when standing next to it and a subtle humming could be heard in the back of your mind; it made the hairs on the back of Jon's neck stand on end. When he moved back, the humming stopped, along with the goose-bump sensations. They were all enthralled by it; both Trapper and Tracker put their hands up towards the shield, taking care not to touch it, and felt a trickle of energy running up their arms, which caused an itching sensation. Other than the humming of the energy shield the place was silent, disturbed only by the noise of the horses as they skittered nervously in their harnesses. The drivers pulled the coaches back further away from the edge so as to keep the horses calm and tethered them to a tree.

As the drivers were walking away from them to rejoin the group, the horses whinnied and kicked out in fear, startled by something as yet unseen by them. They all turned to see what was startling them; Braun drew his broadsword, whilst the two dwarves had already taken up a defensive position around Hamill and Ebon, who still slept under the influence of Hamill's potion. They waited, nervously anticipating an attack from gnomes, or worse; the horses were tethered near a rocky outcrop and were reacting strangely. Then the rocks began to move; two stone giants stood from being seated on the rock. Bearer and Petros approached them, they had blended in so perfectly that they had

324

not been noticed. They greeted the metal master cordially and nodded in acknowledgement of the others.

'Bearer, Petros, it's you, thank goodness; you gave us a scare,' Braun replied, visibly relieved to see them again. The others likewise were relieved and relaxed their readiness for action, not that Jon had given much thought to what he would have done if it had been gnomes, but Anna had been ready with her slingshot; he felt rather ashamed that he had stood there defenceless, whilst Anna was ready to fight.

'It is good to see you again, my friend,' Bearer boomed out to Braun. 'We have been waiting for you since dawn, making ourselves comfortable and keeping watch in the event that there was a problem, but we have seen no one else this day, other than yourselves.'

'We are likewise pleased that all is well with you both. Has Urim not arrived?'

'We have seen no one, as I have said.'

Ebon started to come to his senses and sat up from were he had been laid, moaning that he was thirsty. Carefully and minding not to give him any chance to try any of his tricks, Tracker gave him a drink then backed away from him to a healthy distance, keeping an eye on him all the time.

Tom, the driver, had come across to see what was going on when he heard Ebon moan. As he drew abreast of Anna he grabbed her and placed a gnomish blade against her throat.

'Stand clear of the master.'

He threatened to harm Anna, using her as a shield as he worked his way across to Ebon. The dwarves, recognizing the blade, kept their weapons sheathed and warned the others to take care. Tom was a turncoat; for all his friendly banter and cheerful smile, he was a traitor to them and in the service of Ebon. What could they do? One false move and Anna would feel the cold steel of the assassin's knife. Anna clutched at his arm that was around her shoulders, wide-eyed with alarm and powerless to prevent Tom from holding her.

Jon made a slight move to try and get to Tom and save Anna but Tom was too alert for that and turned her towards Jon, placing the blade's sharp edge closer to her skin, causing it to yield under his pressure.

'Not so fast, Jon, I'm sure that you would not want anything to happen to your girl. Harry, see to the master, quickly, man,' he shouted over his shoulder.

'No, you're much better at the powders than I am, I'll take the girl, hand her over to me and you see to him. All right, now then, you lot, any funny business and the girl dies; is that understood?'

They all nodded. Jon swallowed nervously and noticed the dwarves making subtle hand signals to each other; Tom also saw it and, shouting at the dwarves, said that he meant what he had said. They decided to back down rather than risk Anna being harmed.

Harry drew his own blade and stepped up behind Tom to take Anna from him; he wrapped his arm around her, taking care that she could not escape without harming herself, and laughed in her ear. His horrid breath turned her nose as it assailed her senses; she could see in her mind's eye his blackened teeth, rotting from the effect of the chewing tobacco as he placed his head up against hers. She started at the words he whispered in her ear.

'Do not be afraid, I am with you, but I must pretend that I am still with Tom in this thing; play along with me and you will come to no harm, I promise you.'

He winked several times at the dwarves and nodded very slightly in the direction of Ebon and Tom.

'You heard the man, don't go getting any ideas that you can jump me or my partner, I've got the girl now.'

What he was really meaning was that Anna was safe now and that if the dwarves were going to make their move, it had better be now.

They did not need another sign, catching the drift of his remarks; they swiftly drew their knives and dived for Tom, taking him completely by surprise but not altogether quickly enough for he managed to block their initial attack and, stumbling back, managed to regain his stance.

Letting Anna go and apologising for any hurt he may have caused her, Harry motioned for the dwarves to stand aside and let him deal with Tom.

'Captain Perkins told me to keep an eye on you; you thought I was with you, didn't you, well I played your little game, but I'm not playing any more.'

The two men grappled with each other, pulling and scratching at each other, ducking and weaving, all the time searching for a way through the other's defences. Several times both Tom and Harry scored hits on the other, catching an arm or a leg. Everyone kept their distance, not wanting to interfere for Harry's sake in case Tom were able to take advantage of their intervention, but they stood ready to help should Harry need it. The fight was intense as Tom was desperate to keep out of the reach of Harry's blade; it was clear that Harry was the more experienced and had the edge over Tom; he bided his time, wearing his opponent down and not expending too much energy himself. He was a sight to see, a skilled fighter: were the duel not so serious, it would have been a delightful spectacle and demonstration of tactical fighting. All it needed was for one false move; several more times hits were scored, mostly by Harry on Tom. Blood trickled into his eyes from a cut on his forehead and he shook his head and wiped the blood away with the back of his hand. Lunging with an almighty effort in a last attempt to win or lose, Tom thrust his knife up towards Harry's throat but changed at the last moment and went for his heart. Harry cried out in surprise and Tom grinned in triumph, the two of them sinking to the ground. Tom remained still with the fixed grin on his face, eyes staring lifelessly up to the sky. Harry had seen his chance and taken it, but it had cost him as well; leaning back from Tom and clutching at his side, he rose and staggered a few feet before collapsing. Hamill rushed to his side to inspect the wound and was relieved to find that it was superficial, painful, but not life threatening; he had collapsed more from fatigue than anything else. Tom, however, had paid the price of his gamble and been found wanting; lodged firmly up to the hilt in Tom's chest was Harry's knife; he had made the move that Tom had intended to make on him and struck him through the heart.

While Hamill was tending to Harry's wound, he told them about his orders from Captain Perkins.

'He had suspected that there would be an attempt to stop you and had had his doubts about the two drivers who had volunteered to drive you. He arranged for one of them to be "taken ill" and put me in his stead. I had already been working undercover within the fortress for some time so it was easy for me to fall in, as it were, with Tom's scheme, as he believed me to be one of the dissidents. I was able to convince him to replace the poison he was planning to use against you with a sleeping agent or you would all be dead now. I told him that it would take a lot of explaining if that were to happen; better for you to be just unconscious. As it was, Jon was able to raise the alarm and Ebon's gnome was dealt with; that left it up to Tom to do something. The gnome was the one who searched through your room the other night; apparently Ebon wants something that Urim took from him and thought that you might have it.'

Having made Harry comfortable, Hamill made sure that he was placed in one of the coaches and gave him something to help him sleep. This time he had no qualms about administering the draft; this time it was perfectly permissible in order to aid his recovery.

A distant rumble of thunder threatened bad weather and a breeze sprang up, chilling them through their clothes; strange cloud formations gathered over the Heights as the air turned cold. Lightning so white it looked blue struck against the barrier and rebounded off, hitting the trees at the edge of the woods, felling a large branch with a loud crack. The wind gathered in strength and blew with icy fingers off the mountains; it swirled into a funnel not twenty lengths from them then settled. Urim stepped out of the midst of the storm and it subsided into nothing, he held two staffs, one of them his, the other belonging to Ebon.

'Greetings, my friends, welcome to Seers' Tower, I wish it could have been under better circumstances, then we would have given you a more cordial welcome. As it is, I am pleased to see you safe and well.'

He walked across to where they stood and thanked them for coming then, looking at the two dwarves, said, 'I am particularly grateful to you dwarves; you have proven loyal at every step and shared in our trials when there was no call on you to do so. I will be forever indebted to you and your song shall be heard loud and long across the camp fires throughout the ages, recounting your bravery and your sacrifice.'

They thanked him but insisted that they felt it their duty to be of service and that it had never been seen by them to be a sacrifice. Whatever ill they might have suffered, they had done it willingly and would continue in so doing, so long as there was a need.

Urim thanked them again and blinked rapidly as his eyes moistened.

Braun addressed Urim somewhat formally and in a measured tone, saying, 'Excuse me, seer, there is something I must ask you.'

Chapter XX

Coming of Age

Braun looked steadily into Urim's eyes. A mood of disappointment, of betrayal, played at the edge of his emotions. He was not sure whether he really wanted to know Urim's response to the question he knew he must ask, for fear of the answer.

Urim answered him quietly, a sadness in his eyes.

'My dear friend; I know what it is that you seek of me and I hesitate in saying that it is a possibility that I was responsible for the razing of your forge shop. If indeed it was by my action that this occurred then, I am truly sorry; it was not intentional on my part. You see I had to secure the chest that belonged to Terra Standfast so that it did not fall back into Ebon's hands; so I waited until you had all gone before using the power in my staff in sending it to a place of safety. By doing so, some of the residual power may have remained where the chest had been standing; it would not have taken a great deal of persuasion by someone who was skilled in the art of arson to have fanned it into a fire, but it would have needed feeding in order to build into a fire big enough to have really taken hold. It is my belief that the gnome returned with the intention of retrieving the chest but on seeing that it had gone, decided to burn the place down. He probably saw the chance of blaming the incident on me should it ever be necessary. So you see, in a way, it was I that caused the fire, though not by intent. I did not tell any of you this in case it was revealed to Ebon in some way by any of you that I had the chest secure. I sent it to Jon's home: the only place I could think that it would remain undisturbed until I recovered it once this was all over.'

He paused and looked questioningly at Braun.

'I take it that the gnome told you that I had started the fire?'

'He did, but I can see the logic in what you have told me and I

329

believe you; the gnome would no doubt have burnt my shop down just for spite. He told me that the shop was already on fire when he got there; what you have told me would fit perfectly well into his story. Thank you, Urim, I feel relieved to know the truth and do not hold you responsible; I believe that the gnome had every intention of doing it himself and he has paid for it with his life.'

Braun took Urim's hand in his and shook it with a firm, friendly grip.

'Hah! You're all fools; you all think that he's so good; that he's your friend. He only wants what suits himself, of course he wanted your shop to burn down; how else could he get you to go with him; you're all players in his game.'

Ebon spat the words with venom. Though still groggy from the sleeping agent and the length of time he had been under its influence, he was gaining strength fast.

Urim strode towards him, the two staffs, one in each hand, thumping into the hard turf. 'You shall not betray anyone again, Ebon; the time has come for you to answer for your deeds and no amount of falsehoods will prevent that.'

Urim lifted Ebon's staff in front of him and handed it to Hamill, saying, 'I entrust you with this staff until it is returned to the Council of the Sight. Do not try to use it in any way, for you have neither the skill nor the authority to do so.'

Hamill was speechless but took the staff carefully from Urim, gulping at the responsibility that had been invested upon him.

Ebon sneered and laughed cynically.

'I don't need my staff anyway, or my stone, by the end of the day you will all be dead and I shall rule here, not the Sight.'

He struggled to free himself from the grasp of the two dwarves.

Urim waved them away and said, 'Let him go; he is full of empty threats.'

The dwarves stepped aside but the two colossi moved closer, standing just behind him in case he tried anything; Ebon straightened himself, puffing out his chest and proudly squaring his shoulders in defiance of Urim.

'Empty threats are they, deceiver? It is you who are full of empty promises. Don't forget that I know who you really are, coming here at this time, pretending to be someone who you are not; the lad should be told the truth don't you think?'

'Enough!'

Urim raised his voice and passed his hand over his staff, whereupon Ebon was silenced and though he tried to speak, found he was unable. Turning to Jon, Urim said with quiet reserve, 'What Ebon has said is partly true; that is how he deceives us and would cause us to doubt one another; therefore I have silenced him for now. Do you recall me telling you that the time would come for you to know the truth and that I would tell you all you needed to know?'

Jon nodded.

'Well, that time is not now, but soon. When we have released the seers and returned home together, you shall know all that there is to know. Will you trust me until then?'

Jon turned to look at Ebon who tried to speak but could not and was shaking his head animatedly, trying to influence him to say no. Ebon advanced on him but was grabbed by the sure grip of Bearer and Petros, restraining him. Jon looked at all the others, one by one, leaving Anna till the last. She nodded encouragingly. Looking back at Urim, he said, 'I don't need anyone else to decide for me or to seek for anyone else's advice; I know of myself that I trust you, Urim.'

Then looking aside at Ebon and raising his voice to emphasise his reply to Urim, 'It doesn't matter who you are, you have proved yourself true to the cause of freedom and to all of us; I believe you when you tell me that I shall know eventually; I can wait until then.'

Urim breathed a small sigh of relief and smiled warmly, placing a friendly hand on Jon's shoulder.

'You have proved yourself well, Jon, and shown to me that you are your mother's son; she would be proud of you.'

Jon shot Urim a glance, searching for something; he saw it in Urim's eyes; a melancholy that sat deep within. Urim gripped Jon's shoulder a little tighter and blinked back a tear that had started to gather in the corner of his eye.

Hamill shouted out a warning in alarm, pointing away behind the others, towards the east.

'Listen! kite-folk, coming this way!'

He looked at the others and paled.

'That's not all.'

They turned and looked in the direction he had indicated;

there from around the trees were a score of trolls headed their way in full armour but instead of their customary clubs, they carried long metal-tipped pikes.

'Leave these to us; we will take care of them.'

Bearer left Ebon in Braun's charge before striding off to meet the threat with Petros no less eager to stop the trolls from getting through.

Urim hurried them towards the trees.

'We can do little to assist them and the kite-folk will be upon us soon. If they catch us out in the open then we will not stand a chance; best get under the shelter of the trees; bring Ebon and keep him close, watch him for any tricks.'

They rushed for cover and managed to get under the trees as the kite-folk arrived; their chattering filled the air as they swooped down, trying to locate them. Some landed on the grass between the trees and the water's edge, sniffing at the ground. They picked up their scent, their heads bobbing up and down as they walked awkwardly and nervously towards them.

Swoosh!

One of the nearest kite-folk went down, a stone lodged in its skull. Swoosh, swoosh; two more succumbed to the deadly accuracy of Anna's sling before the creatures flew up into the air in alarm; they would not be trying that again in a hurry but now they knew their quarry was hidden in the trees; all they had to do was to get them to come out, but how?

A number of them flew off towards the battling trolls whilst the others remained either circling overhead like scavenging vultures or standing, at a safe distance, on the ground, keeping watch on the trees in case of an attempt to escape.

From the shelter of the trees, they could see that the creatures had managed to get four of the trolls to peel away from the fight with the colossi and go into the trees behind them. It would only be a matter of time before the trolls found them and either drove them out into the open or killed them in their attempt at releasing Ebon. Against one troll, they had a very good chance of success; against two would have been difficult but possible; but against four, they stood no chance. Then Anna signalled that she had an idea. She signed to Jon who translated for the others. What she had in mind was to draw the trolls off one at a time as they made their way through the woods; they could then deal with them on a single basis and not all at once. She waited expectantly as Jon finished the translation and smiled with satisfaction when her idea was accepted.

'That's a brilliant idea, Anna, how do you propose we do it?'

Trapper was generous in his praise for her quick thinking, which encouraged her to expand on her idea. She signed to Jon who translated and impressed upon them all the need for perfect timing as well as the need for both Hamill and Jon to stay with Ebon and guard him, whilst the others helped her in the execution of her plan.

They all agreed, though Urim was somewhat reluctant to leave Ebon; after a little reconsideration Anna suggested that he stay with Hamill to guard Ebon and Jon could assist them. Urim was more comfortable with that idea, reinforcing the need for care to be taken by them all.

With each of them knowing what was required of them they headed off towards the trolls; they were to try and get them to separate so that they could be dealt with more easily. Not long after leaving Urim, Hamill and Ebon behind, they heard the approach of the heavy trolls. The ground undulated in steep banks and gullies; they were not very big, but large enough to slow a troll.

Jon made sure that he was spotted at the top of one of the banks by one of them who grunted to the others that he was going off in pursuit. So far so good; it came after Jon, who ran down the other side of the bank, timing it so that the troll saw where he went. The creature followed at a pace, careering down the bank and between two trees; as it went through, the two dwarves pulled a vine they had cut down, up across its path, and the big oaf went sprawling, hitting its head and knocking itself unconscious.

Trapper was impressed by how well Anna's plan was working.

'That went better than I thought it would; well done, Anna, well done, Jon.'

They used the vine to tie the creature up, making certain that it could not escape, before hurrying on after the others; encouraged by the ease at which they had brought the first one down, they opted for the same tactic on the next. It worked according to plan and another troll came scampering down the bank and through the bushes where the dwarves tripped it with another vine. This time the troll managed to roll forward and come up on its feet. Caught somewhat unprepared for this, the dwarves sat in bemusement for a moment before scrambling to their feet. The troll, angered by their attempt to bring it down, rushed forward only to be thrown sideways by Braun, who thudded into the brute by swinging across the gully on another vine. Both of them tumbled to the ground but Braun was the quicker of the two in getting to his feet and swung his broadsword at the troll in a great arc, separating its head from its body.

'That's two down and two more to go. You carry on; I'll catch up with you once I've got my breath back.'

Braun rested on the hilt of his sword; he had winded himself after colliding with the creature.

'Are you sure you'll be all right?'

'Yes, fine; now get after those trolls.'

Braun pushed Jon away to help him off after the others.

The last two, however, would not be separated and no matter how they tried to get one of them to follow them, they would not and continued on towards where the others were waiting Anna let loose some stones at them but they had very little effect, other than to annoy them.

Their only chance was to join forces and tackle the trolls together. Jon and Anna threw stones at one of them making it raise an arm to defend itself from the stones, as they hit home like stinging insects; as it did so the dwarves ran out from concealment and slashed at its legs, bringing the creature down by cutting the tendons at the back of its knees. The heavily built creature fell like a tree, crashing into the one in front and knocking it off balance. Seeing an opportunity, Trapper sprang on to the back of the one in the lead and plunged his knife into its neck between the armour plates covering its shoulders and its helmet. Shrieking in pain, the troll threw itself against a tree to try and dislodge him but Trapper hung on and stabbed again through the neck, this time severing the spinal cord whereupon the creature simply went limp and folded up like a canvas chair, hitting the ground with a thud. Trapper rolled into a ball and came up on to his feet, ready for action should there be a need, but the fight was over; other than to deal with the maimed troll that sat holding its legs, wincing in pain.

They did not have the heart to kill it but did not want to leave it here injured either. They gathered in a huddle to decide what to do; the troll saw their indecision and attempted to throw a pike at Jon but never managed it. The creature coughed and rolled its eyes before falling forward onto the ground; standing behind it was Braun, his sword bloodied from the thrust into the brute's back; he had come upon them in the nick of time.

'Never leave a wounded troll; especially do not turn your back on one.'

Hamill and Urim were still watching over Ebon, who was sitting on a fallen tree trunk, not daring to confront Urim all the time that he was without his staff; Hamill kept a respectable distance from him. The kite-folk were still waiting for the expected rush from concealment, having sent in the trolls to flush them out but Jon nodded to Urim that their plan had worked and they stood wondering what they should do next; they could not very well stay here for the rest of the day standing idly by. A shriek from a kite-folk circling above them in the air alerted those on the ground to danger and they sprang up to take flight, two of them did not get very far and plummeted to the ground with long pikes impaling them. The two colossi were returning having been successful in despatching and frightening away the other trolls: two more of the creatures fell to the earth similarly skewered by pikes; this proved more than enough for them and they scattered in panic now that they realised that the trolls had been fought off and the two colossi were back. Petros signalled to them that the kite-folk had gone and it was safe for them to come out. Grabbing hold of Ebon, the dwarves escorted him out of the wood, the others following on behind.

Bearer and Petros really looked as though they had been in a battle, their clothing was ripped and splashes of troll blood covered them; Hamill did notice, however, that they had chips and scratches on their legs and arms, as if a stonemason had taken a cold chisel to them.

'Never fear, Hamill, these are but a small price to pay for this day and we will carry these marks with pride at having been of service. We wait on your next move, Urim, Seer of the Sight. I believe it is to you that we owe our thanks for reuniting us with our brethren.' Bearer bowed slightly towards him.

'Indeed it is, but do not think any more of it; I did it for the sake of all who live on this land, for without the intervention of the colossi, both you and those who arrived with Amorphous, the battle would have been lost at Northill. We now have the chance to secure the future for all by releasing the Sight from their imposed imprisonment and ensuring that Ebon never again becomes a threat.'

Turning towards Ebon, who was being held firmly by Tracker, Urim stepped closer, placed the foot of his staff firmly on the ground and in a commanding voice said, 'Ebon Lodestone, will you of your own free will release the Sight from the force that you have placed around them?'

Urim passed his hand over his staff and Ebon found that he could speak again.

Standing defiantly between the two dwarves he glared at Urim.

'By what right do you come here to challenge me? I do not recognize your authority here, go back to where you came from and I might consider letting the boy live; if not, then he will die and you shall not have the power to stop me.'

'You know that is something I cannot allow; I am here to prevent you from bringing all peoples under your subjection, the very fact we are having this conversation here and now stands as a witness to the fact that you will not succeed.'

That remark stung Ebon to the core and for the first time Jon saw fear in his face: fear that what Urim was saying was true, that he was not invincible and that he might fail in his aim to rule the land.

Ebon screamed at Urim like a mad man.

'Never! I'll never give in and you won't stop me, either of you.'

He burst free from Tracker's grip and, whipping around, managed to steal the dwarf's knife from out of his belt. In a flurry that was too quick to be prevented by the war-wise dwarf, Ebon held Tracker in an arm lock and pressed the blade against his throat, backing away from the group towards the energy shield. Trapper cried out and made to rush Ebon to release his brother from his grasp but Ebon only squeezed the blade closer to his captive's throat. The whiskers of the dwarf's beard almost covered the knife, but they all knew it was there, ready to slice into his neck should anyone make a false move.

'No surprises now, Urim, you know that I'm serious when I say that I'll kill him without a moment's hesitation.'

'What is it that you want, Ebon?'

'You can't be serious, Urim, you can't give in to him – whatever it is he wants he'll not keep his word,' Jon shouted out before he could stop himself.

'Ah, spoken like a true member of the Carter family; that is you name, Jon, isn't it – Jonathan Carter of Ashbrooke? What's your name, Urim, keeper of the Golden Tome? Do tell; we'd all like to know I'm sure.'

'My name is not important at this time, what is important is that I know that you will not succeed in what you aim to do, which is why I will do nothing to stop you. I will not need to; you will manage that all on your own.'

'Is that so? Well I might just surprise you.'

With that he drew the blade across Tracker's throat and shoved him into his brother's arms then sprang for Anna and grabbed her around the waist, placing the bloodied knife against her throat.

'Not again,' Jon groaned, remembering that she had gone through this not long ago, panicking that Anna would receive the same lack of respect that Tracker had received.

The poor dwarf lay in his brother's arms; Trapper's tears streamed down his face, begging his younger brother to live. It was not to be; bleeding badly from the cut that had gone through a major artery, with his life blood spilling out onto the ground and with no way of preventing it, Tracker looked up into his beloved brothers eyes, smiled and slipped away.

They all felt his pain as Trapper wailed in frustration and grief, cradling his dead brother to him and rocking to and fro. Urim hung his head in sorrow at the act whilst the others stood in stunned silence; were it not for the fact that Ebon had a knife held at Anna's throat and the callous seer had just showed how ready he was to use it, Braun would have snapped his neck with his bare hands; his rage was clear for all to see.

Hamill boiled over inside with anger and, not thinking, he went for the rogue seer with Ebon's own staff that Urim had given him to look after, swinging it like a club at the malevolent seer. It was the very thing that Ebon had hoped would happen and he grabbed it as it came within reach, yanking it out of Hamill's grasp.

'So you see, Urim, once again I find myself in possession of my staff and have the upper hand I think, in that you would not wish any harm to come to your young friend.'

'You must do whatever it is that you think you must do,' Urim said, not making any sense to any of them by his remark. He started to advance towards them. Ebon backed away, threatening to harm the girl if he did not stop. Urim raised his staff. Ebon, still backing away, edged ever closer to the energy shield; they could all hear the gentle hum of its power increase the closer he got. Still Urim advanced. Panicking, Ebon sent a blast of green energy at Urim, which was countered by the blue shield from his staff. Jon shouted out for Urim to stop for Anna's sake but he kept on going forward, chanting words under his breath, summoning power from within his staff as it grew brighter and brighter.

'I give you one last warning, Urim, I will kill her, I will.'

Ebon was frantic in his fear of the apparently unmoved Urim and, summoning all his might, swung his staff around behind him in order to send a massive blast at Urim. The tip of his staff entered the energy shield and was flung across the field landing thirty paces away. They watched in horror as the energy field seemed to wrap its way around the frightened seer, engulfing Anna too, and draw them in to its folds of energy.

The shield crackled and sputtered as they passed into it. For a moment they were outlined in pure energy; Ebon screamed in terror and struggled desperately to avoid the irresistible pull of the barrier. He let go of the knife that he had held against Anna's throat and it fell to the ground.

Anna tried to resist the pull of the barrier too, her eyes wide with fear; Jon rushed forward to grab her and was astonished to hear her call out.

'Jon, save me.'

It was the first time he had ever heard her voice, for as he reached for her and she for him, the barrier collapsed and she, along with Ebon, disappeared; the energy field folded in on itself with a clap of thunder that rocked the ground and reverberated around the lake, echoing into silence and was gone. The shimmering veil had disappeared, the Tower and its occupants were freed from their confinement but Anna had gone, as had Ebon.

No one moved or spoke for some while; they were all far too shocked at what had happened, almost unbelieving, stunned and surprised. Urim stood holding his staff in one hand, his head in the other; a groan escaped his lips as he sank to his knees on the ground and cried.

They were a sorry sight and an air of deep melancholy settled over them. Jon stood rooted to the spot staring at the place where Anna had disappeared, tears falling freely, though he did not cry. Hamill went and stood by Trapper's side and took Tracker from him; he was beyond any help that Hamill could ever administer so he laid him gently down and pulled the dwarf's cloak over his body, saying a silent farewell to the brave little dwarf and placed a comforting arm around Trapper's heaving shoulders.

The two colossi stood at a respectful distance, waiting to be told what, if any, help they could be; Braun sat with his knees up to his chin, hugging them close, and stared out across the lake, lost in his own kind of grief.

Petros was the first to notice movement on the other side of the lake and indicated to Bearer where to look. At the gateway into the Tower several cloaked figures could be seen looking across at them. The colossus strode over to Urim and with a sensitive hand brought the seer to his feet, saying that he needed to speak to those who had appeared across the lake. Urim brought himself under control and thanked Bearer for his support. Braun also noticed that people were gathering at the gateway and he too got to his feet and made his way over to stand by Urim.

Urim called to Hamill and asked softly with a careworn expression on his face, 'Hamill, please collect Ebon's staff from where it has fallen and bring it to me. Braun, I would ask that you remain here with the others until I return; it may be some time before I do. Is that agreeable with you?'

'Gladly, seer; I will do whatever you ask of me.'

He smiled at the seer and placed a reassuring hand on his shoulder.

Hamill returned with Ebon's staff and offered it to Urim.

'Here you are, Urim, I'm sorry that I messed things up; I shouldn't have gone after Ebon like that. Because of me Anna has gone; I don't know how I'm ever going to look Jon in the face again.'

Hamill stood before the seer in abject misery. His shoulders drooped and he stuttered his words. Looking up, Urim motioned for Jon to join them, which he did though he was still in a state of shock.

'Hamill here thinks that it is his fault that Anna has been lost to us and he is unsure how he will look you in the eye.'

Urim brought the two of them to face each other. Jon reached out and hugged his friend. Sobbing into his ear, he reassured him. 'Oh, my dear friend, how could you ever think that I would blame you; you who have been such a good friend to us both; it is Ebon I blame, not you.'

He held him at arm's length and looked him in the eye and they both cried.

Urim approached Trapper and knelt down to speak with him.

'I am truly sorry for the death of your brother. If I could have prevented it I would have done; I would have given my own life in exchange for this not to have turned out the way it has. Would you like us to bury him here at Seers' Tower, or would you prefer something else?'

'Thank you, Urim; your offer is a kind one and one that I think he would like to accept. You have been a true leader and friend to us dwarves and we will be forever in you debt. I attach no blame to you for this, and neither would my brother were he still here and it was I who had been killed.'

Trapper kept his head down as he spoke with a firm conviction but when he finished his last sentence he looked Urim in the eye; tears stained his face as he mourned for the loss of his brother.

Getting to his feet, Urim made his way back to Jon and Hamill.

'Jon, I crave your indulgence for I must leave you for a while and go into the Tower to meet with the Council of the Sight. I would take you in with me but it is not possible to do so at this time, but one day you shall enter in and see what lies inside. I say this to you for I need to take Hamill in with me.'

Jon looked up with a question on his lips but he restrained himself and simply nodded before replying.

'No doubt you have a good reason for doing so, Urim, and I respect your wishes; the fact that you have told me helps, so I will await the time when we can go inside together.'

Urim patted him on the shoulder and went to walk away but turned and hugged him, then took a bewildered but excited Hamill across the dark lake on the ferry. Jon watched with the others as they disembarked and walked up through the gateway and into the Tower. A group of people used the ferry to cross over to them and approached, carrying boxes; they also had bags slung over their shoulders. Upon reaching them they began to set up tents for each of them and a griddle for cooking on, inviting them to take their rest; all of this was with the compliments of the Council of the Sight and they offered their apologies for not being able to entertain them within the Tower at this time. Harry, the driver, was tended to and placed on a more comfortable cot and received every attention in order to make him comfortable. He had a shelter to himself. Tracker's body was treated respectfully and placed temporarily in a wooden casket that they brought across on the ferry; they placed it in a separate shelter for the night. In the morning they would take it to the Tower to prepare the body for burial.

Darkness fell and Jon sat on a chair in the entrance to his shelter, his stomach filled with a roasted meat banquet that the people from the Tower had provided them with. The evening was cold and promised to grow colder but he did not feel it, he was still numb from the loss of Anna and of hearing her voice; he would never forget that voice, so sweet and gentle amidst the fear she must have felt at the time. He wiped away a tear, believing that he would never stop crying.

They all had shelters of their own, apart from the colossi who were perfectly happy to stay outside and sleep under the stars. There were a great many of them, as Jon looked up into the sky and wondered at their beauty; a shooting star sped across the night sky and was lost in the blackness. He sighed and turned in for the night, though he thought he would not sleep, but he was wrong.

Morning brought no relief from the pain he felt at being without Anna, but he did feel rested and was grateful for the breakfast that was provided by the workers from Seers' Tower. They went about their business with a respectful hush to their voices, taking care to tend to the needs of those who had succeeded in freeing them from Ebon's grip.

The morning passed slowly and they kept themselves to themselves, not wishing to intrude on each other's thoughts. It was near midday when Urim was spotted crossing back over the lake on the ferry with another seer. They recognized Urim straightaway; the other seer remained hooded.

341

Urim introduced him to them as Ebon Lodestone, which caught them by surprise and Trapper went for his knife, but Urim laughed then apologised and they gasped in surprise as the seer lifted his hood to reveal himself as Hamill.

'What kind of game is this, Urim?' Braun asked in disbelief.

'I promise you that this is no game. Hamill is indeed the new seer in the Council of the Sight and he takes upon him not just the name of Ebon, his predecessor, but his mantle too; hence Hamill is no longer Hamill, he is Ebon Lodestone and he will heal the wounds of the land in the way that Ebon before him should have done instead of using his powers for his own ends.'

Jon realised that his jaw was gaping open. Closing it, he stammered out, 'Well done, I mean congratulations, Hamill, I mean Ebon. Is it really true? Are you really the new Ebon as Urim says? This isn't some kind of prank?'

Hamill grinned from ear to ear and looked pleased as Punch, yet he also looked scared.

'Yes. No, it's true, I can hardly believe it myself and it took a lot of persuading to get me to accept, I can tell you. We were up half the night arguing it out but finally Urim's unique understanding of things and his sound logic won me over, so I have indeed taken the vows of a seer. I have Ebon's staff and his stone; I'm not quite sure what to do with them yet and the thought of using them and being one of the Council of the Sight scares me to death. What happens normally is that the outgoing seer grooms the new one and passes on all that he needs to know; seeing as how Ebon didn't do that means that I have to learn everything from scratch. The other seers have all promised to help me settle in and become accustomed to my new role; I couldn't have better teachers than that, could I?'

Braun and Trapper congratulated the new seer wholeheartedly while Urim drew Jon aside.

'This is I know a disappointment to you, Jon; there is no need to be afraid of how you feel, it is only natural that you should feel a little envious of your friend. Trust me when I say that you will spend a great deal of time with him yet; you have not lost him as a friend, far from it, you have gained another ally.'

Urim winked at him and said no more; just as he always did when he wanted the conversation to be over.

*

Well, Jon supposed that it was over, now that the seers had been freed and Ebon was gone, replaced by someone who Jon agreed with Urim would make a very good seer, so long as he didn't have to get up early in the morning. He sat in his shelter that evening thinking over the events of the last few weeks; it had seemed like a lifetime, yet it had passed so quickly. The thrill of their task being completed was lessened considerably by the very large price they had had to pay for it. Anna and Tracker were lost here in their fight with Ebon at the Tower; Captain Quentin and Marshall, among others, gave their lives defending Northill; and his friend Mason, the dwarf who had had such a desire to discover the past. He promised himself that he would return to Ffridd-Uch-Ddu to visit with Digger; Jon thought that maybe he would even accompany him on one of his expeditions.

There was so much that he wanted to do and see; coming on this trek had given him a taste for furthering his knowledge and meeting different people. He definitely wanted to go back to Northill and see Captain Perkins, if only to see what he had achieved in improving the defences there. He would like to visit the colossi in the mountain city and witness the rebirth of their commerce between them and the 'fleshers' as they called Jon and his like. Oh yes, there was plenty to keep him amused for some time to come; his only regret, and it would follow him all of his life, was that Anna would not be there to see it with him.

'I'll be with you, Jon, always.'

He heard the voice as clear as day and jumped out of his chair as if he had sat on a wasp. He searched around for someone who might have been playing tricks on him, but there was no one around; that voice, he could never forget how it had penetrated his head. It was Anna. He knew it though he had never heard her speak in all the years that he had known her; but now she had spoken to him.

'Anna, is that you? Can you hear me?'

Silence filled the air; he listened for a while but gave up not long after and put the experience down to his being tired; he *was* tired, more tired than he could remember being before. He watched as the sun set over the Hammerhead Heights and got into his cot when the light faded.

He was soon asleep and dreaming of Anna; he saw her in a beautiful garden filled with the most wonderful flowers whose scent filled his nose with a heady fragrance. She stepped through a pergola that had a rambling rose covering it and ran to him, calling his name again and again.

He woke up with a start, his shelter was filled with light and there, sitting in the chair watching him, was Anna. He could not believe his eyes and thought he must be dreaming still; he closed his eyes and opened them again, but she was real.

'Hello, Jon.'

'Tell me you're not dead and that I'm not dreaming or I think I might go out of my mind.'

She laughed, the sound of her laughter filled his mind, but it was not a mocking laugh, rather it was playful, happy.

'You are not dreaming, my love, and I did not die, rather I have simply been taken from one place and put in another, though I am unable to return; you saw where I am in your dream. I am able to talk now, Jon; I have the power to communicate in a way that was unknown to me before. Do not grieve for me, this is truly a marvellous place and I am happy; I have made new friends here and there is no unhappiness, no tears and no pain.'

'But what about Ebon? What happened to him?'

Jon was concerned for her safety and feared lest Ebon held her captive.

'Ebon – he's not here, no one like him is here, I told you, there is peace here. My only regret is that we cannot be together; the barrier between us is too strong. I must go now, Jon; my time with you can only be fleeting, but I will come to you again soon, my love, only to you; farewell.'

'Wait, don't go.'

He reached out after her but she vanished and the shelter plunged back into darkness; tears stung his face and he sobbed into his pillow until he fell asleep.

In the morning Urim was the first to greet him; he was sitting on a chair outside Jon's shelter wrapped in his cloak. He looked as though he had gone without sleep as his eyes were all bloodshot.

'Good morning, Jon, did you sleep well?' he asked and stirred himself into a better sitting position.

'Good morning, Urim, yes I did, or rather, after a while I did. How about you? It looks like you've been here all night?'

344

'I have. I am so pleased that she came back, Jon; I heard her voice as she spoke to you and I just wanted to say to you how sorry I am; sorry that I could do nothing to prevent her from passing through the barrier.'

He hung his head a little lower and chewed his bottom lip to stop the tears that he knew were just below the surface.

They sat in front of Jon's shelter for some time, neither of them saying a word, just sitting together in silence; they watched as the rest of the group emerged from their shelters until all were ready for the day.

Urim called a meeting and announced that he planned to leave after Tracker's funeral later that morning, to return with Jon and retrieve the chest that belonged to Terra. He requested that Braun return with Bearer and Petros to the mountain city and act as an ambassador between them and the rest of the folk throughout the land, saying that the colossi would have need of a good master smith. Braun gladly accepted the assignment and promised that he would build bridges between them so that never again would there be a divide amongst those who served the right to be free.

Urim addressed Trapper.

'As for you, my good friend, I have no mission for you to fulfil other than perhaps you might wish to stay here amongst us, or be free to return to your own kind; the choice is yours.'

Trapper thought for a moment then said, 'If it's all right with you and the other Seers, I would like to stay here for a while, perhaps then I might feel like returning home at a later date.'

'That is perfectly acceptable and we welcome you to our home, feel free to roam anywhere as you will, there is nowhere you will not be allowed to enter. I have been authorised to offer you the freedom of the Tower.'

Trapper held his head high and squared his shoulders, honoured to have that privilege bestowed upon him.

The funeral service was brief but poignant, a fitting end for a brave dwarf. Tracker would feel honoured to be the only dwarf who was not a seer to be buried in the tombs of the Sight; the tombs were situated in a valley a little way from the Tower. There were many tombs that held the seers of the past, each of them had the title name of the seer above the entrance. Inside, engraved on the stone lid of their coffins was the name by which they had been known before adopting their title. Trapper was privileged to be laid to rest in the tomb of those who were known as Terra Standfast and given a position near the doorway so that Trapper and others who may come to pay their respects could do so without disturbing the rest of the tomb. Following the service, they gathered at the camp where they ate a last meal together before saying their final goodbyes to each other; Jon and Hamill hugged and slapped each other's backs playfully.

'Think of me sometimes, Jon.'

'I don't think I could forget you; though one thing I will not miss about you is your snoring.'

'I don't snore, do I?' Hamill teased, knowing full well that he did.

'Why don't you come with us, I'm sure the seers would let you have some time to yourself before you start training.'

'Hamill will be required to remain here and to continue to learn his duties and to practise his skills; as for the rest of us, I thank you one and all for your assistance, your loyalty and your strength. I could not have achieved this without you; you are free to follow your path to wherever it may lead you, good luck be at your side and safety in your hands, farewell my dear friends.'

They all promised to meet up again one day, then commenced their separate journeys: Braun with the two colossi to the north and Jon with Urim to the east. A volunteer from one of the local villages had been employed to drive Braun, whilst Harry, their driver and protector from Ebon's attempt to escape, was sufficiently recovered to drive Jon and Urim to Ashbrooke; from there he would return to Northill and his family.

Hamill stood at the ferry and waved until he saw them disappear over the ridge.

'Goodbye, Jon; good fortune be with you until we meet again.'

He crossed his fingers then turned and walked back into Seers' Tower, still not quite taking in all that had happened to him and the great responsibility that he was about to shoulder; that of being a seer. How it could be that he of all folk should have been chosen to replace Ebon, he did not fully understand; he hoped one day that he would.

Chapter XXI

Urim's Secret

Jon opened his eyes and smiled as he stretched, he could hardly believe that he was home in his own cot. The familiar surroundings comforted him and he sighed contentedly, the luxury of it made him want to wallow for a while in self-indulgence. Mixed emotions flowed through him: this house had many memories, mostly good ones but it was tinged with the sadness of the absence of his mother; she had been the very heart of the place, now that heart had stopped; instead of a home, it was now simply a house. It could stay that way if Jon allowed it too. He had wanted it to be a home again, but now that hope had perished: Anna was no longer with him. Then he remembered that he was only here because of the efforts of others.

The mission to release the seers from their enforced seclusion had been accomplished now that Ebon had been stopped from subjecting the land to his rule and the barrier had gone. Urim had been able to recover three of the talismans Ebon had purloined: the scroll that belonged to Terra Standfast (they had sent the chest they had obtained at the forge in Foundry Smelt back to the Tower upon their arrival at Jon's house yesterday); the crystal had been collected from the Sprite Queen by Emerald, the water sprite seer; and Urim had passed the whistle to Auger Wind-rider when he had entered Seers' Tower. They were now safely in the hands of their rightful owners. Four talismans still needed to be recovered but Urim had said that it was the responsibility of the seers to whom they belonged to do so; his task was done and there were other duties for him to perform elsewhere.

Ebon had gone and along with him Anna, though according to what Anna had told him, they were not in the same place and Jon took some comfort in knowing that she was happy where she was. His thoughts turned to the things that they had gone through together and how they had grown closer; he had hoped that they could have spent their time together as a couple and raised a family after the seers were freed but fate had stepped in and took her away from him. He smiled as he thought of Hamill and his annoying ways but he had grown to be very fond of him: Jon was still in shock at Hamill being selected as the successor to Ebon; he had no idea that the half elf physician, of all folk, would become a seer. Hamill had been as shocked and surprised as they were. That said, he was a good person: one who cared for those who needed his help; on reflection, he made a fine choice as the new Ebon.

It still irked him a little that Hamill had gone into the Tower with Urim and yet he had been left outside; he knew that Urim had a good reason for doing so and maybe he would find out what that reason was; he anticipated learning a lot from Urim today as he had promised to explain things to him. His mind whirled with thoughts of what would be revealed, imagining all kinds of things and wondered, now that Hamill had become a seer, whether he too might venture to be one someday and to follow in Urim's footsteps. 'Ridiculous,' he heard the words coming out of his mouth, 'who would entrust a clumsy country boy with a responsibility of that magnitude?'

He recalled how he had felt a change in Hamill when he came out of the Tower: he went in as a halfer with nothing more than a desire to heal those who had been hurt. He could also of course be an irritating pain in the neck but was essentially someone to whom one could not help feel friendship and a sort of love towards. When he came out, he was different: he emanated authority and purpose; for the first time since Jon had known him, he was confident in himself. Jon was pleased for him, and somewhat envious if the truth be told. He would have loved to have gone into the Tower and seen his induction into the Sight; to have met with the other seers; maybe one day he would. He resolved that he would return, if nothing else but to see Hamill, Ebon that is; now that really was going to take some getting used to.

Urim had insisted that Jon and he return to Ashbrooke together, saying that he needed to see to the return of the chest, but he still didn't understand why Urim had sent it here, so far away from the Tower. Maybe that was it: being so far removed from the Tower, it was considered safe. As ever he kept his own counsel and only said what was necessary: all he would say was that there was something Jon needed to learn; that he could only start the next stage of his life by returning to his home; from here he could begin to piece together the loose cords of his past and move forward.

How could he move forward without Anna? She had always been there to support and encourage him; his life would never be the same again because of losing her; that would be a hurt that might never heal. Seeing her that night when she appeared in his tent and spoke to him seemed surreal; he determined that he would do all he could to get her back. There must be a way of retrieving her, though she had said that there was none; he could not bear the thought of her trapped there; he was not going to give her up as lost, no matter what Urim said. Maybe together they could get her back; perhaps that was why Urim had travelled here to Ashbrooke with him; could it be that they were going to seek help from the colossi or the sprites? He did not have the answer to any of these questions; typical of his life these past few weeks: there were always more questions than there were answers.

Urim had had a significant impact upon his life; he'd turned it upside down and Jon wondered whether he would ever be the same again; he doubted it.

He cradled his hands behind his head, leaning against the headboard and wondered what did lie ahead of him. As he lay there pondering these things, the sound of the gate being opened then closed gently roused him from his reverie; as if whoever was using it didn't want to make too much noise. He jumped out of his cot and looked out of the window but could see no one in the alleyway. He pulled on a gown and stepped onto the small landing. The door to Urim's room was open and the cot empty. He panicked: was Urim leaving him, and without saying goodbye?

He rushed to the window in Urim's room, flinging it wide so that he could peer out better; he searched up and down the lane for him, leaning out, trying to catch sight of him but he was nowhere in sight. Jon's heart sank as he began to close the window. A movement in the shadows under the tree in the churchyard caught his attention. Sunlight speckled the ground as it filtered through the leafy canopy, Urim stood at his mother's grave resting his hand on the headstone, head bowed, as if in prayer.

Jon dressed hurriedly; he was curious as to why Urim should be there and didn't want to run the risk of him disappearing. He had a habit of doing that; a sense of foreboding ran through him that he might leave and never see him again.

He had grown close to Urim, a bond had been forged and he felt it returned but he still was unsure of him, even after all this time. Had Urim been entirely truthful to him? Ebon had been so sure that he had misled Jon about being his uncle but had not revealed anything else; that had bothered him for such a long time. Now that it was all over he wanted to know for certain who Urim was; he felt he was owed that much.

Their search for the way to release the seers from the Tower had indeed brought them together, not just as 'players in the game' as Ebon had called it, but as family. Still the question remained, Who was he? He wanted to lay the ghost of his father down: if Urim was his father, as he hoped and suspected, then now was the time to know. He had to ask him. His throat went dry and his pulse quickened; chewing nervously at his bottom lip he crossed the lane into the churchyard and made his way towards the seer; he approached quietly.

Jon stood opposite Urim over his mother's grave. The seer had his head bowed, hands clasping his staff before him.

'Hello, Jon. I knew you would come,' he whispered softly and with difficulty cleared his throat.

Jon was surprised to see tears brimming in his eyes, held back by sheer force of will. Urim passed a hand across his brow.

'My eyes are streaming today: it must be the grass. It has been a very long time since I have visited this place; too long.'

He smiled weakly and gathered himself emotionally, squaring his shoulders.

'Jon, it is time I answered another question; one that has been bothering you ever since we met and the answer may cause you some concern. When I introduced myself to you as Urim of the Council of the Seers, I was truthful. When I said I was your uncle, I was not.'

Jon's head felt like it was in a spin, his heart quickened and he could feel a hot flush to his cheeks.

'Ebon was right then.'

'Yes. On this he did not lie, but he didn't tell you who I really am did he?'

Ever since they had met, Jon had had his suspicions but had dismissed them as wishful thinking, of hoping beyond hope that he had at last found the answer to the question. What became of my father? He knew now, or rather, hoped he knew, and with Urim's confession that he was not his uncle, it was the only possible conclusion.

'You're my . . . father?' Jon asked hesitantly, hoping beyond hope that he sounded more confident in his tone than he felt and that the question was not as fantastic sounding as it seemed.

Urim looked straight at him and said hesitantly: 'Jon, I am unable to tell you who I am; if I were to do so . . .'

He left the sentence unfinished and chewed hard on his lower lip.

'I cannot deny that we are closely related, you and I, yet I am Urim of the Council of Seers, Keeper of the Golden Tome, and I must return to my duties; I cannot tarry here with you.'

'Then I will come with you,' Jon half stated, half asked. All the time feeling, knowing what Urim's response would be; so he was a little surprised when Urim said that he would.

'Yes, Jon, you will follow me.'

Jon's heart quickened and he lifted his head, a broad grin on his face.

'But not at this time.'

He crashed back to earth with a heavy heart, disappointment etched deep within him.

'But why can't I come with you, Urim? There's nothing else for me to do here; not now Anna's gone.'

His voice faltered and his chin quivered; he wanted to cry, to release all the emotion he felt. Without Anna, without Urim, what was there for him to do?

'This is a difficult thing I ask of you I know. Believe me, Jon, when I say that I really do appreciate how you feel, but it is not possible for us to walk this path together. You have to find your own way.'

'But I have so much to learn and there is so much more that you could teach me.'

Jon felt the tears starting to gather and pleaded with Urim to take him with him.

Urim continued gently but with reassurance in his voice.

'There will come a time when we can be together again and you will see things from a different perspective then. Were we not to part now, the future would be a very different place. The Council has cautioned me on this prior to my being sent on this venture. You and I must abide by that or what we have achieved together will be for nothing. Her loss will count for nothing.'

He paused and drew a deep breath filled with suppressed emotion.

'I tried to stop her Jon, you saw how I tried to stop her; I knew she would not come back if she went on our quest. I fear she is gone despite all I could do. I tried, Jon, I tried but she was so stubborn, she wouldn't listen to me. I risked damaging the Binding to save her. Do you remember, Jon . . . ? The energy force that lies deep beneath Seers' Tower? It is a barrier between two worlds. Ebon used it to imprison the other seers; it keeps us safe and I risked that, Jon, so that she might be with us still . . . but it was not to be, instead she has passed through that barrier into the other world and I fear she is lost to us forever. There will be times when she will come to you again, have no fears, that much I can tell you.'

It took a few moments for what Urim had said to sink in; Jon reeled at the confession. Why had Urim done that? To risk jeopardising the integrity of their very world in order to save Anna? Jon could not understand why he should do that. He recalled now that Urim had indeed argued strongly for her to remain behind and that he was so frustrated at her following them. He trusted Urim beyond any doubt but this shocked him.

'Why, Urim, why did you take such a risk?'

'Because I knew how much she meant to you. Because I knew that she would fall through the barrier that Ebon had created into the other world if she came with us,' he replied after he'd taken a moment to compose himself.

Jon recalled how Urim had reacted when Anna had been engulfed by and slipped through the energy field and that he had blamed himself for it. He had been as desperate as Jon had been at her loss.

They stood opposite each other unable to speak, both of them reliving their emotions of that day. It would take a long time, if ever, for Jon to deal with his feelings over this. He had been through a roller-coaster of emotions these past few months and it wasn't getting any easier. He had been at rock bottom at losing Anna just as they should have been feeling euphoric at what they had accomplished, at completing what they had set out to do. Now he was feeling good that his suspicions that Urim was his father were right: to have found him after all this time. He had but one more question that remained unformed on his lips. Why had he abandoned them? He looked at Urim with pain in his eyes.

Urim must have discerned his thoughts for he reached out and clasped his arm tightly.

'I know you may find this hard to accept but I am unable to explain any more to you at this time, you will understand why before too long but I cannot tell you now.'

Jon knew by now better than to try and press him any further; he had already learned so much, more than he could cope with for the one day. He decided to put his trust in him one more time. What Urim promised, he delivered; he would have to accept what was being said. Urim hugged him, then held him at arm's length and chewed at his lower lip. He smiled self-consciously as he became aware of it. Speaking softly, he said: 'Be strong. Walk the path that you have started on, seek for that which is in your heart to become and you shall achieve it. Along that road we will meet again, I promise you.'

He picked up his staff, took one last glance at the headstone and whispered under his breath, 'Farewell, mother, till we meet again in the next life. I think you have a son you can be proud of. Farewell, Jon, 'till we meet again.'

He walked out of the churchyard towards the west; returning to Seers' Tower. Jon wanted to go with him; he wanted to rush after him, to stop him from walking out of his life a second time; but his feet rooted him to the spot at the foot of his mother's grave. Tears blurred his vision and stained his cheeks; he felt his heart was breaking and would never mend. How cruel, he thought: to have lost his father then found him after all these years only to be told that he could not stay and neither could Jon go with him. Now he was losing him all over again. Urim had promised that they would meet again and Jon believed him; he just wished that it would be sooner, rather than later. He also believed that he would see Anna again and he would count the days until then. He would do as Urim had suggested: he would seek the ways of the Sight and become a seer. He watched Urim until he rounded the corner of the street. He did not turn to wave or look back; he just carried on going, back to Seers' Tower and his next assignment, whatever that might be.

Jon considered his future: would he indeed become a seer, like Urim? He heard the echo of the seer's voice from the first time they had met; Urim had said of his readiness to succeed that time will tell. That was just what Jon would do: he would set his mind on obtaining that which was in his heart, to be like Urim, to be a seer.